UNLOCKING THE TYCOON'S HEART

ELLA HAYES

A MOTHER'S SECRETS

TARA TAYLOR QUINN

MILLS & BOON

First Published in Great Britain 2020
by Mills & Boon, an imprint of HarperCollinsPublishers,
1 London Bridge Street, London, SE1 9GF

ISBN: 978-0-263-27889-7

0720

FSC
www.fsc.org
MIX
Paper from responsible sources
FSC™ C007454

This book is produced from independently certified FSC™ paper to ensure responsible forest management.

For more information visit: www.harpercollins.co.uk/green

Printed and bound by CPI Group (UK) Ltd, Croydon, CR0 4YY

UNLOCKING THE TYCOON'S HEART

ELLA HAYES

For Caro... happy memories of Amsterdam 2014!

CHAPTER ONE

'A SIGNALLING FAULT?' Mia's heart caved. She turned away from her laptop, swapped the phone to her other ear. 'Bloody hell, Ash! Have they said how long?'

'No…but I've got a bad feeling…'

She glanced at her watch. One-fifteen! No wonder her brother sounded tense. After an early-morning business meeting in Kent, he was now stranded on a train on the outskirts of London when he was supposed to be on his way to a two o'clock meeting with Theo Molenaar—in the city centre!

The opportunity to pitch to the CEO of Dutch IT giant MolTec was a massive deal for Ash. If the pitch was successful, it would boost his software development business into the stratosphere, and after everything he'd been through with Harold Kogan it was a boost he sorely needed.

Cheating Hal!

Mia pushed away her pain and refocused. Ash needed solutions, not regrets.

'I know… What about offering to meet Molenaar in Amsterdam on Monday?' She tried to sound upbeat. 'Come back with me on Friday! Stay the weekend! It's ages since you've been over and… Cleuso misses you.'

'Cleuso's the stupidest cat alive! He wouldn't recognise me if he fell over me which, let's face it, is quite likely.'

She stifled a chuckle. 'That's harsh.'

'The truth often is. We both know that.'

Mia's momentary lightness evaporated. 'Halgate' had blown up eighteen months before but the bitterness lingered. She could hear it in Ash's voice, could still taste it in the back of her own throat.

Ash had thought that Hal Kogan was going to be the perfect business partner, and she'd thought so too. Smart, articulate Hal—full of energy and confidence. He could hold a room, steer a conversation, handle people without them knowing they were being handled. In business, he was magnetic. In private, he was irresistible. When he'd trapped her in his steady blue gaze, she hadn't wanted to free herself. He'd filled a space in her heart, and after everything she and Ash had been through it had felt like destiny: Ash and Hal building a business; Mia and Hal building a life. They were a little family. Perhaps she'd wanted it so much that she hadn't been able to see anything else. Guilt squirmed inside her belly. Perhaps she hadn't wanted to see it.

'Besides,' Ash was saying, 'much as I'd love to come to Amsterdam and share a cramped cabin with Clueless, Monday's no good for Molenaar. He'll be in the States by then. This was the *only* window he had… Hang on! They're saying something…'

Through the earpiece, Mia could hear a crackly announcement playing over the speaker in her brother's carriage. She held her breath.

'Up to an hour's delay… Damn it! I'm going to have to cancel.'

The anguish in his voice was tearing her apart.

'No! You *need* this. There *has* to be a way…' She eyed her laptop. 'I'm putting you on speaker, okay?' She propped the phone against her coffee mug and typed

'Theo Molenaar' into the search bar. The screen filled with MolTec stuff: bulletins and business reports. Nothing about the man, until…

MOLENAAR HAS HIS EYE TO THE TELESCOPE!

She clicked the link and scanned the article, waiting for words to jump out: pioneering IT solutions; environmental interests; satellites; black holes; the expanding cosmos.

'Bingo! Molenaar's a star-gazer.' She retrieved the phone. 'He's into astronomy.'

'And that helps how?'

'I'm not sure… Let me think…' She got to her feet, drifted to the window. A white van was parked in the mews. *Southeast Satellite & Broadband Services* was written on the side of it in big purple letters. In her head the words clustered around the grain of an idea. 'Ash, you're coming in from the south east, aren't you?'

'Yes.'

'The observatory's in Greenwich.'

'So?'

She felt a smile coming. 'Tell Molenaar you've been delayed but can make it to the planetarium in an hour. If he meets you there it'll save both of you a lot of time and, if you *are* held up for longer, then at least he's in his happy place among the stars. Everybody wins.'

'For pity's sake, Mia—you're talking about the CEO of MolTec! I can't ask him to trek across London on my account. I'll just have to postpone.'

Something inside her snapped. 'No! I'm not letting you do that, not for the sake of one little hour.' Her mind was racing. If she could deliver Theo Molenaar to the planetarium, give Ash his chance with MolTec, maybe that could be her atonement. Atonement for blindly believing that

Hal had funded all their fancy trips to Paris, Prague and Berlin with an unexpected bequest from a distant relative.

'*I'll* meet him.' She hurried into the hall and started pulling on her jacket. 'I'll make him see that going to Greenwich makes perfect sense.'

'Mia, you can't. He'll think it's weird.'

'Maybe.' She pushed her feet into some shoes, grabbed her bag. 'Or maybe he'll think it's a…creative solution!'

'It's certainly creative.' The smile she could hear in his voice faded to a sigh. 'You're crazy, you know that?'

She opened the door, squinted into the city sunshine. 'But you still love me, right?'

'Always.'

She smiled, then rummaged for her sunglasses and slipped them on. 'Now, tell me where Molenaar's staying, then get yourself to the planetarium.'

She preferred these small, boutique hotels to the generic glamour of the bigger five-star places. The reception lobby of this one was particularly nice. It had a cosy vibe—quirky art on the walls, comfy-looking sofas upholstered in dense fabric. If Molenaar felt at home in this hotel, it meant he wasn't flashy. She liked that.

A desk clerk in a blue shirt looked up as she approached. 'Hello. Can I help you?'

'I have a meeting with one of your guests.' She smiled. 'Theo Molenaar.'

'Your name, please?'

She paused for a beat. 'Ashley Boelens.' There'd be time for explanations later.

The man nodded and stabbed an extension code into the phone.

She drew in a slow breath, trying to quash the tremble that had just started in her knees. Hatching a plan to help Ash was all very well, but there was no getting away from it: Molenaar was expecting a business meeting, not an impromptu jaunt to Greenwich. He might be offended. Or dismissive. Maybe this wouldn't help at all. Maybe she was messing everything up…

There was a little throat-clearing noise. The desk clerk was looking at her, his eyebrows slightly arched. 'Mr Molenaar will be down in a moment. Please take a seat.'

In the seating area, she lowered herself onto a sofa, pulling her bag onto her lap. *Mr Molenaar...* A knot tightened in her stomach. She didn't know what he looked like—or how old he was. There'd been no pictures with the article she'd read and in her five years as a features writer she hadn't come across him. Of course, since she didn't write about tech or astronomy, that was hardly surprising. She shifted on the sofa, running her fingers through her fringe. If she could just switch off her stupid nerves she'd be fine, but her nerves seemed to have developed a mind of their own and they were jangling chaotically.

She glanced at the lift doors and saw the floor numbers flashing…counting down. He was on his way!

She straightened her spine and lifted her chin, suddenly noticing the bulky weight of the bag in her lap. Lotte would be laughing at her: *Mia! You look like Mary Poppins!* Hurriedly, she turfed it onto the sofa, but her phone spilled out along with a lipstick and two pens. Frantically she raked them back inside, yanked the zip shut and then she looked up.

Blink! Breathe!

A thirty-something gorgeous man was standing in front of the closing doors looking right at her. He was tall, clean-shaven. His dark-blond collar-length hair was swept back from his forehead, so it was easy to see his brow furrowing as he gazed over. And then his eyes moved on, sweeping the lobby, clearly looking for the real Ash Boelens.

She knew she ought to go over and introduce herself, but for some reason she couldn't move. Why couldn't he have been much older or at the very least a stereotypical computer geek? What she'd come here to do was audacious enough without having to contend with Molenaar's movie star looks.

Helplessly, she watched him go over to the desk, exchange words with the clerk, and then he was turning, looking at her again.

Breathe.

She forced herself up onto unsteady feet.

He was walking towards her, eyes narrowing, softening, and then he was holding out his hand.

'Ash…?' His eyes were green, filled with confusion and curiosity. 'I'm Theo Molenaar. But I'm…' He hesitated. 'I was expecting…'

His tone was friendly, his accent light. There was kindness in his face, a smile hiding at the corners of his mouth. She felt her lips curving upward. She liked him, just like that. Easy as pie.

'You were expecting my brother.' She put her hand into his. 'I'm Mia Boelens.'

His fingers flexed around hers, warm and just firm enough.

'So, Mia…what's the story?' Something in his eyes wouldn't let her go. 'Are you Ash's business partner? Is he coming?'

'Ash *is* coming, yes—and, no, I'm not his business partner.'

A wisp of hair was tickling her neck. She tucked it behind her ear and glanced at her feet, noticing the hem of her slouchy grey trousers skimming her patent loafers.

Theo was smartly dressed in a blue suit and crisp white shirt. His brown shoes were well-polished. She'd been in writing mode when Ash had called and that was how she'd left the house. Without looking, she couldn't even remember if she was wearing a plain white tee-shirt under her jacket, or the black one with the feminist slogan. Certainly, she wasn't dressed to impress. There hadn't been time.

She lifted her eyes to his. There was warmth behind the intensity of his gaze; something else too which was playing havoc with her pulse. 'Unfortunately Ash has been delayed. He's stuck on a train. It's not his fault—it's a signalling fault.'

His eyebrows quirked. Maybe he was amused. She moistened her lips. 'This meeting is very important to my brother, Mr Molenaar—'

'Stop!'

The breath caught in her throat. She'd screwed up.

'My name is Theo.' He was smiling properly now. White, even teeth.

She exhaled slowly, feeling a small wash of relief. He *was* going to listen. Maybe she was actually going to pull this off.

'Okay, *Theo*.' She smiled. 'As I was saying, this meeting is very important to Ash. I came here hoping to persuade you to change the venue…' if only he'd stop looking at her so intently '…to split the difference, time-wise. Ash doesn't want to postpone or cancel. He said this was the only window you had.'

His eyes narrowed. 'So, what are you proposing?'

She swallowed hard. 'Greenwich.'

'Greenwich…?'

'Ash's train is coming in a stone's throw from there, so going to him will save time, and…' She took a deep breath. 'I thought you'd like it because there's a planetarium.'

For the first time he broke her gaze. He shifted on his feet, pressed a hand to the back of his neck and when he looked at her again his eyes were cooler, guarded. 'What makes you think I'd like the planetarium?'

Her heart clenched. She'd unsettled him somehow, just when she needed to keep him onside. She considered his hotel. Small. Exclusive. *Discreet!* There'd been no photographs of him online… He was a private person, intensely private. Maybe he was made that way, or maybe he was hiding something…

Hal had been good at that. Hiding. Stealing from the business to fund his gambling habit. Throwing her off the scent with expensive weekends away paid for out of a bogus inheritance. Ash had been the one paying…and when he'd started noticing discrepancies in the balance sheets, when he'd raised his doubts about Hal with her, what had she said? She'd said that Hal would *never* do such a thing, that he was too smart, too honest, too much in love with her ever to hurt her or their little family.

But she'd been wrong—catastrophically wrong! Was Theo Molenaar hiding something too? Was he another Hal?

He was looking at her intently, green eyes full of complications. Maybe it didn't matter what he was. The only thing that mattered was securing Ash's chance to pitch to MolTec.

She smiled, gave a little shrug. 'I saw an article about you having your eye to the telescope and I thought—'

'That I like the stars?' The tension faded from his eyes. 'That article was going with a metaphor about business expansion.' He hesitated, eyes fixed on hers, and then his face took on a boyish shyness. 'But, as a matter of fact, I *do* like astronomy. The big bang theory, the expanding universe…' He smiled. 'The oldest planetarium in the world just happens to be on the ceiling of a canal house in Franeker—can you believe that? I went when I was a boy, and ever since I've been fascinated by the stars; I even have my own telescope. So, actually, you weren't too far off the mark.'

He'd trusted her with something private. The touch of colour at his cheekbones gave him away, or maybe it was that tiny glimmer of vulnerability she could see behind his eyes. She searched for some moisture in her mouth, something to swallow so she could speak. 'I just want to help my brother, Theo…and the planetarium seemed like a happy compromise.'

He shifted on his feet. 'Your brother's lucky you're willing to go the extra mile for him.'

She was close, she could feel it. All he needed was one last nudge. 'Actually…' Her fingers tightened around the strap of her bag. 'The observatory's six miles from here.'

He lifted an eyebrow, a smile touching the corners of his mouth. 'Six miles? In that case, I'll order us a car.'

Theo pressed the phone tightly against his ear as a police motorbike weaved through the nearby traffic with its siren blaring.

'See if you can fix something for Wednesday and, if that works for Thorne, change my flights.' He pictured his assistant's face. 'I'm sorry, Trude.'

Trude laughed. 'I've no doubt your gratitude will be reflected in my imminent pay rise!'

A smile tugged at his lips. 'If you can reschedule the meeting without ruffling Thorne's feathers, I'll consider it.'

'Leave it with me.' She lowered her voice. 'I'm dying to know why you're postponing Jason Thorne—it must be something *very* important!'

He glanced at Mia then turned to watch the view unfolding through the window of the luxury saloon. Trude never stopped trying to prise him open but it wouldn't work; he was a clam. 'Let me know how you get on with Thorne, okay?'

'Okay, Theo. Bye for now.'

He slipped his phone into his pocket. Disruptions usually annoyed him, but instead he was caught somewhere between admiration and bemusement. That Mia had gone out on a limb to help her brother resonated with him deeply. She was clearly the kind of person who couldn't sit on the sidelines if she could do something to help, and he understood that impulse all too well. He felt the dark stirrings of a memory… His father… His older brother, Bram… Hard fists… Purple bruises… He'd learned at an early age the intolerable frustration of powerlessness.

Perhaps Mia's fighting spirit on its own would have persuaded him to reschedule his afternoon appointments and head across London to meet Ash Boelens, but there'd been something else too: the way she'd looked at him; that glimmer of vulnerability woven through the steely threads of her determination. She'd had him from the start, and he wasn't used to being had. He didn't know what to make of it.

He turned to catch her eye, but she was gazing out of the window. Her shoulders were rigid, her chin lifted. Tenderness bloomed in his chest. She was only pretending to be confident…

'I just want to help my brother.'

He sighed softly and studied the back of her head. Her light-brown hair was wound up chaotically, speared with a pointy thing, and there were strands hanging loose against the side of her smooth neck. He pictured her face—the clear, brown eyes, the constellation of tiny freckles across the bridge of her nose, the perfect fullness of her lips.

He dropped his gaze. Her outfit was rather boho: black patent shoes, loose grey trousers, a battered military jacket. At the hotel he'd glimpsed a slogan on her black tee-shirt, but he didn't know what it said because he hadn't wanted to stare at her chest.

She turned suddenly, sensing him, perhaps. 'I'm sorry you've had to cancel your next meeting. I didn't think things th—'

'It's okay. It can be fixed.'

She was fingering the strap of her bag and then her eyes widened. 'At least the traffic's not too bad.'

The driver braked suddenly and they pitched forward in perfect unison. She caught his eye, started to giggle and then he was chuckling too. He motioned through the window. 'We'd have been quicker on bicycles.'

She pulled a face. 'I'd never cycle in London—it's far too dangerous!'

'So many stationary cars! Very dangerous!'

She mock-scowled. 'It *is* dangerous. They're putting in cycle lanes but London's a long way behind Amsterdam.'

She was right about that. She was obviously familiar with his city. He shifted in his seat. 'So… I'm intrigued! You have a Dutch name but no trace of an accent…'

'Ash and I grew up in London.'

'Where's your family from, originally?' He checked himself. 'If you don't mind me asking, that is.'

'My father's family is from Texel.'

'I have a beach house there…' His tongue stuck to the roof of his mouth. He hadn't meant to share that, or the story about his childhood visit to the planetarium at Franeker, but there was something about her that drew him in, made words fall from his mouth. He'd have to be more careful.

'We used to spend our summers there.' Her smile was a little wistful. 'It's a lovely place.'

'And your mother's family—where are they from?'

'England.' She faltered. 'Actually, I wonder if talking about my family is altogether appropriate.' She pressed her lips together, blushed a little. 'You're about to go into a business meeting with my brother.'

He cursed silently. He hadn't meant to make her feel uncomfortable. 'You're right. I'm sorry. I was only making conversation.'

She dropped her gaze to her hands, twisting the ring she wore on her thumb. Loose strands of hair grazed the soft hollows beneath her cheekbones. She was undeniably lovely. Looking at her face, seeing the way the light danced in her eyes when she was talking, was so much better than staring out of the window.

'Can I ask you about yourself, then?'

She looked up and shot him a little smile. 'What do you want to know…?'

'I'm wondering what you do when you're not running diplomatic errands.'

Her eyes clouded momentarily and then her expression settled. 'I'm a writer.'

A muscle in his jaw twitched involuntarily. She didn't seem to have the sharp elbows of a newshound, but he'd have to be careful—for Bram's sake. He drew a steadying breath and managed an interested smile. 'Of books? Or are you a journalist?'

'I write magazine articles and features. Blog posts. A bit of copywriting.' She smiled. 'There's no sign of a book yet…'

He pressed a finger to his temple. 'What sort of features?'

'A mixture.' She gave a little shrug. 'Popular culture, art, design, interiors…that kind of thing.'

Relief loosened his joints. The arts were a million miles from the gutter where the paparazzi and their cronies hung about. 'So, what are you working on at the moment?'

She angled herself towards him on the seat, pulling one leg up under the other. 'Have you heard of *Dilly and Daisy*?'

Her eyes were wide and full of light. It was hard not to get lost in them.

'No, I haven't.'

'Okay, well, the D&D brand is all about sustainable fashion; it's how they made their name. But now they're moving into homeware—so that's furnishing fabrics, cushions, cookware…'

'Wow!' He arched an eyebrow. 'I had no idea that's what homeware was…'

Her eyes narrowed momentarily, and then she burst out laughing, rocking forward, hands over her mouth, and it was as if all the tiny tensions orbiting around them had suddenly vanished. Then he was laughing too, right from the bottom of his belly; he couldn't remember laughing like that for the longest time.

When she'd finally gathered herself, her eyes were still glistening with smiles. She put her hand on his arm. 'I can't believe I was actually explaining homeware! I'm so sorry. It must be nerves…'

Her eyes held his through an endless moment, a moment he couldn't shake himself out of, and then she seemed to notice that her hand was still resting on his arm and she pulled it away quickly, her cheeks colouring.

He looked down, felt his heart thumping. It had been a spontaneous gesture—a friendly touch, nothing more—but then it had turned into something else and he'd felt that cosmic pull, like planets drawing together. *Dangerous!* Admiring Mia's eyes and the way she smiled was one thing, but it had to stop there. He'd been sucked into the vortex before and he was never going there again.

She was tucking loose strands of hair behind her ears. 'Anyway, I'm doing a piece about them—how they started, their design influences, how they see things progressing… I interviewed them yesterday.' She shrugged a little. 'But I suppose you know how that goes. You must get mobbed by tech writers all the time.'

She had to be joking. Putting himself into the hands of a journalist was the last thing he'd ever do. 'No. I don't do interviews.' He tried to keep his gaze level. 'MolTec has a PR department; no one needs to talk to me.'

It was a relief to be out in the fresh air and sunshine. Accompanying Theo to Greenwich hadn't exactly been part of her plan, but when he'd said, *'I'll order us a car,'* she hadn't wanted to object. He *had* changed his plans for Ash, after all.

And the car had been nice and roomy, and the journey had been fun—at least up to the moment when she'd put her hand on his arm. She hadn't meant anything by it but there'd been that long moment, something in his eyes that had made her senses swim. She'd felt disorientated, unsure of the signals she was sending out, unsure of the signals she was receiving. She'd been glad when the car had pulled up at the observatory entrance.

She slipped her sunglasses on and turned to watch him. He was busy surveying the London skyline, eyes fastened to the talking telescope. His face had been a picture when he'd spotted it, full of boyish delight.

No one needs to talk to me.

He seemed to be an intensely private person. She'd

noticed a momentary glimmer of discomfort in his eyes when she'd told him she was a writer. He was a star in the business world. You had to be pretty fearless to survive in the world of tech. What could he possibly be scared of?

She felt her phone vibrating in her hand, saw Ash's face on the splash screen. 'Hey, you!'

'Dare I ask…?'

'We're here, at the observatory.' She grinned. 'Theo's got his eye to the telescope right now.'

'I owe you big time!'

After Hal? He had to be kidding. 'You don't owe me anything. Where are you?'

'Fifteen minutes away.' He was happy; she could tell. 'I've managed to book a meeting room inside the planetarium. They're doing coffee for us, so just go in when you're ready.'

'Perfect timing! Theo's just relinquished the telescope to a sobbing child…' He was looking around, clearly trying to spot her. She raised a hand and, when he saw, he broke into a smile, started walking towards her with a long, easy stride.

Ash laughed. 'Is he that tyrannous?'

'I was joking—he isn't tyrannous at all.' A toddler with a spinning helium balloon ploughed into Theo's legs. She watched him absorbing the impact, dropping to his haunches, laughing, talking to the tot, smiling away, pointing to the bobbing balloon. 'He's sharp as a tack, but he has a heart, otherwise he wouldn't have come.' She dropped her gaze, noticing a scuff mark on her shoe. 'When you arrive, I'm going to disappear, okay?'

'Is everything all right?'

'Of course it is. It's just that…' *Theo makes my head spin* '…you don't want me hanging around while you make your presentation. I'll only heckle and make a terrible nuisance of myself.'

He chuckled. 'We'll catch up later, then?'

'Yeah—just make sure you smash it out of the park, okay?'

CHAPTER TWO

Three weeks later...

MIA TOOK HER coffee onto the deck and settled herself into the old wicker chair. Cleuso leapt up and wedged himself into the non-existent space beside her. She tickled his throat, listening to his purr as she gazed across the canal.

It was early—before six, her favourite time of day. The city was peaceful. All the small noises were delightfully random: the lollop of water against the side of the houseboat; the cry of a bird; the distant rattle of a window shutter. Once the day got underway the soundtrack of Amsterdam would change. The streets would fill with the *dong, dong, dong* of the trams and the rumble of suitcase wheels rolling along pavements. The babble of a hundred different languages would rise into the air, punctuated by the insistent *dring-dring* of bicycle bells. But in that moment, watching the early sun filtering through the mist on the water, Cleuso's soft body warming her thigh, she felt as if the city was unfurling just for her, inviting her backstage.

She sipped her coffee, savouring the deep, rich taste of it, and then she smiled, just as she'd smiled every morning for the past three weeks. It was because she couldn't drink this coffee without thinking of Theo...

He'd been standing in the meeting room at the planetarium, cup and saucer in his hand, surveying the curved walls lined with books. He'd lifted the cup to his lips, sipped and a shadow had crossed his face. She'd known why. The coffee was disappointing. They'd set their cups down at exactly the same time.

She'd caught his eye. 'It's not the best, is it?'

'No.' He'd held her gaze for a long second then turned away, tipping his head back so he could look at the skylight. 'I always get my coffee beans from Koffiemeester's on Van Baelerstraat. *That's* good coffee.'

She'd turned away to hide her smile. She knew Koffiemeester's. It was where she bought her coffee too, but something had stopped her saying it. For some reason she didn't want him to know that she lived in Amsterdam. It seemed safer to let him believe that she was based in London…and it wasn't entirely untrue. She stayed at the mews house frequently enough when she was covering events or interviewing designers in London. It would always be part of her—the family home—but after 'Halgate' she'd needed a fresh start and she'd always loved Amsterdam. Her grandparents had given her their houseboat. They preferred to stay in Texel all year round these days and they knew how much she'd always loved the barge.

She looked along the water towards the bridge. The trees beside the canal were pushing out leaves, and in the pots crammed onto the deck of the boat green tulip tips were nosing through the compost. Spring! The season of beginnings. She sipped her coffee again. Somewhere in the city, perhaps nearby, Theo might be drinking his coffee too. Perhaps he had a view of the trees and the canals. Perhaps he was thinking about her.

Cleuso twisted onto his back, stretching his limbs, spreading his toes. She touched her finger to the plump pads of one paw and felt his claws flex in a gentle warning. *Beware!*

Warning signs were everywhere. You just had to tune in to them. Like Hal saying, *'We're going to Paris this weekend... I've got tickets for the opera...'* ten minutes after Ash had told her he thought there was something amiss with the business accounts. Like Theo's face turning ashen when she'd told him she was a writer. *Why?* She sighed. Hal's actions had made her hyper-alert to any kind of shadiness but, still, something about Theo's intent green eyes was tormenting her. She'd tried to put him out of her head, yet here she was again, thinking about him—the way he'd looked at her when they'd said goodbye.

She drained her cup, set it down on the deck. So, they were both coffee snobs—what of it? It didn't mean there'd be other things they'd have in common. Besides, now that Ash was going to be working closely with MolTec, giving Theo a wide berth was absolutely the right thing to do. Her feelings for Hal had blinded her to things she should have questioned and nearly driven a wedge between her and Ash. She couldn't go through that again, dividing her loyalties between her brother and a lover. She couldn't protect Ash from the past but, after everything that had happened, falling for his new business associate would be utter madness.

Cleuso writhed suddenly and sprang from her lap. He stretched his hind legs then jumped onto the rail, teetering for a moment before springing upward onto the barge roof. He paused to wash his face, then trotted off to the far end of the boat and disappeared from view. She gazed after him. It had been the right decision not to tell Theo that she lived in his city, yet somehow she couldn't get him out of her head. The way his face had brightened when he'd spotted her at the observatory; the way he'd smiled as he started walking towards her. There'd been openness in his smile, a feeling of connection, as if the stars had already settled into a new alignment.

She pushed him out of her head. The first trams were moving, and she needed to get moving too. She had her Dilly and Daisy article to finish, a blog post to write for a sportswear client and after that there was the big charity event for the women's refuge. All in all, there was more than enough to keep her mind off Theo Molenaar.

It was hard not to see traces of Mia in her brother. Their eyes were the same shape, although Ash's were a clear blue, and Ash's hair was a shade or two lighter than Mia's. Theo wondered if Mia had inherited her brown eyes from her mother, and then he wondered why he was even thinking about that when he was supposed to be concentrating on what Ash was saying. He refocused.

'We need to make sure that the software doesn't become a prophet of doom.' Ash was leaning forward, his eyes narrowing. 'What I really want is for it to be used in a positive way, to demonstrate how small environmental changes can make a significant impact.'

Ash's environmental-impact modelling software was still in development but Theo could see many potential applications. He'd been so impressed with Ash's presentation at the planetarium that he'd jumped at the chance to get involved. Now it was a question of putting a strategy in place, providing Ash with the technical support he needed to put the prototype through its paces.

He rocked back in his chair. 'We're definitely on the same page, Ash. The world needs creative thinking tied to practical applications and that's exactly what your software is going to deliver.' He smiled. 'We need to get you to Amsterdam soon, to meet my technical team.'

'No problem. I could come the week after next.' Ash's eyes were merry. 'Mia will be very happy—she's always telling me I don't visit often enough.'

The words were plainly spoken but Theo couldn't make sense of them. He pressed a finger to his temple. 'She likes you to visit Amsterdam?'

Ash was powering off his laptop. 'She likes me to visit *her*.' He looked up. 'Mia *lives* in Amsterdam—didn't she mention it?'

His heart bumped. 'No…she didn't.' He opened his briefcase and slipped his notes inside, keeping his eyes down. Why hadn't Mia told him that she lived in his city? They could have talked about it, the places they liked and didn't like. For some reason it stung that she'd kept it to herself. Sensing Ash's gaze, he looked up, forced a smile onto his lips. 'To be fair, she was rather preoccupied.'

'That's Mia! Unstoppable when she gets the bit between her teeth.' A shadow crossed Ash's face. 'We're very close, you know. We've been through a lot…' He seemed to drift momentarily and then his face brightened. 'Do you have brothers and sisters?'

'One of each.'

Ash slid his laptop into its case. 'And what do they do?'

He hesitated. There wasn't enough time for that conversation even if he'd felt inclined to have it. He closed his briefcase. 'I'm sorry, Ash. I have to scoot. I've got a plane to catch.' He wondered if he'd sounded a little brusque, so he added, 'I'm having an early dinner with my sister, actually, and I can't be late.' He stood up, held out his hand and smiled. 'We'll sort out the Amsterdam meeting, okay? Get things moving.'

In the car to London's City Airport, Theo sank back into the seat and loosened his tie, considering what Ash had just revealed. In his mind, he went over the conversation he'd had with Mia on the way to Greenwich. They'd talked about cycling… She'd told him she'd never cycle in London. She'd even remarked that London was a long way behind Amsterdam for cycle paths, but she'd framed it in a general sort of way. He'd assumed that she was familiar with Amsterdam, given that she was Dutch on her father's side at least—they'd never got as far as talking about her mother's family—but he'd also assumed that she was based in London, like her brother, and she'd done nothing to dissuade him of it.

Why?

Suddenly the words he'd spoken in the hotel reception area came back to him: *'I'll order us a car.'*

He swallowed hard. Had he overstepped a line without realising it? What if she'd never intended to accompany him to the planetarium, had felt pressured to go? If that was how she'd felt, she might have been worried that, if he knew she lived in Amsterdam, he'd ask to see her again…

He groaned inwardly. It was the last thing he'd intended—to come on too strong, to come on in any way at all. It was just that she'd taken him by surprise, thrown him off-balance with her clear brown gaze and her sweet smile, and when she'd said that the observatory was six miles away there'd been something in her voice, more than just hope in her eyes… She'd trapped him in her warm light, had drawn him in with a teasing glint. That was what had made him think she wanted to go with him…

He turned to look through the window, but it was her face he saw. The way she'd laughed at his lame joke, her hand on his arm, eyes full of…what? If he'd been sending out signals, then she'd been sending out signals too. He wasn't imagining it. In the car, he'd had the feeling that there was a whole other conversation going on between them in a parallel dimension. He hadn't known what to make of it, or what to do about it. All he knew was that for the past three weeks he hadn't been able to get her smile out of his head, and it was confusing, because even starting to think about someone in that way again was precisely what he'd told himself he could never do.

He sighed. Now he wouldn't have to think about it any more. Whatever he thought or imagined he'd felt between himself and Mia, she hadn't wanted him to know where she lived, and that could only mean she wasn't interested in seeing him again. She'd been helping her brother. End of.

He closed his eyes. Some part of his subconscious had misread the situation. No surprise! Experience had taught him that he couldn't trust his own judgement when it came to matters of the heart, even if Mia *did* seem to be the polar opposite of his ex-wife, Eline de Vries. Supermodel.

A fist closed around his heart. It always happened when he thought about Eline. When he'd met her, she'd simply been a pretty student at the same university, the girl who'd stolen his heart. He'd loved her smile, her confidence, the way she could light up a room. He'd proposed to her on her graduation day and nearly died with happiness when she'd said yes.

Six months later, they were married. His only thought had been to make her happy, to be a better man than his father had ever been. That meant never touching a drop of alcohol, never releasing the inner violence that was his legacy. It meant providing stability and financial security—all the things he'd grown up without.

After university he'd started his own software development business, working from a room in the apartment until things had grown sufficiently to require a small contingent of staff. Then he'd taken a small unit by the river and started to build the MolTec brand.

Eline had wanted to be a fashion buyer, but fresh out of university she'd joined a company which specialised in fashion events...for the experience and the contacts, she'd said. At a catwalk show an agency scout had taken her picture, told her she had a distinctive look. She'd laughed about it but within a fortnight she'd been signed to a top agency and after that everything changed.

While he was working eighteen-hour days building the business, Eline was courting the limelight. While he was helping Bram battle alcoholism, Eline was partying. Her confidence turned into haughtiness; her sweetness turned sour. She'd said Bram was weak. She'd said that he should put Bram into rehab and get on with his own life—*their* life. She'd said he was neglecting her, that *she* needed him by her side, but Bram needed him more. Helping Bram through his illness was something he'd *had* to do, something he'd *wanted* to do. He'd thought Eline would support him, but instead she'd had an affair—not a love affair, but a casual thing. She'd done it out of spite, to hurt him. She'd broken his heart.

He opened his eyes to redness—the flank of a bus in the other lane. That was what love did. Filled in the view so you couldn't see around it or through it. There'd been a time when he'd thought Eline would walk through fire for him but instead she'd betrayed him when he'd needed her most. He'd wanted them to be perfect. He'd wanted one perfect thing in his life, but she'd ripped it up, thrown it away.

He'd vowed never to let anyone hurt him like that again, but somehow someone had... It wasn't a big, devastating kind of hurt, more of a little pinprick, but it ached just the same, maybe more for being so unexpected.

In a parallel dimension he must have been nurturing a vague hope that he'd see Mia again. The thought of it gave him a head rush and, as he got out of the cab and paid the driver, it suddenly struck him that in spite of everything that had happened in his life he still believed in love.

Mia felt an arm sliding around her waist, the press of lips against her neck. She caught the distinctive scent of Lotte's perfume and a second later there came the soft, musical accent whispering into her ear. 'Guess who might be coming tonight?'

She wriggled free so she could see her friend's impish face. 'If it's someone important, I should have been told...'

Lotte gave a little shrug and widened her eyes. 'Well, it's not definite, but...' She leaned in, whispered, 'Madelon Mulder!'

Mia nearly dropped her champagne flute. Madelon Mulder had been involved with the Saving Grace women's refuge in Amsterdam for many years. After winning the best actress gong at the Sunshine Film Festival, for her breakthrough performance in Chris Van Kooten's lauded movie *Going Home*, the twenty-nine-year-old was beginning to attract attention from the press, which could only benefit the refuge by association. Mia dipped her chin, keeping her voice low. 'Why didn't anyone tell me?'

Lotte tugged her arm, steering her away from the guests mingling in the middle of the function room. 'Because we only just found out. Madelon's only in Amsterdam for a few hours so there's no time for an interview. She's on her way to Athens to start shooting a new movie, but her agent said she wanted to drop in for a quick photo op to publicise the work of the refuge.' Lotte hitched the camera strap higher up her shoulder and faked a swoon. 'I *love* her. Do you think she might fall in love with me while I'm taking her picture?'

'Everyone falls in love with you.'

Lotte frowned. 'Don't be disingenuous. You know what I meant…'

Mia sighed, slipping her arm around Lotte's shoulders. 'I don't know, Lotte. My grandmother used to say that what's meant for you won't pass you by.'

Lotte twisted round, her eyes wide and wounded. 'You're telling me I was *meant* to be assaulted?'

'No! I didn't mean…' She bit her lip. She'd been talking about finding love, but Lotte had twisted it, made it about *that* night… She shuddered involuntarily, remembering the darkness and the pouring rain, the strangled sob, the sight of Lotte struggling with the big man… That terrible night had brought Lotte and her together, forged a friendship between them that she knew would last for ever, but if their friendship was the silver lining then now wasn't the time to mention it. Lotte was on the edge of tears. It was a side she didn't reveal to anyone else, but Mia saw it all too often. To the rest of the world Lotte projected strength and spirit. She liked to shock people with her forthright manner, but Mia knew the truth. She knew how Lotte's spirit had been broken, how she still looked over her shoulder even in the day time.

She gave Lotte's arm a squeeze. 'Of course you weren't *meant* to be attacked. That's not what the saying's about. It's about good things, like love… It's about destiny.'

'Destiny?' Lotte turned to face her. 'I don't believe in all that "written in the stars" crap, Mia. I never have, and I don't understand how you can believe in it either after losing your mum and dad…and after Hal ripping Ash off like he did, breaking your heart.'

Mia bit down hard on her lip. Lotte wasn't trying to upset her, she knew that, but it was hard to hear the layers of her pain being piled up like mattresses in the fairy tale. *The Princess and the Pea.* Her mum used to read that story to her when she was a little girl, but she couldn't hear her mum's voice in her head any more. It had faded away. Hal and everything that went with him would fade away too, in time. One day, even Lotte might stop seeing menace in the shadows. She looked away, staring into the milling crowd with unseeing eyes. For some reason Theo drifted into her thoughts. Green eyes. Warm smile. She drew a breath, braved Lotte's gaze again. 'You're all out of faith. I understand. Most of the time, I'm the same, but sometimes…' She gave a little shrug. 'Don't you just want to believe that there's a reason for it all? That something good can come out of the bad stuff?'

Lotte stretched out and took her hand. 'You're the only good thing, Mia. You get me…put up with me, even when I'm a mess.' She stepped closer. 'I wish…'

The wide blue eyes held her, and for a moment Mia wished that she could make Lotte's dreams come true, but she'd never be able to do that. She smiled softly. 'You'll find your lobster, Lotte… One day.'

Lotte huffed a sigh and then her mouth quirked. 'Well, I'm not going to find her if I don't start working the room.' She lifted the camera strap off her shoulder, looping it around her neck. 'If I hear any more about Madelon, I'll let you know.'

Mia watched Lotte disappearing into the crowd. Hal, and the man who'd tried to force himself on Lotte, they'd left such a trail of destruction behind, so much damage, so much pain… She sipped her drink, starting a slow circuit around the great room, forcing herself to think about other things. Interviewing Madelon Mulder really would have been something! In the interviews she'd seen, the actress had always seemed so grounded, so completely genuine. At least Lotte would get pictures—another famous person to add to her growing portfolio.

She looked upward and around, taking in the mottled plaster walls, the sharp shiny angles of the suspended lighting rig. The Machine Room at Westergasfabriek was one of her favourite places—a wonderful venue for events. The light through the tall arched window in the gable was turning to a peachy glow. She stared into it, stepping back slowly, losing herself in its warm haze as she thought about what she was going to write…

The Machine Room at Westergasfabriek was the perfect venue for the recent Saving Grace fundraiser.

Two hundred guests attended: contributors, trustees and sponsors of the women's refuge charity which, for the past decade, has offered support and, more importantly, places for women and their children to stay while they find their feet again.

The gathering was 'graced' with an unexpected visit from...

A sudden, solid presence at her back startled her and she spun round.

'I'm so sorry. I hope—' Black denim jacket. Dark V-necked sweater. Smooth, golden skin at the base of his throat. Perfect mouth, straight nose, green eyes. She blinked once, twice, but it wasn't her imagination. Theo Molenaar was standing right in front of her.

'Hello, Mia.'

Her heart was galloping and the floor seemed to be moving, throwing her off-balance. She pressed the balls of her feet into her shoes and swallowed hard. 'Hello, Theo.'

He was looking into her face, a question in his eyes, but there was something else too, a tiny glimmer of hurt, a trace of vulnerability, which made her feel ashamed. She twisted the champagne flute around in her hands, trying to steady her breathing. In a million years she hadn't expected to bump into him and now she had some explaining to do.

She moistened her lips, shot him a little smile. 'Of all the gin joints in all the towns… That's what you're thinking, right?'

His eyebrows lifted. 'More or less.'

She drew in a breath. 'I live here, okay? Well, not *here* in this exact building, obviously, but in Amsterdam.' His expression was softening. 'I grew up in London. I spend a lot of time there, but I moved here a while ago, and I didn't mention it because…'

The amusement in his eyes was making it impossible not to smile. 'Because it was such a bizarre situation: coming to your hotel; making you go to Greenwich…'

'You didn't make me. You convinced me.' Eyes locked on hers. 'There's a big difference.'

She wished he'd stop looking at her like that but, then again, she liked the happy fluttering of butterflies in her stomach, liked the way he made her senses fizz like sparklers.

'I wanted to tell you, really I did. At the planetarium, when you said you got your coffee from Koffiemeester's, it almost broke me because I buy my coffee there too.'

'You do?'

'Of course! It's the best coffee in Amsterdam.' As his eyes held hers, she felt her smile fading, a little frown taking its place. 'I'm sorry I didn't tell you, Theo. I'm not one for secrets—quite the opposite—but at the time it just didn't feel…'

'Appropriate?'

She nodded.

A smile played on his lips. 'It *was* a rather unusual situation.'

She tilted her head. 'We could start over…'

'Start over?'

She smiled, held out her hand. 'Hello. I'm Mia Boelens, resident of Amsterdam.'

Warm fingers closed around hers. 'Theo Molenaar.' He held her gaze, smiling softly. 'It's really good to see you again, Mia—a nice surprise.' For a moment the room fell away and then he released her hand, motioning to the throng. 'So, what brings you to this particular gin joint anyway?'

'I write blog posts and press releases for the refuge.' She tucked a strand of hair behind her ear, wondering if her cheeks were as pink as they felt. 'What about you?'

'I used to be a trustee. Now I support the refuge in other ways…' He shifted on his feet, lowering his voice. 'I like to keep my involvement private, Mia.'

There it was again, that wariness. What was he hiding? After Hal, she had no time for secrets, but there was something raw in Theo's eyes which made her want to put her arms around him. *Impossible!*

'Don't worry. I get it; you were never here!' She lifted her chin. 'I can't pretend I'm not curious, though…'

'Motives get misconstrued, Mia.' He shrugged. 'You buy properties for abused women and children to stay in and you're accused of pulling a PR stunt, or you're accused of dodging corporation tax or whatever.' Weariness in his eyes. 'It's easier to be invisible.'

There was something noble about that. He wasn't completely invisible, though. She'd found one small headshot with a brief profile on the MolTec website, not that she'd spent hours searching or anything.

'Hey, Mia!' Lotte was coming towards them. 'That thing we talked about…' She lowered her voice. 'It's happening!'

'When?'

'Soon.' Lotte's eyes slid to Theo's face. She stepped back, looked him up and down then lifted her camera. 'You're very handsome! Can I take a picture?'

'No!' Mia put her hand on Lotte's arm. 'Mr Molenaar hasn't agreed to pictures.'

Lotte's eyes narrowed. 'Okay.' She lowered her camera and held out her hand. 'Hello Mr Molenaar. I'm Lotte—Mia's friend.'

Mia caught the teasing glimmer in his eyes as he shook Lotte's hand. 'Theo Molenaar. Mia's friend also.'

She was trying not to laugh at the pair of them when a sudden flurry of movement at the far end of the room made Lotte turn sharply and rise up onto her toes like a meerkat.

'She's here!'

In the next instant her friend was plunging into the crowd, holding the camera high so that soon all she could see was Lotte's camera weaving through a sea of heads like a shark's fin.

When she turned back to Theo, he had a bemused look on his face. She gave a little shrug. 'Lotte's very excited because Madelon Mulder's making a surprise appearance tonight.' He seemed unmoved. Ash would have been jumping up and down, fighting his way to the front—he had a massive crush on Madelon Mulder. Maybe Theo wasn't into serious cinema. Hal had been into action movies and wouldn't have recognised Madelon Mulder if he'd fallen over her. Maybe Theo was the same. She smiled. 'Do you know who that is?'

He seemed to hesitate and then he smiled, eyes twinkling. 'Yes, I do… Madelon's my sister.'

'Your sister?'

Mia was staring at him with wide, incredulous eyes. She had one of those animated faces that you found yourself mimicking subconsciously. He forced himself to blink. 'Yes.'

Her eyebrows had disappeared into her fringe and her mouth was slightly open, her lower lip full, and rosy and extremely tempting.

He leaned closer. 'You need to breathe, Mia.'

She shook her head a little, took a long sip from her glass then looked up at him. 'Wow! You must be so proud of her.'

He nodded. 'I am. Very proud.' An image drifted into his head: seven-year-old Madelon putting on her little plays, using her dolls as actors—trying to entertain the family in whichever seedy temporary accommodation their mother had managed to find. 'She's come a long way…'

There was a burst of camera flash at the far end of the room.

Mia tilted her head. 'You probably want to go over, right?'

He looked into her face, lost himself in the warm glow of her eyes. Couldn't she see that he was exactly where he wanted to be?

'Madelon and I had dinner together earlier.'

'Of course you did.' She pressed the heel of her hand to her forehead, rolling her eyes. 'I'm such an idiot!'

He laughed. 'Not at all. To you, she's a movie star. To me, she's just my little sister.' He lifted a fresh glass of champagne from a passing tray and handed it to her, taking a mineral water for himself. 'We get together whenever we can. Sometimes we spend a few days at the beach house.'

'On Texel!' She smiled. 'I remember.'

He nodded. 'Madelon's catching a flight after this so we said our goodbyes earlier.' A thought suddenly struck him. 'But do *you* need to go over? If you're writing something, maybe you need…'

'No…it's fine.' She smiled ruefully. 'They didn't set anything up because there's no time for an interview tonight. It's great that we're getting pictures, though. It'll be good publicity.'

'For sure.' He managed a smile, but he could feel the muscles in his neck tightening. Madelon knew that her recent success had increased her currency; it was why she'd insisted on shoehorning a photo-op into her schedule.

'Theo! Saving Grace will get a massive boost if my picture makes the press and goes viral on social media!'

As always, her intentions were good but, although he was proud and delighted about her critical success, he worried about the exposure that came with it. It was why he'd insisted that they shouldn't be seen together tonight. It was only a matter of time before someone put two and two together and found out that Madelon was related to the CEO of MolTec. After that, who knew what they'd find? For Bram's sake, he had to keep the wolves at bay for as long as possible.

'Are you okay?' Mia was looking at him, a little frown on her face.

'Sure. It's been a long day, that's all.' He smiled. 'I was in London this morning, meeting with Ash. Did he tell you?'

She shook her head. 'We speak most days, but today we seem to have missed…'

Her eyes held him softly, stirring his senses around, making him feel…what? When Ash had told him that she lived in Amsterdam, he'd felt bruised. He'd decided that she hadn't mentioned it because she wasn't interested in seeing him again. On the plane home he'd convinced himself that it was for the best, that relationships only brought heartache anyway. Hadn't his father had almost destroyed his mother? Hadn't Eline almost destroyed him?

By the time the plane had landed at Schiphol, he'd sorted out his feelings, stowed them neatly away, but then she'd walked right back into his life—backwards. And now, there was something behind her gaze, something in her clear brown irises which was melting all the thin ice around his feet. He wanted to spend time with her. God help him, he wanted to know her better.

He sipped his water. 'Do you have to stay until the end?'

She shook her head. 'The work I do for the refuge is voluntary and, since Madelon's photograph is worth at least a thousand words, I think I'll get off lightly this time.'

He put his glass down. He'd know soon enough if he was wide of the mark. 'Do you want to get out of here?'

She looked surprised. 'Didn't you come with someone?' She was blushing. 'What I mean is…are you free…to leave?'

He liked that she'd checked first. He smiled softly. 'If I'd come with someone, I wouldn't be asking you to leave with me.'

She blushed again, screwing up her face into an apologetic little smile. 'Of course. I'm sorry… I didn't mean…'

'I'm not offended, Mia.'

She blew out a sigh and laughed. 'Okay, then…let's go.'

CHAPTER THREE

OUTSIDE, THE NIGHT sky glowed orange over the city rooftops. Usually he'd have noticed how may stars were being hidden by all that light, but instead he was noticing the way Mia's dress lifted in the cool breeze as she walked. He was noticing the little bursts of her perfume escaping into the air as she turned her head. He was so busy noticing things about her that it took him a few moments to realise that she was walking towards the bicycle stands.

'You cycled?'

She smiled. 'I cycle everywhere in Amsterdam.'

She stopped next to a bright-orange bicycle, removed the padlock deftly and dropped it into the basket.

'But you never cycle in London…'

Her lips quirked. 'You remember.'

He remembered everything about their car ride to Greenwich. What they'd said, the way she'd smiled, the way her hair had been knotted up, silky brown strands framing her face. He lifted the bicycle out of the stand for her, instinctively pressing his weight against the handlebars, testing the brakes, running his eye over the tyres, the chain and the gears.

'Will it pass?' Her tone was gently teasing.

He looked up and gave a little shrug. 'Old habits… I

used to look after Madelon's bicycle when we were little. Making sure it was safe.'

'Ash used to do mine.' She grimaced. 'He hated it because I was always getting punctures.'

Theo glanced at Mia's tyres again; thankfully fine.

She was buttoning her jacket. 'So, did you cycle too?'

He shook his head. 'No. I walked.'

'From…?'

'Herengracht—the Jordaan end.'

'Nice!'

'It is.' He pictured the old canal house he was renovating, the peeling walls, the empty rooms. It would be better than nice when it was finished but making every decision on your own was difficult, especially when your architect had rather unconventional ideas. 'Where do you stay?'

'Prinsengracht, near Leidsegracht.'

'That's not so far!'

He smiled to himself. For three whole weeks he'd thought she'd been in England and all that time, she'd been just a fifteen-minute walk away from his house! From the look on her face, he guessed that she was thinking the same thing.

He shifted on his feet. 'So…would you like to go for a drink; get something to eat?'

'You've already eaten, and I've had three glasses of champagne…' She seemed momentarily shy. 'Actually, what I'd really like to do is go home and get changed.' She rubbed at her legs through the skirt of her swishy green dress and shot him a little smile. 'I'm a bit cold.'

He'd taken in the details of Mia's dress while she'd been talking to Lotte. He liked the way it nipped in at the waist, the plain bodice, the modest neckline, but it *was* flimsy. Even with her jacket over the top it wouldn't be nearly warm enough now that the darkness had rolled in on the back of a northerly wind.

'So… Prinsengracht first.' He started pushing the bike, tuned in suddenly to the tap of her heels on the paving. 'Wait! Can you walk in those shoes?'

'I don't know.' She glanced at the bicycle, eyed him mischievously. 'It wasn't an issue on the way here…'

The way she was looking at him made it impossible not to smile. He stopped, considering the bike. 'I think we have two options. You can cycle and I'll run.' She glanced at his polished leather shoes, winced and shook her head. 'Or, we can share the bike.'

'Share it!' She was laughing. 'I haven't done that since I was a kid.'

'Neither have I.' He tested his weight on the frame again. 'It's strong enough.'

She stepped forward and put her hands on the handlebars. 'Okay, then, hop on…'

'Me?'

She looked up, giggling. 'Gotcha!'

Impossible not to like her. He slipped off his jacket, folding it into a pad for the carrier. 'Here. You can sit on this.'

'That's very chivalrous of you!' She settled herself sideways on the carrier while he straddled the bike to hold it steady and then she said, 'I'm so glad I booked first class.'

He laughed, his heart drumming with a sort of childish excitement. 'Right, hold on tight.'

He put his foot to the pedal and pushed off. After a momentary wobble, which made Mia threaten to walk after all, they were going along smoothly enough. He took a route through the park, getting a feel for the bike, getting used to the idea of Mia sitting right behind him.

He twisted round a little. 'Are you okay?'

'I'm fine. You could speed up a bit, though…'

He laughed. 'Give me a chance. I'm out of practice!'

'How come?'

'I have a car.'

She was leaning closer. 'But driving in Amsterdam must be a nightmare…'

'It's okay—it's a compact car.' He faced front again, smiling to himself. He was rather attached to his low-slung classic sports car. It was the kind of car he used to dream of owning when he was a boy and he still felt a buzz every time he started the engine.

She giggled. 'Something tells me it's not a bubble car.'

'I wouldn't fit into one of those.' He turned onto Nassaukade and felt an unfamiliar tightness in his calf muscles. Running was his thing, he could run for miles, but cycling was working his legs in a different way.

'So, do you even own a bike?'

'No.' He tried a change of gear, felt the pedals stiffening against his feet.

'That's terrible! How can you live in the city of bicycles and *not* own a bicycle?'

'I have a rebellious streak.' He changed gear again, pedalling hard until they were flying along, passing lively bars, busy restaurants, closed shops and hoardings covered in colourful graffiti. Mia was laughing, urging him to go even faster, so he pedalled harder, then had to ring the bell frantically at a group of tourists who were standing on the cycle path consulting a map. They scattered just in time.

'Sorreee…' Her yelled apology disappeared on the breeze and then her hand was on his back. 'You nearly killed them!'

'You were the one who told me to speed up.'

'I didn't mean for you to mow down innocent tourists!'

He grinned. 'They didn't look that innocent.'

She laughed. 'How on earth could you tell? You only saw the whites of their eyes.'

He was laughing again, noticing how his cheeks were aching from it. Quads burning, cheeks aching; all the muscles he wasn't used to using. Mia was putting him through his paces, and he was loving every second.

He slowed over a bridge, then stopped. 'Which side of Prinsengracht are you?'

'West, just up from Leidsegracht.'

He pushed off again, cycling more sedately until he felt her hand on his back again, patting gently. 'My boat's just up there on the right. The one with the blue roof.'

'You live on a boat?'

'Didn't I mention it?'

He pulled on the brakes and felt her lurch softly against him. 'No. I don't think you did.'

Mia closed the bedroom door and rolled back against it, her cheeks aching with smiles. Had she just ridden pillion through Amsterdam behind Theo Molenaar? Three weeks ago she'd said goodbye to him in London and now he was on her houseboat—in Amsterdam! She was tingling. That moment when she'd turned around and he'd been right there in front of her…

'Hello, Mia.'

How she hadn't collapsed with shock, she'd never know. There were over a million people in Amsterdam. Bumping into Theo—literally—was a one in a million chance.

One in a million!

She held her breath, listening to him moving about in the salon—little creaks, the thud of his feet as he walked over the rug. On the bike he'd made her laugh until her sides ached. Those little quips he'd made, their easy back and forth as they'd wheeled along. He was funny as well as gorgeous, an irresistible combination.

She pressed her hands to her cheeks. She didn't have to look in the mirror to know she was flushed, and it wasn't because of the champagne, or because of the cool breeze whipping at her face as they'd flown through the streets. It was because of Theo, because she'd been close enough to feel the heat radiating from his body, close enough to catch the scent of his cologne. Twice she'd touched his broad back, felt his muscles working beneath the dark cashmere sweater. It had been hard not to slide her hand upward to touch the hair curling at the back of his neck.

She kicked off her shoes and slipped out of her dress. That boyish delight on his face as he'd stepped onto the barge, his eyes shining as he'd come down the steps into the salon—like a kid at Christmas. How different people could be. Hal had always found the boat too cramped when they'd stayed for a weekend, and Ash could only tolerate it for a day or two. But she'd always loved it. Loved the smallness of it—everything scaled down—like a playhouse. It was magical, and from the look on his face she could tell that Theo thought so too.

She wriggled into her jeans, felt a sudden stab of uncertainty. What was he expecting now? He'd asked her to leave the fundraiser with him. He'd suggested going for a drink, or getting something to eat, but she'd brought him home. All she'd wanted was to change out of her dress, but maybe he was thinking… What? She flung on a slouchy black sweater and lowered herself onto the bed. What kind of signals had she been sending out?

She closed her eyes, groaned silently as her own words came back to her: *'Didn't you come with someone?'*

It had been a knee-jerk reaction because she'd assumed that a man like Theo would have a date, but mouthing over the words again, remembering the conversation that followed, she realised that she'd basically asked him if he was single—and he'd basically replied that he was.

She sighed. Two single people on a barge in Amsterdam. Strangers who'd shared a car, then a bicycle… He *was* a stranger, and yet she felt a connection with him, had felt it from the start. Something about him drew her in, stirred her heart… It was why she'd left the fundraiser with him. But…he was also Ash's new business associate, and hadn't she determined just that morning to give him a wide berth for exactly that reason?

She got up, crossed to the mirror and started tidying her hair. Mixing personal relationships with business didn't work. Hal had manipulated her. He'd known she'd convince Ash that the financial irregularities he was seeing on the spreadsheets were nothing to do with *him*. Unwittingly, she'd bought him time, time he'd used to almost bankrupt the company. Ash's face—all the light draining out it—the way he'd looked at her when it all came out.

She swallowed hard. Falling for someone was a risk, especially if they were in business with the only person you had left in the world. How could she even be thinking of going there again…?

Her eyes slid to the photo hanging on the cabin wall—her parents laughing together, young and in love. That was what everyone wanted, wasn't it? To be loved; to have a home. It was what she wanted…in spite of Hal, in spite of all the heartbreak she'd been through. She couldn't stop herself hoping. She stretched her fingers to the frame, straightening it. If only she could ask her parents for advice, but she'd lived without them for longer than she'd lived with them, and as the years rolled on they were only growing more and more distant. She stared at their faces, trying to conjure their voices, trying to pull them back into her heart, but the space was too big to fill. Hal had filled it for a while, but then he'd blown it apart, made the hole even bigger, even more ragged around the edges.

She pictured Theo's intent green gaze, the kindness in it. He wasn't Ash's business *partner*. He was an *associate*. *He* was investing in Ash, funding the software development. It wasn't the same as Hal... Or was it? She couldn't think straight.

She'd liked Theo instantly. Something in his eyes made her heart sprout wings, but he was a complicated man. Successful. A multi-millionaire businessman. Brother of Madelon Mulder! But he was guarded. Secretive. She had no time for secrets—and yet, she'd kept a secret, hadn't she? In the car to Greenwich it would have been the most natural thing in the world to tell him that she lived in Amsterdam, given that they were talking about it, but she'd kept it to herself. That was lying by omission, which was still lying, even if she'd had her reasons at the time.

She swallowed hard. Lying was a shameful act, rarely justified. She'd seen hurt in Theo's eyes and it had felt like a thorn in her heart because the last thing she'd ever wanted to do was hurt him. She didn't want to hurt anyone.

What's meant for you won't pass you by.

What to think...? Fate seemed to have thrown Theo across her path again, but what did it mean? Perhaps Lotte was right: she ought to be scorning the stars; after all, they hadn't shone too kindly on her so far. Maybe it was time to sweep away the stardust along with all her fanciful notions of a grand destiny. Stardust was like any other dust—blinding if it got into your eyes. This time, she'd keep her head, wouldn't give her heart away until she knew exactly who she was giving it to. Theo Molenaar might be her one in a million, but she had no intention of falling for him on the strength of odds alone.

* * *

He looked up, a trace of amusement in his eyes. 'You sure have a thing for house plants.'

He was standing exactly where she'd left him, in the centre of the red Persian rug which covered most of the cabin floor. He was still holding his jacket. *Subtle!* He was putting put the ball in her court. Staying in, going out: it was to be her decision. If only she knew what to do. She folded her arms and looked around, seeing what he was seeing: a tall variegated fig bursting out of one corner; an assortment of ferns dotted about; a peace lily sharing a low table with a baby yucca; a glossy cheese plant on the floor in another corner; and her latest acquisition—a collection of miniature succulents lined up on a narrow shelf over the sofa.

She met his gaze, gave a little shrug. 'They're a sort of legacy.'

'A legacy?'

'The barge belonged to my grandparents.' The full beam of his attention was messing with her pulse, making it hard to concentrate. She spied her indoor watering can on a shelf, picked it up and started trickling water around the base of a frothy maidenhair fern. 'My grandparents had a lot of plants. Some of these are the descendants…' she moved on to a delicate asparagus fern '…and I've added a fair few of my own since I moved in, so now I've got Kew Gardens!' She moistened her lips, braving his gaze again. 'Is it a bit much?'

He smiled. 'Not at all. You must have very green fingers!' He leaned over the sofa, surveying the row of succulents. 'I've never owned a plant. I wouldn't know where to begin.'

'Aloe vera's a good one to start with.' She shook the last drops out of the watering can. 'It's great to keep in the kitchen in case you burn yourself. You just snap off a bit of leaf and squeeze the juice onto the burn. It's magic!'

His eyes caught hers. 'Cool!'

She felt her lips parting slightly and quickly clamped them shut. She held up the watering can. 'I need a refill.'

In the galley, she turned on the tap. So much for keeping her head. The salon felt far too small with Theo in it, charging the air with his smile, and that gaze which made her forget how to breathe. She needed to wrestle back control, put herself firmly in the driving seat. She turned off the tap and leaned backwards by degrees so she could peek at him through the doorway. He was flicking through a book on house plants, jacket over his arm, a little frown on his face. There was something endearing about the way he was taking an interest, something about him which made her want to…

His eyes snapped up.

She swallowed a little gasp. 'How about some coffee?'

He grinned. 'I'd love some.'

That settled the going-out-staying-in conundrum!

When she went back through with the coffee, he was sitting at one end of the sofa with his legs stretched out over the rug, the plant book on his knee. He looked at home and for some reason that warmed her, made her want to be close to him, to find out about him.

She handed him a cup then settled herself at the other end of the sofa. She sipped her coffee, savouring its dark richness. 'So, if I promise never to write about it, will you tell me why you and Madelon are both so involved with the refuge?'

The planes of his face seemed to sharpen suddenly. A trick of the light, perhaps…

He sipped his coffee slowly, then met her eye. 'We're

involved because we've been there.' A tiny quiver touched the corners of his mouth. 'We've got the tee shirt.'

It's the last thing she was expecting, and it took a moment for the words to sink in. 'You mean…?'

His eyes narrowed. 'My father was a drunk and a brute. He liked to beat my mother when the mood took him.'

Telling her about his father had cost him something. She could see it in his eyes, in the firm, grim set of his mouth. 'I'm so sorry.'

'It's not for you to be sorry. It's in the past.' He took another sip from his cup, swallowing slowly. 'When I moved to Amsterdam and heard about the charity, I had to get involved, and then Madelon came on board too. I became a trustee because I wanted to help. Women and children in that situation need support; they need an escape route. Being trapped…being so powerless…is…' His gaze shifted to the floor. He seemed to lose himself in his thoughts for a moment and then he looked up. 'How about you? You said you volunteered?'

He was deflecting. It was understandable, she supposed, given that they hardly knew each other, but there was clearly more to his story than he was telling her. What had he and Madelon been through? What had they seen and heard? Unimaginable. She felt a sudden urge to put her arms around him, but instead she wrapped her fingers more tightly around her cup.

'That's right. I got involved through Lotte. She's a professional photographer. She volunteers at the refuge if they need publicity photos. It's a worthy cause, so I threw my hat into the ring too.'

'Commendable. Both of you.' He shifted on the sofa, his expression brightening. 'Lotte's quite the character. How did you meet her?'

Mia's heart seized. They seemed to be jumping from

one sombre subject to another, but she wasn't going to sidestep his question. There could be no more omissions. She parked her cup on the floor, felt darkness draining through her. 'It's not a very jolly story, I'm afraid.'

He leaned forward, eyes searching hers. 'How so?'

For the second time that evening she was travelling back in her mind. Yet again she heard rainwater splashing over the tops of the gutters, splattering onto the cobbles. 'It was a horrible evening. Cold and wet and windy. I'd not been in Amsterdam that long. I hadn't bought my bike yet. I was hurrying home, trying to hang on to my umbrella, when I heard a noise coming from a side street. A struggle: someone crying.' Her pulse was climbing. 'I was scared, but I couldn't ignore it.'

He was shaking his head. 'You should have gone for help—phoned the police.'

'There wasn't time—it sounded bad.' She snatched a breath. 'Thankfully my brolly isn't one of those midget things; it's quite sturdy. I folded it then made my way towards the noise.' She could still smell the aroma of hot oil and garlic from the restaurant kitchens on the main drag. She could still see steam billowing through a vent in a wall—details trapped in her memory like insects in amber.

She swallowed. 'There was one of those big industrial bins, and on the other side of it I saw Lotte struggling with this big guy. He was all over her, pulling at her clothes.' Theo's eyes were burning into hers. 'I just reacted—thwacked him with the umbrella—gave him such a shock that Lotte was able to get free. She kicked him in the crotch and then we ran for it. I brought her back here.' Lotte's face, streaked with tears, teeth chattering, lips trembling… She pushed the image out of her head.

'We reported it, and after the police had been Lotte stayed the night. We bonded over brandy and a mutual hatred of scumbag men.'

'Did they catch him?' Theo's eyes were dark, his lips pale.

'No. He was a tourist. Lotte had met him at a photography exhibition. They'd started chatting. She'd told him right away that she wasn't into guys and she said he'd seemed cool about it. They went for a drink, just hanging out, and then he'd said he wanted to take some pictures of a side street for a photography project he was working on. That's why she went with him—because she was interested in his project. But then, when they were out of sight, he jumped her.'

Theo's face was rigid. She looked down, saw that his hands were clenched into fists. Maybe she should have edited the story a bit. It was clearly stirring things up inside him that she could only begin to imagine.

She moistened her lips, went on quickly. 'Afterwards, Lotte found it difficult to go out on her own. She got panic attacks; she was scared all the time. She went to talk to one of the counsellors at the refuge and the sessions helped a lot. She's still got a way to go, but at least she can go out without panicking now, which is good… Anyway, that's why Lotte started volunteering at Saving Grace. She wanted to give something back.' She smiled. 'She's always trying to give back. Trying to help the people who've helped her.'

Theo was staring at her. Tentatively, she touched his arm. 'Are you all right?'

He took a breath, seeming to come back into himself. 'I can't believe you did what you did. He could have had a knife, Mia—anything.'

'But he didn't! We got away. If I'd waited for help to come...' She pressed her lips together. What could have happened didn't bear thinking about... She took her hand away from Theo's arm and gave a little shrug. 'I know I can be impulsive. Ash is always telling me to think first...' She thought of Greenwich, felt a blush warming her cheeks. 'But it isn't that I *don't* think. It's just that if there's something I can physically do I'd rather do it than waste time with "what ifs".'

He smiled softly. 'Mia the brave...'

'Not brave. Impatient.'

'*Brave!* Brave enough to ride on the back of a bicycle with a very rusty chauffeur...'

'*Impatient* to get back and put on a warm sweater, you mean.' She smiled. 'Some risks are worth taking.'

He laughed and then the light in his eyes dimmed. Hesitantly, he stretched out a hand and laid it over hers. 'But not all risks, Mia.' His eyes held her, drawing her in. 'You were lucky that night with Lotte, but it could have gone very differently. Promise me you'll never do anything like that again.'

His hand on hers felt warm and protective. For a long moment she held his gaze, losing herself in it. It was disarming that he seemed to care so much about what happened to her, but she'd made a promise to herself, a promise to keep her head and not give her heart away until she knew who she was giving it to. She didn't belong to Theo and, even though she could tell his intentions were good, he didn't have the right to ask her for promises.

She moistened her lips. 'I'm sorry, but I can't.'

There was a quick beat of uncertainty in his eyes, a flicker of realisation. He lifted his hand away from hers and pressed it flatly onto his thigh. 'No—*I'm* sorry. I was being intense.' He faltered, smiled sheepishly. 'Madelon's always telling me I'm heavy going. What I should have said was, *be careful*. Will you at least say you'll be careful…?'

He'd stood down, tucked all the awkwardness into his own pockets. No wonder he was so successful in business. He had emotional intelligence and the tenacity to extract a portion of what he'd originally pitched for. It was impossible not to smile. 'Yes! I'll be careful.'

He looked at his watch. 'In that case, I'll quit while I'm ahead.' He threw her a smile then rose to his feet, lifting his jacket from the arm of the sofa. 'Thanks for the coffee.'

She stood up, battling disappointment. It seemed too soon for him to leave. 'You're welcome. Thanks for bringing me home.' Suddenly her heart was drumming. How would they say goodbye? It wasn't as if they'd been on a date. They'd simply left the event together. Hesitantly, she stepped forward, opened the door then skipped back quickly as Cleuso streaked across the threshold, meowing loudly.

Theo laughed. 'Were you expecting visitors?'

How different his face looked when he was laughing; all the shadows filled in with light. She smiled, grateful for the distraction. 'Cleuso's not a visitor; he lives here.'

'Cleuso? What a great name for a cat. He's…erm…'

He didn't seem to be able to find the words. She followed his gaze to where Cleuso was sitting under the cheese plant, butting his head against the underside of a big, glossy leaf. She felt a smile coming. 'He defies description, really. When I went to choose a kitten, I knew straight away that he'd be picked last, so I took him…'

She sensed Theo's gaze and turned to face him. The

light in his eyes was soft, a little hazy. His chest was rising and falling. Rising. Falling. She held her breath, waiting, not sure what she was waiting for, and then he leaned in slowly and kissed her cheek.

'Goodnight, Mia.'

CHAPTER FOUR

THEO POURED HIS coffee and leaned into the warmth of the old Dutch range. His interior designer, Direk, was trying to convince him to go for a sleek, streamlined kitchen design—black gloss units, black granite work surfaces—but that didn't seem sympathetic to the spirit of the old canal house. Direk kept telling him that it would be cool to *'subvert expectation'* but a kitchen was for cooking; a kitchen was the heart of a home. Why subvert it? Besides, he didn't want his home to have a black heart.

He picked up his cup and eyed the deep window-sill over the sink. An aloe vera plant might fit there. Mia had said that it would be a good plant to start with. He'd looked it up in her plant book: leaves like fleshy blue-green lances, little serrations along their edges. It was a desert plant. They could grow to quite a size, but he supposed there'd be a way of containing the growth—she'd know how to do that.

She'd filled every nook and cranny of her compact sitting room with plants. 'Kew Gardens', she'd called it.

He smiled. He'd liked her plants. He'd liked her barge. Everything scaled down, cleverly designed to fit the narrow space. There'd been something of the playhouse about it, something magical, and yet it had felt like a proper home. The sofa had been comfortable; the faded Persian rug on the floor had felt plush under his feet. He'd looked around while he waited for her to get changed. Her books were the classics, mostly, and collections of poetry. There'd been a stack of interiors magazines and a few copies of the *Paris Review* on a side table, and along the top of the bookcase there'd been photos of Ash and herself as kids in smart school uniforms, then in shorts and tee shirts at the beach. He'd noticed in particular a picture of a happy young couple—her parents, presumably—taken in a dry, exotic location. India, or Africa maybe…

He set his cup down and surveyed the old plaster walls around him, the myriad shades of ancient. It was two days since he'd cycled through the city streets with her laughing and squealing behind him. He smiled at the memory: the way she'd yelled an apology to the scattering tourists; the warmth of her hand on his back…

When he'd asked her to leave the fundraiser with him, he thought he'd known what he was doing. He'd wanted to spend some time with her. He'd wanted to get to know her better but, on the barge, his feelings had started to run away with him. As she'd recounted the tale of how she'd stopped Lotte's attacker, he'd felt a ferocious tangle of emotion. Admiration for her bravery, fury that she'd put herself into such a dangerous situation and…tenderness. He'd felt an overwhelming desire to protect her, but then he'd overstepped the line, asking her for a promise he'd had no right to ask for, and in that moment he'd realised he was in trouble.

He was so drawn to her, to the warmth in her eyes, to the courage in her heart… Caring so much about someone he barely knew—someone who seemed to be able to draw things out of him with just a look and a smile—had thrown him into a flat spin. He'd felt out of his depth, unsure of what was happening to him. He'd had to leave; take some time to sort out his thoughts and feelings.

He pushed himself away from the stove and walked slowly around the huge scrubbed table where he cooked and ate. He couldn't get it out of his head: Mia confronting Lotte's attacker…

The scumbag could have turned around, blocked the umbrella strike, smashed his fist… He could have thrown Mia to the ground, used his feet… He stopped, felt a cold shudder travelling through him. She'd have understood why he'd asked her to make that promise if she'd seen what he'd seen.

He closed his eyes, trying to block out the sound of his mother's sobs, chairs crashing, Bram launching himself at their father, fists flying, shouting at him to take Madelon away… He'd grab Madelon's hand, pull her from the house clutching her dolly.

'Let's run a race, Maddy...fast as we can to the canal... One, two, three... Go!'

He'd once asked his mother why she'd married his father. She'd told him that things had been different in the beginning. She'd said she didn't know what had triggered the drinking, but that when his father had started turning up to lectures drunk she'd known it wouldn't be long before he lost his job at the university. When it happened, she said, he'd been angry, angry all the time, lashing out more and more. Afterwards he'd be full of remorse, begging for forgiveness. For the sake of the man he'd been, she'd held on, hoping that things would change. They didn't. The irony, she'd told Theo, was that his father had always sworn that he would never be like his own father, Theo's grandfather, who'd also been a violent drunk.

This was his legacy: a chain of violence and misery. Even his heroic brother, Bram, had succumbed and there were moments when he was sure that he could feel the darkness of generations creeping through his own veins. It was why he spent his life boxing at shadows, keeping himself on the ropes, not letting what was inside him see the light of day. It was a matter of self-control.

Madelon was always teasing him about being so buttoned up and that worried him too. Was his intensity overbearing?

Eline had once told him that he was good, kind and noble, but on the day she'd left she'd looked at him scornfully. *'You want to control everything, Theo. It's boring as hell.'*

He pushed through double doors into another empty room—a family room for a man with no family. Was he boring as hell? Was he too controlling? He pictured Mia's face on the barge. When he'd tried to extract that promise, she hadn't looked intimidated. She'd looked…surprised. *Bemused.* And then she'd looked him squarely in the eye and refused.

For a moment he'd wanted to open himself up to her—tell her more about his father, the way he'd been, what he'd done to the family—but he'd stopped himself. He was ashamed of his background and he wasn't ready to reveal that shame to Mia, even though he felt safe with her, even though kindness and empathy shone through her eyes like starlight. When she'd told him about why she'd chosen Cleuso, his heart had melted. It had taken every ounce of willpower he possessed not to pull her into his arms and kiss her. He'd kissed her cheek instead, so full of emotion, so disorientated that he'd left without asking her for her phone number.

And now he was pacing from room to room, veins throbbing with restless energy. Since Eline, he'd been tight as a clam, but something about Mia made him want to unseal himself. But he was scared too. Opening was hard for him, even by degrees, even to someone who seemed as sweet and trustworthy as Mia. Eline had turned against him, broken his heart just when he'd needed an ally. People changed: his father, Eline, Bram… How could you see a person's true colours when the kaleidoscope was always turning?

At the door, the way Mia had looked at him, that uncertainty in her eyes mingled with gentleness, openness… If he'd tilted her chin, touched her lips with his, would she have pulled away or kissed him back? Just the thought of it made him dizzy. She was lovely. He wanted to see her again, wanted to know her better. He'd have to take it slowly, scope things out, but he couldn't do anything without her phone number. Asking Ash for it would be too weird…

He pressed his hands to the crown of his head, spun around slowly. She lived close by. If he was to drop in unannounced, would she think he was stalking her? He tipped his head back and stared at a jagged crack in the ceiling. He needed to go for a run. Running was his thing. He always felt better afterwards, clearer in his mind. He'd think about Mia later.

Mia jingled her bell three times then braked gently, waiting for the tourists to realise that they'd strayed onto the cycle path. They suddenly broke stride, jigged a little dance of shock then scurried to the side. She smiled, waved and pedalled on. Lotte wouldn't have slowed down; she'd have sped up, scowled her way past. But then Lotte was a native, impatient with tourists, especially the drunken men and the stag-nighters who gawped at the girls in the red-light district; and the flocks of raucous hen-weekenders cavorting around the streets in their cheap pink sashes, brides to be; bridesmaids; mothers. The city had become a magnet for the wrong type of tourists. That was what Lotte said.

She rang her bell again, smiling at more scuttling tourists. She wasn't as jaded as Lotte. The city still excited her. It was a vibrant place, a magnet for artists, makers, creators and innovators… *Like Theo!* Her heart jolted. It happened every time she thought about him which was getting to be a little inconvenient. She cycled slowly, scanning the canal railing clad in bicycles of all shapes and sizes for a gap where she could park hers.

Up ahead, a man was unchaining his bike, lifting his little boy into the seat positioned over the front fork. Whole families could fit onto a single bike if it had the right attachments, like the bicycle in the children's book her dad used to read to her when she was little. The story was about an inventive woman who kept adding gizmos to her bike to make it better. She'd loved that book, the way her dad had used to do the woman's high, squeaky voice, his gold-rimmed reading glasses glowing in the light pooling from the bedside lamp… At least that was what *she* remembered. Ash said that their dad's spectacles had been silver, not gold. They used to argue about things like that, trying to tie down memories that always seemed to be a confusion of the real and the imagined. If they'd got some of their parents' personal items back, maybe it would have helped somehow, but they hadn't.

The man with the bike was strapping his little boy into the seat, listening to the child's chatter, smiling and nodding. She looked away, eyes misting. The passage of time was diluting so many of her recollections, turning them into mere impressions, like paintings. She'd have done anything to bring those memories back into focus, even for a moment, but she couldn't. She caught a tear on the back of her hand. Maybe the colour of her dad's readers didn't matter. What was important was that he'd read her the story, done the voices, made her feel loved. He'd always listened with great interest to her childish babblings. He'd always made her feel important. He'd been a good man. Patient, clever, and kind. Maybe that was why he'd been so well regarded in the diplomatic service. He was a natural!

She swallowed hard, smiling at the man and his little boy as they finally vacated the space, then she slotted her own bike into the gap and chained it to the railing.

The day was bright and warm. That was what she needed to focus on! She looped her bag across her body, straightened her hat and set off walking. There was blue, blue sky and sunlight glinting through fresh green leaves glittering on the dark choppy water of the canal. She loved the canal houses that lined the banks. Tall, narrow with curved or stepped or oblong gables, and so many windows, as if light was everything. It was the sunlight that had drawn her outside. She'd needed to escape from the barge, from the memory of Theo's face as they'd said goodbye. That moment at the door, softness in his gaze, something raw behind it, his chest rising and falling… And then he'd leaned in slowly, kissed her cheek. What to make of *that*? Two days had gone by—two whole days—and she couldn't concentrate, couldn't write. She didn't know what to do with herself.

She hadn't wanted him to leave. It was obvious that he thought he'd crossed a line trying to extract a promise from her, but he hadn't. She'd seen on his face that he was genuinely concerned for her safety. Ash had been the same when she'd told him about it—a lot more vocal, actually.

On a different day she would have found Theo's protectiveness endearing, but she'd been so busy flexing her new 'head over heart' muscle that she'd failed to tell him that she appreciated his concern—that she was fine with taking care of herself. She could have added that the real danger lay in trusting someone else to take care of you, but that would have opened the door to a different conversation, and she wasn't ready for that.

At the entrance to the Bloemenmarkt the crowd bottlenecked but she didn't mind. The flower market was best viewed at a leisurely pace. You needed time to take in the riot of colourful flowers, the stiff tulip stems with their bullet heads in jewel-brights and milky pastels. The scent was intoxicating but difficult to describe, even for a writer. Fresh, wet, sweet, musky…fragrant.

She wandered on, faltering at the sound of a raised voice filtering through the crowd. She turned, caught sight of a man sitting at a table outside one of the eateries. Two glum children sat beside him, an overturned glass on the table between them, pink milkshake flooding the surface and splattering onto the ground. The man was mopping at the mess with his napkin, shaking his head, grumbling at the kids.

It was nothing but it made her think about Theo… Had his alcoholic father shouted at him, or worse?

We've got the tee shirt.

He hadn't volunteered any further information, and she hadn't wanted to ask, but if personal experience had motivated him to become a trustee of the refuge then maybe… She shuddered.

Seeing Theo in his fine suit and impeccable shoes, every inch the successful businessman, it was hard to imagine that his background could have been anything but privileged. Was that why he was so guarded? Was he concerned about his image? She stepped under the striped canopy of her favourite stall, perused the selection of house plants. She conjured a memory of him barrelling along on her bright orange bicycle with herself behind, laughing and shrieking. Hardly the behaviour of someone who was concerned about his image.

She trailed her fingers through the fronds of a fern then went to look at the succulents. When she spied a baby aloe plant at the back of the display, Theo came to mind yet again. Aloe—the plant she'd told him about. She huffed a little sigh. He was under her skin, in her thoughts, and now he'd found her here among the plants. Those eyes, the way they'd held hers before he'd kissed her cheek… How would it have felt if he'd kissed her lips instead? She closed her eyes, felt her heart jolt for the umpteenth time. It was trying to tell her something and it was being very insistent. If she listened to her heart, admitted to herself that she wanted to see him again, then there was still the niggling problem of not having his phone number. She picked up the aloe and twisted it this way and that, checking that it was a good one. He'd said he'd never owned a plant and for some reason this one seemed to have his name written all over it.

What's meant for you won't pass you by.

A smiled edged its way onto her lips. She'd buy it—for him. If she bought it maybe the stars would guide him to her door again.

The willow trees around the lakes in Vondelpark looked vivid in the afternoon sunshine. The park was busy: families, tourists, cyclists, skaters. They were all out enjoying the spring weather. On some paths Theo had to duck and weave as he went along, but it felt good to be outside, moving, pushing his body to its limits. His tee shirt was damp, cool, against his skin when the breeze rippled, but he liked the simple cause and effect of working out and sweating. It was satisfying. Pleasurably predictable.

When he got to De Vondeltuin café he slowed to a walk,

swiping the sweat off his forehead. He took a long drink from his water bottle. He liked De Vondeltuin, especially in the evenings. It was where he and Madelon used to meet. A casual dinner on the terrace, talking as evening fell around them. Now that she was famous, they wouldn't be able to do that any more, at least not without being disturbed. A knot tightened in his stomach. The price of fame could be incalculable. Just one photograph of Madelon and him together could open a door to misery for Bram. The press would have a field day.

Esteemed actress is sister of MolTec millionaire and a deadbeat.

They'd twist the facts, just as they'd done with Fred Zucker…

He'd met Fred through Eline. Fred was a great guy, friendly, good-natured, a popular professional cricketer who'd done a charity catwalk show along with other members of his team. Fred was generous with his money and his time, but that didn't stop him from being pilloried by the press on account of a shady relative. That was what the gutter press did—destroyed good people.

Theo felt his jaw tightening. If the hacks joined up the dots, they'd be staking out Bram's house in no time, knocking on his door, making his life hell… Madelon would weather it, *he* would cope, but Bram wasn't strong enough to deal with it. That kind of attention could wipe out all the progress he'd made, set him back by miles. Theo wouldn't let it happen. He'd storm the gates of hell itself before he'd let his brave, damaged brother go through that.

He took another pull from his water bottle, found himself staring at a girl with light-brown hair twisted up the way Mia wore hers. The girl was laughing with her friend, waving her hands about, bracelets jangling on her wrists. He turned away.

What did Mia do with herself on Sunday afternoons? He could see her hanging out at the quaint, bohemian waterfront café that Madelon used to like: Hannekes Boom. She'd fit right in there, being a bright young thing. Not that *he* was old, but he felt old most of the time. He'd always felt old, had always been beset with grown-up worries. He'd worried about where they could go to hide when his father came in drunk and spoiling for a fight; he'd worried about Madelon seeing things a little girl shouldn't have to see; he'd been horrified at the sight of Bram's bruises. The magic of childhood had passed him by, but that was the reality for kids from homes like his. It was why he'd got involved with the refuge; why it would be a lifelong commitment.

He ran a hand through his hair, set off running again. Mia was bound to be out somewhere, doing something, but with whom? It was hard to believe that she was single.

And then it came back to him, what she'd said when she'd told him about that night with Lotte's attacker.

'We bonded over brandy and a mutual hatred of scumbag men.'

Having a general hatred of scumbags was understandable, but maybe she'd been talking about a specific scumbag.

He gritted his teeth, ran faster. The thought of anyone hurting Mia made his blood boil. She reminded him of Bram, jumping into situations without thinking of herself. She'd intervened to make sure Ash got his chance to pitch; she'd braved a dark side street armed only with an umbrella; she'd stopped Lotte taking his photograph at the fundraiser; and she'd picked the kitten that no one else would have wanted… How could anyone ever hurt a girl like that? She was a sheltering sky, a haven, a beautiful soul. No wonder he felt her magnetic pull; no wonder he wanted to spend time with her. She felt like home, and a home was all he'd ever wanted.

As he neared the Leidsegracht-Prinsengracht bridge, he saw a group of tourists staring into the water. There was an air of anxiety in the craning necks, in the hands fluttering and hovering around mouths. He slowed, leaning over the railing to see what they were looking at. Something was splashing about in the water, splashing and sinking, flailing its paws, wailing. He glimpsed sharp white teeth, a pink tongue and wild, frightened eyes before the creature slipped under the surface.

It was a cat, drowning right in front of him! His pulse exploded. He bolted to the edge nearest to where it was struggling, looked around frantically for anything to throw, anything at all that it could sink its claws into, but there was nothing. He considered his tee shirt, pulling it quickly over his head, ripping the side seams apart so that he had the longest possible rope, then he flattened himself on the ground and threw the loose end over the water towards the cat.

'C'mon, kitty! Grab it. *Grab it!*'

The cat lashed about. The tee-shirt rope wasn't quite reaching.

He yanked the wet fabric back and looked over his shoulder at the spectating crowd. He caught a man's eye. 'Grab my ankles; hold on tight.' With the stranger's hands locked around his ankles, he pushed himself over the edge of the bank so that his torso was clear over the water. He threw the makeshift rope towards the cat again, and this time it was close enough. The cat yowled, sank, then came up, clawing at the fabric.

Relief rushed through him. 'That's it! Hold on. Hold on, kitty…don't let go.'

He pulled in the tee-shirt rope slowly, not wanting to jerk the fabric out of the cat's claws. When the animal was near the bank, he bent from the waist and reached out his hands, stretching and stretching, but the canal side was too high. His fingertips were just inches away from the frightened animal, but he couldn't quite reach.

'Come on, cat…*try!*'

The frantic eyes locked on his and with a burst of super feline strength the cat launched itself upward, sinking its claws into his forearms. He gritted his teeth, then gritted them again as the cat clawed a route all the way up his arm to his shoulder. He ducked his head, squeezing his eyes shut as the cat's claws raked the skin along one side of his face, and then it was over.

He shimmied back onto the bank, breathing hard, heart pumping, face stinging. There were lancing pains in his arms, and his stomach muscles were burning from planking over the water, but the cat hadn't drowned and that was all that mattered. As he got to his feet a little ripple of applause filled the air and then a movement in the crowd drew his attention.

A girl in a trilby hat was working her way to the front. Her head was down and she was crooning softly to the damp, furry bundle in her arms, a furry bundle which, on closer inspection, looked vaguely familiar. And the girl… her height, her figure, the curve of her cheek beneath the brim of her hat… He felt the pavement shifting beneath his feet, the blood galloping in his neck. Could it be that in a city of over a million cats he'd somehow saved Cleuso? What were the odds? He couldn't calculate it any more than he could stop the smile spreading painfully across his cheeks.

* * *

'You…?'

That was all she could manage. It was hard to speak when your lips wouldn't move. He must have been the one who'd saved Cleuso and, from the look of things, it hadn't been an easy rescue. There were long, red scratches on his arms and on his left shoulder, another trio of scratches along the left side of his face. He had to be hurting, but his eyes were twinkling, and he was smiling such a smile.

'Hello, Mia.'

There was a length of wet grey fabric dangling from his hands—what was left of his tee shirt, she supposed, given that his torso was bare. It was impossible not to notice his smooth golden skin, the washboard stomach, the trim, well-muscled legs. He must have been out running; that would account for the shorts and the trainers. The sight of him practically naked would account for the inconvenient rush of heat she felt. She adjusted her hold on Cleuso, wishing the onlookers would disappear, but if anything they were pressing closer, evidently curious as to what would happen next.

'I…' She stepped closer, trying to block out everything except his eyes, his smile. 'I can't thank you enough. If I wasn't holding Cleuso, I'd give you a big hug.'

Why was he laughing? And then she knew why. Someone was lifting Cleuso out of her arms, pushing her forward gently, and suddenly she was laughing too, laughing, and blushing and stepping forward, putting her arms around him, carefully because of the scratches. Almost immediately she heard the soft slap of wet fabric hitting the ground, and then his arms were drawing her in, warm and tight. He was hugging her right back, and it was heavenly. Her hat fell off as she rose to kiss his damaged cheek, then she startled at a burst of cheering and clapping from the people watching because she'd forgotten they were there.

He looked at her for a long moment then released her, smiled and gave a little bow. Following his lead, she turned to face their audience, bobbing a little curtsey. And then a lady with grey hair put Cleuso back into her arms and the crowd melted away.

What to say next? She gave Cleuso a little hug then turned around. Theo's arms were a mass of raised pink wheals, his shoulder too. It had to be stinging. She wondered if his tetanus shots were up to date.

'Thank you again…so much.' She glanced at Cleuso, rubbing his head softly. 'This cat's a total liability but I love him. I'd have gone mad with worry if he hadn't come home.'

'I know cats hate water, but I thought they could swim.' He picked up her hat, brushed it off and placed it gently on her head.

She lifted her chin so he could seat it properly. 'Probably most cats can…but Cleuso isn't "most cats".' He was taking his time with the hat, but it gave her the chance to study his face. The scratches had narrowly missed his left eye. She wasn't up to speed with the accepted wisdom around the hygiene of cats' claws, but canal water was dirty, and Theo's skin was broken all over. Antiseptic would probably be a good idea. 'We should get something on those scratches.'

He stepped back, examining his arms. 'I'll live.'

He bent to pick up his ruined tee shirt, biceps, abs and hamstrings shifting like gears in a well-oiled machine. She moistened her lips. 'But you might get septicaemia… When did you last have a tetanus?'

'I have no idea.' He wrung out his tee shirt and made to put it on.

'You can't wear it! It'll be full of germs.'

He hesitated, amusement in his eyes. 'It's all I've got. Walking topless through the streets isn't an option.'

She lifted an eyebrow. 'Lots of people wouldn't mind…'

He laughed roundly. 'Are you objectifying me?'

She shook her head, widening her eyes. 'Of course not.' She glanced at the railing where she'd hurriedly propped her bicycle. 'But you saved my cat, you've ruined your tee shirt and you're risking septicaemia if you put that on. It's no distance to the barge. Come back with me. We'll deal with those scratches; I'll dig out something of Ash's for you to put on, and I'll make you *the* best cup of coffee you've ever had. What do you say?'

He grinned. 'Coffee sounds good.'

'I wish I'd seen you planking over the water… You need to close your eye.'

'Why?'

'Because I don't want to get this stuff in it.'

He grinned, doing as he was told. 'That's not what I meant—and you know it.'

She carefully dabbed antiseptic along the scratches on his face, ignoring his sharp intake of breath. It was all she could do to control her own breathing, to stop her eyes from sliding over his naked torso. 'I just wish I'd seen you in action, that's all. I only saw the crowd, then Cleuso streaking towards me looking like a soggy dish mop.'

She moved on to his shoulder, trying to keep her fingers tight around the wad of cotton wool. If they so much as brushed his skin, it would be impossible not to run them over the smooth swell of muscle… 'But planking like that…for so long…you must have abs of steel. No wonder you drew a crowd.' She re-wetted the cotton wool ball with fresh disinfectant, stroking it slowly down the length of a deep scratch. Looking at his steely abs was not an option. He'd notice and, even though they were flirting a bit, she had to keep her head.

He winced again. 'They were watching the rescue.'

A girl in the crowd had filled her in while she'd been gathering up Cleuso. *'Some hot guy just saved this cat... planked over the edge so he could reach. He was awesome.'*

She giggled. 'You can keep telling yourself that if you like.'

He lifted an eyebrow. 'Are you objectifying me again?'

'Not *me*.' She held in a smile. 'But I can't speak for that crowd!' The way the woman had taken Cleuso from her... pushed her towards Theo...that heavenly hug... 'Those people were enjoying the spectacle, is all I'm saying.' She grinned, handing him the bottle and a fresh piece of cotton wool. 'You can do your arms now but don't miss anywhere. I don't want you getting sick.'

He sniffed the bottle. 'I don't think there's much chance of that. This stuff is caustic.'

'It's *effective*.' She stood up. 'I'm going to get you something to wear and then I'll make that coffee.'

She felt his eyes on her back as she walked through the galley and into the guest cabin. There might have been a flicker of disappointment in his eyes when she'd put the antiseptic bottle into his hands but what else could she have done? Much as she'd enjoyed trailing the cotton-wool ball over his skin, tending the scratches that he could easily do himself would have changed the landscape, charged the atmosphere even more—it was already crackling.

She pulled out the drawer under the bunk, rummaging for something decent that Ash had left behind. The grey marl tee shirt he wore to the gym would do. She found it and held it out. Ash wasn't as broad as Theo, but he was about the same height. She nudged the drawer shut with her foot and sat down on the bed. She needed to take a moment.

Somehow, she and Theo had progressed to casual flirting…and she liked it! She liked seeing the playful light in his eyes, the smile hovering on his lips every time he looked at her. That hug by the canal had changed things. They'd folded into each other so naturally, so easily. Signals transmitted and received without thinking. But her head had to catch up. She couldn't let Theo's heroics blind her. She still knew so little about him. She looked down at the tee shirt in her hands. The sooner he was wearing it, the easier it would be to keep her head.

In the salon, she found him sitting with Cleuso curled on his lap.

He looked up, eyes shining with a child-like delight. 'I think he likes me.'

She smiled. 'I should hope so. He owes you his life.' She handed him the tee shirt and went to fill the kettle. Cleuso didn't usually take to men but there he was, sleeping on Theo, completely chilled out. Was it a sign?

She scooped coffee into a jug, calling over her shoulder, 'It was lucky you were passing.'

'I guess.'

She made the coffee and took it through. The tee shirt was a neat fit but at least it seemed long enough. She handed him a cup. 'So, is Sunday your running day?'

He shook his head. 'I run every day…but I usually go early in the morning.'

She settled herself at the other end of the sofa. 'It's the best time, isn't it? Quiet…peaceful. It's when I do most of my writing.'

He nodded, stroked Cleuso's head.

His fingers were long, his nails clean and neatly trimmed. There were fine, golden hairs on the backs of his hands.

'I wasn't just passing, Mia.'

Her heart fluttered. 'I'm sorry…?'

'I was in Vondelpark and I decided to drop in on you. That's why I was at the bridge; I was on my way here.'

His steady gaze sent a flush of warmth into her cheeks. So he'd been thinking about her too… It hadn't been just her, thinking about him.

'I wanted to see you because when I left the other evening I forgot to ask you if I could take you for lunch some time.'

Lunch was safe. He was playing it safe. Maybe he was as scared as she was. For some reason the thought warmed her. She smiled. 'I'd like that.'

He drained his cup and gently lifted Cleuso off his lap. 'I have to go, but if I can have your number I'll call you soon, okay?'

'I'll give you my card.' She got up and retrieved a business card from her bag. When she turned around, he was on his feet. She stepped towards him. 'Thanks again—you're a hero.'

His eyes clouded. 'No. No, I'm not.' He took the card, tucking it into the pocket of his shorts. When he looked at her again, his eyes were warm and bright. 'You're the hero…heroine, rather. You've saved me from an almost certain death by septicaemia.'

She pressed her fingers to her eyes, laughing. 'Goodbye, Theo.'

'Goodbye, Mia.' He looked into her face for a long second, then leapt up the steps and disappeared through the door.

CHAPTER FIVE

LOTTE'S EYEBROWS ARCHED. 'You mean the handsome guy… the one who didn't want to be photographed?'

Mia nodded slowly. 'Yeah.'

'Wow! Even *I'd* make an exception for him.' She ripped open a sugar sachet and emptied the contents into her coffee. 'And you're having second thoughts because…?'

Mia ran a finger around the rim of her cup. So many reasons… Because she didn't know how Ash would react. Because she already liked Theo too much, risked liking him even more if she went to lunch with him, and that scared her because a casual lunch was exactly how things had started with Hal.

She met Lotte's clear, blue gaze. 'I don't know… Maybe it's just the thought of starting all over again. Once bitten and all that.'

'Stop projecting!'

Lotte was stirring her coffee and biting into her *hagelslag* sandwich, talking with her mouth full because she was pressed for time. She had a shoot across town, some sort of fashion thing.

'He hasn't asked you to marry him. It's only lunch.'

Only lunch!

That was the problem: there was no 'only' where Theo Molenaar was concerned, but Lotte didn't know that, because Mia hadn't kept her in the loop. She hadn't told Lotte about cycling home from the fundraiser or about Cleuso in the canal. It wasn't that she was being secretive on purpose. It was just that Theo was so private, and Lotte was, well, Lotte was Lotte.

She lifted her cup to her lips. 'So you think I *should* go?'

Lotte shot her an incredulous look. 'Hell yeah! You've lived here for eighteen months and you haven't been out with a single person in all that time. Of course you should go!' She dabbed a finger around her plate, picking up the stray chocolate sprinkles. 'Anyway, I thought you were a fatalist—*what's meant for you won't pass you by*, remember?' She daintily licked the sprinkles off her finger. 'If you look at it that way, there's nothing to decide. You can just let everything unfold because the future's set!'

Mia sighed. She'd hoped for something else from Lotte—some unbridled cynicism, some consensus about what a bad idea it would be to have lunch with Theo.

Lotte was frowning at her watch. 'I'm sorry but I've got to go.' She shimmied out of her seat, hoisting her camera bag onto her shoulder. When she looked down again her gaze was soft, full of warmth. 'Lighten up, Mia. Just have fun. Theo seemed really nice to me.' She bent down, kissed Mia's cheek quickly and then she was weaving her way through the tables, disappearing through the door.

Mia sipped her coffee, let out another little sigh. She'd learned to her cost that 'seeming' wasn't the same thing as 'being'. If only you could see a person's true colours without having to weather a rainstorm. The rain had washed Hal's colours away, had left her with nothing but grey. A shiver hovered at the base of her spine. Could she bear to go through all that again?

Stop projecting!

Her eyes drifted to a young couple two tables away. She could see the invisible bubble around them. They were in the thick of love, oblivious to the clatter of cups, deaf to the screech and burble of the coffee machine, to the funky jazz playing over the sound system.

Theo at the canal, scratched and smiling… She'd risen up onto her toes to kiss his cheek, had been startled by the sound of clapping from the crowd, because for that moment she'd been in a bubble of her own.

Dangerous!

She turned to look through the window. People were going by with chins down, braced against the breeze. The trees were swaying, wind tugging at branches and leaves, tussling with the flowers in the café's hanging baskets. He'd saved her cat… No! He'd saved *a* cat. On their way back to the barge, he'd said that he hadn't known it was Cleuso until she'd emerged through the crowd with him in her arms. So he was a man who saved random cats. A man who couldn't bear to see suffering. Surely that was a real thing; a vibrant, shining thing about him? A true colour!

She put her cup down and twisted it back and forth on the saucer. Everything about Theo drew her in. She was right on the edge of that bubble, could feel it closing around her every time she looked in his eyes.

'I thought you were a fatalist.'

It wasn't what she'd wanted to hear from Lotte, because if fate was playing a hand in all this then there was no arguing with the facts. She'd literally bumped into Theo at that fundraiser then, of all the cats in Amsterdam, it had been *her* cat he'd rescued, just as she'd been cycling by. Serendipity might well be making a fool of her, but there was only one way to find out. She'd have to keep that lunch date.

* * *

Theo hiked up his coat collar, scanning the street for Mia's bright-orange bicycle, but there were no bikes to be seen, just people scurrying along with umbrellas. He'd offered to pick her up in his car but for some reason she'd been adamant about meeting him at the restaurant. Maintaining independence was understandable, he supposed, but cycling in this squall had to be a nightmare, and it wasn't as if this was a blind date that she might want to escape from. They'd spent time together. Enough to have weighed each other up a little bit.

He touched the scratch at the side of his eye, felt a smile coming. There'd been more than a little weighing up going on when she'd been bathing his battle scars. Every look she'd given him had made his heart pump faster. The way she'd trailed the cotton pad over his skin; the bite of the antiseptic; the tingle lingering on…pain and desire burning through him with every long, slow, stinging caress. He hadn't been touched in a long time, hadn't wanted her to stop, but he could understand why she had. When she'd handed him the bottle, the air had been thick with something more than the smell of antiseptic.

It was why he'd suggested lunch, not dinner. Lunch was safe. Lunch would level things up, give them a chance to talk casually. Being in a confined space with Mia—in the car to Greenwich; in the small sitting room on the barge—played havoc with his senses, set his imagination going, leaping ahead, weaving scenarios. Maybe she felt it too. Maybe that was why she'd refused a lift. Hadn't he told her that his car was compact?

He turned his back to the breeze, watching the rain sheeting across the canal. At least there was a canopy over the restaurant entrance. He hadn't wanted to wait inside, leave her to walk in on her own—that wasn't his style. He glanced at his watch, felt a twist in his gut. For a splintered second his head filled with a vision of wet cobbles… a tangled bicycle… But his father had been drunk, had blundered straight into the path of the tram. The weather had been incidental. He drew a long breath and pushed away his dread thoughts. Mia was far too sensible to end up under the wheels of a tram. She was late, that was all. Or…maybe she'd changed her mind.

He swallowed hard, turning to look at the street once more. Still no bicycles, but there was a figure walking quickly along the pavement, drawing near. She was in a trench coat and dainty black boots and she was holding a red umbrella that had a price tag dangling from its innards. He couldn't see her face, but he didn't have to. The way she carried herself and the way she moved already seemed to be imprinted on some part of his brain. And then she was right there in front of him, tilting the umbrella back, looking into his face and smiling. It was like being struck by a meteor shower.

'You're here!'

She shook her umbrella, folded it and stepped under the canopy. 'Of course I'm here.' Wet drops glistened on her cheeks, clinging to the strands of hair that fell about her face. 'Did you think I wasn't coming?'

'It crossed my mind.' He smiled. 'But I was hoping you would…'

Her tongue touched her bottom lip. 'I'm sorry I'm late. I had a puncture, so I had to abandon the bike, and then it started pelting down, so I had to buy an umbrella.'

Her lips were red, dewy from whatever she'd put on them. 'If you'd let me pick you up…'

'I know. I've been reflecting on that all the way here.'

'You should have called… I'd have come.'

Clear brown eyes held his. 'I know you would, but…' She glanced at the door. 'Shall we go in?'

'Of course.' He opened the door, stepping aside for her. 'I'm sorry, I wasn't thinking. You must be cold.'

'Your face is healing well.'

It had been over a week since the episode at the canal. He'd left a few days before calling her to arrange a date. He'd been going for casual, meanwhile he was anything but! He ran a finger over the taut little ridges near his eye. 'Thanks to you.'

She laughed. 'What can I say? Florence Nightingale made a big impression on me when I was a kid.'

He pictured her rescuing injured birds, bandaging her teddy bears. 'I'd like to have seen you as a kid.'

Her eyes clouded. She turned away, looking around the restaurant. 'It's lovely in here, isn't it? Very cosy with the candles. Perfect for such a horrible day.' She picked up the menu, scrutinising it closely. 'What do you recommend?'

She'd thrown up a wall. For some reason it made him think about the photographs he'd seen on the barge: Ash and her in smart school uniforms, the architecture of the buildings in the background… Boarding school? She'd told him about summers on Texel but maybe there were things about her childhood that were less than rosy.

He glanced at the menu. 'I like the ravioli with the shaved truffles, but the risotto's good too.'

She smiled. 'The ravioli sounds perfect.'

'Wine?'

'No, thank you. I'll have a sparkling mineral water…' She shot him a mischievous look. 'But I'm totally having a dessert. I love *zabaglione*.'

When she looked at him that way, he couldn't help smiling. 'You can have as much *zabaglione* as you want!'

Her eyes held his. 'Worth walking through the rain for, then.'

'Definitely…'

It was happening again—the effortless back and forth, the subtle flirting. Candlelight in her eyes, a touch of pink in her cheeks, that luscious mouth. It was easy to lose himself in the changing geometry of her smile, in the muted colours of her soft dress and in the warm fragrance she was wearing, but feeling attraction wasn't enough. He wanted to feel more, wanted to know who she was inside, because she was doing something to him, tilting him off-centre in the best possible way.

When the waiter had taken their order and disappeared, he watched her watching the bubbles rising in her glass. That night on the barge she'd asked him a straight question about why he was involved with the refuge charity, and he'd answered truthfully, even though he wasn't in the habit of revealing his family history to anyone. But she'd just deflected his light-hearted attempt to talk about her childhood. Did she still think it was inappropriate to talk about her family because of Ash and their business connection?

Ash himself hadn't been as circumspect. When they'd met in London, he'd remarked to Theo how close he and Mia were, had told him that they'd '*been through a lot*' together. There'd been sadness in his eyes, an awkward pause… Maybe he should have picked up Ash's baton, asked him what it was that he and Mia had been through, but it wasn't in his nature to ask personal questions. He'd cultivated a habit of incuriousness because he couldn't reciprocate, couldn't share his personal past or his present without fear of exposing Bram to the kind of scrutiny that could send him spiralling back into his old habits. Being private had become second nature, but now he felt restless, trapped in a cage of his own making.

She suddenly looked up, cornered him with her clear brown gaze. 'I'm surprised you asked me for lunch today.'

'Why?'

'Because it's a week day.' Teasing light in her eyes. 'I thought you'd be busy with important CEO stuff.'

'I took the day off.' He pointed to the scratches on his face. 'Sick leave!'

Her mouth fell open. 'You pulled a sickie?'

He grinned. 'Don't tell the boss.'

'I won't.'

The light in her eyes faded, but her gaze held him fast, and suddenly he knew that if he wanted to break out of his cage he'd have to risk a piece of himself.

'Mia…' *Breathe.* 'The truth is that I took the day off for you.' Just saying the words out loud made him feel lighter, triggered a warm glow of surprise in her eyes which warmed him right back. 'I didn't want to be fitting you into a schedule. I wanted to spend some time with you.' He smiled. 'I thought it was time to take control.'

She smiled back shyly, a flicker of something akin to gratitude in her eyes. 'I'm glad…although I'm not so sure that we ever control anything. Mostly I've found that fate takes the upper hand.' She sighed. 'We just get to react to whatever it dishes out.'

She'd opened a door. 'Such as…?'

A shadow crossed her face. 'You said you'd have liked to see me as a kid…but you wouldn't have enjoyed the view.' She dropped her gaze, twisted her glass around by single degrees. 'I lost my parents suddenly when I was eight, so a lot of the time I was a sad little thing.'

The photos: the young couple…her parents… *That* was what he'd noticed: how young they were. There'd been nothing recent and it had struck him as strange. 'I'm so sorry, Mia. What hap—?'

'Helicopter crash.' She looked up, cheeks pale, eyes dry. 'We never found out exactly what happened…' She shrugged. 'It's a loose end—but it niggles a bit, not knowing.'

She was wearing her composure like a mask, but he could see the hairline cracks. 'Where did it happen?'

'In Africa… Angola.' She sipped her water. 'Dad was in the diplomatic service. The Angola post was supposed to be temporary, but then it was extended, so Mum went out for a while. They'd been on consular business outside Luanda, were on their way back to the embassy when the helicopter went down.'

Her tears were dry, but he could still see them. Maybe on some level he'd felt it about her from the very beginning: the way she'd intervened for her brother; the curious combination of strength and fragility he'd seen in her eyes. That protective instinct she had, her warmth, her ready empathy. He didn't want to cause her pain, push her too far, but he wanted to know more. He searched her face. 'Do you mind talking about it?'

She shook her head. 'It's not my favourite subject but it's part of who I am.'

Mia the brave.

'So after that…?'

She fingered the silky ruffle at the neckline of her dress. 'Boarding school in London; weekends with my maternal grandparents in suburbia; summers with my Dutch grandparents on Texel. Then university. We both studied in London so we could live together. We inherited the house, you see. Ash still lives there—me too when I'm in London—but after Hal I had to get away.'

His curiosity spiked. 'Who's Hal?'

She looked down, flushing, a sudden tightness framing her mouth. Clearly she hadn't intended to mention Hal, whoever he was, and *he'd* fired out his question at point-blank range. It was too late to take it back. She was biting her lower lip, wrestling with something, and it was on the tip of his tongue to say that he shouldn't have asked, that it was none of his business, but he swallowed the words because he desperately wanted to know who Hal was… Why his name had affected her so profoundly.

After a moment she lifted her eyes, tucked a strand of hair behind her ear. 'Hal's my ex. My former fiancé…'

'Oh. I see.' It made sense that she'd been with someone. She was too lovely, too special, not to have been cherished, but he couldn't bring himself to say he was sorry about the break-up because he wasn't. He was glad that Hal was history, but it was hard to see the bright flare of old hurts in her eyes. He wanted to know what had happened, but he wasn't going to push. Maybe she'd tell him in time. He unscrewed the bottle cap, poured her some more water. 'So you moved to Amsterdam?'

'Yes.' She sipped her water. 'A fresh start on an old boat with an accident-prone cat.' She grinned. 'Ash calls him Clueless, but that's *so* rude! He might not be the sharpest knife in the box, but he's got emotional intelligence, and that's more important.'

He remembered the barge. Cleuso, still damp from the canal, rubbing against his bare legs then jumping onto his lap. Maybe it had been the cat's way of apologising for the scratches.

Emotional intelligence...?

The main thing was that Mia's face was radiant again and he was glad. When the waiter brought their ravioli, she was all smiles, full of praise for the flavours, the textures and the presentation. Her pleasure warmed him. This was his favourite restaurant. He liked that the tables were well-spaced; he liked the warm, hushed ambience and unobtrusive music. He always felt relaxed here, could see that Mia was falling under its spell too.

When she tasted the *zabaglione*, he realised he was watching her mouth.

'This is so good.'

'I'm glad you like it.'

She scooped up another little mound of the pale, creamy dessert. 'It's divine!'

Her lips closed around the tip of the spoon, then she touched the corner of her mouth with her finger, ran her tongue…

He put his spoon down. He couldn't taste anything, couldn't think of eating, because something unsettling was running through his veins, a burgeoning torrent of emotion that was skewing his senses. His eyes slid to the silk ruffles touching the milky skin along the neckline of her dress, the smooth rise of her breasts just visible.

He picked up his glass and took a sip. He'd thought lunch in a restaurant would be safe, but it seemed that where Mia was concerned there was no safety. Whenever he was with her, his thoughts ran away with him. He tried to switch them off, but it was no use. He was picturing his vast, empty bedroom, the king-size bed, Mia cocooned in acres of white bed linen, hair tumbling around her face.

'What are you thinking?'

Her face came into focus, clear brown eyes locked on his. He sipped his water, put down his glass. He'd have to go for a white lie. 'I was thinking about my house…thinking that you might be able to give me some advice about what to do with it. You write about interiors?'

'I do.' She put her spoon down next to her empty dessert glass. 'Are you remodelling?'

He nodded. 'At the moment it's a shell. I have an interiors guy but some of his ideas are...' He shrugged. 'I just can't seem to decide on anything...and you have a flair for it. I like what you've done with the barge, the feel of it.'

She smiled. 'It's easy to make a barge feel like home. For one thing, it's very small. I'm assuming your house isn't...'

He laughed. 'Not small, no, but not massive either. It's a canal house—four floors and an attic, which is my observatory.'

Her eyes widened. 'I remember! You have a telescope.'

'Yes. The observatory's the only space that's finished.'

'Now why doesn't that surprise me?' Her eyes were full of mock consternation.

He grinned. 'It's not a "toys for boys" thing, honestly! It's also my office. It's a functional space. Everything in it is there for a reason. The rest of the house is...a challenge.'

She tilted her head and shot him a little smile. 'Well, if you give me your address I'll come by some time, take a look.'

'What about now?'

Damn! What was happening to him? He might have been thinking it, but he hadn't meant to blurt it out. It sounded too eager...pushy. *Controlling.* His heart clenched. Maybe she'd think he was pressuring her. That was the last thing he'd ever do. That wasn't the kind of man he was. White noise was buzzing in his head. What kind of man *was* he? He'd spent his life trying not to be his father's son, but in that moment, trapped in Mia's warm, steady gaze, he wasn't entirely sure who Theo Molenaar was. He cleared his throat quickly. 'Or...just whenever.'

She considered for a moment, then she smiled. 'I'd like to see to your house, and since you've taken the day off maybe now's as good a time as any.'

Her smile filled him with light. 'Only if you want to. I mean, I wouldn't want you to feel—'

'I don't. Whatever it is that you're worried about.' She grinned. 'I'm just hoping that you have a kettle and a cafetière.'

Theo pushed open a set of double doors. 'This is one of the sitting rooms…'

Thankfully, it was very large—unlike his dark-blue sports car. Maybe it was the rain streaming down the windows that had made the atmosphere in the car so very intimate, or maybe it was the way he'd caught her eye, the way he'd smiled. Whatever it was that had electrified the atmosphere within that plush leather interior, she was relieved to be out of it, glad that he was walking to the opposite side of the room. It was easier to breathe when he wasn't beside her.

He stopped at the fireplace, rested his hand on the broad, empty mantelpiece. One side of his face was in shadow, the other was washed by the grainy wet weather light spilling from the two tall windows which overlooked the canal. He looked like a painting of a lonely man. She turned away, gazing at the exposed brickwork in a corner recess. She'd thought lunch would be safe. She hadn't expected him to invite her back. Why had she come? Her eyes slid over white walls that were peeling in places. No skirting boards. When he'd told her that he'd taken the day off for her, she'd felt a rush of happiness because he'd laid down a cornerstone, something they could build on.

How quickly their conversation had deepened after that, or at least *her* conversation had. She'd opened a door into her past, told him about her parents, because she'd wanted him to see that he wasn't the only one who'd had a difficult childhood. She'd been trying to lead him into talking about his father, his family, but she'd tripped, inadvertently opened the Hal door. At least he'd had the sensitivity to see it, hadn't pursued her about it, but then he'd changed tack, started talking about his house…

She dropped her gaze to the wide, wooden floorboards. They were mostly sound. They'd benefit from sanding and sealing, then they'd need something to draw out the tones… Wax would do it, well-buffed.

When he'd told her that he liked the barge, she'd considered how it reflected *her*, filled as it was with all the things she loved: her treasured books, photos, plants. Everything she owned told a story. And she'd got the idea into her head that his house would tell her his story. That was why she'd come, but she was looking at a blank page. He'd said the house was a shell but for some reason she'd thought he'd been exaggerating.

Her eyes settled on the two cream armchairs brazening it out in the middle of the room, a pale rug on the floor in front of them. The chairs were accessorised with tribal print cushions—charcoal diamonds woven through a coarse cream fabric. On the floor beside one of the chairs was a black decorative birdcage. She frowned. It was an incongruous little tableau.

'The chairs were Direk's idea. He's my interior designer.' Theo shrugged, starting to walk towards her. 'He's trying to help me visualise living in these spaces.'

'So, in this room he sees you relaxing with one friend and a canary?'

He chuckled. 'Poor Direk's been driven to desperate measures because I can't make decisions.'

She met his gaze. 'You're the CEO of a global business. I think you're underestimating yourself.'

'Business is different; I find business decisions much easier.'

'Maybe you just need time. Once you've lived in the house for a while, things will come to you.'

'What constitutes a while?'

'A few months…enough time to get a feel for things.'

He exhaled a long sigh, regarding her with a baleful expression.

She frowned. 'How long *have* you been living here?'

He rubbed the back of his neck. 'Three years.'

'Three…years?'

He nodded. 'Bear in mind that I'm away a lot.'

She couldn't think of anything to say. Coming home to this emptiness had to be dispiriting. From the outside he looked like a man who had everything, but instead… She glanced upward. Thick white beams. Why was he alone in this vast unfinished house? She wanted to ask him, but something stopped her.

She scanned the room again. 'You need a jumping-off point…a piece of furniture you like, or an object, or a colour. Once you've got that, you can start pulling ideas together.' She met his gaze. 'You must have a favourite thing…?'

'I don't.' He shrugged.

'A favourite colour?'

His eyes swept over her. 'I like the colours in your dress…'

She felt a blush coming and looked down at the subtle hues of plum, ochre and olive in the silk skirt of her dress. Why did it feel like he was saying something else? She cleared her throat, looked up. 'Okay, well, that's a start.'

He shifted on his feet. 'Do you want to see the rest of the house?'

Maybe the other rooms wouldn't be as bare. She smiled. 'Absolutely.'

The rest of the house was hardly better than the first

sitting room he'd shown her. The vibe was archaic minimalist, occasional items of furniture swamped by white space. There was a huge bed in the master bedroom, a vast wardrobe, a massive chest of drawers and through a peeling door, a sizeable *en suite* bathroom which looked starkly functional. With every step she took, she felt sadder and sadder. If a house reflected the personality of the person who lived in it, then Theo was either empty inside—which she knew he wasn't—or he had no idea of who he was, which seemed so much worse. Maybe it was the size of the place that amplified its emptiness, but in it Theo seemed so alone, so lost, that it was hard not to ache for him, hard not to want to hold him.

In the kitchen, which at least had a sink, an old range, a table and chairs, she couldn't hold back any longer. 'Why did you buy this house?'

He set the kettle on the range. 'It was an investment.'

Her throat closed. She'd been trying to reach out, but his reply had almost felt like a rebuff. She turned to look through the window. It was still raining, drops ticking against the glass, running down. She swallowed hard. She was being too sensitive. *Projecting!* The house was undoubtedly an excellent investment and just because she couldn't imagine herself rattling around in it for three years didn't mean that Theo minded. As he'd said, he was away a lot.

She folded her arms, paced slowly towards the table, watching him. He was busy spooning coffee into a cafetière, getting cups out. What was Ash always saying? *Men are from Mars, women are from Venus...* Maybe he hadn't been deflecting. Maybe he just hadn't caught the drift of her question because she hadn't phrased it properly.

She drew a breath, ignoring her thumping heart. 'Theo, why are you alone?'

He paused for a beat, then turned around and leaned against the range. For a long second his eyes glittered with shards of something that looked like bitterness but as he held her gaze his expression softened. 'I'm alone because my ex-wife soured the milk and it's stayed sour for a very long time.'

It made sense. Not that he was divorced—far from it—but that he'd been married. What would turn a wife against a man like Theo? He was handsome, caring, protective. Clearly, he saw himself as the injured party, but then again everyone saw themselves that way. Hal would probably say that *she* hadn't given him a chance to explain, that she'd thrown her engagement ring at him and cut him off completely.

She pulled out a chair, sat down at the table. 'So the house. Was it...?'

'No; it's not a sad relic of my marriage. Eline and I divorced five years ago. I bought the house for myself because it's on the best street in Amsterdam.' He faltered, a glimmer of vulnerability in his eyes. 'When I said it was an investment, I wasn't talking about money...' He pressed his palms to his thighs, smiling sheepishly. 'The pathetic truth is that it's a status thing.' His gaze seemed to turn inwards. 'I suppose I've never been able to shake off the poor kid's desire for a smart address and a fast car...the feeling that in a house like this nothing bad could ever happen.'

She felt tears budding behind her eyes. He was confiding in her, trusting in her, and it was disarming; it made her want to wrap her arms around him.

He hooked his thumbs into his trouser pockets and cast his eyes around the kitchen. 'The trouble is, now that I've got the address, I don't know what to do with the inside.'

She stowed her emotions and took a steadying breath. 'It's a huge project but at least you've found some colours you like.' She plucked at the neckline of her dress, threw him a little smile. 'It's a start.'

He chuckled, turning to tip boiling water into the cafetière. 'You'll have me making mood boards next.'

'Pinpoint's the way to go—you can do it on the computer—it should be right up your street.' He was putting the cafetière and the cups on a tray. She tilted her head. 'Are we going somewhere?'

'Yep.' His smile was mischievous. 'I've saved the best till last. We'll take our coffee upstairs, in the observatory. Follow me!'

CHAPTER SIX

HER EYES WIDENED. 'You *definitely* saved the best till last!'

The only thing this space had in common with the rest of the house was the colour of its panelled walls—but this white was fresh and crisp, its expanses punctuated with bright abstract paintings. It took her a full minute to assimilate everything: the pale, plush carpet; the huge burnished-leather sofas; the imposing desk and bookcase; the wall-mounted television which was larger than the screens she'd seen in some small cinemas.

He set the coffee tray on a low table. 'I pretty much live in here.'

'I'm not surprised.' She smiled. 'I'm relieved, actually.'

His eyebrows lifted.

'What I mean is that I'm glad you've got somewhere comfortable. I don't like to think of you…' She pressed her lips together.

'What?'

A blush tingled in her cheeks. 'Not being…' He was doing it again, looking at her as if he could see right through her. She swallowed. 'Not being comfortable…'

She broke his gaze. She might as well have told him straight out that she cared about him. How had that even happened? He was practically a stranger…and he was divorced! He might seem inordinately kind and noble—

not to mention sexy—but it was entirely possible that his marriage had fallen apart because of *him*. That bitterness in his eyes…

'My ex-wife soured the milk...'

Her instinct was to believe him, but she'd trusted her instincts before and it had cost her dearly. She touched the sofa back, eyes drifting as she tried to stop the doors in her mind revolving. At the far end of the room there was a short flight of steps that she hadn't noticed before. She turned, caught his eye. 'What's up there?'

'The dome—where the telescope lives!'

She felt her brow creasing. She'd thought *this* was the observatory. She scanned the room again. *No telescope.* How could she not have noticed? Too busy tying herself in knots over Theo and his big empty house, that was why. She pressed her teeth into her lower lip. Maybe if she got him to show her his observatory it would divert him, make him forget that she'd expressed care and concern about his comfort.

She turned to look at him. 'Can I see it?'

He seemed to hesitate, and then he smiled. 'Of course.' He walked across the room and she followed, trying not to notice the breadth of his shoulders, the way his hair curled slightly at the nape of his neck.

At the top of the steps was a small landing, just enough clearance for the door he was opening. He stood aside. 'After you.'

There was a moment of disorientation. Going from the vast white room into the compact circular pod was like stepping into a different world. In the centre, a huge white telescope sat on its mount like a king on a throne. The ceiling was domed, like the observatory at Greenwich, but much smaller—a diameter of ten feet or so. There were various gizmos, pieces of electronic hardware and a laptop computer connected to a black box.

She turned. 'When you said you owned a telescope…'

He was right there, barely a foot away. The floor seemed to tilt. She caught the clean smell of his skin, felt the heat radiating from his body. She tried to step back, but her heel struck the telescope mount. She swallowed hard. 'I thought you meant a telescope on a tripod…' She swallowed again. 'Near a window or something. Not like a whole dome with…' Green eyes were locked on hers. She waved her hands about, drowning not waving. 'This is some very serious kit.'

She thought he might have stepped back a bit, but he seemed to be rooted to the spot. She moistened her lips, trying to ignore the butterflies taking flight in her stomach. He looked very much like he was going to…

'It is. Very serious.' For an instant, his gaze dropped to her mouth, then he lifted his hand, stretching his fingers to her cheek.

Her heart exploded softly then a gentle warmth flooded her veins. She wanted to close her eyes, melt into his touch, but she was supposed to be keeping her head… Wasn't she? It was why she'd had mineral water at lunch instead of wine. It was why she'd asked him to show her the dome. It was meant to distract him. She shifted her foot, felt the immoveable bulk of the mount behind her heel.

'It's a research-grade telescope…very powerful.' His eyes held hers as he slid his fingers along her jawline to her neck. 'On a clear night, you can see the Sombrero Galaxy…' His voice was a lullaby, his touch unhurried. She hadn't been touched like this for a long time and his fingertips felt so warm, so perfect, that she couldn't not surrender a little. She took a baby breath, resting her hands lightly on his chest.

He bent his head so that their foreheads were almost touching. 'The rings of Saturn…'

She could push him away, but he was stroking her cheekbone with his thumb and it was making her weak.

'Sometimes the Horsehead Nebula…otherwise known as the Nebula of Orion…'

There was no keeping her head now. She was undone. She lifted her face so he could close the infinitesimal distance between them, and instantly his lips were on hers. She closed her eyes, lost herself in the warm, sweet taste of him, the scent of him, the sensation of his mouth taking over hers. When he pulled her closer, deepening his kiss, she pressed her body against him, sliding her hands up the hard barrel of his chest and over his powerful shoulders…and all she could think was that she didn't want it to stop. She didn't want to think, she only wanted to feel, because nothing had ever felt like this.

When he broke away, his breathing was ragged. He stepped back, eyes burning into hers. 'Do we need to talk about this?'

His eyes were full of everything. Talking… Thinking… They could do that later. She shook her head, somehow found her voice. 'No.'

'Good.' He smiled, and then she was being swept up, being carried down the steps, through the room and down the stairs to the vast, empty bedroom; that vast, empty bed.

He hadn't planned it, only thought about it. At lunch he'd had a vision of Mia in this bed and now she was beside him, wrapped in white sheets, her hair long and loose around her face. She was lying on her side, gazing at him, cheeks flushed, eyes glowing softly. He wasn't used to being looked at like this, as if he was someone special, but it was how she made him feel. The way she'd kissed him, the way she'd touched him, the way she'd given herself to him so tenderly. Two hours ago she'd asked him to show her the dome, and he'd hesitated, because it was yet another small space. In the car, coming back from the restaurant, it had been almost impossible not to slide his hand over hers, not to lean in and kiss her when the engine died.

He'd known being in the confined space of the dome with her would challenge his self-control. He'd failed, hadn't been able to stop himself reaching for her. If she'd stilled his hand, he would have stepped back, but she hadn't. They'd collided like stars, exploded like meteors.

He touched her hair, winding a tendril around his finger. 'It's the first time I've seen your hair loose.'

She smiled. 'There've been lots of first times today.'

Her smile was full of light and he felt lucky to be the one bathing in its warmth. If fate had twisted in a different direction, she might have been married by now. Could he afford to break his own rule, permit himself some curiosity? There'd undoubtedly be fallout, but he couldn't help it. He wanted to know everything about her. He leaned in and kissed her softly. 'Tell me about Hal.'

'Hal?' The light in her eyes drained away and two little creases appeared on her forehead. She took a breath, hesitated, then exhaled slowly. 'He was Ash's business partner.' She lowered her gaze and for a long moment she was silent. When she looked up again, there were tears behind her eyes. 'He was...the kind of person who made you believe in possibilities. He was good for Ash...in the beginning, anyway. They were a good team. Friends as well as colleagues. The three of us spent a lot of time together.' She smiled softly. 'We were already like a family when Hal asked me out. When he asked me to marry him, it felt like we were completing the circle.'

She seemed to lose herself for a moment. Rain pattered on the windows. He held his breath, listening. Waiting.

'But Hal wasn't what he seemed.' Her fingers clenched the sheet. 'He was cooking the books, stealing from the company.'

'Stealing?'

She met his gaze. 'He was massively in debt: gambling; high-stakes poker… I didn't know he gambled, had no idea he was in debt, because he was always splashing money about, booking trips for us to lovely places. His family was well-off, you see. He told me he had money in shares, trust funds, investments. He once said he'd had a surprise bequest from a distant family member, but he hadn't been to any funeral.'

Her mouth wobbled. 'I should have worked it out, especially after Ash told me that there were inconsistencies in the company accounts. At the time it caused friction between us. I couldn't believe he would doubt Hal's honesty.' She chewed her lip. 'But then I realised I'd never seen a single bank statement of Hal's—only the statements from our joint account. He told me that his family's accountant always handled his finances and I'd just accepted it.

'I decided to test him. I said that we ought to be looking for a place to buy for after we were married; that we ought to be lining up a mortgage. I told him that I'd arranged an appointment with the bank. He got flustered, started saying that there was plenty of time, that we shouldn't be rushing into anything. I saw it then, the blind panic in his eyes, and I realised that Ash had been right all along.'

She pressed her fingers to her eyes. 'It all came out after that. The gambling, the debts. He'd cleaned out his trust fund, sold his shares, and when it was all gone he'd started stealing from Ash. I broke off the engagement. Hal's family settled out of court, but Ash and I took a real knock over it. We mended our fences, but I felt terrible. For so long, I'd been telling him that he was wrong about Hal, and he'd chosen to believe me. If it hadn't been for me, he'd have challenged Hal much sooner.'

'Oh, Mia…' She wasn't to blame. It had been an impossible situation; loyalties divided between lover and brother. He understood that situation all too well. He touched her shoulder, running his fingers lightly along her arm. 'Now I understand why you came to my hotel that day, why you interceded so compellingly for Ash.'

She sighed. 'Atonement.'

He pulled her close. 'A little, maybe, but mostly you did it because you love your brother, and you wanted to help him. It's what you do, Mia—you help people. You push back, you shape fate.'

'Is that what you think?'

He kissed her hair. 'Let me see… You convinced me to meet Ash in Greenwich, which secured him development funding and will conclude in a valuable contract for both of us. You saved Lotte from a serious assault. You saved me from having my picture taken as well as saving me from septicaemia. As for Cleuso…'

She lifted her head. 'You have a nice take on things.' A smile touched the corners of her mouth. 'I haven't helped much with your interior décor situation, though, have I?'

He glanced at the silk dress on the floor. 'That's a work in progress, and I can say hand on heart that there's absolutely no rush.'

'It wouldn't wash if you did… I mean, *three* years!' She shifted a little and ran a slow finger over the back of his hand. 'Seriously, though, until I saw I your man cave I was feeling sorry for you…living here, in all this emptiness.'

'Man cave?'

She nodded. 'It's a thing!' She flattened her hand over

his and fixed him with serious eyes. 'Where did you live before…when you were married?'

His felt his shoulders stiffening. She'd told him about her parents; she'd told him about Hal. He'd known she'd come back to him with questions about himself. It was the contract of conversation, only natural, but it was the kind of conversation that made his temples throb. Sweet, brave Mia. She wanted to open him up, she wanted to know him, but all he could think about was how he was going to dodge the bullet that he knew was coming.

'We had an apartment near the river.'

'Furnished?'

In spite of himself, he chuckled. 'Yes.'

'What was it like?'

Eline had done it all. Modern, clean, elegant. She'd had a thing about elephants—sculptures, paintings, small ornaments. They had to face the right way—towards the door, towards the window. Ironically, he couldn't remember. He'd had his hands full with caring for Bram.

'It was…streamlined.' He thought of the old Dutch range in the kitchen downstairs. 'Very different to this, although Direk's trying to persuade me to go for a modern streamlined look in the kitchen. He's rather fond of black granite.'

'Black? You mustn't do that. You've got that lovely old stove. I'd start with that. You could have it reconditioned; re-enamelled. It's such a lovely blue. Very Delft.'

'And it works well, as long as you're not in a hurry.'

She smiled. 'I know what you mean—my grandmother had one.' Suddenly she was sitting up, wrapping the sheet around herself. 'What did your wife do that hurt you so badly?'

For some reason his heart didn't shrink at the mention of Eline. Maybe because his focus was elsewhere.

Mia looked so lovely in the fading afternoon light, loosely wrapped in white, hair tumbling around her shoulders. He felt the fresh stirrings of desire but pulling her down, losing himself in her again, was too obvious a diversion tactic. And, after everything she'd told him about Hal—the secrets and the lies—he wanted to trust her with something real.

'She had an affair.'

'Why?'

Wide eyes held his. He drew in a slow breath. Neglect. That was what Eline had accused him of. But if he told Mia that, then he'd have to tell her about Bram: the drinking, the drugs, the despair. He'd have to explain why he'd bought the isolated beach house, why he'd spent weeks at a time there with Bram, drying him out, trying to keep him away from his addictions.

Wide eyes held him gently. She'd understand, and he wanted to trust her, but something was holding him back. Perhaps the roots of his pain ran too deep after all.

Eline had been sweet and understanding at first, but she'd grown impatient with him, and with Bram, and then her impatience had turned into bitterness, and the bitterness had turned into cruelty. She'd taunted him, fanned the flames of his shame.

'For pity's sake, lighten up, Theo. Have a drink!'

He shuddered inwardly.

'I suppose I wasn't what she wanted in the end… It happens.'

Mia frowned.

He sat up, adjusting the pillow behind him. 'Look… She was my first serious relationship. We got married straight out of university. I'd had a bad start in life, and I suppose I was trying to make up for that, trying to create something of my own…' He shrugged. 'I was working twenty-four-seven, building the business, and then she got spotted.'

'Spotted?'

Damn! Why was conversation such a minefield? Why was he surrounded by famous people when all he wanted was to keep himself and his history private?

'Yes. Eline worked in fashion. A scout liked the look of her…so she started catwalk modelling.' He pressed a finger to his bounding temple. 'You've no doubt heard of Eline de Vries…'

'Your ex is Eline de Vries?'

He nodded.

'Seriously?' Her eyes were wide as saucers.

'Yes, seriously!' It didn't mean anything. Eline was just a person like everyone else. No more special than himself, Mia or his brother. They were all just people, messing things up. 'After she signed with the agency, she started running with the beautiful people, and then she had an affair. I was the accessory that didn't match her outfit any more.' He smiled, joking at his own expense. 'But I'm not bitter.'

'I can see that.' She wasn't smiling.

He touched her elbow, ran his fingers up her arm to her shoulder. 'Look, it's ancient history—not worth talking about.' There was something in her eyes that looked like distance growing and it threw him. Could she see that he'd given her half a story? He felt panic rising, tightening his chest. He couldn't bear to see her retreating, not after the sublime intimacy they'd shared.

He leaned in, pressed his forehead to hers. 'I don't want to talk about her, Mia. I want to give you my undivided attention.' In a heartbeat her expression softened and he seized the moment, kissed her slowly, savouring the warmth of her mouth, the softness of her lips. When he felt her rising towards him, kissing him back, sliding her hands around his neck, the tension in his shoulders melted away. When he was kissing Mia, he could forget everything else. Everything he wanted was right there in that room with the light fading and the rain tapping on the window.

CHAPTER SEVEN

THERE WAS AN empty table near the window. Mia parked her coffee, sat down and slipped her laptop out of its case. She had work to do, but at home the words weren't flowing. It was probably foolish to imagine that writing at Hannekes Boom would be possible, although maybe the bustle of the trendy riverside café-bar would give her something to pit her concentration against. At least getting here early meant she'd secured a table, although Ash would probably want to sit outside and dangle his legs over the dock like the students and the hipsters did.

She switched on the computer, gazing through the window while it clicked and whirred. Across the river, the Nemo science centre rose up like a blue cigarette butt stubbed out in the heart of Oosterdok. She liked its blunt lines, the canted roof. A blue building against a blue sky. An old blue stove in a run-down canal house. *His* house.

She pushed the thought away, opened the blog post she was working on, but the words on the screen kept rearranging themselves into his words.

Do we need to talk about this?

Impossible!

Impossible to work because she was missing him, aching for his touch, his kiss, his smile. Why did it feel as if she'd been on a collision course with chaos from the moment they'd met? The car to Greenwich. The fundraiser. Cleuso in the canal. Spending an entire afternoon in bed with him after what she'd thought was going to be a safe lunch. She dropped her head into her hands and massaged her forehead. She'd gone back to his house because she'd wanted to get to know him better but getting to know the smooth curves and hard lines of his body hadn't been part of the plan.

She reached for her coffee, remembering the coffee he'd made which they'd never got around to drinking. Had she been reckless, giving herself to him so easily? She'd never done anything like it before. She put the cup to her lips and sipped slowly. The truth was that she'd always been a little bit scared of loving people because she was frightened of losing them, as she'd lost her parents. Not that staying away from love had been a deliberate policy; it had been more of a subliminal thing—self-preservation.

And the thing about Hal was that, when they'd started going out, she'd been eased in already because she'd spent so much time with him and Ash. He'd felt like family, had filled her longing for a circle that was wider than just Ash and herself. And she'd thought he was a known quantity—safe to love. Wrong, wrong, wrong.

When Theo kissed her in the dome, when he'd made clear what was on his mind, maybe he'd caught her in a defiant mood. Maybe some part of her had decided that she might as well be hung for a sheep as a lamb. She stroked the touch-pad of her laptop, waking the sleeping screen. But, no, that was wrong. It hadn't been about defiance. It had been about feelings, about expressing all the things she couldn't say to him in that moment: like how her heart had ached when he'd shown her around his empty house; like how she could see through the skim of bravado he used to cover his vulnerability. It was about that connection she'd felt between them from the very first day.

Maybe Theo *was* a risk, but she'd felt something real when he'd lifted her into his arms, when he'd loved her so tenderly, so passionately. Maybe it was that her heart had been ahead of the game, had run a risk assessment and given her the green light.

Would Ash give her the green light? For some reason, she'd avoided the subject of Theo with her brother, but now she'd have to tell him, and the thought of it was making her palms clammy. From the outside it would look as if she was falling down the same old rabbit hole: falling for another of his business associates. She pictured his face—the wide, serious eyes; that thing he did with his thumb, biting the pad of it—not the nail. When he did that, it meant he was concerned.

She nudged the computer off standby for a second time. Never mind Ash, she had concerns of her own. For all the physical chemistry between them, for all the feelings of intimacy and genuine connection, there were things Theo was holding back. She could read it in his eyes, in the way his shoulders had stiffened when she'd asked him about his ex-wife. He'd attributed his divorce to a youthful marriage, to Eline switching tracks, leaving him behind, but she couldn't help wondering if there'd been more to it than that. She wanted to believe that Theo was blameless, but her experience with Hal had made her wary. She couldn't stop wondering why Eline had had an affair. If she'd fallen in love with someone else, wouldn't she simply have left? An affair seemed so untidy. Had Theo driven her to it somehow? And, if so, what had he done?

Guiltily, she'd searched online for information. She'd found one small photo of Eline and Theo together. A candid shot, taken backstage after Eline's first catwalk show. Eline's arms were draped around Theo's neck, a cocktail in her hand. Theo was looking off-camera, smiling; even white teeth, his hair shorter, his face not quite so lean as now. He'd have been twenty-six, perhaps. Young and so handsome.

She'd turned up a brief article about their divorce, but it had been frustratingly short on detail. No details in the press; no real details from Theo. The fist in her heart clenched. In her limited experience, secrets spelled lies, set her nerves jangling like nails scraping down a blackboard. If only he'd told her more, she wouldn't have been reduced to searching online.

Later, in a calmer mood, she'd reasoned to herself that she and Theo were freshly minted lovers, that she couldn't possibly know everything about him, but still her senses were on high alert and her mind was rattling the gates of every possibility. Fate had brought them together time and again. Was there a reason, or were the stars just stirring fate around as part of some huge cosmic joke?

She slumped backwards in her chair. It was said that actions spoke louder than words. If that was right, then maybe she needed to put the brakes on, stop worrying…

They'd abandoned the bed as the last wisps of daylight had melted into darkness. He'd wanted to cook for her, but she'd had to get back to feed Cleuso, so he'd driven her home. In the car she'd stroked the back of his neck; on the barge he'd kissed her dizzy. He'd said he'd fetch her bicycle from across town where she'd abandoned it, so she'd given him the key to the padlock. The next morning she'd found the key underneath the designated plant pot, the bike secured against the railing of the barge. The punctured tyre had been fixed.

* * *

'I'm buzzing!' Ash's eyes were bright with excitement, his smile wide and white. He took a long swig from his beer bottle, set it down on the wooden planks of the dock. 'That was such a great meeting, Mia. Theo's techies are awesome and the atmosphere at MolTec is fantastic. There's a real can-do vibe.'

She squeezed his shoulder, ruffling his over-long hair affectionately. It was good to see him like this. After 'Halgate' he'd lost his sparkle, but this was the old Ash—handsome, happy, brimming with optimism. He'd propped her up when she was little, carried her emotionally, been her rod and staff. Her heart swelled for him and swelled for Theo, too, for giving her brother a boost just when he'd needed it the most.

He raked his hair back into place. 'It's a pity Theo's away. I was going to ask him to join us for a cold one.'

She toyed with her beer bottle, took a small sip. 'He's in Hamburg…and then he'll be Paris. He won't be back until Friday.'

Ash was staring at her. 'And you know this how…?'

She angled herself towards him. 'Because… I'm sort of seeing him.'

'Oh.' Ash picked up his bottle, lifted it to his lips lowering it again without drinking. 'Since when?'

'Um…since Monday—officially—but things have been heading that way since I ran into him at a charity event…' She told Ash about the fundraiser night; about Cleuso in the canal; about having lunch and about going to look at Theo's canal house. She didn't tell him how things had ended up. *Too much information!* He listened with interest and he didn't bite his thumb, which she took as a good sign. 'I was a bit worried about telling you, to be honest.'

'Why?'

'Can't you guess? Déjà vu!'

'It's not the same situation.' He swigged his beer. 'Theo's not my business partner, and my gut tells me that, even if things don't work out between the two of you, he wouldn't let it affect our business dealings.'

The breath caught in her throat. It hadn't occurred to her either until that very moment and now her heart was flapping like a fish in a landing net. If things didn't work with Theo, would Theo want to maintain a business connection with her brother? Feasibly Ash could come a cropper all over again and it would be *her* fault—again! Ash's faith in Theo was admirable. If only she could share it to the same degree, but suddenly she was thinking about Eline again, the feeling she'd had that Theo wasn't telling her everything about why his wife had had an affair. She pressed her beer bottle to her forehead and rolled it slowly. Right from the start, she'd had the feeling that Theo was a man with something to hide but she couldn't share her misgivings with Ash. He'd only say that if she felt like that she shouldn't be getting involved with Theo at all.

'Mia…?'

She came back to herself, meeting Ash's concerned gaze. 'I'm fine.' She lowered the beer bottle and smiled. 'I'm relieved that you're okay with it.'

'It's your life, Mia.' He slid a beer-chilled hand over hers. 'For what it's worth, I like Theo. He seems like a decent guy.'

A decent guy...

Theo *had* been involved with the women's refuge for many years; he'd rescued her cat; he'd fixed her puncture… Decent acts. Her tension eased. Ash always did that: made her feel better. She smiled, leaned closer. 'He's not only a decent guy but he's a decent guy with a famous sister…'

Ash's eyes widened. 'Who…?'

She lowered her voice: 'Madelon Mulder.'

'No!' His eyebrows leapt up. 'No way…'

She nodded deeply. 'It's true.'

'Jeez, that's really something.' He tipped the remains of his beer into his mouth. 'In London, Theo told me he had a sister and a brother, but he didn't give me the juicy details!' He paused for a moment, thinking. 'He did say he had to dash because he was meeting his sister for dinner…' His eyes locked on hers. '*That* was the night of the fundraiser, when *you* bumped into him.' He grinned. 'So weird.'

A brother?

Theo hadn't mentioned a brother. She racked her brains, trying to think of any moment when it might have been relevant to their conversation, but she drew a blank. So many blanks, like the walls of his canal house.

Ash was snapping his fingers in front of her eyes. 'You need something to eat, sis. You keep zoning out. It's a sign of low blood sugar. We should go inside and order. Pizza would totally hit the spot right now; what do you reckon?'

She let him take her hand and pull her to her feet. 'Pizza sounds great.'

Theo dropped his key card onto the console table and contemplated the room. Trude had done well; had found him another of the small, exclusive hotels he liked. He didn't care for the huge places; he liked the feeling of being tucked away.

He slipped off his suit jacket and loosened his tie. The colours of the décor reminded him of the colours in Mia's dress. He hesitated then pulled out his phone, moving around the room taking pictures, amused with himself because he was thinking about mood boards. When he'd shot every angle, he scrolled through the photos, warmed by the thought of Mia's smile. If he showed her these it might help them brainstorm ideas for the house…

His finger stilled. He rewound the thought. When had he started thinking of his house as 'the' house? A joint project. He threw his phone onto the bed and yanked off his tie. He needed to stop that kind of thinking. It was jumping the gun by a mile.

He stripped off his shirt, caught his reflection in the console mirror. The scratches on his shoulder and on his arms had faded, but the little knot of concentration between her eyes as she'd bathed his torn skin was burned into his memory, as was the image of her wrapped in his sheets, hair tumbling around her shoulders. She'd been asking him about Eline…and he'd given her a half-story. He pressed his temple, swallowing hard. She deserved more. She'd told him about Hal, not holding anything back. He'd seen the hurt in her eyes, the tears brimming there, the devastation on her face. She'd let him in, shared her pain, but he hadn't returned the favour.

He lowered himself onto the bed. Half-stories and half-truths…that was his life now. If only he could let go, allow himself to trust again, but he couldn't because this wasn't about *him. He* was strong enough to take life's knocks, but Bram wasn't. Everything he did, the precautions he was forced to take, was all for his brother. And he was happy to do it, because Bram had always had his back, not just at home, but at university too. When he'd been an impoverished student Bram had helped him out, even though he hadn't been earning much himself. He used to bring delicious food round, pretending to be after Theo's opinion about some new ingredient he'd discovered. That was Bram, looking after him. It was what he'd always done. His brother was the most selfless person he'd ever known, and the fact that he was ill didn't change that. It just made Theo even more determined to pull him back from the brink, to protect him while he healed.

He'd compelled Eline to sign a non-disclosure agreement as part of the divorce; she was forbidden to mention or allude to himself or any member of his family, be it on the radio, on television, in the press or online. She'd called him a crazy control freak, but control was what drove him. It was what having grown up powerless did to you. It made you burn for the opposite. If that made him a freak, then at least he was a freak with good intentions.

He got to his feet and fished a tee shirt out of his suitcase. Madelon's success was going to be a problem but she was mindful. That was how they both had to be until Bram was properly back on his feet again. He unhitched his belt and took off his trousers. Would that day ever come? A wave of weariness swept over him. It was all the false starts that had exhausted Eline's patience. So many times they'd thought Bram was clean and every time they'd been wrong. He'd kept falling back into his old ways and then it was picking up the pieces, starting all over again. Weeks on end at the beach house, running the business from his laptop, babysitting his brother.

He pulled on some jeans. But now Bram had been clean for eight whole months—the longest stretch he'd ever managed—and he'd told Theo to leave him be.

'You've got a life you're not living, a house that you barely spend time in. And it's because of me. I've been weak, unforgivably selfish. Poor little brother... I've dragged you through every miserable moment, but I'm not doing it any more. I know I've promised you so many times, but this time I'm doing it for you, Theo, and because I'm doing it for you, not for myself, I'm going to make it.'

He'd seen a new resolve hardening in Bram's eyes, a

firmness of intention that had rowed him right back into their childhood, to the days when Bram had been the protector; himself, his mother and Madelon, the protected.

He'd agreed to leave Bram to his own devices on the condition that he saw someone every day; not a healthcare worker—Bram hated that idea—but the young woman, Marta, who went in to clean twice a week. He'd asked Marta if she'd check in with Bram on a daily basis, and she'd readily agreed, but she'd refused to take any payment. She'd said it was no trouble to call in, that she passed the beach house every day anyway.

With Marta keeping tabs on Bram, he'd started allowing himself to hope, but he couldn't let his guard down. Bram was as fragile as a tower of cards. The slightest breath of an adverse wind could trigger a total collapse.

And so, no matter how he longed to open himself up to Mia, he couldn't risk loosening his grip, couldn't risk taking an arrow to the heel. But holding out on her was making his heart ache because she deserved better. She deserved trust, loyalty, love and happiness. More than anything, he wanted to give her those things, but it was going to take time and the one thing he hadn't taken was time. He'd lost control, jumped on the accelerator like a total idiot. And now the intimacy they'd shared had sharpened the edges of his confusion. He was in a tangle: thinking about her all the time; missing her; burning with desire for her sweet body, her touch, the taste of her lips. It was ironic. He'd spent his whole life avoiding alcohol, even prescription drugs, but now he was in the grip of an unforeseen addiction and he had no idea how he was going to conquer it.

'I've been reading your blog.'

'Why? You're in Paris. You've got the Louvre, the Moulin Rouge…'

'It's impressive, Mia.'

Little pause. 'Really?'

'Yes.' He pulled his computer onto his lap and opened the pages he'd bookmarked.

'I'm especially taken with your essays. I've never read anything like these before.'

'They're just half-formed ideas…meandering thoughts…' There was shyness in her voice.

'But there's a thread that ties everything together. They're not random.'

He'd been mulling over his Mia 'addiction' when he'd remembered that she had a website. Two clicks later he'd found himself in her professional world. Pacey articles, deft observations, sharp humour and boundless humanity. Her blog space was devoted to work of a different slant. The writing was almost experimental. Lyrical, captivating…personal. One item had caught and held his attention.

'I really liked your latest post: *Empty Rooms*.'

'Oh.' A moment unfurled slowly. 'What can I say? I found your house inspiring…'

He'd read the piece over and over again, felt moved by it. 'I love the phrase "dust aches between floors". I don't know anything about poetry, but your writing is poetic; beautiful.'

'I'm blushing.'

'I wish I could see that.'

'I'm glad you can't! Beetroot doesn't suit me. How's Paris?'

Changing the subject. Maybe she was as spooked by the suddenness of their togetherness as he was. He glanced through the window and saw a piece of sun sinking between the rooftops, a section of the Eiffel Tower stretching skywards. 'I haven't really seen it. I've been in meetings all day and now I'm at the hotel—in my room.' His eyes slid to the empty pillow beside him. 'I should have brought you with me. We could have found something to do...'

'Like what?' Her tone was teasing.

How easy it was to slip into the froth of casual flirting. It was their safe place; their comfort blanket. 'We could have walked romantically by the Seine.'

She laughed. 'How do you walk "romantically"? You can walk quickly, or slowly, but I'm struggling to picture romantic walking.'

He chuckled. 'Well, I'd put my arm around your shoulders, and you'd put your arm around my waist, and then we'd walk very slowly, and of course we'd have to keep stopping...'

'To...?'

He grinned. 'To feed the ducks!'

'I've been to Paris and I don't remember ducks on the Seine.'

'They're part-time ducks.'

'I see.' She was chuckling. 'So, if there weren't any ducks, would we still keep stopping?'

'Yes.'

'Why?'

'Because it's the law.'

He imagined her frowning, smiling that squashed little smile that went with it.

'Which law?'

'The one that says that lovers have to kiss every ten metres.' Silence. 'Mia?'

'There's no such law. I just checked online. I always check facts—it's a writer thing.'

He turfed the laptop off his legs and settled back against the plush headboard. 'Okay, so I might have been making it up, but if I was walking along the Seine with you I'd kiss you every ten metres...maybe every five metres.'

'It'd take us a long time to get anywhere.'

'I wouldn't care. Would you?'

'No…no, I wouldn't…'

Her voice trailed off in a whisper.

Maybe talking about kissing had been a bad idea. It was stirring the wrong pot, especially since they hadn't really talked about what happened; how they were feeling. The day after their extended lunch date, he'd had to fly to Hamburg, but he'd made sure to retrieve her bicycle and fix the tyre before he left. He'd wanted to show her that he was there for her, that whatever it was they'd embarked upon wasn't a meaningless thing. He'd told himself that they'd talk later but until now their conversations had been snatched. He'd been on the move, busy with meetings… or maybe that was just an excuse.

The truth was that he was out of his depth. Perhaps she felt the same. Maybe they both needed something real to hold onto and he knew it was down to him to offer up a piece of himself, as it had been in the restaurant. A simple truth to wipe away the half-truths, to make her understand that he wasn't playing games. He stared at the darkening Parisian skyline, at the lights glowing from distant windows. 'I miss you, Mia…'

He held his breath, heard the tiny catch in hers.

'I'm missing you too…'

He could feel her smile; he felt warmed by the tiny flame of honesty he'd kindled between them. 'Are you free tomorrow evening?'

'I thought you'd never ask.'

He smiled. 'The skies are set to be clear. It's going to be a perfect night for stargazing and… Indonesian food! Do you like *nasi goreng*?'

'It's one of my favourites!'

'That's handy—it's one of the few things I make quite well.'

He felt a lightening of spirit. Perhaps this was the way forward—through his actions. He could only deal out little truths until Bram was strong again, but he could show Mia how much he cared through the things he did. His actions would have to do the talking until he could explain everything.

CHAPTER EIGHT

THE SKY OVER Van Baelerstraat was cobalt blue. Cloudless. It was a wide street, with grand red-brick buildings, so different from the tall narrow houses squeezed shoulder-to-shoulder along the canals. On this street there were lanes for cars, lanes for bicycles, tram tracks and pavements, a feeling of expansiveness. It was why Mia had chosen to walk to Koffiemeester's instead of cycling. She'd wanted to stretch her eyes to a wider view, fall into the rhythm of her own footsteps, acclimatise to the weightlessness she was feeling.

I miss you, Mia.

Something in his tone had derailed her for a moment, then flooded her with happiness. His words had reassured her that what had happened between them wasn't a casual thing. It had living roots, an onward momentum. And he'd be back tonight…disarming her with his smile, his eyes. She'd feel those strong arms around her, his lips on hers. She tingled, smiling to herself about 'romantic walking'. If only he knew that his little declaration had her walking on air. Walking on sunshine. Yes, there were things to talk about, things she wanted to know, but right now she was high on feeling, high on anticipation. It almost felt as if she was…

Her phone vibrated against her hip. She wrangled it

out of her pocket, eyeing the screen. 'Hi, Lotte! How's it going?'

'Fabulous as always, darling.' Lotte loved mimicking the drama queens and models she worked with. 'Where *are* you? I was passing and thought I'd drop in, but the only one here's Clueless.'

Poor Cleuso. One day he'd prove them all wrong. 'I popped out to buy coffee, but I'll back in a jiffy...if you can hold on.'

'I can...but get your skates on because I've got something exciting to tell you.'

Lotte stopped scrolling and looked at her. 'So, what do you think?'

'They're certainly different!' The footwear Lotte was showing her on the laptop was made from recycled plastics and fabrics. Bright. Innovative. Interesting. 'I love them. I'd wear them.'

Lotte arched an eyebrow. 'I'll bear that in mind.'

Lotte was always being given clothes and accessories after her photo shoots, quite a lot of which came her way because Lotte's own tastes were very particular. For one thing, Lotte didn't do dresses. That was how *she'd* ended up with the gorgeous dress that Theo had liked.

'So...? What's the story?'

Lotte kicked off her shoes, crossed her legs and dropped her knees out Buddha-style. 'Okay, so the designer's called Kris Haynes. He's one of the designers taking part in a showcase of—' she scratched quotes into the air '—fashion with a conscience. They're calling the event Watch your Footprint, and it's going to be held at Tobacco on the fifteenth of September...proceeds going to charity.'

'So you'll be photographing the show...?'

Lotte nodded. 'And I'm doing publicity photos for the

designers ahead of the event. There's going to be a social media push and a printed programme—on recycled paper, of course!'

'That's great! You're nailing it, and rightly so. Your work is amazing.'

Lotte waved her hands dismissively. 'Thanks, but yada yada…' She grinned. 'I wanted to give you the full brief because I've told them *you'll* write the copy for the programme.'

It took a moment for Lotte's words to sink in. 'Me?'

'Hell yeah! I pointed them to your Dilly and Daisy write up, and they loved it. They want a similar approach: some background on the designers, something about ethical fashion, the move away from fast fashion et cetera… You can expect a call from the organiser very soon.'

Her heart ballooned. 'Aww, Lotte…thanks so much.' She leaned across the sofa and gave her friend a hug. 'You're so sweet.'

'It's nothing to do with being sweet. You're a fabulous writer and you're the perfect fit for the gig. You'll love doing it and you'll make some great contacts.'

'Contacts are always useful.'

Lotte rocked forward, an impish grin on her face. 'Which brings me to the best bit.' Her eyes danced. 'The organiser is Eline de Vries!'

Mia's lungs collapsed. 'As in the super—?'

'Yep!'

A boat chugged past, its vibrations filling the air. A welcome moment of respite. She swallowed hard, trying to look thrilled. 'Wow! That's such a…' The words got stuck so she forced a wide smile onto her lips. 'That's so great!'

Lotte beamed. 'Isn't it? I mean, Eline freaking de Vries! That's *got* to open some doors—for both of us.' She folded her laptop, poked it into her bag then stood up, sliding her feet back into her shoes. 'I'm sorry but I've got to go…' She adjusted the bag strap across her shoulder, then she looked up, eyes narrowing. 'Are you okay, Mia? You've gone pale.'

She wasn't okay, but it wasn't Lotte's fault. She'd been all over the place after her lunch date with Theo, so she'd only given Lotte a tightly edited version. Lotte had no idea that Eline was Theo's ex.

She got to her feet and managed a shaky smile. 'I'm shell-shocked, that's all. As you said, Eline freaking de Vries!'

It was warm and sunny on the deck. She didn't usually sit out in the afternoon, because there were too many people going past, too many curious eyes, but Lotte's news had thrown her into a flat spin and she'd needed some air. Cleuso had wasted no time in joining her in the old wicker chair, and now he was sitting on her knee purring, his eyes closing.

'You can't go to sleep.' She rubbed his throat, tilting his face upward, but his lids determinedly stayed shut. She released his chin and stroked his head. 'I was hoping for some advice…' He shifted, turned a slow circle then curled into a neat furry bundle; a warm, soft weight in her lap. She slumped backwards, stretching to reach her cup of camomile tea from the base of an upturned plant pot. Camomile wasn't her thing, but her nerve ends were fraying fibre by fibre and she'd thought it might help.

Eline de Vries!

Of all the people in the world, Lotte had set her up for a job with Theo's ex, had inadvertently handed her the mother of all conundrums. To tell him or not…? To take the job, or not….? She sniffed the tea, shuddered and set it down again. If she told him he wouldn't take it well; she knew that instinctively. It wasn't unreasonable, she supposed, most people wouldn't want their current partner meeting their ex, but she had a feeling that Theo's reaction would go beyond ordinary discomfort.

There was something he wasn't telling her about the reasons for Eline's affair; she was sure of it. What he'd said about them marrying too young, about Eline's career driving a wedge between them… It had sounded like a cliché and it didn't tally with the bitterness she'd seen in his eyes when they'd been talking in his kitchen. At the time, she'd felt that his pain was genuine, but she had been wrong about someone before. She'd fallen for Hal's masquerades, jetted off to Prague believing that the money he was spending was his to spend. Even though it was hard to believe, it wasn't beyond the possibility that Theo had hurt Eline first…that her affair had been a reaction to something he'd done.

A small boat puttered up the canal towards her. The helmsman gave her a jaunty wave and she nodded, tried to smile…and failed. She stared at the wake travelling across the water. Hal had broken her heart with his secrets and she couldn't go through it again. If only Theo would talk to her, really talk to her, but he switched gears whenever things got personal and she was running out of time. Just that morning she'd been walking on air because he'd said he was missing her and there'd been that inkling of recognition…

She was falling in love with him, but she was scared because he was holding something away from her; something important. Maybe meeting Eline would help in some way…even if it was just allowing her to get a measure of what kind of person Eline was.

She bit her lip. Lotte had been so thrilled to gift her this job—always trying to pay back for the night of the assault—so there was no way she could turn it down. Besides, refusing to take it would make Lotte look bad with Eline, and there was no way she could do that to her friend.

A girl cycled past and threw her a cheery smile. She turned away, tears thickening in her throat. She didn't deserve a stranger's smile. Keeping this secret from Theo went against everything she believed in. It made her a hypocrite, but what could she do? She was trapped.

The airport lounge was busy. Theo parked his holdall between his feet, leaned his shoulder against the plate-glass window and gazed across the runway. The tinted glass robbed the blue sky of its vibrancy, but it couldn't dull his excitement. That night he'd be seeing Mia, and he had a surprise for her!

He took out his phone and read Madelon's message again.

Confirming for tonight—seven p.m.!

He hadn't expected to see his sister until the following week, but her shoot in Athens had wrapped ahead of schedule. She was back in Amsterdam. They'd had a long talk on the phone that morning. He'd told her about Mia.

'Can I meet her?' Madelon had asked, and then he'd had an idea—a thing he could do for Mia that would show her how much he was thinking of her. He'd asked Madelon if she'd let Mia do an interview. An exclusive with Madelon Mulder was bound to give Mia's career a boost. The style of Mia's writing would lend itself well to the measured, in-depth kind of profile that Madelon's work and interests merited. She'd be in safe hands with Mia.

Madelon had agreed readily, but she'd been bemused. 'You're in love with this girl, aren't you?'

For a second his mouth had gone dry. Madelon knew him better than anyone and without even seeing his face she'd twigged something that he hadn't quite twigged for himself. He'd been glad of his hectic schedule. Wall-to-wall meetings filled with absorbing discussions about complex issues had kept his thoughts about Mia on the back burner but now, watching planes slowly trundling over the tarmac, the truth of Madelon's observation broke over him like a warm wave. He *was* in love with Mia. He'd fallen for her in the lobby of that London hotel. He'd stepped out of the lift, noticed her instantly… Her profile; her upswept hair; her neat, straight nose; milky skin contrasting with the dark stand-up collar of her jacket… When she'd turned, caught him staring, he'd almost lost his balance.

In the short time he'd known her, she'd brought him joy, the kind of joy he hadn't expected to feel again. If only he could be the kind of lover she deserved. He wasn't that man yet, but he aspired to be, would work hard to prove himself until the day came when he'd be able to share his whole story with her. Until then, he'd find a million ways to show her what she meant to him.

A female voice over the loud speaker announced that the plane was boarding. He called up Mia's number, quickly tapped out a text:

Can pick you up tonight if you want. Let me know. Can't wait to see you! Theo x

Madelon leaned against the stove. 'If I'd known you were making your famous *nasi goreng* I'd have accepted your invitation for dinner!'

He speared a shallot with the point of his knife and held it up. 'It's not too late. I can make extra…'

She shook her head. 'It's tempting, but I can't. I'm going to see Mama.' Her face lit up. 'I said I'd stay over so we can have a marathon catch-up. I'm going to take her breakfast in bed in the morning—spoil her a bit.'

'She'll like that.' He started slicing shallots. His mother was going to be over the moon to have Maddie to herself for a few hours. Maddie was her baby, the one whose memories of all the bad stuff were the vaguest; the one whose anecdotes, about the movie world, were the most diverting. He peeled another shallot. 'I took her to Concertgebow the week before last.'

'She told me. She said it was wonderful.'

He threw her a knowing smile. 'You know how she loves Mozart.'

After the concert, he'd driven her home. He'd always wanted to buy her something grander than the little house she'd chosen in the city suburbs, but she'd insisted that it was *that* house she wanted. She'd said it had a nice vibe, that it made her feel safe. Safety was still paramount to his mother, even after all this time. As usual they'd talked about Bram, shared their worries and their hopes...

'Here...let me help.' Madelon was nudging him along the table, pushing up her sleeves. 'I feel useless just watching.' She picked up a knife, started stripping papery skin from a fat garlic clove and then the knife stilled in her hands. He could feel her eyes on his face, searching. 'So... have you told Mia about Bram?'

He'd asked her to come early so they could cover these bases before Mia arrived, but he knew it was going to be a tricky conversation. He took a breath, looked up. 'No.'

Madelon frowned. 'Have you told her anything?'

'She knows Pa drank. She knows he was violent.' He shrugged and swept the sliced shallots into a bowl. 'That's all I've told her.'

'What about Eline?'

'Garlic, please...' Madelon handed him two peeled cloves and he thwacked them hard with the hilt of his knife. 'She knows about Eline, knows *who* Eline is, but I haven't gone into the details.' He caught Madelon's recriminatory look. 'We were in...' He rolled his eyes. 'It was an intimate moment, okay? I didn't want to be talking about my ex-wife at that particular juncture.'

'Hmm.' Madelon spliced a carrot and started carving it into matchsticks. 'So, even outside the interview, we can't talk about the family, or anything personal...?'

Madelon was mindful because she had to be, but her natural disposition was to be open and honest. Of course, since her career had always taken precedence over personal relationships, as far as he knew she'd had no experience of being in a situation like his. He rattled his knife over the smashed garlic, micro-dicing it the way Bram had taught him. 'Ideally, no.'

The weight of Madelon's stare was deadening his limbs. He set the knife down, wiped his hands on a cloth and met her gaze. 'What...?'

She sighed, reaching for the spring onions. 'I don't know... I just keep thinking about all the people who knew us before. Any of them could come out of the woodwork at any time...'

'They won't. Not without a reason. Right now you're just a girl they used to know—someone who's making a successful career. They'll be saying, *Hey, I remember that girl from school...* Or, *I worked at the same coffee shop as Madelon Mulder!* That's as far as it'll go. But if someone connects us, finds out that Madelon Mulder and the MolTec boss are siblings, that's when someone'll start joining the dots, asking questions: *Wasn't he married to that supermodel? Wasn't there another brother?* The alkies and junkies Bram used to run with would sell him out in a heartbeat for the price of one lousy fix!'

His heart was pumping, heat rising. He gripped the cloth tightly, pushing at the narrow walls of his anger, trying to subdue his hammering heart. 'The press loves you now, Maddie, but they love a dirty story even more. Can you imagine—paparazzi camping out on Texel waiting for Bram to go shopping? Christ! You'd think they'd find something better to do.' He snapped the cloth hard against the table edge and felt a momentary relief. 'I don't care what they say about me, and you'd ride it out because talent always trumps scandal, but Bram wouldn't cope.'

Madelon sighed heavily. 'You're right but…don't you get tired of it all?'

For some reason he was folding and unfolding the cloth. 'Of course I do, but it's just the way it's got to be, until Bram's…'

'Better?' She looked up. 'What if he never gets better, Theo? Are we to spend our whole lives on lockdown?'

There was no recrimination. It was only a question, a point she was raising, but still his stomach churned. He couldn't go there, couldn't allow himself to believe that Bram wasn't going to make it.

'Eight months clean, Maddie; that's more than he's ever managed before.'

She put her knife down and stepped towards him. 'I want Bram to make it, I really do, but I have two brothers…' She touched his arm, squeezing gently. 'And you've sacrificed so much. You can't go on like this. You're in love. You've got a chance of happiness, but you'll lose Mia if you keep her at arm's length. Why won't you trust her?'

Words he didn't want to hear; a question he couldn't bring himself to answer. He *wanted* to trust Mia, but he'd lost his first love because of his devotion to Bram, and he wasn't ready to risk it happening again. He'd never told Madelon about Eline's cruel jibes; how much she'd stung him. It had seemed like an unnecessary detail—Madelon had found Eline's affair heart-breaking enough—and it was pointless talking about it now. All he knew was that for the moment he couldn't face telling Mia about Bram.

'I'm dealing with it, okay?' He swallowed hard. 'We can't widen the circle…not yet. Not when Bram's almost—'

The doorbell rang, cutting him off.

Madelon shrugged, eyes heavy. 'Okay…but, for the record, I think you're making a terrible mistake.'

'Mia!'

Her heart leapt as he gathered her into his arms, hugging her warm and tight. Everything felt better when his arms were around her. She nestled against him, breathing in his clean skin smell. It was hard not to slide her fingers under the hem of his tee shirt.

He released her slightly, smoothing a strand of hair away from her face. 'You're a sight for sore eyes.'

'So are you.' She slipped her arms around his neck, happy to be in the moment, not worrying about Eline or the secrets he might or might not be keeping. She just wanted to lose herself in his warm, green gaze.

He pulled her in again, lips against her ear. 'I missed you so much.'

Something in his voice, a depth of emotion that made her heart quicken. Perhaps she wasn't the only one on the brink of…

He released her for a second time, took hold of her hand. 'Let's go inside so we can say hello properly.'

'Wait! I've got you something.' She'd been so preoccupied with the Eline de Vries situation that she'd almost forgotten to bring him his present. She pulled her hand out of his and picked up the gift-wrapped pot plant she'd stowed near the door. She held it out, bobbing a curtsey. 'Ta dah!'

Recognition flared in his eyes and then he was smiling. 'Aloe Vera, right?'

She nodded. 'For your kitchen windowsill.'

'Thank you.' He took it from her, giving it the once over. 'My first ever plant…'

'It'll be the first of many. Aloes breed like rabbits.'

He laughed and then his eyes grew serious. 'Come on… let's go inside.'

As he closed the door behind them the chug of boats on the canal fell away. The hallway was quiet and cool; a little gloomy. Tingling, she watched him setting the aloe down on a table that hadn't been there before.

'Is that new?'

'Direk likes to sneak things in when I'm not here.'

'He's got a good eye; it works beautifully.'

He came to stand in front of her, putting his hands on her shoulders. 'I'll tell you what works beautifully…' He eased her closer. 'You.'

She caught his forearms in her hands, lost herself in darkening green eyes. He bent his head, leaned in until their noses were almost touching. 'I'm so glad you're here.'

And then his mouth was on hers, his lips warm and insistent. It was like melting; melding together so that she didn't know where she began and he ended. She let go of his arms, ran her hands over his torso and under his tee shirt, fingertips connecting with warm, smooth skin. For an instant, his lips softened against hers, coaxing hers apart, and then he deepened his kiss, slowly propelling her backwards until her shoulder blades touched the wall. She felt his hands moving to her waist, travelling upward. When his thumb slid over her nipple, her pulse spiked, a volley of white-hot darts shooting through her belly. She was on fire, losing control, burning with an immeasurable need. Breathlessly, she pushed at his shoulders, breaking their kiss. 'Can we take this upstairs…?'

'Definitely…' He kissed her again softly, then stepped back a little, a mischievous glint kindling in his eyes. 'But it'll have to wait. First, I've got a surprise for you.'

She dropped her hands to his waist, not wanting to let him go. 'What sort of surprise?'

'It's a sort of professional gift…' He straightened her blouse across her shoulders and then he smiled. 'I've arranged for you to interview a certain award-winning actress…'

A pulse-beat. 'No!' Her insides were hopping like fire crackers. 'Madelon? Is she coming?'

'She's already here. Come…' He held out his hand. 'She's dying to meet you.'

Her heart was pounding. Meeting Madelon was the last thing she'd expected. It felt like a grand gesture, not because Madelon was a star but because she was his sister. He was trusting her with his family.

As they walked towards the kitchen, her mind was racing, sifting through anything she could remember about Madelon's career. He'd given her a wonderful opportunity, but this wasn't how she was used to working. She felt hopelessly unprepared.

'Hello, Mia!' Madelon kissed her on both cheeks then stepped back, smiling.

It was hard not to feel a little star-struck. The slender blonde with the golden skin and warm curious eyes was someone she'd only ever seen on the big screen. In the flesh Madelon was smaller, less statuesque than her screen persona. Her resemblance to Theo was tangible.

'It's lovely to meet you, Madelon.' She glanced at Theo. 'I'm blushing, I know. It's just that this is a little unexpected.'

Madelon touched her arm. 'Apologies! Theo's learned to strike while the iron's hot!' Her eyes were darker than Theo's, more hazel. 'I always seem to be on the move these days. It can be hard to plan ahead.'

'Impossible, more like!' Theo was cracking eggs into a bowl. 'Remember that time we were supposed to meet in London?'

'No! Don't!' Madelon was laughing, her eyes pleading for understanding. 'We'd been planning it for weeks… a few days in London after my final show in the West End…'

'I'd broken my journey especially…' Theo started beating the eggs.

Madelon threw him a conciliatory look. 'Poor Theo! He'd been in LA, was travelling back to Europe.'

Frenetic whisking. 'Jet-lagged, of course!'

'Rub it in, why don't you!' Madelon shook her head. 'We'd planned to see the sights because you know I never have time when I'm doing a show…'

It was impossible not to like Madelon; she had an easy manner, an infectious, throaty laugh.

'So it was the last night, final curtain… I was looking forward to seeing Theo but then my agent called! She said I needed to get myself to LA "immediately" to audition for a movie. Theo was mid-air, couldn't take a call, so I had to text him to let him know I was catching the red-eye to LA…'

Theo set down the bowl. 'We ended up having coffee in the airport, and it wasn't even decent coffee!'

She laughed, giving him a pointed look. 'Well, that would've *definitely* been the last straw!'

Madelon's eyes flashed. 'You obviously know him very well…'

She caught Theo's eye. 'I'm *getting* to know him…' He winked and turned towards the stove.

Seeing Madelon and Theo together, how close they were—their easy conversation—reminded her of how she was with Ash and somehow it was reassuring. Madelon's whole demeanour was open, her eyes warm and interested. Madelon was like Theo without the clouds. Would Madelon so patently adore a brother who'd done something bad, something that he needed to hide?

Watching them now—Madelon's hand on his arm, their low laughter, their obvious affection—she couldn't help feeling that maybe she'd been searching for skeletons in empty closets…

In bed with Theo that afternoon, she hadn't fully bought into his story about why Eline had had an affair—'I was the accessory that didn't match her outfit any more'. She'd wondered if he might have been to blame, but perhaps that was what Hal had done to her: made her mistrustful. She sighed. It was entirely possible that Eline's fame had changed her. That kind of thing happened all the time. She bit her lip. When Theo had said that Eline was ancient history—not worth talking about—she'd thought he was deflecting, avoiding the subject, but maybe that hadn't been it at all. She drew a slow breath, tingling at the memory of warm fingers tracing a line from her elbow to her shoulder; of green eyes locked on hers. He'd said he'd far rather be giving *her* his *undivided attention* than talking about his ex-wife. She held in a smile, losing herself in the memory, and then another memory surfaced…the thing that Ash had said.

She stepped forward, catching Madelon's eye. 'You have another brother, don't you…?'

The momentary silence felt like a glitch, then Theo spoke. 'That's right.' His eyes held hers for a long second, searching, then softening. 'Ash told you?'

She nodded. 'He was over during the week, seeing your technical team.' She turned to Madelon. 'Ash is my brother and, for the record, he's a massive fan.'

'I'm always grateful for fans…' Madelon smiled, lifting her chin slightly. 'Theo told me they're working together?'

'Yes. Ash writes computer programmes…and that's all I know!' She glanced at Theo, then back to Madelon. The atmosphere in the room seemed altered. She hooked a loose strand of hair behind her ear. 'So, what does your other brother do?'

Madelon pressed her lips together. 'He's a chef.'

'Cool!' She looked at Theo. 'Did he give you lessons?'

'As a matter of fact, he did.' His smile didn't quite reach his eyes. He looked at his watch. 'Do you girls want a drink, something to take upstairs with you?' His gaze rested on Madelon. 'I'm just thinking, you should probably make a start…given that you can't stay long.'

'You're not staying for dinner?'

Madelon shook her head. 'Sadly, I have other plans, but I said I'd do the interview.' Her eyes slid to Theo, suddenly mischievous. 'Theo wanted to give you something so that you'd know how much he—'

'Wine? Beer? Mineral water?' Theo jostled Madelon aside, started tickling her. Madelon was laughing and squirming, then she broke free, grabbed Mia's arm.

'Come on. Let's go upstairs and let the chef have his kitchen back.'

They watched Madelon waving from the taxi as it pulled away.

'She's so lovely.' Mia slid her arms around his waist.

'Thank you so much for arranging it, Theo. Honestly, I'm buzzing!'

He closed the door, wrapped her in his arms. 'It went well, then?'

'It did.' Her eyes were shining, her cheeks slightly flushed. 'Usually I'd have researched someone before interviewing them, but Madelon was amazing. She filled me in on all the shows she'd done, and the movies, right from the early days. She was sweet and generous and interesting and so…well-earthed.'

He couldn't help smiling. She might have been describing herself. He released her, guiding her down the hallway. 'So, what happens now, in terms of placing the interview?'

'I've got a couple of editors who'll be interested for sure.' She stretched up, kissing his cheek. 'I can't wait to write it up! I was thinking that maybe I could catch Madelon when she's here again, so that Lotte could take pictures to go with the piece. Wouldn't that be great?'

'Yes…' That was Mia, already thinking about how she could share the glory. What he couldn't let her share with Lotte was his own connection to Madelon. He bit back a sigh. Madelon was right; living under lockdown was tiresome. He'd talk to Mia about all the provisos later. At that moment he just wanted to enjoy her company, live a little. He brought her to a halt. 'So, while you've been hanging out with the glitterati, I've been hard at work…' He opened a set of double doors and moved aside.

She stepped into the room then looked back at him, her smile full of happy light. 'Wow! Theo, this is lovely.' She crossed to the middle of the room. 'Is this the table from the hall?'

He nodded. After she'd gone upstairs with Madelon, he'd paced around the kitchen, frustrated with himself for telling Ash that he had a brother. At the time he'd simply been answering a question; he'd had no way of knowing that in a matter of weeks he'd be in love with Mia, that she'd be bringing up the subject of Bram at such an inopportune moment.

Restlessly, he'd paced out of the kitchen and along the hall, spotted Direk's table and suddenly realised that it would make the perfect dining table for two. After he'd shifted it into the room the ideas had kept on coming. He'd found a bag of tea lights, set them up around the room then put a few on the table, using drinking glasses as holders. The candlelight had transformed the huge, empty space. Now it felt intimate. A little bit special. Worthy of his very special dinner guest.

He pulled out a chair for her. 'I thought it would be nicer to eat in here than in the kitchen.'

She settled herself, touching the linen napkin. 'Candles, music, table linen… Direk would be proud of you. Excellent romantic visualisation!'

He laughed, taking his place opposite her. 'It's much easier to visualise a room when you've got a reason to use it…' The light in her eyes was soft and glowing. Maybe it was the candlelight. He reached for the bottle chilling in the ice bucket. 'Wine?'

Her eyes flicked to the water glass he'd set out for himself. 'Are you having some?'

'No.' He drew a slow breath, held it in his lungs. Maybe it was time to tell her. 'I don't drink alcohol, Mia.'

'Ever…?' He could see her taking it in, turning it over in her mind. 'Why?'

'I'd have thought it was obvious.'

Her tongue touched her lower lip. 'Understandable, perhaps, but not obvious.' Her eyes held his, questioning.

'Look, my grandfather was an alcoholic…my father was an alcoholic. There's clearly a gene, a weakness that runs in my family, and I'm not interested in putting myself to the test.'

Bram, eyes dulled with drink, knuckles white around the hilt of a cook's knife, slashing at shadows.

He refocused. 'I prefer to stay sharp.'

Eline's taunting eyes… *'Lighten up, Theo.'*

He pushed the images away. 'I like to be in control. Is that so wrong?'

She covered his hand with hers and squeezed it gently. 'No, not at all.' Her touch was reassuring and when she smiled there was nothing but acceptance in her eyes. 'I'll have a glass of water, please.'

She'd made it so easy, hadn't thought that he was strange or uptight. As he filled their glasses, all his little tensions gave way to a warm, steady pulse of happiness.

'Are you hungry?'

'Starving!' Her eyes danced. 'Madelon bigged up your culinary skills so I'm looking forward to this.'

He grinned, lifting the lid off the serving dish. 'Voila! *Nasi goreng,* Theo-style.'

'So, what gives the planets their colour?'

She was peering through the telescope. He was unashamedly enjoying the view of her cute behind. He liked her in jeans, but he liked her in dresses too. Most of all, he liked her without clothes.

'It's to do with what they're made of, and how the chemicals found in their atmospheres reflect and absorb sunlight.'

She shifted slightly. 'So, what *are* they made of?' Something in her voice, something about the way she was moving… 'Venus, for example?'

He held in a smile. 'Venus is a grey, rocky planet, but you can't see any of that because its atmosphere is very dense with swirling sulphuric acid. The sulphur reflects sunlight, so Venus looks yellow.'

'Hmm. What about Neptune?' She shifted again and suddenly it was too much. He stepped behind her, slid his hands into her back pockets. She giggled, pushing her bottom into his hands. He felt a stab of desire and had to work at keeping his voice steady.

'Neptune is a ball of gas, literally. There's a lot of methane in its atmosphere, which absorbs red light from the sun, leaving only the blue. The blue's reflected, so that's why it looks like a blue planet.'

She was rotating her hips, distracting him deliberately. 'That's very interesting.' She arched her back. 'And what makes Mars red?'

He swallowed hard. 'Iron oxide…dust…it gets blown into the atmosphere.'

She abandoned the telescope and fell back against him, spine curving, shoulder blades nesting into the barrel of his chest. She was shifting her hips from side to side, pressing against him, driving him wild. Her voice was a low tease. 'Science at school was never as good as this.'

He smiled into her hair as he took his hands out of her back pockets. He knew how to tease her too. Slowly, he smoothed his palms over her taut abdomen and upward to her small, round breasts. The neckline of her silk blouse was low, but not low enough. He undid the small covered buttons, one by one, felt a tide of heat rising through his body as he slipped his fingers into the black lace of her bra. She moaned softly, and then she was twisting out of his hands, turning to face him, her eyes hazy with desire. 'Could we take this downstairs?'

He pulled her hard against him, so she'd know exactly what she was doing to him, and then he kissed her, a hungry, hot kiss that made her moan softly into his mouth. He liked how much she wanted him. Her need made him feel strong, powerful in a way he hadn't felt for a long time, but he couldn't hold out on her for much longer. He needed her too, wanted her with every fibre of his being. When he broke their kiss, she was flushed and breathless, but no more than he was. He lifted her up, felt her arms and legs wrapping around him tightly.

'Downstairs, you said…? Let's go.'

CHAPTER NINE

MIA OPENED HER eyes, pushed the hair away from her face. She blinked, taking in the whiteness, the space, the quietness…a quietness broken only by the sound of steady breathing. She turned her head on the pillow. Theo was sleeping on his side, a peaceful expression on his face. *Cloudless*. She shifted a little so she could gaze at him.

Had she ever felt so thoroughly wanted, needed, desired? In bed, he held nothing back and, because he didn't, she didn't either. Physically, his devotion, his tenderness, his passion was absolute. It was almost as if he was trying to make up for his verbal reticence, as if he was trying to show her… What? His love? Was that what Madelon had been about to say when he'd stopped her with his tickling?

Was Theo in love with her?

She stretched out a hand, hovering it over his shoulder. He hadn't said he was in love with her, but last night she'd felt it in his kiss, in his touch. She'd seen it in his eyes. She felt a smile growing on her lips. Yesterday, she'd been worried about falling in love with him, but this morning she could see it was too late. Love was already there, growing, unfurling inside her, a living, breathing thing. Maybe it had been there from the very first day…

She drew her hand back. Waking him would usher in the clouds, and she loved to see his face like this… Loved him. Period. She sighed softly, studying the smooth arc of his eyebrows, the gentle set of his mouth, the closed lips… He *was* keeping something from her. Yesterday, the thought of that had frightened her, but for some reason it didn't any more. Maybe it was because of Madelon…

During the interview, Madelon had been open about her career but she'd been casually oblique about personal matters. It seemed that she was afflicted with the same reticence as her brother. There was comfort in that, because if they were both hiding it pointed to a reason that went beyond Theo's defunct relationship with his ex-wife. After the interview, she'd felt calmer about things, more confident about loving Theo.

His eyelids were flickering. Such a handsome face… No, beyond handsome. She wanted to kiss him, hold him, tell him she'd always be there. If she had to wait for him to tell her the things that he was too frightened to share, then it was fine. There was no hurry. As for the Eline de Vries assignment…she'd cross that bridge when she came to it. The event was a full four months away. It was unlikely that Eline would be calling any time soon. She might even change her mind, choose someone else to write the programme.

He was stirring, then his eyes opened and he smiled sleepily. 'Hello, beautiful.'

'Good morning.' She snuggled against his chest, kissing his sandpaper chin. 'You look like a kid when you're asleep.' She traced her fingers across his forehead. 'Everything smooth…no crinkles.'

'Crinkles?' He knitted his brows together then laughed. 'You mean my frown lines…?'

'Maybe they're laughter lines.'

His eyes twinkled. 'Only when I'm with you. You make me laugh, Mia. You bring me joy…'

Something behind his eyes; endless depths. She took a breath. '*You* bring *me* joy too.'

For a heartbeat he held her gaze and then his hand cupped the back of her neck, drawing her in for a kiss. It was slow, warm, gently arousing, a loving kiss that was tugging her into the warm shallows of desire, but she couldn't let him love her again. Cleuso would be hungry; she had to go home.

She pulled away gently. 'I can't…'

His eyes narrowed. 'Why?'

She felt her lips twitching upward. 'Because of my dependant.'

'Your dependant?' He broke into a smile. 'Ah… You mean you're turning me down for a cat?'

She nodded. 'He'll be hungry.'

He threw her a deeply suggestive look. 'So am I…'

'I'm sorry.' She wriggled out of his arms and sat up, looking at him over her shoulder. 'I can come back later.'

He rolled up smoothly and swung out of bed. 'I've got a better idea. I'll walk you home.'

She eyed his naked buttocks wistfully. 'You might want to get dressed first.'

The sound of the door being closed shattered the quiet for an instant, and then the hum of not-quite-silence resumed, broken only by the soft scuff of his shoes on the path as he walked towards her. She liked him in jeans and a tee shirt, his hair mussed, the planes of his face softened with stubble. He smiled. White teeth, green eyes…making her senses swim. She looked away, squinting into the low sun. 'Isn't this just the nicest time of day?'

He slung an arm around her shoulder. 'It's why I go running early. No one around. So quiet. It's like a different city.'

She wrapped her arm around his waist and they started walking, slowly. 'It's like there are two different cities: the early morning one, then the crazy, busy one. I love them both.' She tilted her face to catch his eye. 'Have you always lived here?'

'No. I was born in Delft.'

'And…?' Silence. 'Then…?'

A shadow crossed his face. 'I'm sorry, Mia. I don't mean to be…' He stopped walking, turned towards her. 'I'm not trying to shut you out. It's just that I find it hard to talk about my childhood.' He folded her hand into his, his eyes full of gentle compassion. 'I know you had a hard time too, losing your parents without warning, not knowing what really happened… That must be so hard to live with, but somehow you do. The great thing about you is that you seem to have accepted it. It's part of who you are—that's what you said.'

She gave a little shrug. 'It's not like I had a choice…'

'No, but you wear it, and I admire that in you.' His gaze seemed to turn inward. 'I don't feel that way. I don't want anything from my past to be part of who I am.' His eyes dimmed. 'I'm ashamed.'

That raw edge in his voice; childhood sores still weeping. Her heart ached for him. 'But it's not your fault, Theo—what your father did. You're not *him*; you've got nothing to be ashamed of.' She could tell from his eyes that he needed more than platitudes. Maybe she could steer him to a fresh slant on things. 'Look at what you've achieved! MolTec's a global business! Maybe some of the drive and determination it took to build it grew out of what you went through as a child—and think about Madelon. You've both done so well.' She took her hand out of his, slipping her arms around his neck. 'Sometimes adversity breeds strength… You can't change the past, but maybe you need to look for the good in it.'

A smile touched the corners of his mouth. 'You're good at doing that. I can't…'

'You can.' She released him, tugging his hand so they were walking again. 'When we were in London, you told me about the planetarium in Franeker.'

'You remember?'

'Of course I do—you went there when you were a boy. So…who took you? How old were you?'

'Six, maybe.'

'And…?'

He sighed. 'My father took us.'

'You and Madelon and your brother? Does your brother have a name, by the way?'

He nodded. 'Bram.'

Progress!

'So, was your father into astronomy?'

Another nod.

A bicycle slid past, wheels humming rhythmically. She watched it growing smaller and smaller, counting the seconds, counting their footsteps: seven, eight, nine, ten…

'He was a university lecturer.'

For some reason that surprised her—a reaction he must have read on her face because he let out a short, bitter laugh. 'I know. Such a *respectable* profession!'

There was no point going into that; she was after something else. 'What was his subject?'

'Physics and maths.'

Theo's strong suits too… Perhaps he owed his intellect to his father, which was a sort of positive. It was worth a try. 'So he took you to the planetarium when you were six…and now you have your own observatory.'

He smiled faintly, then his mouth became a line. He

released her hand, went to stand at the side of the canal. She gave him a moment then followed. 'Did I say something wrong?'

'No.' He shot her a glance and moistened his lips. 'I'm sorry.' He hooked an arm around her shoulders, kissed her hair. 'It's just that, when it comes to my father, there's no right thing to say.' He sighed, shuddered. 'You meant well but I don't like being reminded of the things I have in common with him.'

She stared at the water, tears thickening in her throat. This wasn't about maths or science or astronomy… She remembered their conversation at dinner, his confession about why he didn't drink alcohol. First his grandfather, then his father… No wonder he kept himself on a tight leash. He was frightened of himself, scared of what might be lurking within. If only he could see himself through her eyes, he'd know there was nothing to fear.

'I'm guessing you don't see him…'

'No.' He turned, held her gaze. 'He's dead.'

What to say…? 'I'm sorry.'

'I'm not.'

She could see in his eyes that he meant it, that the conversation had run its course. She walked back to the pavement, waiting for him to come. The sun was higher now, hazy and golden. She tuned in to the clang of a distant tram, thought about the times Hal had told her things that she'd accepted without question. She'd believed him so easily; *chosen* to believe him because she hadn't wanted to put a dent in what they had; hadn't wanted to risk losing everything because she'd lost one family already. But now she knew that being scared of losing someone wasn't a good enough reason not to ask the difficult questions. Loving someone meant loving the whole person. The bad, the good. The weaknesses as well as the strengths.

He was coming towards her, his hair close to copper in the slanting sunlight. If he was ashamed of his father, feared his father's legacy, it was understandable. But his father was dead, and it seemed that his death hadn't brought Theo any closure. Something else was keeping the wound open, and she had to find out what that was. It would mean more difficult questions, but she'd bide her time. Bombarding him wasn't the way.

'Hey.' He tugged her close, concern etched on his face. 'Are you okay?'

She nodded. 'Of course. I was just giving you your space.'

'Thank you, but I prefer my space when you're in it…' He kissed the tip of her nose and pulled her even closer, his eyes darkening, a smile touching the corners of his mouth. 'In fact, the smaller the space we're in, the better.'

She chuckled; she couldn't resist faking asphyxiation. 'Okay. But breathing…is…important.' He released her, laughing, catching her face in his hands. 'It sounds like you might need some mouth-to-mouth resuscitation…' And then his lips were on hers, warm, insistent, hungry. His need was a hot wire, drawing a rush of heat through her that made her forget where she was. She slid her hands into his back pockets, pulled him closer. He groaned, deepened his kiss, moved his hand from her face to her waist, then lower, fingers moving under the hem of her blouse, warm and perfect.

A bell jangled. 'Get a room!'

Startled, they broke apart, staring after the kid who was speeding off into the distance. Theo grinned, reached for her hand and pulled her on. 'I think he's right. When we get to yours, I want you to show me your private cabin…'

Her stomach dipped. 'You're insatiable!'

'And whose fault is that?'

That gaze, turning her insides to liquid. She felt a blush coming. 'I feel embarrassed, being reprimanded by a teenager.'

'I don't.' He grinned. 'I feel young.'

'You *are* young!' A chuckle rose in her throat. 'Youngish, anyway.'

His eyes flashed with mischief. '*Youngish!*' And then he was on her again, fingers probing her ribs, finding her ticklish spots.

'No! Please… Theo, no, no, no!' She tried to jerk away, but his hold on her was tight. He was laughing, enjoying himself, tickling her mercilessly. 'Please stop… I take it back. You're very young.'

He released her, breathing hard. 'Not *very* young. I'm thirty-three, but youthful, I hope!' He ran a hand through his hair, arching his eyebrows. 'Dare I ask…?'

'Twenty-seven.'

'*That's* very young.' He draped an arm around her shoulders, moving her on.

She watched his feet on the path, the way he was adjusting his stride to hers. 'It's funny; I've never really felt young. I've always felt like a grown-up.'

'Me too.' He touched his head to hers, kissing her hair. She read the gesture, heard what he wasn't saying out loud: that their experiences had robbed them of their childhoods, had given them old heads on young shoulders. She slid her arm around his waist and gave him a hug. Instantly, she felt an answering squeeze and then he shrugged. 'Maybe it's why I got into astronomy. When I was a kid, the night sky felt like a place I could let my imagination run free… Now, I love the science of it all: the expanding universe, the Big Bang… It's fascinating.'

'Do you ever dream about finding a place beyond the stars?'

'What?'

She smiled. 'You know, like Neverland...? *Peter Pan*...?'

'Ah...of course.' He chuckled. 'Maddie used to be frightened of Captain Hook...and the crocodile. I was always more preoccupied with how the clock managed to keep ticking inside the crocodile's stomach.'

'That's because you've got a scientific mind!'

'True.'

She thought about the illustrated copy of *Peter Pan* that had belonged to her mother. It lived at her grandmother's house, and after her mum died she'd take it into her room or into the garden and spend hours looking at it, trying to guess which pictures her mum had liked best. Tinkerbell! Wings to fly, silver fairy-dust trailing...

'I was besotted with Tinkerbell, and I loved Nana the dog...' There was that part of the story where Mrs Darling was telling the children that night lights were like a mother's eyes, guarding them. Had Theo's mother guarded *him*, and Madelon and Bram, or hadn't she been able to? She came back to the moment, found Theo gazing at her. 'But I was always rather concerned about the Lost Boys...'

He smiled softly. 'That's because you're like Wendy.'

'I can't believe it took three quarters of an hour to walk less than a mile!' She was in the galley kitchen buttering thick slices of bread, sprinkling them with *hagelslag*.

He stepped behind her, sliding his arms around her waist. 'It's because we were walking *romantically*.'

She paused, laughed, carried on shaking chocolate over the bread. 'So I can strike it off my bucket list?'

'Not yet.' He lifted her hair away from her neck and kissed the warm, smooth skin behind her earlobe. 'We need to work on our technique...to get the kissing-to-walking ratio exactly right.'

He closed his eyes, breathing her in. He couldn't get enough of her. Her body, her lovely face, her smile…everything she was. Although their childhood experiences had been radically different, she knew how it felt not to have been truly young or carefree, and it was a relief to share that understanding. Eline had had everything: two parents who'd loved each other; a beautiful home; advantages at every step. Perhaps that was why she'd struggled to empathise with Bram's situation and his own response to it. But Mia could. She *got* him, even though he wasn't able to be completely open about everything.

She wriggled out of his arms. 'I need to make the coffee…'

'I'll do it.'

'No.' She picked up the plate of sandwiches. 'You take these on deck and guard them against marauders! I'll bring the coffee out.'

'Aye-aye, Captain.' He took the plate and in a matter of moments he was outside—on deck! Why was that thrilling? It was a small space. Two blue wicker chairs were surrounded by a sea of planters and pots crammed with jewel-bright tulips, their heads nodding stiffly on their stems. There was that sense of a playhouse…a secret den… childish things that he'd been aware of as a boy but which he'd never fully experienced. His childhood had always felt peripheral to his anxieties, his anger, his shame.

He put the plate down on a chair, then it was two strides to the hand rail. There was some movement on the bridge now, random bicycles, early-morning pedestrians, the city getting itself into gear. Soon it would be thronging; so different from their peaceful walk through the dawn. Except that it hadn't been completely peaceful…

Mia's intentions had been good—trying to focus him on the positive aspects of his past—but he was done with looking for positives because there weren't any. Yes, he'd inherited his love of science and maths from his father, but it wasn't his intellectual legacy that kept him awake at night. It was fear and anger. Fear of who he was inside; fear that Bram would never get better. Anger with his father for being so weak, so brutal; for leaving him with such a cocktail of anxieties and insecurities.

Outside of MolTec, who was he? For pity's sake, he couldn't even choose furniture or paint colours. He didn't blame Bram for getting sick, but Bram's illness had changed everything. For the past eight years, practically all he'd thought about was getting Bram better, keeping him out of harm's way until he was strong again. Watching his brother slide backwards over and over again had only fed his anger, made him hate his father even more. The only positive thing to have come out of it was MolTec, because expanding the reach of the business, building the brand, had been a blessed distraction from all his inner turmoil.

He leaned on the rail, stared into the water until the choppy glints of sunlight turned into bright blurs. Madelon had warned him not to keep secrets from Mia, but for some reason he was struggling to tell her about Bram… and it wasn't because Eline had hurt him so badly over it. He knew Mia well enough now to know that she'd never be like that, yet still he couldn't find the words. When it came to his brother, his head was a maze. Blind alleys of fear, shame, disappointment, heartbreak, Bram in the middle of it. If he could find his way through it all somehow, separate everything, then maybe he'd be able to…

'Cleuso!'

Mia's indignant yelp spun him round. She was in the doorway, holding two coffee mugs. He followed her gaze, nearly choking on own his laughter. Cleuso was standing on the chair making short work of the sandwiches.

She lifted her eyes to his. 'I told you to watch out for marauders!' She was trying to look cross.

'I'm sorry.' He wiped his eyes, struggling and failing to look apologetic. 'I got distracted.'

She put the mugs down on an upturned plant pot, shooed Cleuso off the chair then handed him the plate. 'You might as well stick it on the roof for the birds. We can't eat it now.'

He held in a smile and did as he was told. 'I thought cats were carnivores.'

She rolled her eyes and made a little tutting noise. 'You had *one* job…' Her lips twitched into a smile. 'I should make you walk the plank.'

He stepped in front of her, cupped her face in his hands. 'I'll make it up to you somehow…' He leaned in and kissed her slowly.

'Hmm.' Warm hands slid to the back of his neck. 'You could make it up to me in my cabin…' She pulled him in again, ran her tongue along his lower lip. He felt heat kindling in his belly, spreading to his chest, surging through his veins. He imagined her cabin… Cosy…confined…the sound of the water on the hull…the sound of her sighs… She pulled away again, nuzzling his nose with hers, and then she smiled impishly. 'Hold that thought…'

Mind-reader!

She sat down and reached for her coffee. 'I'd have caught Cleuso sooner if Ash hadn't called.' She took a sip and then her eyes widened. 'He was very excited to hear about Madelon!'

His heart stumbled. He'd forgotten about Ash: the potential repercussions of Ash knowing that Madelon was his sister. A wave of weariness washed over him. All he'd wanted was to sit with Mia, enjoy her company, but now there was yet another fire for him to fight. How had his life become so complicated?

'Are you okay?' She was staring at him.

'Of course.' He sat down beside her and picked up his coffee. He took a slow sip, trying to calm his racing heart. 'Mia, do you remember what I said at the fundraiser about keeping my involvement with Saving Grace private?'

'Yes.' She looked puzzled. 'What are you saying?'

He moistened his lips. 'I'm saying that I'd also like to keep the connection between Madelon and myself private. I don't want anyone to know that we're related.'

She frowned. 'So you didn't want me to tell Ash?'

'It's fine for Ash to know, but he can't tell anyone else.'

'Why? Why does it matter?'

He was relieved that she knew something of his history. It meant his explanation would stack up. He set his coffee down on the deck. 'For the same reason I keep my charity work private. In the wrong hands, facts can get twisted. I don't want to expose the rest of my family to the wrong kind of scrutiny. Bear in mind our background, Mia. A deadbeat father, so drunk that he cycled in front of a tram and killed himself. Why do you think Madelon changed her name?'

Her eyes held him softly. 'I'm so sorry about your father, even though I know you're not.' She put her mug down and slipped her hands over his. 'To be so lost, to be so beyond help… I find that very sad.' For a beat she looked away and then her eyes were on him again, recognition flaring. 'It's why you didn't want to go over to Madelon that night, isn't it? You didn't want to be seen with her, photographed with her?'

'Partly.' He laced his fingers into hers. 'But it was also because I didn't want to leave your side.'

Her expression softened momentarily but then she was frowning again. 'I don't think people would care about your background, Theo. Quite the opposite. I think people who've conquered adversity and go on to become successful—they inspire others.'

'You're right, but we're not talking about *people* generally.' A knot tightened in his stomach. 'We're talking about the press. The media loves to destroy its icons. Fred Zucker—remember him? Cricketer, role model, patron of his own charity for young people. Fighting gang culture through sport. He's a friend of mine; a thoroughly good person. But he had an uncle who'd been engaged in dubious activity with young boys. When the press found out, Zucker's whole family was dragged through the gutter. There were insinuations that Fred had known what was going on…' He disentangled his fingers from hers, rubbed the back of his neck. 'The sins of the fathers, Mia. They come back, especially if there's money to made out of it.'

'It's a minefield.' Her tongue touched her bottom lip. 'So…what about Lotte?'

His heart stumbled again. Last night she'd mentioned Lotte… He'd been going to talk to her about provisos but then they'd gone to watch the stars. He tried to keep his voice even. 'Does she know about Madelon?'

'I haven't told her anything about you.'

Relief washed over him.

'But I wanted to offer her a shoot, remember, to go with the interview piece…?'

'You can still offer her a shoot. Just don't tell her that Madelon's my sister, okay?'

'But… Lotte's my friend.' Her brow furrowed. 'How do you live like this? Where do you draw the line with who can know what? Doesn't it drive you crazy?'

If only she knew. Suddenly his head was pounding. Since Eline there'd been no one, and now he remembered why he'd sworn off relationships. Being close to someone widened the circle, made everything much more complicated. More than anything, he wanted to be with Mia, but at that moment he needed space; needed not to be answering questions. He got to his feet. 'It's hard, yes, but it's just the way it has to be.'

'Are you leaving?' She rose from her seat, putting her hands on his forearms. 'I thought you wanted to see the cabin…'

Her gaze was open, traces of pain and confusion behind her eyes. His chest tightened. The thought of hurting her frightened him more than anything, but he couldn't stay. He was suffocating. Direk was coming to the house at eleven to talk about ideas for the sitting room. If he bent the truth a bit, he could spare her feelings.

He took her face in his hands. 'I *do* want to see the cabin, but Direk's coming over with paint and goodness knows what else. I'd completely forgotten about it until now.'

Her eyes searched his, turning him over, and then her gaze softened. 'Don't let him talk you into black, okay? I'll text you a photo of my dress so you can show him the colours you like.'

He kissed her softly. 'He knows the colours already, but send me a photo anyway…of yourself.' He tasted her lips again, felt desire thrumming in his veins. 'Something to keep me going until I get back.'

Her eyebrows arched. 'Are you objectifying me?'

That was her gift—the way she could make him smile even when his head was throbbing. 'Of course not. I'd never do such a thing.'

CHAPTER TEN

HER PHONE WAS VIBRATING. She stopped typing, glancing at the unfamiliar number before swiping the screen. 'Hello? Mia Boelens…?'

'Mia! It's Eline… Eline de Vries.'

Her heart stalled. 'Hi!' She cleared her throat. 'How nice to hear from you. Lotte said you might be calling.' She gritted her teeth, trying to breathe calmly.

'There was no *might* about it! I *loved* the Dilly and Daisy write-up you did, and I've been *devouring* your blog. It's terrific!'

'I'm glad you like it.'

'So…we need to meet! I know the event's a while away, but I have to plan well ahead because of my schedule. I like to be organised.'

Mia glanced at her open journal. Ticks, asterisks, underlining. Being well-organised was in her DNA so she couldn't hold it against Eline freakin' de Vries. 'I'm the same.' Her professional instincts must have kicked in because she was speaking competently evenly though her heart was throwing shapes in her chest. 'When do you want to meet, and where?'

'Could you make this Friday? Early evening, at my apartment? I hope you don't mind but it's easier that way. Public places can be a nightmare… I'm sure you understand.'

'Of course.' Going to Eline's apartment was the last thing she wanted to do, but she couldn't argue. Lack of privacy was the price of fame. No wonder Theo kept a low profile. 'Where's your apartment?'

'It's near the river but I'll send a car for you. Shall we say six?'

We had an apartment near the river.

She swallowed hard. Had Eline got *their* apartment after the divorce? Was that the apartment she'd be going to—Theo's former home? Her stomach churned. 'Sounds great. You'll want my address…'

'Lotte gave it to me already. Totally cool, by the way, living on a barge.'

'It is.' Eline's friendliness was throwing her off-balance.

'So… I'll see you on Friday evening, then?'

'Yes. Great!' She swallowed hard. 'Bye for now.'

Heaviness tugged at her chest. She slumped back in her chair, rolling her phone over and over in her hands. She didn't want to meet Theo's ex, didn't want the job, but she was committed because of Lotte. How on earth was she going to get herself out of this mess?

For the past week she'd been turning things over in her head, trying to come to terms with Theo's paranoia about his family's privacy. After he'd left her on the barge that morning, she'd sat for a long time considering what he'd said about Ash, Madelon and poor Fred Zucker. His words had been calmly spoken, flawlessly logical, but he'd been tangibly edgy, his finger tapping the side of his mug, tightness in his shoulders and around his mouth. His body language had pointed to some deep-rooted internal anxiety and, when he'd said he had an appointment with Direk, for a second it had felt as if he was running away; running scared.

She'd wondered if he was leaving to avoid her questions, had even wondered if he was telling the truth about meeting Direk, but there *had* been an appointment. He'd come back with photos on his phone: pictures of the colour patches Direk had painted on the walls—damsons, ochres, and olives—and a hand-blown glass vase that Direk had brought because he'd thought it would work well on the sitting-room mantelpiece. And then she'd felt guilty for doubting him.

So the dust had settled. There'd been dinners out and early-morning walks. Star-gazing in the dome followed by long nights in his bed. Or in her bed, with watery moonlight glancing through the cabin windows. He'd told her a little about his mother—a librarian, he said, living a quiet life on the outskirts of the city. And he'd told her about Madelon—how she'd used to make up plays with her dolls, doing funny voices, making them laugh. Happy memories.

She'd told herself that in time these little glimpses would form a picture, that if she was patient he'd show her what he was hiding inside, trust her with all the things he found so hard to talk about. And she'd told herself that when that day finally came she would put her heart on the line and tell him that she was in love with him.

But Eline's phone call had just changed the landscape.

When Lotte had first told her about the job with Eline, she'd resolved not to tell Theo about it, but now that the moment had arrived there was no way she could keep him in the dark. She didn't want to hide anything from him. She switched off her computer and got to her feet. Telling him about the Eline situation would surely make him see that he could trust her, and maybe he'd be open with her in return, tell her more about what had happened between him and Eline. Perhaps this curve ball would actually be the making of them…

She pulled on her jacket and contemplated the grey sky

through the window. Clouds storing up rain. That was Theo…storing rain. If only she could make him see that, for him, she didn't mind getting wet.

The doorbell jangled. Theo startled then stilled, listening to the sound of the door being opened, the weighty clunk of it closing. Only two people had a key, and Direk was in Utrecht.

'Mia?'

He felt a glow of happiness as her voice ballooned up the stairwell. 'Hello-o-o! I've brought you something!'

He saved his work and coasted his chair away from the desk. He hadn't expected to see her until the evening, but he didn't mind the interruption. She was his favourite distraction. He started down the stairs, light-hearted, loose-limbed.

She was in the bigger of the two sitting rooms, arranging tulips in Direk's fancy vase, her shirt sleeves rolled back, the white cotton skimming her smooth forearms as she worked. Her jeans were loose on her hips, turned up at the ankles, her bare feet sheathed in blue loafers. The air was fragrant with her perfume, or maybe that was the flowers. He leaned against the door frame, watching, but she must have sensed him because she looked up and cornered him with a smile. 'What do you think?'

'I think you're amazing.'

'I was talking about the tulips…'

He walked towards her. 'I think you're amazing the way you can put tulips into a vase and transform a room. You've made it feel like a home.'

'The way you did with your improvised romantic dining room!'

He smiled and pulled her into his arms. 'Move over Direk!' He felt her hands sliding over his shoulders, warm fingers threading through the hair at his nape. He leaned in and kissed her, felt an instant thrill of desire. 'Hello, by the way…and thank you for the flowers.' He kissed her again, not wanting to stop. 'I wasn't expecting you till later.'

'I know, but I need to talk to you about something.' She took her hands from the back of his neck and eased herself out of his arms.

For some reason his heart bumped. He dug his hands into the pockets of his chinos and rocked back on his heels. 'Okay. What is it?'

She carefully laced her fingers together then met his gaze. 'I've got a job coming up; something that Lotte put me forward for.'

'Right…' The edginess in her eyes was making him nervous.

'Lotte didn't know, you see, because as I said before I haven't really told her anything…'

'About…?' His heartbeat was rising, pulsing at the base of his throat.

'About you… I mean, anything private about you…like how Madelon's your sister and about how you were married… Divorced…' Her tongue touched her bottom lip. 'So it's not her fault at all. She had no idea about Eline.'

His mouth dried. 'What's Eline got to do with anything?'

'It's the job she's committed me to. It's a fashion event. Eline's organising it.' Her eyes were searching his, checking. 'Lotte's doing the photos and I'm writing pieces about the designers for the programme…' Her voice trailed away.

'I see.' He swallowed hard, trying to see through the mist in his head. 'So you'll be talking to the designers…?'

She nodded and gave a little shrug. 'I'm not sure about the exact brief until I've had a proper chat with Eline.'

His heart bumped again. 'You'll be talking to Eline?'

'She called me an hour ago to arrange a meeting. I didn't expect her to get in touch so soon…' She scraped a strand of hair out of her eyes and folded her arms. 'It's why I came straight over, to tell you…' Her tongue touched her lower lip again. 'I'm going to Eline's apartment at six on Friday. She said meeting anywhere public would be tricky…'

Suddenly, the air was too thick to breathe. He turned away, squeezing his eyes shut, willing himself to stay calm, but there was something boiling up inside him, livid white noise dancing behind his eyelids. Eline was the enemy; she'd betrayed him, broken his heart, and now what? Mia was going to meet her. Work with her!

'Are you all right?' She was in front of him again, taking him apart with her eyes. 'I know what you're thinking…'

No, she didn't…because she didn't know anything about Bram, about how cruel Eline had been. If she knew the pain Eline had caused him, she'd never have taken this job. He swallowed. 'You have no idea.'

Her eyes narrowed. 'I do! You're thinking that meeting Eline is an infringement of your privacy…' She drew in a breath, put a hand on his arm. 'But there's nothing to worry about.' She pressed her lips together. 'It's only a job, Theo. Like any other job. We won't be touching on anything personal.'

He stepped back and raked a hand through his hair. What she was saying made sense. She'd just be a writer talking to a model about a fashion event…there'd be no reason for Eline to talk about Bram or him. She'd signed the non-disclosure and in five years she hadn't breached it. He drew a steadying breath, but in the next instant any iota of rational thought was swept away on a fresh wave of panic. He felt his guts writhing, tasted bile in the back of his throat. Something inside him was collapsing, curling into a ball, trying to shut out the torrent of desperation, the crushing sensation of powerlessness.

Get a grip!

Wide, worried eyes held his. For some reason Cleuso popped into his head, the kitten that no one else would have chosen… Mia was a beautiful soul. He couldn't stop her meeting Eline but maybe he could appeal to her empathy, could make her reconsider. He stepped forward, taking her hands in his. 'I'm not thinking that at all. This isn't about privacy, or infringements…' He swallowed hard. 'Mia, this is someone who cheated on me, someone who caused me immeasurable pain. If I was standing here telling you that I was meeting Hal, doing business with Hal, how would you feel?'

'That's so unfair!' She pulled her hands out of his, tears glistening at the edges of her eyes. 'The difference is that I've told you everything about Hal. *Everything!* So, you'd know exactly what you were doing to me if you took up with him. But I don't think you've told me the whole truth about what happened with Eline. You didn't want to talk about it. You never want to talk about anything.' She blinked, swiping at her eyes. 'You haven't trusted me. You won't let me in. How do you think that makes *me* feel?'

Hurt in her eyes and *he* was the cause of it. His heart was aching. Why couldn't he make himself tell her the whole story? Why wouldn't the words come? His palms were sweating. He couldn't think for the buzzing in his head. It was all sliding away, draining him out. Everything. He swallowed hard, his voice cracking. 'Isn't it enough to know that she hurt me?'

Her face softened for a moment, and then she drew an audible breath. 'No—no, it isn't.' A sudden steeliness flashed in her eyes. 'You see, aside from thinking you'd be mad for wanting to do business with Hal, I actually wouldn't care because I have no stake in my past. But you do, don't you?'

He was losing her, he could see it in her eyes, and still the words she needed to hear wouldn't rise on his tongue.

She picked up her bag, and when she met his gaze again tears were winding down her cheeks. 'I thought we had something, Theo, but I can't be with someone who's keeping things from me. I've done it before and I'm not doing it again. I deserve better.' Her eyes held him as she walked backwards, step after step after step, until she was standing in the doorway.

His heart was a hollow drum, beating fast then slowing as a strange calm claimed him. She was right. She deserved better—someone whole. Someone who could be everything she needed them to be. He wasn't that person. She'd be better off without him. Suddenly he wanted her to go. He couldn't stand the way she was looking at him, her eyes wide and wet, full of fading hope.

'Goodbye, Theo.' Her words were barely a whisper, then she disappeared through the door. He heard the key going down on the hall table, the door closing with a weighty clunk.

'You're English!' The driver was looking ahead, twisting slightly so that his voice would carry in her direction.

'Yes.' Mia didn't want to talk. She rooted in her bag for her notebook and pen.

'So what are you doing in Amsterdam?'

'I'm a writer.' She managed to catch his eye in the rear-view mirror. 'I'm sorry, I hope you don't mind, but I need to do some work…' She flipped open a page of the notebook as if she was about to start reading.

He nodded, gave her a wink then settled forward, focusing on the traffic.

Mia stared at the blank page. She hadn't heard from Theo since she'd walked out of his house three days ago. *Three days!* She'd thought he'd come after her, call her at least, but he hadn't. Showing him honesty had blown everything apart. Clearly, her judgement was shot where men were concerned. Hal had abused her trust and her love, and now the man she'd thought Theo was on the inside, that noble, kind, protective, ardent lover she'd fallen in love with, had proved himself unequal to the deeper intimacy she wanted.

She lifted her eyes, watching the trams and the bicycles going by. How could it be over? That connection she'd felt from the very beginning, the tenderness she felt in him every time he held her, kissed her, made love to her—she hadn't imagined it. So, if the unspoken love she'd seen in his eyes was genuine, why was he holding back? What was he scared of?

She sighed heavily and doodled a box on the open page of her notebook. If only Lotte hadn't set her up with this assignment, then she and Theo would still be together. She drew another box inside the first one, then another and another and another, then she sighed again. The problem wasn't with Lotte or the assignment. Theo had allowed her to walk out of his house because of something inside himself. What had he said by the canal that morning—that she was able to 'wear' her pain? He'd said that he admired her for it; that he couldn't do it.

She closed the notebook softly. That smile…intent green eyes…the way he made her feel. When she was with him, everything felt right. She needed to tell him that, tell him that she was in love with him. He'd said to her once that she was the kind of person who shaped fate.

Maybe it was time to put it to the test. He loved her, she could see it in his eyes, but he was boxed in somehow. If he couldn't reach out to her, then she'd have to reach in. It might be a dark side street, but she'd braved dark side streets before and she'd survived. All she had to do was get through this meeting with his ex-wife, and then she was going to go to the canal house to tell him that she wasn't giving up.

'I'm sorry it had to be a Friday evening. My schedule's crazy; this was the only bit of free time I had this week.'

Eline was gliding into the sitting room ahead of her, long-limbed in dark palazzo pants, abundant blonde hair tumbling down her back. Her silk wrap-blouse was tied tightly around her tiny waist—a waist that Theo's arms had circled. It was hard to think about that, about the important place Eline had occupied in his life. Had this apartment been theirs? It *was* modern, streamlined, glamorous in an understated way—just as he'd described. She tried not to picture him lounging on the cream sofa.

'It's fine… I don't mind.' Finding something neutral to talk about—that would help take her mind off Theo. Her eyes slid over the shelves. 'You've got a lot of elephants…'

Eline turned around, smiling. 'I've loved elephants ever since I went on a safari with my parents when I was sixteen. Three amazing weeks in Botswana! After that, I became a collector!' She motioned to one of the cream sofas that dominated the sitting room. 'Please, take a seat. Would you like a glass of wine, or mineral water?'

Two bottles poked out of an ice bucket set on the large, low table between the sofas. There was a glass of wine already poured, moisture beading around its rim. It looked tempting but staying focused was essential.

'I'll have mineral water, please.'

Eline poured a tall glass for her, then dropped onto the opposite sofa, crossing one leg over the other. 'So, it's lovely to meet you, finally! I *love* your writing, Mia, and your blog especially. That brilliant piece about what "self" is…! *"Nobody sees anyone as he is. They see a whole—they see all sorts of things—they see themselves."*'

She felt her heart shrivelling. She'd written that piece after Hal had revealed what *he* really was.

She broke away from Eline's clear blue gaze to retrieve her note pad and pen from her bag. 'It's not mine; it's Virginia Woolf…from *Jacob's Room*.'

'Yes, of course… I saw the acknowledgement…but I like how you used the quote as a springboard for talking about what identity is; what it means.'

She shrugged. 'They're just things I think about sometimes…but I'm glad you liked it.'

'I did because, you know, I think about those things too.' Eline sipped her wine, her hand circling in the air. 'I often think about what I was… What I am now…'

'Were you thinking of a bio for the front of the programme?'

'No. When you've spent as much time as I have in the limelight, being adored for all the wrong reasons, you get rather tired of yourself. I'd rather focus on the designers.'

A relief! She was undeniably curious about Eline's past as far as it concerned Theo but talking about the designers and the event was something she could do with a clear conscience. It was what she'd told Theo she'd be doing. She smiled. 'Okay.' She pulled her notebook onto her lap and readied her pen. 'So tell me about the designers.'

'You know, I started out wanting to be a fashion buyer…'

She pressed the tip of her pen hard into the pad. Not the designers, then. She lifted her eyes. 'Oh?'

Eline took a hearty sip from her glass. 'I did a business degree then took a position with a fashion event company to get experience and to make contacts. I got spotted by an agency scout at one of our shows and, before I knew it, I was being signed by Models Ten. It was crazy. My then-husband and I were like, *Can this be real?*'

Her heart tripped. She hadn't expected Eline to mention Theo. She drew in a slow breath, trying to stop the colour rising into her cheeks. She had to look interested, but she didn't want to provoke a further outpour by asking a question. She'd specifically told Theo that this would be just another job; that his privacy wouldn't be infringed. She forced herself to smile. 'Wow!'

Eline sipped from her glass again, eyes sparkling. 'Wow, wow, wow more like! It was so exciting, Mia! It all seemed so glamorous. The designers, the clothes, the catwalk—I loved it!' Her eyes clouded suddenly. 'But, you know, everything comes with a price tag.'

To pick it up or let it lie… Her nerves were jangling. She slowly drew a circle on her note pad then met Eline's gaze. 'I suppose there must be down sides.'

'And then some! Everybody wants you when you're in the limelight. You get used to being the centre of attention. I'm afraid fame went to my head. I lost sight of…' She smoothed a perfectly manicured hand over the leg of her trousers. 'There were things that I didn't handle well. Things I regret.'

Mia didn't want to delve into Eline's past; it was too close to the bone. She picked up her glass, sipped slowly. There was no subtle way of shifting the conversation back to the designers. All she could do was try to defuse the bomb. She set her glass down. 'Everyone has regrets.'

'Yes, but some are harder to live with than others. Like

when you know you hurt someone very badly…and you can't take it back.'

Mia moistened her lips slowly. Eline hadn't mentioned his name, but she knew that this was about Theo. 'Maybe we should talk about the designers…?'

'We'll get to the designers, but I want you to understand how I came to be organising this event. My disillusionment with the fashion industry and all the things I regret have played a part.' Eline's perfect mouth hardened for a moment. 'Nothing of this must go into what you write, but it's context, and…' her lips softened into a wistful smile '…it's good to talk, right?'

Mia nodded, heart pounding. If Eline knew about her and Theo, she wouldn't be talking like this, but she couldn't close her ears, or just up and leave. She was trapped and…was it wrong to be a little bit curious?

Eline topped up her wine glass and took a long, slow sip. 'My husband was a wonderful man. Handsome, kind… noble.' It was unsettling to hear Eline using the same descriptors Mia used in her own mind when she thought about Theo. 'He'd had a poor start in life—a violent, alcoholic father—massive insecurity. He rejected everything about his childhood. He was very driven. He craved financial security, built a very successful business on the back of his disadvantages. We married fresh out of university because he wanted… I don't know…to feel safe.'

She tucked a strand of hair behind her ear, sipped from her glass again. 'Because of his father, *he* would never touch alcohol, but his brother did; too much and too often. Around the time I started modelling, he realised that his brother was becoming dependent. He wouldn't hear of rehab. Instead, he bought a house on one of the northern islands. He took his brother there, spent weeks at a time trying to straighten him out. He never gave up trying, even though his brother kept falling off the wagon.'

She lowered her eyes and fingered the stem of her glass. 'I got impatient. I wanted my husband's undivided attention. I wanted him to come to my fashion shows, and to the parties, but his brother always came first. It seemed that everyone loved me, except him. I was jealous and then I grew bitter. I had an affair—to get back at him, I suppose—and I said things…cruel, hurtful things…that I'll regret for the rest of my life.'

Bram, the chef—an alcoholic! The strange glitch she'd felt that night in the kitchen with Madelon and Theo…the way the atmosphere had changed when she'd asked Madelon about her other brother. The beach house on Texel… He'd bought it for Bram, had looked after him personally for weeks at a time. Such devotion. Rehab would have been the obvious solution, but he'd chosen his brother over his wife, and she'd lashed out, hurt him badly when he'd only been trying to do the right thing. And now Bram was the secret he couldn't bring himself to share…

'I see why you write so well, Mia.'

Blue eyes came into focus. 'Excuse me…?'

'You're crying. You feel things deeply. It's why your writing is so…absorbing.'

Mia wiped her eyes with her fingertips, took a small sip of water. 'It was a sad situation…' It would be impossible to explain the twist of fate that had brought her here, the real reason for her tears.

'It *was* a sad situation, made worse by me.' Eline shifted on the sofa. 'I was so caught up in the fickle trappings of the crazy world I was in that I didn't see it until it was too late…'

'See what?'

'That I'd lost the best thing in my life.'

Suddenly Eline's china-blue gaze felt like a prison. She wanted to pick up her things and run to Theo's house on Herengracht, but she had to see the job through for Lotte's sake. She put her glass down and picked up her note pad. 'I suppose we all have experiences that change the way we think about things… With this event, you're taking a stand against fast fashion; you're promoting designers who work with recycled and sustainable materials. Shall we talk about that now…?'

CHAPTER ELEVEN

THEO STEPPED BACK and studied the wide stripe of pale olive paint he'd just applied to the wall above the fireplace. It seemed right for the room. A calming sort of colour but rich enough, saturated enough, not to be boring. He loaded the roller again and worked it over the wall, expanding the patch of colour. There was something satisfying about the sticky glide of the roller, the fresh paint smell, the instant transformation. Mia would approve, he thought. Direk would be peeved. He'd say that Theo was the client, that he wasn't supposed to be painting…

But he'd been restless. A long run hadn't helped and, when he'd tried to focus on work, his thoughts had kept drifting to Mia, to the look on her face as she'd slowly backed out of the room. She hadn't turned her back on him, but held his gaze to the last, giving him chance after chance to stop her. But he hadn't; he'd let her go.

He'd given up trying to work and roamed the house instead. He'd been pacing up and down the hall when he'd felt a sudden compelling need to control something, an overwhelming desire to assert himself. He'd spotted the paint tins through the sitting room door, and that was it. He'd moved Direk's vase off the mantelpiece and set to work painting the chimney breast. Pathetic, really, slapping paint on a wall to exorcise his demons. He knew what was wrong with him. It was half-past six. Mia was at Eline's apartment, which had been *his* apartment once, and he had absolutely no control over what was being discussed…or revealed.

He coated the roller again, driving it over the wall, wet pinpricks of paint peppering his face. For three days he hadn't been able to think about Mia without seeing her tear-stained cheeks as she'd stood in the doorway. For three days he'd tried to convince himself that she'd be better off without him, but if he believed that then why hadn't he been able to draw a line under everything? Why couldn't he stop thinking about her? He paused for a beat. Because he knew all the way to his bones that they were better off together. It had been the coward's way out, trying to write off everything they'd shared, because he was too scared to turn his gaze inwards and deal with the hard stuff.

Hard stuff!

He powered the roller over the wall.

Deal with it!

Eline… The thought of her didn't turn his blood to ice any more. Yes, she'd stung him with her attitude to Bram, and she'd broken his heart with her casual affair, but it was time to face the truth. Ancient hurt over Eline wasn't the reason why he hadn't told Mia about Bram. It had been a ready-to-wear excuse, that was all. Mia was sweet, kind and empathetic. He'd always known in his heart that she would never think badly of Bram; would never see Bram as a tiresome liability, as Eline had. For pity's sake, Mia had even expressed sadness at the death of his father, something he'd never been able to do himself.

He poured more paint into the roller tray and moved on to the next section of wall. His father had been a waste of space. At twelve years old Bram had been more of a man than his father had ever been. Bram, protecting them all, wading in to divert his father's drunken fists from their mother, hollering at him to take Madelon away so she wouldn't see… And he'd always done as he'd been told, hadn't he…? He'd always run away knowing full well that, when he got back, Bram would be…hurt. The roller froze in his hand. To this day the sharp scrape of chair legs on tile made his heart lurch. The sound of breaking china made him buckle inside.

He stared at the glistening green wall, felt his ten-year-old self shrinking back, heartbeat ramping, mouth tinder-dry. He'd been a coward. He'd never done a single thing to help Bram put their father down. He'd never raised a finger or answered back. The noise and the swinging fists had frightened him. So he'd let Bram do it, had let him take the blows and the curses, and when Bram had congratulated him for getting Madelon out of the house he'd glowed because Bram's approval had meant everything. In his eyes, Bram had seemed unbreakable, like a superhero. He'd seemed like someone who could weather a storm and come out smiling. He'd been reliable, dependable. Strong.

But Bram wasn't a superhero. He was mortal, broken and scarred on the inside. He'd been pretending all along to make his cowardly little brother feel better…

Theo lowered the roller, felt it slipping from his hand. Bram the hero; Mia the brave. He'd never noticed before, the vocabulary he used in his head. He was drawn to strength and bravery because strength and bravery were attributes that he didn't possess. He could see it clearly now: his unswerving determination to fix his brother at any cost had been a desperate attempt to atone for his own failings. It was messed up but that was why he hadn't been able to tell Mia about Bram, because sharing Bram's story with her meant sharing his guilt, admitting his own weakness…

He drew in a long breath. His abhorrence of violence and abuse; the properties he'd bought for the refuge so that women like his mother, and kids like Bram and Madelon and himself, would have somewhere safe to go; his need to control things and protect his family: they were shoots grown on a rootstock of crippling guilt.

He bent to pick up the fallen roller, set it back on the paint tray then stepped over the green splodges on the floor and lifted Direk's vase back onto the mantelpiece. He pictured Mia's smile, the way she'd looked at him when she'd caught him watching her filling the vase with tulips. He wasn't worthy of her love, but if she knew how much he loved her, how utterly shattered he'd felt when she'd closed the door behind her three days ago, would she give him another chance? If he told her everything about Bram; if he dared to show her the darkest side of himself, the side he was most ashamed of, would that make things right between them?

Bram had told him that it was time for him to let go of the reins and live his own life, and Madelon had said she was tired of living under lockdown. He was tired too, bone-weary of it all. Maybe redemption *could* be found in just being, in living, loving and rising above the past. No one wanted him to be the gatekeeper any more. Perhaps they never had…

Mia glanced at the clock in the lobby as she hurried towards the exit. *Half-past seven!* No wonder she felt shredded; she'd been in Eline's apartment for an hour and a half and it had felt like torture. She'd been desperate to leave, desperate to get to Theo's house so she could tell him that she was in love with him.

She hitched her bag onto her shoulder, pushed through the lobby doors then toppled to a teetering halt. The car by the kerb wasn't the black saloon that had brought her here; it was a familiar low-slung classic sports car and leaning against it, in a paint-spattered tee shirt and jeans, was Theo.

Her heart couldn't beat fast enough. The only person in the world she wanted to see was standing right there in front of her, looking messy, tired and completely perfect.

He smiled, hesitation hovering at the corners of his mouth. 'Hello, Mia.'

'Hi.' She swallowed hard. If he was here, it could only mean one thing—that he didn't want it to be over either. A little bubble of joy quivered in her chest. She stepped towards him, tears gathering behind her eyes. 'It's funny… I was going to ask the driver to drop me at your house…' She glanced left and right, smiling. 'Where is he, by the way?'

'I killed him.' He dusted his hands together, a playful glint in his eye.

She clutched her chest, pretended to be mortified. 'But he was such a nice man…chatty and everything… He didn't deserve to die.'

Theo laughed, rocked forward off the car and stepped towards her. 'I didn't really… I just told him he wasn't needed.' Closer. 'I told him that I'm the one you need…' Closer still, soft light in his eyes. 'Because I'm the one who loves you, and I shouldn't have waited so long to tell you that.'

There was no holding her tears in now. They were falling like rain. 'And I love you too, Theo, but I mean all of you, not just the bits you want me to see. And I was coming to tell you that, because I realised I hadn't, and maybe you just need to hear it.'

'Oh, Mia, *you're* what I need. I'm sorry I hurt you; I'm sorry I made you cry. I swear I'll never make you cry again.' And then he was pulling her into his arms, holding her tightly, and it was sublime, the best feeling in the world. Like coming home. She could feel his heart beating against hers, his warm breath in her hair, and she wanted to stay like that for ever; but then he was shifting on his feet, disengaging. 'We should go.' His eyes held hers. 'We've got a lot to talk about and this isn't the place…'

Something in his eyes. 'Was this where you and El—?'

'Yes.' He'd read her mind. 'Eline kept the apartment after we split.' He shrugged. 'The views were great, but the memories weren't…' He opened the passenger door for her, motioned her inside. 'I prefer my house. And yours.'

She slipped into the seat, breathing in the rich smell of antique leather. In a heartbeat he was beside her and then the engine was roaring. He caught her eye and frowned a little. 'I forgot something…'

'What?'

He leaned in. 'This…' and then his lips were on hers, warm and firm, and there was that tiny sandpaper rub of his skin against hers, warmth flooding through her, desire pooling in her belly. She slipped her hands to his face, pulling him closer. He made a low noise in his throat, deepened his kiss; and he tasted so good, smelled so good, that if she could have stopped time, stayed for ever in that moment, she'd gladly have done it. But all too soon he was pulling away, eyes cloudy with desire and love. 'We need to go.'

'To your place?'

He shook his head. 'To yours first. You'll need some stuff for the weekend, and you'll need to make arrangements for your dependant…' A ghost of a smile touched his lips.

'Arrangements…? Stuff for the weekend…? I'm intrigued.'

He grinned. '*Then* we're going to my place.' He rubbed at the flecks of paint clinging to the hairs on his forearms. 'I need to clean up.'

'I was going to get to *that*. You've actually been painting?'

He nodded. 'I stuck a toe in the water. Have you eaten?'

She'd hardly eaten for three days. 'No.'

'Hungry?'

'I am.' She felt a smile coming. 'In so many different ways.'

He laughed. 'Okay…so, barge first, then clean-up duty, then dinner and then…'

She slipped her hand to the back of his neck and buried her fingers into his hair. 'Just drive, Theo.'

She turned the vase on the mantelpiece a quarter of an inch and shuffled the tulips into a pleasing fan shape. They'd lasted well and the colour looked perfect against the green. Theo's paint job was a little patchy, but it was nothing that a second coat wouldn't sort out. She turned around slowly, furnishing the room in her head. Large, comfy sofas in fabric, not leather; a mirror—nice and big to bounce light around. Shelves full of books; a rug—pale to push the walls out; lamps with shades in old gold silk to make the woodwork glow. In the corner, a statement plant with glossy leaves. She sighed. It was going to be wonderful. A proper family home…

'There you are!' Theo appeared in the doorway, his hair damp and tousled. Clean jeans and tee shirt. His forearms and fingernails were scrubbed clean. He came to stand beside her. 'So, what do you think…?'

'I like it a lot, but mostly I like the fact that *you* did it—that you took the leap.'

He smiled. 'It was a cathartic experience.' He turned to

face her, a familiar look in his eyes. She drew a measured breath. They'd eaten takeaway in the kitchen, and then he'd gone to shower, but they hadn't had a heart-to-heart yet, and it felt as if they could so easily slide back into their old ways. She could feel his eyes on her mouth, his hands going to her waist. He wanted to take her upstairs to bed, and she wanted it too, but first they had to talk.

She moistened her lips. 'You haven't asked me about how it went with Eline.'

'It doesn't matter.'

Was he really stonewalling her again? If they loved each other there could be no more hiding.

'Theo, I know about Bram…'

His eyes narrowed.

'Eline was telling me about her disillusionment with the industry, what her career had cost her…' He seemed calm. She took a breath and continued. 'No names were mentioned but I knew what she was talking about.' She put her hands on his upper arms. 'I know what you did, Theo: the sacrifices you made…how you lost Eline because of it. Trusting someone again… I understand why it's been so hard for you.'

He seemed to consider for a moment and then he gently took her hands from his arms, giving them a little squeeze before letting them go. 'Whatever Eline said doesn't matter because I'm the only one who knows the truth about what I did and didn't sacrifice…'

He threw a glance at the wall. 'When I was painting this room, I was examining myself, trying to work out why I'd let you walk away, why I couldn't face telling you about my brother—you of all people, the person who took in a lame kitten.' He raked a hand through his hair, met her gaze. 'And I realised that I've been hiding behind

Eline's mistakes because hiding was easier than being honest with myself.'

He walked to the single unpainted wall in the room and slid down it. He drew his knees up, traced a finger through the dust on the floor and then he looked up. 'You said you want to love all of me, not just the bits I want you to see… So, because I don't want to lose you, I'll tell you the truth about myself and my brother so you know exactly what I am…'

Seeing him like this, his back to the wall, knees drawn up, it struck her that she was seeing him as a child, and it was turning her inside out. She went to sit beside him and hooked her arm into his.

'I've been angry my whole life, Mia. I thought it was because I was just like my father. It's what I fear more than anything…the violence inside myself. I thought that if I didn't drink I'd be able to control it. But it's there all the time, simmering. It's why I run—why I work like a dog. I don't want to give myself any corner. I have to be in control; I have to know what's coming.' He glanced at her, smiled faintly. 'I didn't see you coming…'

She squeezed his arm.

'When Bram got sick, I bought the house on Texel, looked after him, but you mustn't think I was being noble, or self-sacrificing. I was just trying to make amends.'

'Amends?'

He angled himself towards her. 'Bram protected us all and he paid a heavy price for that. My scumbag father used to…' His mouth stiffened. 'I'll spare you the details.' His chest was rising and falling, rising…falling. 'Bram wasn't scared of him…' His gaze swerved to some distant point in the room. 'Not like me. I was a useless little coward!'

'No, Theo, no.' Tears were thickening in her throat. 'What are you saying…that it was all your fault?'

His eyes snapped to hers. 'I should have done something to help, two of us against him would have been better, but I always had to take Madelon away…'

'So you protected your sister…which *was* doing something.' She shuddered. 'Where was your mother when all this was going on?'

His eyes glazed over. 'In the corner.'

'Oh, Theo…' She knelt in front of him, took him in her arms and felt a shuddering sob working its way through his body. It was unimaginable, what they'd all been through, and he'd heaped layer after layer of guilt onto his own head, just as she'd done over Hal and Ash. There seemed to be so many parallels between them, yet there were so many things she didn't understand… Had there been no help from the authorities? Maybe Theo's family had slipped through the net somehow. No wonder he and Madelon had involved themselves so passionately with Saving Grace.

In time she'd find out but, whatever had gone on, the experiences of his childhood had given him a seriously unbalanced picture of himself. He was no coward. He was strong, noble, kind and compassionate. He needed to see himself through her eyes. That was her job now, to correct his vision.

She released him slowly. 'Do you remember us talking about the day I came to your hotel to ask you to meet Ash in Greenwich?' He nodded, rubbing the back of his neck. 'I said that I'd been trying to atone for Hal, and you said that maybe atonement had a little bit to do with it, but that mostly I'd done it because I love Ash and wanted to help him… And then you said something about how I help people…about how I push back. You had a lovely expression which I remember… You said that I "shape fate".'

She lifted her hand to his face and stroked his cheekbone with her thumb. 'That's you too, Theo… *You* help people. You buy homes for families who have nowhere to go; you rescue drowning cats… And, when the person you'd looked up to more than anyone else in the world needed fixing, you got stuck in. You didn't shirk or give it to someone else to do. You did it yourself. You never gave up trying, and if that isn't shaping fate then I don't know what is.'

She took his hands in hers, gripping them as tightly as she could. 'And, if you feel angry all the time, is it any wonder? You did the *right* thing by Bram and Eline punished you for it.' Such a mess, such a trail of devastation. She took a breath. 'Would it help to know that Eline is sorry…that she bitterly regrets hurting you?' Rain in his eyes again, tightness in his jaw, but behind the clouds a glimmer of light. 'You've had a lot to feel angry about in your life, Theo, but maybe you can start to let it go now.' She leaned in, kissed him softly. 'It's time to cut yourself some slack.'

CHAPTER TWELVE

THE LUMBERING CLANK of the Texel ferry moving away from the dock stirred an unexpected sadness inside her… Memories of that first summer on the island after her parents had died. That feeling of displacement because everything that had been important in her world had been swept away. That first summer hadn't felt like a holiday because there'd been no home to go back to. Home had been irreparably fractured and, maybe because of that, a feeling of home was all she'd ever wanted.

A shiver fingered the base of her spine. She'd blamed Hal for cheating and lying, but had she been any less dishonest? Hal's gambling had put him on a ruinous path, but he'd never lied about loving her. He *had* loved her, but had she really loved him?

She watched the sunshine glinting on the water, tugged her cardigan tighter against the breeze. If she'd really loved Hal, she'd have paid more attention. She'd have seen the fear behind his eyes, noticed the brittle edge on his voice, the way he'd laughed a little too loudly. If she'd really loved him, she'd have seen through the veneer, noticed the sorry state he was in and she'd have helped him. She bit her lip, felt a humbling wash of guilt. Her own need for hearth and home had given her tunnel vision. She'd only seen the Hal she'd wanted to see and that wasn't love.

'Nobody sees anyone as he is. They see a whole—they see all sorts of things—they see themselves.'

Virginia Woolf had been right. Personal experience was the lens that refracted everything: the way people saw each other, the way they saw themselves. Talking honestly was the only way to colour in the picture…asking the right questions and really listening to the answers.

She leaned against the rail and lifted her eyes to the horizon. She and Theo had made a start and already everything felt better. Knowing what had happened between him and Eline—and, more importantly, *why* it had happened—had opened a door to a deeper, closer intimacy between them.

Theo! Just the thought of him made her heart swell with love, made her lips curve upward involuntarily… The green room had been full of moonlight and shadows by the time they'd got to their feet, and when he'd pulled her close and kissed her she'd felt the warm glow of his love spreading through her, all the way to her bones. He'd swept her into his arms, carried her upstairs and, as they'd lost themselves in each other, she'd realised with a shock that home wasn't a place. Home was the feeling you got with the person you truly loved, and it didn't matter whether you were in a vast empty bedroom or on the deck of the Texel ferry.

She heard a footstep and felt his arms sliding around her, the soft rub of his stubble against her ear. 'Hey! Sorry I was so long; there was a breakdown on the car deck—ensuing chaos!' He cuddled her in. 'Are you cold? You can have my jacket, if you want…'

His body felt warm against her back. 'I'm fine, thanks.' She nestled in, tugging the open halves of his jacket around herself. 'See—we can share!'

'Hmm... I like sharing with you.' His hips pinned her to the rail. 'You're giving me the feels, baby.'

'The *feels*?' She giggled. 'You're so down with the kids.'

His lips brushed her cheek. 'Well, now that I'm letting go of my anger, something has to take its place. I'm going to familiarise myself with millennial-speak. Maybe I'll design an app...'

She wriggled round to face him. 'You are *so*...' There was only one word for how he looked. 'Happy!'

He smiled. 'I have a number of reasons for that...all of them called Mia.'

Green eyes, making her blush. She pushed her hair away from her face. 'Not all of them are called Mia. At least one of them is called Bram.'

Bram—the brother she'd known so little about just twelve hours ago and now they were on their way to meet him. Theo had planned the Texel trip before he'd intercepted her at Eline's apartment building, hoping, he said, to show her that he was deadly serious about letting her in, trusting her with his deepest, darkest secret.

His forehead touched hers. 'You're right. I'm beginning to believe that he's going to make it this time.'

She took his face in her hands and kissed him softly. 'He will, my love. Have faith.'

Theo pulled off his loafers and dug his toes into the cool golden sand. A simple act, but there was such a sense of freedom in it. He rolled up his jeans around his ankles, got to his feet and started walking towards the water.

Free!

A feeling of weightlessness. It was impossible not to smile, impossible not to feel euphoric. Bram was all right. After all the false starts and disappointments, this time

Bram really seemed to have turned a corner. It would always be one day at a time, Theo knew that, but still, he wanted to jump for joy. His brother was back! He wanted to shout it out loud. He started to run, felt the sand scuffing under his heels, the sea breeze in his face. Bram was all right! More than all right. He looked well. Fit and healthy, lightly tanned. He'd taken up kite surfing, he said, and he was running—had actually challenged Theo to run a charity marathon with him—and he was excited about a café and gallery he'd seen for sale in De Koog. Would Theo invest? Damn right he would! Bram's plans were totally on point: healthy food, freshly cooked. Smoothies and juices; vegetarian and vegan... He'd got it all worked out. He even had a business partner who was going to run the gallery side of things.

He slowed to a walk, dawdling at the water's edge, enjoying the feeling of froth tickling his toes. He held in a smile.

Marta! How could he have known that the girl he'd employed to clean the beach house twice a week was a talented artist? She'd been supplementing her income through small cleaning jobs, and over the time she'd been going to the beach house she and Bram had become close. After he'd asked her to visit Bram daily, they'd become closer still, and then they'd fallen in love. Bram was a dark horse; he hadn't told him a thing until that morning. He chuckled softly. He was an accidental matchmaker! Marta's seascapes were mesmerising; worked in acrylics on canvas, they were vibrant, dramatic, powerful. Mia was already lining up to do a piece about her for an arts magazine, the two of them chatting away like old friends...

He'd left them to it, wanting some time to himself to take everything in. Bram in a good place at last, and himself...? He took a few steps forward until the cold water drowned his ankles. He gritted his teeth, waiting for the cold to stop biting, and then his body was unwinding like a spool of thread. He felt his limbs loosening, calmness washing over him. He lifted his eyes to the horizon, to the high, clear sky. He was in a good place too and it was because of Mia.

She was a light on the shore. A clear, bright beam guiding him home…and a home was all he'd ever wanted. He closed his eyes and saw her arranging tulips in Direk's fancy vase; the deftness of her fingers, the way her hair touched the side of her neck, the light in her eyes when she'd looked up and found him watching her. Somehow, she'd come into his life, and since then everything had been better. He couldn't imagine going back to a life that didn't have her in it.

He opened his eyes. She'd turned his own phrase back on him, told him he was a person who shaped fate… He drew in a lungful of sea air. She was absolutely right. He was going to try his hand at shaping fate because some things were too precious to leave to chance.

'That looks really cold…'

Mia!

He spun round and felt a vigorous swell sloshing up his legs. She was standing a little distance away, her white jeans turned up around her ankles, her hair blowing back in the breeze. She had a way of looking at him that turned him inside out. A loving glow in her eyes. He'd never tire of seeing it. It felt new every time.

He glanced down. 'My feet are numb. I can't feel anything.'

'I was worrying about you.' She took a step towards him, winced as a wavelet swirled between her toes. 'Are you okay…?'

He felt a steady warmth building in his chest, spreading through his limbs. 'That depends…'

She took another step forward, flailing and gasping. 'On what...?' She steadied herself, met his eye again.

He smiled. 'On your answer...'

She took another cautious step forward, then she looked up at him, her brow furrowing. 'My answer...?'

She really had no idea. He took a breath then crashed to his knees in front of her. The shock of the water rushing up his thighs was nothing to the shock on her face.

'No...' Her hand was over her mouth and her eyes were glistening.

'What...?' He gasped as a wave drenched his crotch. 'You're not allowed to answer until I've asked.'

Both hands were over her mouth now, tears winding down her cheeks. At least she wasn't saying no any more, which was a good sign.

He took a steadying breath. 'Mia... I love you so much. You are the kindest, sweetest, most wonderful person I've ever met.' He swallowed hard. 'I can't believe you love me. I know I don't deserve you but, if you'll have me, I'll spend the rest of my life trying to deserve you.' She was crying and smiling now. His heart leapt. 'Mia Boelens, will you marry me?'

And then she was falling to her knees in front of him, gasping and laughing, wiping her eyes. 'Yes! A million times, yes.'

And then her lips were on his and he forgot about the cold chewing through his bones because she was warmth and light and love... He was home at last.

* * * * *

A MOTHER'S SECRETS

TARA TAYLOR QUINN

For my mother, Agnes Mary Penny Gumser, who is the most giving, selfless person I've ever known. I learn from you every day. And I love you, always.

Chapter One

Okay, so we're doing this?

The definitive answer, a yes, came in the sound of ocean waves as Dr. Jamison Howe pounded out his morning jog on the beach. Sand sprayed. His tennis shoes thudded a regular rhythm in the thick substance, rubbing against the small toe on his left foot.

And in the sunrise, he saw Emily's grin, ear to ear, her eyes glinting with the happiness she'd never lost, even during the grueling brain surgeries she'd had to endure after her biking accident. She'd promised him, seconds before they'd put her under for that last surgery, that they were going to have their baby. Their family. She'd made him promise that

that's what he'd be thinking about while the surgeons worked on her.

The future. The baby they'd been trying so hard to conceive. It was going to happen, she'd told him. She'd been so certain that he'd really believed her. And had spent every second of those hours focused on a nonexistent baby. Imagining a boy or a girl. Playing with names. Picturing scenarios with a running or biking stroller, backpacks that held a little one.

Disneyland rides. Swimming lessons. He and Emily standing quietly, watching their baby sleep.

Which was why, when they'd told him she hadn't made it through the surgery, he hadn't believed them. Even after he'd been allowed in to see her lifeless body.

The truth had hit when he'd arrived home that night instead of sleeping in a recliner chair by her bedside at the hospital as they'd planned. When he'd climbed into their bed alone.

And he'd been bereft.

There was no baby. And no Emily, either.

Pounding feet. May sun half blinding him. Ocean breeze cooling his skin. Cloying humidity.

And still, *yes*.

Christine Elliott was not overly fond of exercise. It wasn't that she hated physical activity, it was just that most forms of regular daily exertion—running, bike riding, machine incline exercises, weight lifting—bored her. As the owner of a prominent, privately run fertility clinic, she was in tune with the need for good health. But she'd just allowed any other responsibility in her life to take priority over time at the gym. Or on the streets.

Until she'd discovered racquetball. Not as a sport or a game, but as a solitary physical expenditure of energy. She was up to five days a week, any week that would allow the time, alone in the little high-ceilinged room, banging the little rubber ball off the walls. Again and again. She'd upped her shot over the past year. Purposely hitting it so it would be impossible to return and then racing to return it. Sometimes succeeding, sometimes not. But always trying. Always upping the ante on what she expected of herself.

Always needing to prove that she could do more. Do better.

Yeah, she got that this was a character flaw: her inability to accept herself as she was. The incessant need to always prove her worth to herself. Surrounded by doctors—psychiatrists and gynecologists—and counselors at her job, she knew all of the rhetoric.

And there was nothing wrong with loving her solitary racquetball time.

Except when she failed to set her alarm and she ended up late for her Tuesday afternoon appointment.

That wasn't cool.

Nor was it completely true. The appointment existed, but she always built in extra time, and was only at her desk fifteen minutes before her four o'clock appointment was due to arrive, instead of the scheduled half hour.

Newly, though quickly, showered, and back in her tie-dyed sundress and heeled flip-flops, her shortish brown hair still slightly damp on the ends that curled up in the back, she opened the file on the top of her desk.

Dr. Jamison Howe. She remembered him and his wife, Emily. She'd attended high school with them, though, as they were both two years ahead of her, they didn't know her. She hadn't recognized them, either, when she'd met with them two years before. They'd been through all of the genetic testing, and while no apparent reason had presented for their inability to conceive, they'd wanted to speak with her about options offered through her clinic—The Parent Portal.

Reading the file, she instantly remembered details. The two, who'd been best friends since they were eight years old and too cute for words together, had decided to try in vitro fertilization after struggling with infertility. They'd gone through the embryonic process and had been due back into the clinic for implantation the day after Emily's bicycle accident. They'd chosen to freeze her embryos, for use as soon as she was deemed well enough to sustain a healthy pregnancy, but that hadn't happened. Emily Howe had died on the operating table the previous year.

The embryos had been in frozen storage ever since. Waiting to be destroyed, as was common practice in such situations.

Per the legal contract, between each of the Howes and The Parent Portal, Jamison was now sole owner of the embryos and the only person who could make that difficult decision.

A phone call, a notarized signature to the lab, would make that happen. He needn't visit The Parent Portal, but Christine wasn't all that surprised by the fact he'd requested to come in person. In the years she'd been in business, she'd come to understand the full emotional depths that people went through when dealing with their own fertility, their future. Most couldn't just destroy what, to them, once represented the beginning of their child, with a phone call. Some hung on to embryos for years. And while Christine had her degree in health management and was not a counselor, her clients often sought her out when they had difficult decisions in front of them.

She'd present the facts, most of which they already knew, in a way that allowed them to step back. She'd give them a glimpse of a fuller picture, one in which science and biology couldn't create people alone. Without the final component of a loving mother and a womb in which to grow, the embryos were just science and biology. Oftentimes she was able to help them see their way more clearly to a decision they'd probably already subconsciously made before they'd entered her office.

It was all part of the job she'd created for herself and taken on with her whole being. Her clients were all looking to create families of their own. The Parent Portal was her family. Her progeny. Her future. Her love and happiness.

Her purpose.

There'd been a time when she'd envisioned being a mother herself one day. But then an excruciating young love had put her on a completely different path.

A buzz from the reception desk interrupted her contemplation, letting her know that her client was on his way in and the knock on the door sounded a full five minutes before Jamison Howe was due.

She was ready. Had been in since six that morning to prepare for the day, as per her general routine.

She'd mentally chosen to conduct this meeting on the tan-colored leather sofa and chairs on the other end of her office. Something more comfortable and homey for what was sure to be an emotionally difficult conversation. There was nothing legal to discuss here.

Opening the door, she stepped back.

Jamison Howe, his thick, long, dark hair tipping the collar of his short-sleeved dress shirt, barely gave her a glance as he took seemingly purposeful steps right past her and lowered his tall athletic frame in one of the two leather chairs in front of her massive, light wood desk.

So much for homey and compassionate.

But that was fine.

Anything she could do to make this difficult time easier for him…

He looked completely different than she remembered. But when she looked back, mostly what she remembered from her one visit with the Howe couple was…Emily. The woman's unbounding joy in life. Her smile, which seemed completely genuine, from the inside out, even when discussing the possibility of failure of the in vitro process. The two-year-old impression of Jamison stored in Christine's brain was of a quiet man who seemed truly happy to give his wife whatever she wanted.

As she remembered, he'd been a PhD in math. Taught some kind of spatial art class at the local, privately run, but nationally known, art college in town. Also had a math professorship at a university in Mission Viejo, or LA. Someplace with a bit of a commute.

He'd had super short hair then, too, and wore dress pants with his shirt and tie, instead of the jeans his shirt was currently tucked into. He'd had a beard before, she remembered that. The clean-shaven look suited him, showed the strength in his jawbone as he flexed it.

Nervously?

The kindest thing she could do for him was get him through the next few minutes and out of there as quickly as possible. She had a notary on standby—an employee of the clinic—and they could fax the paperwork to the lab for him.

"Thank you for seeing me," Dr. Howe said before she'd even taken her seat behind her desk. "I'd like to say that I won't take up much of your time, but, if you can even consider indulging my request, that won't be the case."

She dropped a little heavily into her seat. A little less gracefully than usual.

"I have time," she said, meeting his dark-eyed gaze with the professional courtesy she offered everyone who stepped through her door.

The office was hers. The appointment, the need, was his.

He had her curious, though. What request could he possibly have of her? A notary took seconds. Faxes, the same. It was all standard procedure.

But not to him. For the father of the embryos under consideration, the choice he was about to make could seem like a matter of life and death.

Maybe he wanted her to talk to someone for him? She'd do whatever she could. Of course she would.

Her clients, every single one of them, even those she only knew by name, were dear to her.

Which was why she always tried to meet each of them, at least once.

"My request is quite unusual, and I've been rehearsing all day, in between summer session classes, trying to come up with the best way to break it to you. But if there is one, I've been unsuccessful in finding it."

Okay, so now she was really curious. The man seemed strangely energized. Not broken.

Sitting forward, her arms on her desk, she said, "Well then I suggest you just ask." Hoping that whatever it was, she could grant the request. The man was endearing. An unusual combination of vulnerable, strong, sexy and…a bit unsure?

"I've decided to use the embryos that Emily and I had frozen. To go forward with our plans to have a family."

She nodded, buying herself time while she assessed him. He seemed perfectly rational. Calm, even, as he made the statement.

"I take it you've given this a lot of thought."

"I have. For months. And I have no doubts. No hesitation."

She was getting that.

And absolutely hated to have to deliver her next piece of information. The Parent Portal was not a surrogacy clinic. They could do the fertilization process, would happily do so, once he found a surrogate, but they didn't hire women to have babies for others. She could refer him, though…

Searching her mind for the best option, she was already reaching for her drawer to pull out a brochure when he said, "You don't approve."

"My approval isn't even a consideration here," she quickly told him. "But for the record… I think I do approve, though I still don't like that word. More to the point, I think it might be a great choice for you."

Not for some, certainly, but perhaps for this man… "You and Emily…you've been a pair since you were in grade school." She said out loud what she'd just read again a few minutes before. "It seems fitting that you would continue on with what she so clearly wanted more than anything else…to have a child that was a part of both of you."

He nodded, cocking his head a bit as he seemed to assess her. Her words. "You get that," he eventually stated.

Her shrug was accompanied by a smile. "It'd be hard not to, even after having only spent that one hour with the two of you."

"Before that last surgery…" He broke off speaking, but didn't break eye contact. "She made me promise that I would believe that we were going to have our baby," he said. "For a while there, after she died, I was thinking she was just being her…you know…thinking of everyone else, of me…giving me something good to think about during surgery, but later, it dawned on me what she was really doing. She was, in her own way, begging me to continue on with our plans, whether she made it through the surgery or not."

The words brought her a second of unease.

"So…you're doing this for *her*," she said, careful to keep her tone even. Having a child to honor his dead wife was…perhaps…a self-sacrificing noble gesture. For the wife. But a baby…a child…a life…

"You're afraid I'm being selfish…thinking only of how badly I want this child…and trying to justify using Emily's embryo without her specific consent."

"Legally you have her consent, on that contract you both signed. Just as she had the sole and legal right to determine what would happen to your frozen specimen in the event of your death."

He frowned. "So, what's the problem?"

"Who said there was one?"

"Your tone of voice…"

So neutral hadn't been a good choice. Either that or the man was uncannily observant.

"I just wondered, though it's honestly none of my business, whether you were just doing this out of grief, and to honor Emily, as opposed to really wanting the child yourself. Like I said, none of my business…you have all legal rights to do as you've stated. But a child…that's a lifetime commitment.

And doing it alone…that's not easy. None of it's easy. It's hard. And messy. And frustrating. And…"

"It's standing by the crib alone, watching my child sleep," he said, his gaze direct. "Having to do all of the middle of the night feedings alone. All the baths. Mastering all the learning curves. Cheering him or her on alone, making all of the tough decisions alone. And it's bringing to life the miracle that will make life worth living," he said. "Trust me. No one wants a child more than I do," he said.

So maybe, back then, he hadn't just been happy to give his wife whatever she wanted. He'd been happy because he'd known they both wanted the exact same things.

For a second there, Christine envied him—the widower sitting across from her. At least he had a memory of knowing what that felt like—to have someone in your life who not only shared your hopes and dreams but really needed them, too.

Having been alone for most of her adult life, pursuing her career and what drove her, she could hardly imagine how great such a shared life would be.

"Okay, so I assume you're here to get the process started," she said, pulling out her bottom right hand drawer, reaching into the proper file for the pamphlet she needed. They were all there, clearly labeled, easily accessible. "Unfortunately, we don't provide surrogates here at The Parent Portal, but this would be my recommendation for a clinic that does. If you don't like At Home," she said, naming the clinic, "there are dozens of others in the state, and I'm sure one of them will work for you. Once you've chosen the surrogate, if you want us to oversee the fertilization process, on up through the birth, since that was Emily's wish, we'll be more than happy to do so." When he didn't immediately take the pamphlet, she slid it through the small pieces of three-dimensional art populating her desk to lay it in front of him.

He was nodding. Watching her. Pressed his lips together. Bit the lower one and then pressed them together again.

This was the emotion she'd expected when he'd first come in the door... Everyone reached that point differently.

She'd give him as long as he needed. Glanced at a multicolored porcelain horse, part of her collection, at her angel figurines, scattered in various spots on her desk, at a small metal heart-shaped sculpture...

"I've actually chosen the surrogate," Dr. Howe said, in an odd tone of voice that had gone suddenly scratchy sounding. "Or, at least, I know who I want her to be," he said. "She hasn't yet said she'd do it."

He met her gaze, but not as openly as he had before. Signaling clear discomfort.

"You need me to talk to her." She finally got what this meeting was about. He wanted her to talk his female choice into having his baby.

"No," he said, sitting back, both arms resting on

leather, his hands gripping the edges of the chair. His knuckles were white. She stared at them. At their whiteness, as though it was a signal to her, something vital.

"I don't need you to talk to her," he continued, paused.

"I need you to *be* her."

Chapter Two

"Excuse me?"

Jamie heard his cue, but was too busy fighting an unusual case of jitters to jump in with the explanation he'd mentally perfected over the past few months. The hard part was done. The part he'd found no good way to do—letting her know what he wanted to do.

The rest was supposed to flow smoothly.

And then, perhaps, maybe some nerves would come into play as he awaited her final response.

"I'm afraid you've misunderstood, Dr. Howe. I'm not for sale here. Nor is anyone else at this clinic. There are certified, viable clinics that help with surrogacy, but The Parent Portal isn't one of them."

The words should have stopped him. Propelled him out the door while uttering an abject apology.

They didn't. While her shock was evident, he heard no anger in her tone.

"You suggested surrogacy as a possible option down the road. When Emily and I met with you. You said that if it turned out that tests proved her uterus to be inhospitable, surrogacy would be a way for us to have the baby we wanted."

"It would have been. Still is," she amended, her expressive eyes wide and filled with compassion. "I'm sorry if I misled you, but I was only listing options, not in any way suggesting that I was available to perform them..."

He nodded. Remained in his chair as he'd started, leaned back, arms down. Mostly because he was a bit uncomfortable with the swarming in his stomach, the way just looking at her started a bit of a maelstrom inside him.

Emily had gotten emotional over everything. He'd always been the calm one.

So now that he was pinch-hitting on earth for both of them, he was suddenly going to be experiencing the emotions his wife would have, as well? The idea, while pleasant in some kind of bonding way, was not one he welcomed. Losing Emily had changed him irrevocably, to be sure, but some parts of himself had to remain as they'd been.

"I understand." He found his voice, because the

only other option was to sit there and let the idiocy tumble around inside him. "I fully understand," he assured her. "I was just hoping you'd hear me out."

"I don't see…"

"Please." He held her gaze steadily. He needed her to listen.

When she nodded, the odd sensations in his stomach settled.

"I'm not a fanciful man. I'm a mathematician. One who excels at and thrives on proving that everything lines up. And makes sense. There have been a series of events, starting way back when Emily and I were kids, that have all added up to this point. To my being here with you. I'm not about to sit here and tell you that she was some kind of psychic or angel on earth, or anything more than a human being just like you and me, but I can tell you that she'd look at me in a certain way, speak in a certain tone of voice, and whatever she said came to be. I don't think I realized it when she was alive, but since she's been gone, when I look back, I see that it was there."

"That's not all that uncommon." Christine's tone was filled with warmth, but also respect. She wasn't humoring him as many might have done. He wasn't at all surprised by that.

But that warmth in her gaze… It wasn't at all personal, but felt that way to him. His body reacted.

What in the hell was going on?

His life was a neat and clean spreadsheet. Not a

jumbled mass of inexplicable impressions. More than that, he honestly liked who he was.

"When one loses a loved one, the past becomes more concrete. It's a whole picture, not part of a moving and changing one. That life becomes finite to us."

He recognized the words. "You've been through grief counseling."

She didn't respond.

"When you have the completed picture you can study it more easily, and the mind naturally tries to make sense out of the things that stand out to us. For some people, the lucky ones, the mind succeeds."

She was throwing him off course. Yet, he couldn't argue her logic.

"Not to get too deep or heavy here, but I think that we all know more, deep down, than we consciously see," she continued as though they were there to discuss life after death.

Avoiding the real topic on the table?

He took encouragement from that.

Because if she was just going to turn him down, without consideration, there'd be no reason not to just get it done.

Right?

"So maybe that's why, after someone is gone, it's easier for us to see the places in her life where she was acting from that deeper place. Maybe it's those truths that stand out to us when we look at the whole picture that that life represented."

She was looking at the trinkets on her desk. And there were a lot of them. Colorful fake flowers in a colorful vase, too.

He got the distinct impression that he needed to rescue her. From this conversation, not from the flowers.

And that was bordering on him not being himself again. He was more recluse than rescuer.

"I first met Emily in the emergency room when we were eight," he said, off plan, but not completely. "She'd been bitten by a dog. I was there because my father was in kidney failure again. It wasn't my first time hanging out there by a long shot. I saw them bring her in. But I can also remember, to this day, her words as they wheeled her past me. 'Don't let them hurt the dog,' she said. Like I could do anything about any of it. Anyway, I kept walking by the cubicle where they'd taken her, and one time, the curtain around her was open. She asked me if I wanted to see her dog bite up close. Which, of course, as a kid, I did. She asked me if I wanted to be her friend, and I nodded. We got to talking, and when her mom came back from having used the bathroom, Emily announced that she and I were friends and her mom smiled and asked me my name, as though I belonged. I spent most of that afternoon in her little cubicle while they waited for whatever they were waiting for. When they finally came in to stitch her up, I got up to go and she asked me to stay. And when she was released and in the wheelchair on her way out, she told me to remember that we were friends. I remember thinking she was a bit goofy to think that we'd ever see each other again, but I liked the sentiment. I told her goodbye. And she said, 'See ya.'"

Not goodbye. "See ya." As though she'd known…

"A month later, when I went back to school, there she was, the new girl in our third grade class."

"What happened with your father?" Christine asked.

"I imagine he spent the night at the hospital, though I don't have specific memory of that. He most always did when he went into failure. He'd been in a bad car wreck before I was born. Both of his kidneys had ruptured. He had another transplant the year that I met Emily, but he died when I was in junior high."

"I'm sorry."

He shrugged off the sympathy. In some ways his childhood had been hard, with so much time spent in hospitals due to his dad being so sick, but in others, it had been the best. His mom and dad had always been there for him. Doing fun things with him. Giving him a solid base of love and security. His mom was still that. As was his stepfather, the man who'd been his father's best friend.

"Emily somehow knew we'd meet again," he said, getting the conversation back on track. "She knew that our friendship was real. And she took comfort from it that day, squeezing my hand and not crying at all as they stitched her up, letting me watch."

He'd almost cried, she'd hurt his hand so bad.

"I think she also knew, when she went into that surgery a year ago, that she wasn't going to make it. Or at the very least, she knew she had to provide for me in the event that she didn't make it. Her last words were a promise to me that our baby would be born. She made me promise that I believed her."

Christine's gaze narrowed. She swallowed.

But she seemed to have no calm and steady words of compassion to offer.

Dr. Jamison Howe was either one hell of a con man, or he was about the most unusual person she'd ever met.

He wasn't a scammer. There was no reason to con her. He could get what he wanted, a woman to carry his child, in any number of legally vetted health clinics across the state.

Which left *unusual*.

He was getting to her.

It was a first.

She had no idea what to do about it.

Except do what she did. Listen. Try to understand. To help. At the very least to empathize. To consider his suggestion fairly, compile the logical reasons she couldn't comply, and then move on with her day. To the next "Jamison Howe" or Emily Hannigan, a former classmate of Jamison's who had also been a client of The Parent Portal.

Life wasn't easy.

But it had moments of pure rightness. Of complete joy. Christine could attest to that.

She wanted him to have his child. Wanted to help him. Would help him. Once she got him past the whole "her carrying his baby" thing. It wasn't the first time she'd been asked. Was something she'd actually considered a few years back. But with her clinic, her position there, surrogacy had muddied her waters too much. There were a lot of great surrogates out there. She'd had clients at The Parent Portal who, after finding their own, had come to the clinic for the insemination, prenatal care and birth.

"I planned to give you a list of many such instances in my life with Emily, times when she'd say something and then it would come to be in one fashion or another, but there's only one that matters here," Dr. Howe said. The man was handsome from the hair on his head on down. His eyes. The deep timbre of his voice. The way he held his torso when he spoke—not upright straight, and yet seemingly straight. Relaxed, but no slouch…

"After we left here the day we met with you, she said that if it came to the last resort and we had to use a surrogate, it had to be you."

"She meant The Parent Portal, but I clearly misrepresented us to the two of you that day. We don't provide surrogates. I mean, we could. We just don't. I run a fertility clinic that insists on open family agreements, not a surrogacy clinic. I think it's best to specialize, and our specialty is not surrogacy."

"You told us you'd given your son up for adoption."

She stared at him. Had completely forgotten she'd told them. But now that he mentioned it… Emily had told her that she'd felt so strongly about using The Parent Portal because of the clinic's policy of acknowledging its patients and their needs, in the present and in the future. The woman had looked her in the eye, smiled and asked Christine if she'd ever had a child.

She hadn't prevaricated, even though she always did. But that day she hadn't. It was the first time since she gave her son up at seventeen that she hadn't. She'd told the Howes about the six-pound baby boy she'd loved so fiercely during his time inside her and then given to a family who'd desperately wanted a child of their own. Every day since, she'd been glad she made that choice, giving her son a family rather than bringing him into a home where his teenage mother was a nursemaid to her elderly grandparents.

"Emily said that we'd be doing you a favor by using you as our surrogate because it would help you to allow yourself to have another child."

He might as well have hit her on the head with a baseball bat.

It would have been kinder.

Chapter Three

Jamie wasn't all that surprised when Christine asked him to leave. The look of blank horror on her face had preceded her abrupt request.

He didn't blame her. As soon as he'd heard himself repeat what Emily had said to him over two years before, he'd known he'd made a huge mistake.

The personal remark, the reference to Christine's own child, had been totally out of line. Definitely not in his rehearsed rhetoric. But then nothing about the afternoon meeting had gone as he'd imagined it might.

At the door to her office, he turned, surprised at the tears he saw brimming in her eyes as she turned away from him. "I'm sorry," he said, knowing that there was no taking back what he'd said. "Emily and I had no business talking about you as if we knew you. And we really didn't, actually. Sit and talk about you, I mean. She just made that one statement and we moved on. I have no idea why it stuck with me. I certainly never meant to repeat it to you," he added. And when she didn't immediately remind him that he'd been uninvited from their meeting, he continued.

"I got carried off course, and absolutely didn't mean to imply that Emily was right in that particular assertion. Or to make you think that I think she was some kind of gifted seer who was always right. She wasn't. She was wrong a lot..." Like when she'd told him that buying their house was the absolute best thing for them to do. He was in the process of putting it on the market so that he could buy his way out of it and move on.

"I was only letting you know why I felt so strongly about asking you to be our surrogate. That statement from her is the only weigh-in on the matter I'm going to get from her."

Christine was sitting back in her chair, hands folded across a completely flat midsection. Ignoring him politely, freezing him out of there? Or listening?

"I'm certain about doing this, about having our family. I have no doubts or apprehensions at all. But finding a woman to carry Emily's child? How do I do that? How do I choose a woman to give birth to the child that my wife conceived and wanted more than anything on earth? It's not like I'm looking for someone to clean the house, here. Or bake my favorite cookies."

"You'd also be looking for someone to provide child care. Which you will presumably need to do after the baby is born as well. For now, you need a caretaker who's willing to do the job 24/7, internally."

His hand dropped from the doorknob.

She was engaging with him?

Should he still leave? Or was it appropriate for him to stay? Was there any chance she'd consider his request?

"Do you have a projected date for implantation in mind?" Her question had him leaning toward sticking around, but he didn't move away from the door.

"Soon," he said. "I have no date, no. I'd just like to get started on the process as soon as possible simply because I'm eager to have a family. I'm thirty-three," he ended, as though his age played some key role. It was Emily's biological clock that had mattered. Yeah, he'd like to be young enough to charge up hills with his offspring, but he expected to be able to do that for the next four decades, at the very least.

"I apologize for my abrupt response a few minutes ago, telling you to leave," she said. "I'm not used to people getting so intimately personal with me. At least not to my face," she said.

Was this really happening? She was coming around? "As I said, I was totally out of line."

Something in his stomach started to flop around again. Not a sensation he appreciated, nor one he'd tolerate once he had a moment or two to work on calming it. He'd definitely be adding some abdomen strengthening exercises to his daily regime.

"You *were* totally out of line with your personal comment regarding my life, and I'll forget it happened if you'll forgive my completely unprofessional response."

He turned to face her. "Done."

She nodded, picked up a pen and pulled a pad in front of her. "If you'll give me some parameters, I can get started seeking out candidates," she said. "This is nothing The Parent Portal has ever handled, as I said, but under the circumstances, I'd like to see if I can be of some assistance. You'll need your own lawyer, I know that much. And the surrogate will need a separate one. Rule number one in this state—whomever you choose, even if it's someone in your family, or someone you know privately, will have to have a full medical workup. The surrogacy clinics all have their own criteria, some based on state law, some based on their experience with successful matches and births."

"I've done the research," he told her, still stepping no closer to her. He didn't want her help finding a surrogate. He needed her to *be* the surrogate. There was no scientific or logical basis for his certainty on that. He just felt certain.

Could be the strain of pigheadedness in him.

Or it could be something more.

Jamie needed time to work on that one. For the time being, he'd accept what help she was willing to give him. Maybe she'd find someone who felt right for him. To him. Maybe.

He didn't think so.

"She has to have given birth before," he said then, to show her he'd really done research. "A lot of the clinics want her to have a child living at home, as it eases her ability to give one up, but I know that's not state mandated."

"It would be best for you if she's had a psychological workup, too," Christine said, holding her pen with a hand on each end as she watched him. She didn't offer him his seat back.

He didn't presume to take it.

The distance between them seemed…okay.

"You'll have a legally binding contract, but she still holds all the cards until that child is born, and you want to avoid as much chance of potential heartache as you can. The baby inside her might not be biologically hers, but her hormones will be working as though it was. You need her to be strong enough to love it for the time she carries it, and then let it go."

Yes. Exactly what he'd concluded. Christine got it. Her focus was on people—their emotional needs—

both those who'd been born and those who hadn't yet. Those who wanted babies and those who were giving them up. It was what made her clinic so different—the contracts she insisted on that allowed all parties to seek out the others, within clearly stated boundaries, in perpetuity.

He wanted her to carry his and Emily's baby. She knew it all.

Was in great physical shape…

He gave himself a mental shake. He wasn't there to assess her body. Before any embryo placement could be made, a doctor would determine whether or not she was physically a viable surrogacy candidate—assuming she agreed to his request, of course.

And that's as far as his knowledge of her body had to go.

"So let's start with a list of what you'd like in a surrogate," she said. "And what you have to offer one."

"I'll pay whatever it takes." That had been a given from the beginning. Not only did he make a good clip, but he'd had a settlement from the insurance company of the driver of the car that had hit Emily. And he'd answer her questions because she seemed to need to ask him, but he couldn't get past hoping she'd have this baby herself. Emily having mentioned her as a potential surrogate…it was as though on some level she'd known…

"I wasn't just speaking financially," she said,

while making a note. "How do you perceive this going? How involved do you intend to be?"

"As involved as I *can* be."

"I'm assuming you want her to be local enough for regular checking in, then?"

He wanted "her" to be Christine. Right there in Marie Cove. Someone who wouldn't get creeped out if he stayed closely in touch, because she understood his situation. Because he was not yet ready to seriously consider an alternative surrogate, he kept the majority of his response to himself, other than a truthful, "Yes."

"Do you want to give her the option to pick her own doctor and clinic?"

Sure, if "she" was Christine. "No, I want the procedure and birth to be handled by The Parent Portal."

He got what she was doing, though. And appreciated her effort. She was seriously committing to helping him find the woman who'd bring his child into the world. Moving closer, he slowly retook the seat he'd vacated. She didn't even look up from the pad upon which she was writing.

"Any age requirement?"

"Thirty to thirty-three," he said, not getting too ballsy. "I want her more mature than twenties and yet still well before the thirty-five age bracket that some professionals say increases risk of problems."

"Do you have any marriage preferences?" Christine asked, looking up at him. "Some couples prefer married surrogates."

"I prefer her to not be married," he said, only because Christine wasn't. In his mind, Christine was it. There'd been no backup plan. How could he not have one, though?

He'd just been so carried away by all of the signs from Emily. The messages he knew he was getting from her.

How could he possibly have expected this woman to carry his child? Was he really that self-involved? Or so into the idea of Emily speaking to him that he was losing touch with reality?

Maybe he needed to go home and grieve some more. Get into the next stage of the process of living after your spouse wasn't.

He didn't feel like moping around. He'd miss Emily every day for the rest of his life, would always grieve for her, but he had to get out and start living life again. To create his new life. He'd been told that was the next stage. Had been assured by the grief counselor he'd seen that his drive to live, even though it meant doing so without Emily, was healthy.

And that, while it was a normal response for him to feel like an ass for having that drive, he wasn't one.

He noticed Christine studying him, those deep brown eyes seeming to touch him somehow, and it struck him that maybe this was what was meant to be. Perhaps Emily *was* leading him to Christine, not as their literal surrogate, but as the woman who helps him find her.

He wanted to think so but felt no conviction.

"If she doesn't live locally, but is willing to relocate to be close to the clinic during the duration of the process, would you be willing to provide a housing allowance?"

"Pay for an apartment, you mean?"

"Yes."

"I told you, money isn't an issue. I'll pay living expenses, whatever is necessary. The woman's putting her life on hold for me, allowing me to use her body..." He stopped when he heard how inappropriate that sounded. Instead, he wanted to tell Christine that he was willing to make a notable donation to The Parent Portal if she'd have his and Emily's baby for them, but didn't want to risk being evicted from her office a second time.

Chances were he wouldn't get a second forgiveness.

She wrote something. And then, pen slightly above the pad, sat there looking at it. Not reading, though. Her eyes weren't moving. It was more of a stare. Like she was deep in thought.

Introspection didn't usually present itself in the middle of business meetings. Unless... Was she considering...

Should he mention the clinic donation he would make?

Would that be tacky?

Or show her that he was willing to do whatever she needed to make their business deal a win-win for both of them?

What could he give her that would be comparable to what she'd be giving him?

"I'd be willing to consider some kind of arrangement whereby she could see the child now and then, if she wanted to do that. To have regular updates. Since, as you say, she will likely fall somewhat in love with the child as she carries it."

Christine blinked, as though coming back to a conscious awareness of where she was. Glanced at him and then jotted on the pad.

"I…please don't take this the wrong way…but I'll be making a donation to The Parent Portal. Not to pay for your help, but because I know, firsthand, how important it is that you're here. Thinking about this place, about those embryos… I think they might have saved me. Or at least helped speed up my recovery. What you do here… I just want you to know that it matters."

He heard himself and wasn't done. "Not to say that I won't pay for your help," he added. "Of course, I will. I intended to do so all along. I just…"

He'd turned into some kind of blabbering idiot.

The comic relief in one of the family dramas Emily used to love to watch.

She'd always been the one with the more obvious sense of humor. He was a numbers guy.

"You already made a donation. After Emily died."

He had, of course. But… "That was before I had the settlement," he said. "I intend to make another, and I should have just done it and kept my mouth shut. I just want you to know I'm a good guy. My intentions are pure and…"

Frowning, she put down her pen and glanced across at him. "I don't doubt your intentions, Dr. Howe."

"Jamie, please. We're in a medical clinic. The 'Dr.' seems a bit pretentious at the moment."

He had his students call him Jamie. Emily had been the only one who used Jamison. The way she'd said it… Like an endearment…

"Look—" he stood "—I bungled this. I'm not myself this morning. I don't normally ramble. Nor am I in the habit of offending people. I am, however, used to narrowing things down to the logical and then acting upon what's there. This isn't that."

"No, it's not." She remained in her seat as he walked toward the door. He had to go. Had to think. Maybe refigure.

"Would you just do me one favor?" he asked, as he turned to tell her thank you. And goodbye.

"I'll try." She'd placed her pad on top of a file. He assumed his and Emily's.

"Would you at least consider my original request? Let it just hang there for a day or so before dismissing it outright?"

It made no logical sense, his need to have her be the one to carry his child. And yet it was the only option that made sense to him at the moment.

Maybe after he met with the grief counselor he intended to call as soon as he was out the door, he'd see things differently.

Surely his emotional insistence that this near stranger was the only woman who could carry his child was merely residual grief. Something someone on the outside would see clearly. Nod his head about. Assure Jamie that he wasn't losing his mind.

Christine was staring at him again. He saw no horror in her expression. Wished she'd stand up and come out from behind her desk—anything that might make it feel like there wasn't an impenetrable gap between them.

"I don't want you to expect me to change my mind about carrying your child for you. Or even have hope that I might."

He heard the *but* she didn't say, which kept him standing there, tense and ready to feel the sunshine on his skin. To run until his feet burned.

"But, of course I'll let your request 'hang' for a

day or two. I expect it will be on my mind for years to come," she finished.

He didn't know if she was being sarcastic, or just plain honest, and didn't wait to find out.

With a nod, he fled.

Chapter Four

The roofers were still at it when Christine got home after six that evening. Two levels were done, the third, almost so. Then they'd just have the turret. And she'd get the final bill.

And was praying it didn't come in any higher than the estimate.

Old houses needed new roofs. And she needed this old house. She also needed money to replace the plumbing.

Still, looking at the new, lighter-colored shingles as she pulled slowly down the old, but statuesque street with its large, beautifully manicured green yards, she smiled. Gram and Gramps had to be smiling down from heaven. They'd loved this place as much as she did. Or close to it.

They, after all, had had each other—and her. She just had the house.

She knew she could get a loan to help to make the fixes. But the idea of borrowing frightened her.

When you only had yourself to count on, and you were your own employer, if something happened to you and you couldn't work, or your business got sued, you'd be unable to make large monthly payments, which could result in foreclosure.

You didn't put yourself at risk like that.

Her dad and her stepmother, Tammy, the woman her father had married not long enough after Christine's mother died, thought she should sell the place. But then they thought she'd been stupid to invest the entire inheritance left to her by her mother's life insurance to open a small fertility clinic rather than accepting any one of the high-paying jobs she'd been offered at a number of health facilities.

They'd said they wanted her close. Wanted their son, her half brother, Tyler, to grow up bonding with her. She loved Tyler's fifteen-year-old smart-ass self, but she'd never felt like a member of their family.

From day one, she'd been a mere visitor from her father's past life.

She'd been only ten when her mother had died at forty, attempting to give birth to a son who had also died, and her father had left her with her grandparents and moved to LA.

He'd moved on by becoming someone else.

Some people dealt with death that way.

Others, like Dr. Jamison Howe—Jamie, he'd told her to call him—moved forward, creating a different life that included who he'd been.

Was that why the man's request had hit her so deeply? Why his remark about her past had made her feel like lashing out and then wanting to retreat and be left alone?

Was he the antithesis of the man who'd hurt her so deeply, let her down so critically?

Was he asking her to help him do what she wished her father had found a way to do? Did he want her to help him take the man he'd been into the new life he must now create by using his wife's choice of surrogate?

The owner of the small roofing company she'd hired waved from the rooftop as she pulled into her drive and then around back to the three-car garage. Parking in her usual spot in front of door one, she noticed the peeling paint on all three garage doors and then thought again about the quote she'd had done to have automatic doors put in.

She just was loath to change the garage.

And hated to see it in disrepair, too.

She could borrow money from the trust that she'd designated for The Parent Portal—but while the clinic was currently supporting itself quite nicely, that trust money was the clinic's security. She couldn't put something she loved at risk.

Shrugging the problem aside, she gathered her brightly flowered leather bag—a knockoff she'd been excited to find at a street fair in LA—and made her way into the only home she'd ever really known via the back door.

It was her night to help out at the local women's center. She was teaching a class in crocheting baby hats, which would be sent to neonatal units overseas. It was something Gram used to do—and taught her to do—before the older woman's hands became so crippled by arthritis that she couldn't work the needle anymore.

And after class, she and Olivia, another friend and volunteer, were going out for a late supper and glass of wine. Who had time to think about a widower asking her to have his baby?

"It was just another day at the office," she told herself as she threw in a load of laundry, dusted the library slash Gramps's den, freshened up for her evening out—and said it again when she was facing Olivia over the booth they'd chosen in their favorite eatery in downtown Marie Cove.

"I hear all kinds of things," she continued, taking her second sip of wine in almost as many seconds. "Couples struggling to have babies are about the most emotional people in one of the most emotional situations. I never know what someone might do or say or suggest. By the time they get to me they're often feeling desperate."

In Jamison and Emily's case, there hadn't been anything making it impossible for them to get pregnant. They just hadn't conceived.

Olivia's dark-eyed gaze softened. "You want to tell me what's going on?" They'd both ordered grilled chicken ranch salads, which should have been there already and weren't. Christine looked around for their waitress.

Olivia insisted she was single because she just hadn't met the right man yet. Christina wasn't so sure. In the six years the woman had been her friend, she'd never known Olivia to have gone on any dates. Though she had a ton of friends, both male and female, and a full social schedule, the young doctor seemed content living alone in her upscale condominium, her mother her most frequent visitor.

"Chris?"

She only realized, as she heard her nickname, that she hadn't answered Olivia's question. And that it was too late for a casual shrug accompanied by "Nothing."

"I didn't quite finish dusting Gramps's den," she said. She only had to do one room a day in order for her to keep the big house relatively clean without help.

"Sheila's ready to add you to her client list anytime you say the word," Olivia said, naming her cleaning woman for about the umpteenth time since they'd known each other.

"And why didn't you finish dusting the den?" Olivia called Christine's gaze back to her.

"I have a client who wants me to have his baby for him." There. It was out. Thank God.

"What!" Mouth hanging open, Olivia's eyes were wide, brows raised as she stared at her friend. And then said, "Is he nuts? He thinks your clinic is some kind of freakish baby-making place, a drive-through? And you, personally? Maybe you should think about calling the cops. The guy sounds scary to me."

As a pediatrician specializing in neonatal intensive care, Olivia had seen as many of the emotional family dynamics as Christine had. Probably more.

"No." And suddenly she didn't want to say any more. Jamison wasn't a freak. His request, while bordering on inappropriate, given the circumstances, hadn't been the least bit frightening. Or even, considering those same circumstances, out of place. "His wife died a year ago. They have frozen embryos. She thought I would be a good surrogate."

"You know her?"

Where on earth were their salads? "I met her once. They were Parent Portal clients."

"You want to do this." Olivia had gone still. Was studying her closely.

"I told him no way." She'd told him to get out

of her office. She cringed every time she thought about it. "But that, even though we aren't a surrogacy clinic, I would help him find his surrogate. I've got people I can call. I can act as his proctor without steering the clinic someplace we don't want to go, or putting us at risk."

Still no salad. Her one glass of wine wasn't going to last through dinner if she didn't hurry up and get some food.

People came and went around them. Someone from another table cackled loudly. Pop music played softly in the background. She felt like she could hear Olivia thinking. Hear every breath she took. Because she feared that her friend was seeing more of her than she was ready to have discovered. Deciphered. Analyzed and picked apart and contemplated.

Some things were best left to wilt and fade away. It just took time.

And yet, she'd blabbed.

Holding her friend's gaze, she searched for words that would defuse the firecracker she'd just figuratively lit on the table between them.

"Here you go! Sorry for the wait." Christine didn't recognize the young woman who arrived and placed their salads with speed and ease. The waitress added, "Someone else took your order, and then delivered it to the wrong table so it had to be remade. She's new and I do apologize..."

Christine, putting her napkin in her lap and picking up her fork, was happy to have her rattle on. Anything to distract her from Jamison's request.

"You want to be the surrogate."

Christine had eaten most of her salad. Was taking small sips of her wine to make it last longer. Had thought the conversation was done. At least the part that included Olivia. Or anyone else.

"I want to help him. The man's a genuinely nice guy. He and his wife… I wish you could have seen them together. They'd been best friends since they were eight years old…"

She hadn't needed the emergency room story to see the connection between Emily and Jamison Howe. But that piece of history had been replaying itself in her mind ever since the man had left her office. She kept picturing that little girl who, at eight, had been so in tune that she'd received an otherworldly message. Or even just willing to be open enough to reach out when her soul mate arrived in her sphere. Whether or not she'd known that was what Jamison was to her, clearly she'd felt something. And had been trusting enough to believe in that feeling.

Children generally were trusting.

Until they learned through painful lessons to harden the sensitive walls that encased the human heart.

"It's okay, you know." Olivia's gaze was always

filled with intelligence and usually compassion. But the empathy…

"What's okay?"

"You wanting to have this baby for him."

"I didn't say I wanted to. I said no way."

"I know. And I know you. If you didn't want to do it, you'd have let it go already. You'd go to work in the morning, make your calls, get the ball rolling to proctor his surrogate search, and we wouldn't be having this conversation."

"With a fee from being a surrogate, I could get all of the renovations done on the house, including a new dishwasher and garbage disposal, new kitchen countertops, electric garage doors…without taking any higher salary from the clinic."

"You need to pay yourself more than you do, but you aren't sidetracking me with that discussion now," Olivia said.

Maybe she told the other woman too much. She had lots of friends. She needed to spread her news around more. Some to one. Some to another.

It was just that she trusted Olivia in the same way she'd trusted Gram and Gramps. Like she'd trust a sister…

"He's willing to pay living expenses for the duration of time I'd be involved, including recovery, which is somewhat common in the surrogacy world. That would mean my entire salary for all those months would be freed up."

Maybe she could get her bathroom updated. Have new tiles put up in the shower. The colors of the old were so faded she couldn't even be sure someone would recognize the pattern if they hadn't been looking at it for thirty-plus years.

The wooden floors throughout the house were solid, but could stand to be buffed and resurfaced.

"And in addition to that, he's going to make a contribution to the clinic—not a surrogacy fee, just a donation..."

"You'd be asking a lot of yourself," Olivia said. "Having your body change, the hormones, morning sickness, fatigue, back pain..."

Yeah, and no wine. She gulped at the liquid barely filling the bottom of her glass.

"It'll only be for a matter of months, realistically," she said. "You don't even show the first two or three months. A lot of women don't even know they're pregnant until two or three months. And the fourth month, okay, maybe some morning sickness, but otherwise your pants just fit a little more tightly."

She stopped herself. Chilled and a bit light-headed as she heard, in her mind, where her words had been headed. Olivia knew a lot about her. But not about Ryder. That was her name for her son, not the one the boy had been given by his parents. She had no idea what name was on his birth certificate. First, middle or last.

No one in her current life in Marie Cove knew

about Ryder. Her father knew, but not because he'd been around. Gram and Gramps had had custody of her by then and had agreed not to tell her father. And going five months without seeing her father, to keep him ignorant of her pregnancy, would have been surprisingly, heartbreakingly, easy. He hadn't seemed to notice when that much time had passed in between visits. But his health insurance company had sent a bill for the ultrasound…

Or rather, she'd thought no one in her current life knew about Ryder.

She'd told Emily Howe—with Jamison sitting there beside her.

"I'm not sure if you want kids of your own," Olivia was saying, blissfully not seemingly in tune with quite every thought in Christine's mind. "But have you even thought about what it would be like to have one growing inside you? To feel him moving, a part of you…how would you not fall at least a little bit in love? And then to have to give it up?"

Now there was an easy answer. "I'd be giving him or her to someone who wants only to love and support him, who has the means and the desire to give him a happy and secure life in a world filled with love.

"And besides," she added, blurting words out of the panic that had nearly consumed her seconds before, "I'm not sure I can be a surrogate. All of the clinics require that you've delivered at least one healthy baby. I'd have to check to see if, in private surrogacy, that stipulation still exists."

"I'm not sure it does," Olivia said.

Not an issue for her. She'd basically just lied to her best friend by omission, and it made her feel kind of sick.

"I guess, when you think about it, no one can stop you from having a baby if you want to. And, legally, you can work out any custody or adoption arrangements you want to, as long as the recipient of the child passes adoption inspections, but with the proposed recipient actually the biological parent, then that wouldn't be an issue. You'd just need to make sure he couldn't ever come after you for child support..."

She'd led Olivia to a wrong path, and her friend, sweetheart that she was, was galloping down it.

"The state of California requires that both parties, no matter who they are, have separate surrogacy lawyers," she said, needing to get them both going in another direction.

Olivia finished her wine. Grabbed the bill that had been left before Christine could do so, and the two of them walked out to Christine's car. They'd driven over from the center together.

She asked her friend about a project she was working on at the hospital, something to do with a research study that measured the health benefits of reading to babies, in an effort to get a library set up in the neonatal intensive care unit. Christine had offered to help to fundraise for books as soon as the project was approved.

And they talked about a two-day Catalina Island cruise Christine was taking the next weekend. She was going with two of her friends from college, one of whom was going through a divorce.

"You want to tell me why you really want to have this baby?" Olivia asked when she was supposed to be getting out of Christine's car back at the women's center and then into her own just a couple of steps away.

"I told you. The money would help a lot. It's not like I have any family or am in a relationship that would be affected by it. And, as you pointed out, I've never been sure about kids of my own so the emotional part wouldn't be such an issue..."

Even if she did want kids of her own, there was nothing to stop her from having another one once the favor was done. Women could give birth multiple times. Her great-grandmother had had fourteen children.

Olivia nodded. Moved to get out. But not before Christine had seen the quickly masked hurt in her eyes. The two of them—they'd bonded over their true desire to live alone. To be single. They were the odd girls out. Those who didn't want to be part of a couple.

And they kept very few secrets from each other.

She had Ryder. And Olivia had whatever it was that kept her single.

"His wife..." she blurted. "Emily. I remember her so distinctly. She got to me, you know?" She'd told her about Ryder. "We went to the same high school. They're from here, but I didn't know them. Still, it felt like she was a friend. And then, to hear that she'd told her husband that if they ever needed a surrogate she thought I'd make a great one..."

Olivia's eyes glistened in the blend of light and shadows.

"Have you ever felt like something stronger than what you can see and prove is at work in a situation?" Christine asked, her voice barely above a whisper. Almost as though she'd taken a lid off the magic potion only to find out that it had no power at all.

"Every day," Olivia said. "I see it in the eyes of the parents who hang on and believe after I've told them that their newborn has little chance of sustaining life. And then, sometimes, in the little ones who prove me wrong."

It was all so confusing. The request. The fact that it was hitting her so strongly. It wasn't the first time she'd had the chance to be a surrogate. There'd been another couple a few years back... They'd both had steady jobs, but an income that wasn't ever going to allow them to be able to pay for one. The fertility testing and drugs had taken all of their savings. Christine had had herself tested, just to make certain she'd be a viable candidate, but before she could offer to help them, the woman's sister had agreed to carry their child…

"You think I'm wrong to be considering this?"

"No. I just hope you really think about it, about how it will feel to carry a baby inside you, to give birth to it and not have it be placed in your arms…"

She didn't have to think about that part. She knew it firsthand. And knew she could deal with it. Which was part of what was pushing her forward.

"That's what I'm doing. Thinking about it. I don't think I'm going to do it. It's like this fantastical episode playing out in my mind, but not real, you know?"

"You're the most practical woman I know," Olivia said, reaching a hand out to her arm, as though knowing Christine needed some connection to ground her back into reality. "If it's on your mind, you're considering it."

Her friend was right. She was considering it. Just wasn't going to do it.

"Whatever you decide, you have my support."

Olivia's parting words were more than a promise. They were like a whisper on the wind beneath Emily's angel's wings, nudging her forward.

Chapter Five

Running forward to make the slam that would win him the match, Jamie came down with his custom-made tennis racket and hit the lime-green ball at just the right angle to make his volley impossible to return. The grunt he emitted was for show.

The score—6:4, 7:5, 6:3. He'd just skunked the man who'd been a father to him for more than half his life.

Dropping off their rackets in the lockers they rented at the Marie Cove Country Club, they walked out to the beachside bar that would be filling up as soon as the day's golfers started to wander in. Saturdays were always the busiest, but it was also the only day Emily's father, Judge Tom Sanders, had free that week. He was heading up to wine country on Sunday for a week of boating and fishing with friends, and Jamie needed to speak with him before he left.

They ordered their customary after-a-match beer, toasted to the win and, rather than settling into a seat at the bar, Jamie asked his father-in-law if they could walk.

"You've got something on your mind," the older man said, his graying hair glinting in the sunlight. A couple of inches taller than Jamie, widower Tom was lean and still drew the eyes of the women at the pool and, farther below, in the sand, as, in their tennis shorts, T-shirts and shoes, they headed down a paved walkway at the top of the beach.

"Let me help," Tom continued, his deep baritone as commanding as always. "I've been waiting for the call that would tell me that you've started dating again, and I just want you to know that not only am I prepared to see that happen, I'm hoping for it to happen," he said, holding his beer by his thigh as they walked. He smiled as a woman passed.

Tom watched the woman go, sipped from his beer and faced forward again.

"You know her?"

"She was in my court a couple of months ago. Tough divorce." While Tom had done his stint in criminal court, he'd opted to sit on the civil bench after Emily's accident. It took less of an emotional toll, he'd told Jamie one night when he'd had an uncharacteristic amount of alcohol to drink.

"So…back to what I was saying… I want to dispel any sense of guilt you might be feeling…"

"I'm not seeing anyone." And he'd thought what he had to say would be easier. Good news. Instead, he felt like a college kid, again, asking the man if he could marry his daughter.

Confident of Tom's regard, just not certain the older man would understand or condone his request. After all, Emily had always had standing in the community and her parents had a lot of money, while Jamie had been the son of a woman who worked five days a week in an office just to make ends meet.

If it hadn't been for the tennis scholarship Tom had urged him to go after, he'd never have made it into college, much less grad school.

Besides, while he and Em had been close since that long-ago day in the emergency room, they'd taken a long time to get from there to admitting they were more than just friends.

Maybe he was premature in his declaration. He hadn't heard a word from Christine Elliott, but then she'd only had three business days to start putting out feelers on his behalf—or considering taking on the project herself—and it wasn't like he'd be her only professional task. She had a slew of clients. A clinic to run.

A life to live.

There'd been more than a few times he'd shuddered over the memory of what he'd done—making an appointment with a woman he hadn't seen in two years, a woman he'd only met once, to ask her to have his baby.

And yet, while he regretted the manner in which he'd done it, he still knew he couldn't possibly move forward with a family without doing all he could to get Christine to agree to be the one to make it possible for him.

He downed a quarter of his bottle of beer. Let the liquid wash the nervousness away. Tom would be as delighted about the baby as he'd been about Jamie and Emily's engagement. And once Jamie told the judge about his intentions, there'd be no going back.

"I've decided to use the embryos Emily and I froze to start a family." He wasn't looking for permission. Wasn't going to change his mind. And Tom had a right to know that he was going to be a grandfather posthumously. After losing his wife and then his only child, he deserved to know that there was good around the corner.

The man stopped, pulled Jamie off the path and leaned back against a guardrail along the back side of it. "Are you serious?"

Grinning, Jamie nodded. "I've given it a lot of thought, and I know that this is the right thing for me to do."

Tom wasn't smiling. In fact, his frown was one

Jamie had seen the older man use in court a time or two. "I disagree." Tom shook his head. "Strongly."

"But..."

"Have you told your mother about this?"

He was thirty-three years old and a successful, respected educator; Jamie most certainly didn't need his mother's permission for anything. "No. I'm not planning to tell anyone until the fertilization procedure is successful. Except you. I wanted you to know. I thought you had a right to know."

He'd hoped to bring some joy to Tom's life. Had hoped for his support. He was giving Tom the only chance he'd ever have at grandchildren...

"You're a young man, Jamie. You've got your whole life ahead of you. Find a woman. Fall in love. Marry her. And then have a family that belongs to both of you."

"But..."

Shaking his head, Tom interrupted. "I'm telling you, this is a bad idea."

So maybe his reservations of moments ago had been warranted. He'd actually expected Tom to be pleased. Once he got over the possible shock of it.

He'd conceded that Tom might think he wasn't thinking clearly. That he was acting out of grief. Had been prepared to assure him that wasn't the case.

So... Strike two on the "talking with others" part of his plan.

First Christine and now Tom. But he couldn't do

it without them. Not in the way he envisioned, at any rate.

"My son or daughter, he or she is going to need their grandpa." He could be as strong as Tom when warranted.

"Let her go, Jamie."

This was going to be maybe one of the toughest things he'd ever done. He looked Emily's dad straight in the eye and said, "I have let her go, Tom. This isn't about hanging on to the past, or seeking comfort due to loss. This is about getting on with the rest of my life. Those embryos are there. And yes, it's a bit unconventional for me to continue with the plans Emily and I made without her, but it's the life I want. I had my soul mate. I'm thankful for the years we shared. All twenty-five of them. And while I expect I'll eventually start dating again, I'm not looking for another life partner. If Emily had been able to get pregnant when we'd first started trying, we'd already have a four-year-old child. And I'd be raising that child on my own."

Tom was still frowning. Shaking his head. But he no longer looked fierce. At least not to Jamie. "But, son…"

"No, Tom," Jamie said. "My mind is made up about this. I'd hoped you'd be excited. But at the very least, you had a right to know."

"I know how hard it is, Jamie. I've been there. Remember?" Tom's green eyes grew moist, the wrinkles at the corners of his eyes more pronounced. "When I first lost Daisy…"

Emily's mother had died from hepatitis when he and Emily were in college.

"I know." Jamie gave the man a minute, remembering how awful that year had been, for all of them, but mostly for Emily and her father. For a while there Jamie had wondered if either of them would ever be truly happy again. Daisy had been the hub on their wheel. And then he said, "It's been almost fifteen years and I don't see you dating again."

Sure, Tom looked at women. He even went out to dinner on occasion. But never once had he introduced another woman to Jamie or Emily.

Lips pursed, Tom nodded. "I'm not going to change your mind, am I?"

"No, sir."

"Do you have any idea of the time frame?"

"Not yet."

Tom started back toward the bar, which was still clearly in view, his bottle almost empty. Jamie dropped his half-full one in the trash as they got close. He had a feeling Tom would be drinking one too many and would need a ride home.

Him. He would be his father-in-law's designated driver.

Funny how life had a way of turning on a dime.

Funny how, even before his child was conceived, he was assuming the role of a father.

* * *

Christine lived alone, but she had a busy life. So much so that she didn't even think it fair of her to have a pet. She wasn't home enough. She spent too much time working at the clinic and women's shelter, plus looking after two elderly couples in the area, having her book club, sitting on a committee that was in charge of overseeing community events and maintaining a slew of friends. Marie Cove, her people, were her family, and she was determined to tend to them as she had her grandparents all those years. Just as they'd all been there for her. That's what family did.

And there was racquetball. Because a woman had to tend to herself, too, if she was going to be any good to others.

One lunchtime the following week, after stopping by the Madisons'—neighbors she was checking in on while their daughter was away on a cruise with her husband—she drove by the high school. Parking across the street, she ate the chicken ranch wrap she'd packed that morning and watched as the high school tennis coach oversaw the summer camp that involved those who would try out for the team in the fall.

She'd signed up her freshman year, but hadn't gone. There'd been so much to do at home, and she'd never have been able to make it to team practices and be gone for all the matches, even if she'd made the team…

Maybe if the coach back then had been as good-looking as Dr. Jamie Howe…

As a coach, Jamie was demonstrating a serve, and those legs… They looked like pure muscle. Lean and strong as iron.

And were absolutely none of her business.

She'd reread his file, in preparation for helping him find a surrogate that would be a good match after she told him no. She was just waiting for him to call and ask her what she'd decided.

She couldn't hear what he was saying out on the court, but the way the kids gathered around him, watched him as he spoke, kept close, approached him, performed for him, she couldn't help thinking he'd make one heck of a good dad.

If he was as patient at home as he appeared to be on the court. And as well-liked…

A person who looked like she might be one of the players' moms approached the court, and Jamie went to speak to her. Her wrap finished, Christine put her car in gear and drove straight back to her office, wiping any thoughts of those male legs out of her psyche.

By the second week since Jamison Howe's visit, she wasn't thinking about the man's legs at all. It had been ten days without a word from him. Seven grueling games of one-person racquetball.

She hadn't figured him for someone who would not call. Had been on edge that whole first week after he'd been to see her, thinking he'd be contacting her at any moment. Waiting for the call. The email. The text. Not because she couldn't get the man out of her system, but because his request continued to linger there. She knew she was going to tell him no, and had to fight with herself, trying not to picture what it would be like if she said yes.

She'd pictured it anyway. The hardships involved with being pregnant. The joy she'd be bringing him. The honor he'd given her—the honor *Emily* had given her. The money that would help her get the house she'd inherited back in pristine condition.

And give added security to the clinic as well.

The hardships would be only temporary.

She thought about them, though, as she cruised to Catalina Island and back with her friends, not that she told either them about the client she'd had or his unusual request. None of them talked about work at all. They spent the two days having fruity drinks by the pool, playing trivia games against other ship passengers, eating decadently and shopping. The other two laughed over stupid things they'd done in college, mostly having to do with guys, and told Christine she'd been the smart one all along to avoid all that heartache.

By the time she returned on Sunday, two days short of two weeks since Jamie had been to her office, she'd quit waiting for the phone to ring. Or for the athletic math professor to show up at her office door. And while she had to admit to being a bit let down—at least to herself—she also knew that if his interest had been that short-lived, she'd been saved making a huge mistake in even considering having a child for him. Or finding another woman to do so.

A baby was a lifetime commitment.

He must have had a change of heart. Maybe he'd realized that it would better to move on and wait to have a family in a traditional way, with a woman who'd be there to help him raise any children they had.

Still, it would have been nice if he'd at least called to let her know. For all he knew, she could have been making calls, finding contacts, maybe even finding surrogates for him to interview. She'd said she'd proctor for him and he hadn't called to tell her not to do so.

That's when it began to niggle at her that something could have happened to him. In the week since she'd spent a lunch hour playing voyeur outside the high school. And peevishness started to stab at her a bit, too.

So thinking, that last Friday in May, seventeen days after they'd met, she called him, intending to inquire as to any further services he might need from The Parent Portal so that, finding none, she could get his file off her desk.

It was time to declutter.

"Christine." He picked up before the first ring

had finished. "I was beginning to think you weren't going to call."

What? They hadn't left it that she'd call him.

They'd just…left it.

With her saying she'd agree to his request to think about his original request. Sort of. And with her possibly checking on some things for him pursuant to surrogacy, yes, but…

Wouldn't you then expect he'd check back in, to see…?

"I was waiting for you to call," she told him. "After we both had time to think. I did speak with my attorney regarding The Parent Portal assisting you with your surrogate search, and made some calls, but when I didn't hear from you again…"

Patients made appointments with medical facilities. That's how it worked. She had a personal service to offer. He had to avail himself of it. And had the right to change his mind and not do so. It wasn't up to her to hound him about it.

Had it been a matter of life and death, then certainly, a clinic or doctor might call a patient as a gentle, or not so gentle, reminder, but in her business…

Infertility was a tough thing. It wasn't her place to push. Clinics had clients who came to them, who seemed to want their services, and then they never heard from them again. It was in the nature of their business.

"I was actually just doing a follow-up, assuming, since I hadn't heard from you that I could close your file…" The emotion storming through her didn't quite give truth to those words.

"No! Please. Nothing has changed, not as far as I'm concerned. Should I make another appointment for us to speak?"

No! Her thoughts echoed his word. "Yes, that would be best," she told him. "I can put you through to reception. Hold on…"

Without giving him a chance to say anything further, she clicked a button on the phone, and another, turned the call over and hung up.

Trying not to notice how much her hand was shaking.

Or to admit that her life was about to take a detour she hadn't expected.

Chapter Six

The first appointment he could get was Tuesday at one—a full three weeks since the last time he'd been to Christine Elliott's office. He'd have liked to have changed from the clothes he'd worn to tennis camp that morning, as planned, but had been waylaid by a student who'd wanted to speak with him. Axel Barrymore, a fatherless kid, was getting pressure from his mother to concentrate on basketball because of scholarship opportunities. This discussion was not something from which Jamie could walk away. He'd ended up speaking with both Axel and his mother, told them that Axel was better at tennis than he'd ever been, a natural, but that the boy needed to choose the sport he loved the most. He'd offered to make himself available in the future, anytime either of them needed anything. And hoped he'd helped.

He was thirty seconds from being late to his own appointment.

"I'm coming straight from tennis camp," he admitted, as he noticed the way the health administrator was looking at his bare legs.

"No, you're fine," Christine said, arranging various papers in front of her—a few side by side, a few in stacks.

To do with him? Surrogate possibilities?

He tried to meet her gaze, to assess her state of mind, but she was too busy to look up. And then her phone rang and she answered it.

Figuring he knew the drill, he sat in the chair he'd occupied twice in the past. Knowing that whatever happened, he was taking the next step forward to having his family. The rush that swept through him took him a bit by surprise.

He wasn't prone to emotional outbursts. Or *in*bursts, as the case might be. Even in grief he hadn't been overwrought. He'd been able to rationalize. To cry alone. And then do what had to be done.

Still on the phone, Christine's conversation was mostly one-sided. She had said little except for an occasional "uh-huh," "yes" and "I'm listening."

He noticed his finger tapping on his knee and stilled. Tried not to put too much emphasis on the fact that, depending on what information was hiding in those papers, he could be closer than he'd realized to becoming a father.

And wouldn't dwell on the disappointment he'd feel if the surrogate were someone other than Christine. Surely Emily would understand that he'd tried…

She wouldn't understand. That wasn't her way. When Emily knew something, she stuck to her guns. Even if she was wrong. Like the house. It was on the market—finally. And he was due to take at least a ten-thousand-dollar hit because of it.

He was tapping again. Watching his thumb and finger for a moment, then stilled them again. Picked at a thread on the hem of his shorts.

He heard the phone drop in the cradle.

"Sorry about that," Christine said, her gaze landing on him with the force of a blow. Those big brown eyes, so filled with…something he couldn't define.

Which put him on edge.

More on edge.

"I was just speaking with my doctor," she said then, standing and heading to the other side of her office—behind him—where he knew a conversation area with a couch and chairs sat. He heard a refrigerator door open, turned to see a small one set into the cupboards set along the far wall.

"Would you like some water?" she asked. "Or juice? I have pineapple, peach and cranberry…"

He preferred orange, hated pineapple, but said, "Peach, please."

He didn't want any juice, really.

Had she just said she'd been on the phone with her doctor? He knew she had. But…

"I've decided to grant your request to be the surrogate for your embryo," she said, sounding like a high school principal or something as she walked slowly back toward her desk, stopping to place a cold bottle of capped juice on the corner of the desk closest to him.

She didn't hand it to him. Why did he notice? Or care?

"That is, if you still would like to consider me as a prospect," she added, watching him as she retook her seat behind the desk. "You'd said that you hadn't changed your mind when we spoke at the end of last week."

"I haven't!" He sat up. Stood up. Reached for the juice. Sat back down. "Did you just say yes?" he asked inanely. He knew there was absolutely nothing wrong with his hearing.

It was the rest of his brain that concerned him. The scattered messages it was sending… Spiked with huge hits of adrenaline…

"I did." Christine wasn't smiling. She didn't look angry, either. Just professional.

Right. Which was what he should be doing. Acting like the professional he was.

"I'm sorry," he said, taking a sip of juice and holding the bottle on the arm of the chair. "I just…you took me by surprise." The grin that evolved out of the waywardness of his mouth almost split his lips. "This is great!" he said. Smiling some more. Nodding. And then, "Seriously, I… Wow. Thank you."

There, finally, something appropriate to the moment.

And then, as though that expression of gratitude righted his mind, a mental list appeared in his thought process.

"So…we'll need to take care of the legalities…"

She handed him one of the piles of papers. "My portion is all here for your lawyer to look over," she said. "I've already had my stipulations drawn up. I'm sure you'll have your own, and when you get back to me, I'll have a meeting with my attorney and hopefully we'll end up with a final document with which we can both be satisfied."

He didn't give a damn if she wanted to name the child. He'd be satisfied. Hopefully appearing a whole lot more calm on the outside than he felt on the inside, he reached for the papers.

Holy hell. He and Emily were going to have their baby! With Christine, just like Emily had envisioned.

His wife hadn't been planning to die. Or even been aware that she might. He didn't think that for a second. But, in her way, when she'd told him that if they had to use a surrogate she thought it should be Christine, she'd still planned their future. Just like that day in the emergency room when she'd called him over and asked him to be her friend. Those words—"see ya" instead of goodbye.

He wanted to pick Emily up and swing her around and around like he had on the dance floor at their wedding reception. To sweep her right up off her feet. To hug her tight.

Glanced to his right. Saw the empty chair sitting next to him.

And welled up with tears.

If Christine hadn't looked up from her papers—she wouldn't have noticed the tears glistening in Jamison Howe's eyes for the second he took to blink.

And then they were gone and he was watching her.

"Anything else?" he asked, not quite smiling, but looking pleased. He held up the papers she'd pushed toward him with one hand, the bottle of juice in the other, and her heart leaped. The man was too endearing to go to waste. He had to find another woman to love. To have her children.

"I've already had the medical exams and tests necessary," she said. "That was my doctor's office on the phone, giving me the final report."

"Your doctor's office isn't here?" An innocuous question. She hadn't realized how badly she'd needed it. Something to get her focus back where it belonged.

"I do see one of our doctors, but I go to her office."

"So you're good to go?"

"As soon as I ovulate." Okay, that was awkward. She'd never talked to a guy about her cycle before. Not even Nathan, Ryder's father. Two loves she didn't allow herself to think about…

Because they were both gone from her life forever. One by his choice, the other by hers.

"I stipulate in there that I want to use my own fertility specialist—the same one who worked with you and Emily so I'm assuming that won't be a problem—and my own ob-gyn for the delivery. You can speak to either of them about the fertilization process if you'd like."

He shook his head. "I'd just as soon hear it from you. That is, if you don't mind and it's appropriate."

Yeah. Right. That. She sighed. "This whole thing is a little…off the normal course…" she told him. "But not at all illegal," she quickly asserted. "As long as we both have separate lawyers who are well versed in surrogacy law, and sign an agreed upon contract, we're fine. I'll be acting as an individual, not in any official capacity with The Parent Portal," she added, getting back on track again. "It was decided that that was best, easiest and the least risk to the clinic. It's all in there." She pointed to the unsigned contract she'd handed him. "I'm choosing to use our fertility specialist and one of our ob-gyns, but as a private client, with private billing. So you'll need to do the same. You'll need to pay the doctors directly, not through the clinic."

Which meant costs could likely be a little higher. Her doctors gave The Parent Portal a preferred rate—as they did all of the fertility clinics they worked with.

"It's generally recommended that surrogacy participants go through an agency for the entire process, but I'm only going to be able to do this for you if we have a private arrangement."

Because she'd made that choice. She wasn't going to do anything that in any way impacted the clinic. Or even had a chance of doing so.

He was nodding. Seemingly unfazed. And she didn't know if she was relieved or not. She was really offering to do this. But did she hope that he'd change his mind? Balk at the stipulations? These were all nonnegotiable, as he'd see when he actually looked at the contract, which started on the page beneath the preface letter from her lawyer she'd seen him looking at.

"You'll notice an escrow agreement in there, as well as your right to prove that I've undergone both medical and emotional screening and have passed both."

There'd been no point in spending time thinking about whether or not she could grant the Howes' request without knowing that she had the ability to do so.

"And there are insurance stipulations as well." He'd need to purchase a special surrogacy plan on her behalf, with all premiums paid up front so that if anything happened to him, or if he was in breach of contract, her and the baby's health would still be covered. If his own health insurance didn't offer a plan, there were plenty in the state of California that did.

She'd been taking care of her "family" for too long to put any of them—her home, the clinic, its employees and clients—at risk.

He still hadn't done more than glance at the cover page of the document. "So what's the process from here? Once I have my attorney look this over and it's signed," he said, holding up the contract.

Glancing down, she took in the other small piles in front of her, deciding which to choose next. Her face warm, she was embarrassed. Feeling his presence like she'd never felt a client—or anyone else—in her life. As though he was touching her from across the desk. As though she wanted him to.

It was because she was planning to have his baby. She knew that. They had, and would continue to have, purely a business arrangement between the two of them. She knew that, too. What they were doing was completely accepted and professional. But when it involved your most intimate parts…

She chose the calendars first—a page for each month she'd be under his employ. "This is the tentative schedule I've worked out," she said. "This is based on all of the information I've gathered and on when giving birth would fit best in my schedule." The dates were all in the contract, too. "This is all assuming that, biologically, everything happens as expected." The contract held a caveat that the dates could change, without consent needed, if things didn't work out the first time around.

He looked at every single page. She hadn't intended him to read the specifics about the various pregnancy-related appointments she'd be having during her prenatal care. Not right then, at any rate.

The last pages were a repeat of July and August, with implantation dates again, instead of ob-gyn appointments.

"What's this?" he asked, holding up those last two pages.

"Those start the original cycle over, a month and two later, in case it takes more than one implantation to result in pregnancy." The contract gave him three tries with her body before they'd reassess her viability.

He went back to the first page. And she slid the last pile of papers across her desk. "This is all reading material I've gathered about the procedure. There's a sheet in the back that gives a list of credible surrogacy clinics if you decide you'd rather go that route. Or even just call and talk to someone before you take this on. They have all kinds of resources available to you..."

He was already shaking his head. "I've done my homework," he said, meeting her gaze openly. And then he smiled. "I just can't believe you said yes," he said. And then continued, "Except that in my mind, I knew you would. I also knew that thought made no sense."

Her life had to make sense. Always. And this did, helping him. She'd held a staff meeting, let everyone know what she was contemplating and why. Every single one of them had offered their support and told her how much they admired her for what she was doing.

Of course, she was their employer, but the doctors who worked with her certainly didn't need her as much as she needed them.

"I'm assuming we'll be doing this on your regular cycle then, instead of having you on fertility drugs that will regulate you to a specific date, since the embryos aren't going to be freshly prepared." He'd ignored the contract, but this he was reading.

"That's right," she said. Which was why his original question about timeline had had her blurting out about her ovulation. "Five days after mid-cycle is best as it generally takes a naturally forming embryo that long to travel through the fallopian tube."

Talking about their reproductivé parts was routine at The Parent Portal. Discussing them with Jamison Howe made her a little uncomfortable. Embarrassed.

And kind of like she was getting a little bit naked in front of him.

Speaking of which…

"I'm assuming you'll want to be present for medical visits, but I reserve the right to have my privacy protected," she said.

The child she'd be growing was his. Not hers. He had a right to be there for each step of its growth.

"You have a choice to make," she told him, gesturing with a nod toward the calendars he'd put on the edge of the desk. "We can do a mock injection to make sure we have timing right with my cycle if you'd like, before using any of the embryos. They implant more than one each time, and since you've got a limited number and no guarantee that it will take, my doctor made the offer… They can follow a non-embryonic injection to see if my uterus is ready to accept implantation so many days after I ovulate…"

Oftentimes the mock trial was done when the embryo was being freshly prepared from a mother's egg, because the surrogate had to take fertility drugs to put her cycle in line with the mother's. But, in this case, because the embryos were so critically limited, her doctor had suggested Jamison might want to do that. Christine was an expert on fertility, as much as she could be without a medical degree, but she'd learned some things over the past couple of weeks.

He shook his head. "No, I'm fine with going ahead," he said. "I don't want to put you through anything more invasive than necessary. And from the reading I did, the mock trial is generally done when the embryos are being freshly prepared…"

She was impressed. And oddly comforted. The man wasn't just acting on a whim. He knew his stuff.

He picked up the calendar again. "So it looks like June 7 is our day?"

Ten days away.

"Assuming we come to a contractual agreement."

He nodded. Stood. Held out his hand.

So she shook it. As she'd done with many, many clients over the years. Probably including him and his wife.

So why, as he thanked her again, holding her gaze, seemingly letting her read into his depths, did she suddenly feel as though, with that simple, professional touch of the hand, she'd just agreed to a crazy kind of love?

Chapter Seven

Jamie had his attorney add one clause to the contract in the coming days, allowing Christine the right to have contact with the child. And also, if at any time the resultant child wanted contact, Jamie could call her and let her know, with the decision to meet up to her.

There'd be a bond there.

And Christine's life work was about the human element involved in fertility science.

His son or daughter was going to know that his or her biological mother had passed away a year before conception. That child might want to know Christine. Conceivably, he or she might feel some gratitude. Hopefully. If Jamie did his job right.

Everything else about the contract was solid. Appropriate. Even the living expense amount—exactly to the penny of the average projected cost in the state of California, according to Jamie's lawyer.

He'd have signed it even if it had been hugely one-sided. Two days after the meeting, he stayed on the court for a couple of hours after tennis camp, hitting balls with anyone who wanted to play with him, while he waited for the call from his attorney telling him that she'd signed the final contract that had been hand delivered to her that morning.

He'd offered, at the beginning of camp, to make himself available to any of the attendees who wanted some one-on-one time with him. He hadn't expected the twelve-student lineup, but allotted each of them fifteen minutes after which they could go to the end of the line and wait for a second session.

The May air was balmy. Low 70s. The court protected from direct sun by the school's amphitheater behind which they sat.

He gave the private sessions a few times every year during camp. Usually setting a stopping point before he began, but that day he didn't. That day he needed the session more than his students did. That day they were helping him.

And when the call came, at just after three, telling him the deal was signed and legally recorded, he shared the news with the seven students left on the court with him. And took them all out for ice cream to celebrate.

He was back in the father game.

And he was going to be a good one.

She was good at her job. Able to care deeply, to empathize, sympathize, bleed compassion and keep a personal distance at the same time. To Christine, doing so was a no-brainer. A happy life meant taking care of who and what you loved.

Others told her she had a gift.

Whatever. She didn't see it that way.

She was just appreciative of her ability to remain personally impassive that first Friday morning in June as she was undressing in the small, a little too cold procedure room in the offices of her fertility doctor's private practice.

She didn't allow herself to dwell on the man sitting outside reception, waiting for his child to be conceived. Other than to remember that she was working for him.

As she'd talked to Olivia the night before, over her last glass of wine for the next nine months, she'd told her friend that she kind of saw what she was doing as the same kind of thing as a soldier going to war. Soldiers gave their lives, their bodies, to their country for the time they spent in their attempts to provide citizens with the freedom they deserved. She was signing on for nine months of service to provide a family with a deserving citizen. She was helping one man win the fight against infertility and a tragedy that had taken away his family.

Her whole life's work was about helping to create families. The Parent Portal was the home that housed all of the people who were "family" to her. And as the doctor and a nurse came in, explained the process one more time, asked her if she was ready, Christine positioned herself as instructed, smiled and nodded.

It was just another task for work.

She'd driven herself to the doctor's office. Jamie had offered to pick her up, but she'd said she was going into work first, taking care of a few things, making certain a few others were ready to go and then she'd meet him at the fertility specialist's office. He'd had the appointment prior to Christine's, to meet with the doctor, hear about the procedure, along with the same list of instructions Christine would be receiving. He'd known that she'd be required to wait awhile after the procedure before she could leave, had offered to go in and sit with her, but she'd opted to work.

He sat in a chair by the window of the reception area and watched videos on his phone. Birthing videos. Pregnancy videos. Diaper changing videos. And a couple of monster truck competitions.

And every time he heard the door open to the inner rooms, he looked up. When he was the last person in the waiting room, he slid his phone into the back pocket of his black dress shorts and paced a bit.

Tom had called the night before, asking if he wanted a boy or a girl. The judge had tried one more time to talk Jamie into waiting to have a family with a woman he could fall in love with and marry, have children with, but Jamie had heard a note of anticipation in the older man's voice that had been missing for a long time.

Maybe since Daisy had died.

This baby was going to be well loved. Boy or girl. Jamie honestly didn't care which. Whether he had a little Emily or a little him, he was good. Tom didn't have a preference, either. But he had a plethora of plans that they could all do together as a family, from Disneyland to touring the country's capital.

When the door finally opened, after all that waiting, he wasn't at all prepared to see Christine. Or, more accurately, prepared for how beautiful she looked to him. Her short hair, all thick and curling in different directions at the end, like she'd just been blown away by great sex. Those brown eyes that showed surprise when they landed on him.

"I didn't think you'd still be here."

"Of course I'm here," he said. "The contract stipulates that I be an active participant from the very beginning. The baby needs to hear my voice so I'm recognized at birth."

"Yes, but…we don't even know if I'm pregnant

yet." She came closer. Looked kind of tired. Which was expected. She'd just spent a good bit of time lying down.

"You have to take it easy for the next couple of days. Rest," he said. Which was one of the reasons she'd chosen Friday rather than Thursday or Saturday for the implantation. So she could take the weekend to lie low.

"I know," she told him, a tad peevishly.

He was being a pain in the ass already. He got it. Walked with her to the door and blinked as the bright sun hit him in the face. If she didn't like him discussing the instructions with her, she really wasn't going to like what he had in mind next.

"I'm planning to make dinner for you tonight," he told her as they approached their separate vehicles. "And to clean the dishes and whatever other chores you might need doing."

With her hand on her car door—a somewhat older burnt orange small SUV—she turned to him. "Dr. Howe. Seriously…"

"It's in the contract," he said. She'd had it drawn up to her specification. He'd read it thoroughly. "You've given me the right to be a part of everything. This rest period between implantation and pregnancy is critical."

"And you only have a limited number of embryos, two of which were used today," she said, nodding. "Plus you're paying for my services and you're right,

I did give you the right to as much access as you wanted. I just didn't envision...well, we'll figure it out as we go. Remember, the success rate is estimated at only around sixty percent, so I might not even be pregnant yet. But...for now, okay, fine. This is all brand-new and we're finding our way. But I already have dinner in the refrigerator. I made up a chicken enchilada casserole last night. You can heat it up and clean up afterward. You stay downstairs and you leave when I've had enough company and need some privacy. That's in the contract, too. *My* privacy."

Grinning, Jamie nodded.

He'd expected to have to fight a lot harder to get in her front door.

And was looking forward to the evening ahead more than he'd looked forward to anything in a very long time.

It was all very practical. The plans. The rationales. The contract. The process.

She'd managed to compartmentalize the actual procedure as little different from an ordinary vaginal exam. In her world, implantation was all part of their day's work.

One key element was unaccounted for, however. What in the hell was she supposed to do with an incredibly sexy and far too endearing man in her home when he wasn't there for anything to do with *her*? It wasn't like she could suddenly install some kind of X-ray system on her stomach that would allow him to watch over the seed inside her while leaving the rest of her life alone.

And what was with all of the sudden spirals going on "down there"? Did having an embryo implanted inside you suddenly make you horny?

She'd expected cramping. Knew hormones could ratchet up the sex drive. But implantation? She'd never heard of that.

He had dinner in the oven. Was opening cupboards in her kitchen, judging by the sounds. While she lay on the couch, tablet in hand, pretending to work.

She'd just had a new life planted inside her. It was all a little nerve-racking.

"Do you eat at the dining room table or the kitchen?" He came through a small hallway from the kitchen, wiping his hands on the hand towel she'd had hanging from the oven door handle.

"I usually sit at the kitchen counter bar." There were two stools. The kitchen table was for when she had guests over. The dining room for special occasions…

He wasn't a guest.

Thank goodness.

The guy just had to breathe and she was aware of him there. In her home. Filling her space. Those tight, firm legs. The backside that followed suit to form a shape made for A-list actors. She stared at it as he left the room.

It had been a while since she'd had sex. A year or two. Clearly too long.

It was a little late now to do something about that. She couldn't very well go have sex while she was carrying another man's baby.

If the procedure was successful, she wouldn't be having sex for another nine months. Just didn't seem right to have another man's body part up there with a baby trying to grow. Didn't seem the least bit sexy to her. That would make it two or three years going without.

She hadn't thought this through well enough.

Why hadn't Olivia reminded her about this?

Olivia. She'd promised her friend she'd text her when she got home. So thinking, she pulled out her phone and let Olivia, who was in San Diego attending a conference, know that all had gone well. That she was home and resting as planned.

She didn't mention that she wasn't heating her dinner herself. Just like she didn't mention most of the business meetings she had throughout her days. It wasn't like she and Olivia told each other everything.

Christine wasn't a "tell someone everything" person. Not since her mother had died.

Besides, every moment in every day came filled with new things to explore and talk about. No need to dredge up the moment that just passed…

Or ones that passed long ago. So it was a bit discomfiting to her, half an hour later, to find herself sitting side by side with Jamison Howe at her countertop bar, and finding nothing to talk about. The awkward silence was choking her as, everywhere she looked, every thought that came to mind, was filled with nonbusiness conversation.

You could only mention so many times that you hoped and prayed the procedure took. Or that it would be a hard two weeks, waiting for a definitive answer. She could take a test in a couple of days. And since her hormone levels would be in a state of flux, an early test could be wrong, either way.

They'd mentioned the fact that they had enough embryos for a couple of more tries, at least five times. Or her brain had. She wasn't certain she'd said all the words aloud.

Jamie, as he kept insisting she call him, didn't seem to mind the silence. Maybe he was one of those quiet, silent guys.

Which, considering she didn't usually go for that type, preferring a guy to step right up and say his piece, boded well for her inappropriate sexual attraction to him. And not at all well for the months ahead. She could handle no drinking, carrying around extra weight, throwing up… But months on end with no conversation…?

"My Gram and Gramps used to sit here every single day for lunch." She blurted out the words like an exploding pressure cooker. "Right here, on these two bar stools, him on the stool where you're sitting and her, here." There. Something got out.

Hopefully the most innocuous of the thoughts she'd been having and holding back.

"This was their house?"

She nodded. Ate with her normal healthy appetite. The enchiladas were especially good this time around. "My mom grew up here," she said. "And so did I. In case you haven't noticed, the place is huge. By the time my mom and dad married, the house was already getting to be too much for my gram and gramps to maintain, so the four of them decided to live together. Mom would one day inherit the house, and it wasn't like she and Dad would be able to afford anything as nice with the way property values had risen here."

He helped himself to another enchilada. She felt kind of good about that. Mostly she was the only one who usually knew whether the dinner she'd made had been a success or not.

"I tried not to be too nosy, but I got a look at the den," he said then. Sitting next to each other, they were facing the kitchen, not each other, and she found that it made conversation with him easier. She just had to be certain that, with their stools as close as they needed to be to fit, she didn't turn and knock her knees into his thigh.

That would not be good.

"All those books…and the woodworking of the shelves, even the desk. It was like stepping back in time to an elegant drawing room…"

"The floors need to be redone," she said, almost light-headed with relief that they'd found something to talk about. "And the rug is threadbare." It was wool, though, and she hadn't been able to afford another like it in that size; settling for synthetic had seemed disrespectful to her parents and grands.

"I'm actually using the money I'm making from you to finish the updates I need to make on the house," she told him, envisioning hours of house renovation conversation. She had lots and lots to say on that topic. Research she'd done. Choices she'd already made and some she had yet to make.

People she'd interview to do the work. Some she'd chosen, some she had yet to choose.

"I'm assuming your grandparents must have passed, since you speak of them in past tense and… they aren't here," he said, interrupting her perusal of her house repertoire right when she'd been debating starting with floor refinishers or the roofers who'd just completed the first portion of the work that needed to be done. All with an eye to the baby's safety, of course.

"They died, one right after the other, when I was in college."

"I'm sorry." Her peripheral vision told her he'd glanced her way. She glanced back before she could stop herself. Read more in his gaze than she generally shared with business associates. Clients.

Or any employer she'd ever had.

Alarm bells rang through her entire system—so loud it was a wonder he couldn't hear them. They had nine months ahead of them, hopefully, at the very least.

No way could she afford to feel things for this man. *Any* things.

Not even the compassion she freely poured over her clients.

He'd already used up his allotted amount.

Chapter Eight

So the man understood grief. Considering their circumstances, that was a given. Didn't mean they had to share a moment over it.

Turning back to her food, Christine attacked the next bite with a gusto she didn't feel. Not for the chicken. "It wasn't unexpected," she said, finding her distance again. "They'd both been failing for a while."

And her turning up pregnant her senior year of high school hadn't helped matters. She'd caused them so much worry…

Not "Jamie Howe on the premises" thoughts. "I'm sure they're both sighing in relief as they look down and see the new roof," she said, managing a real chuckle, as she made her first house renovation conversation choice.

"What about your parents? Are they still local?"

He didn't know her. He knew about Ryder, but he didn't know her. As big and wide as her world in Marie Cove was, she still lived a somewhat insular life. Around people who knew about her mom, at least.

"My mom died when I was ten," she told him. Clinic history. All of her employees knew. Some of her clients did. No reason her temporary employer shouldn't.

Or were they business partners? Their contract put her mostly in the boss position…

"Dad was working eighty hours a week in LA and he and my grandparents thought it in my best interest to keep me with them. Eventually he gave them custody of me." After he remarried.

"I didn't get along with his new wife. Probably my fault as much as hers. I wasn't open to replacing my mother. Or having another one."

"Do you ever see them?"

"Once or twice a year. But we talk at least once a month." She loved her dad. And Tyler, too. Even had developed some fond feelings for her stepmom, who'd been a surprising source of support to her when she'd been pregnant the first time, and again when Gram had died.

But a girl didn't forget how easily she'd been given

up. Or how easily months could pass without being missed. She knew that love didn't always mean having someone who shared your daily life. Or cared about knowing your daily ups and downs.

"How about you?" He'd almost finished his dinner. As had she. Another awkward moment or two and she'd be escaping. She hoped his response came in time, though. She was kind of curious.

"My mom remarried when I was fourteen. They stayed here in Marie Cove until I graduated, but moved to his hometown in Oregon when I left for college."

"Do you ever see them?" She purposely repeated his question.

"Once or twice a year," he said. "But we talk at least once a month."

He was grinning. She grinned back.

And, on that note, excused herself.

He couldn't get her out of his mind. Being on break at the university didn't help. No papers to grade or club meetings to attend. He'd finished putting together his syllabi for the upcoming semester, too. School hadn't yet started.

A guy could only run so much. Tennis camp was done. He'd picked his team the week before the implantation. Axel, the student whose mother had wanted him to concentrate on basketball, was on it. The team was running regular workouts and practice matches. They were done by eleven, Saturday morning.

Heading to the country club, he'd just pulled into the parking lot when he got a text from Tom. His father-in-law wasn't going to make their tennis date. The daughter of a friend of his had just been arrested. Tom wanted to see what he could do to help.

He was there. He could at least get some lunch. The club's chef had a special sauce he put in his turkey wraps…

Phone still in hand, he pushed the newest icon on his speed dial app.

Christine answered on the first ring with: "I'm fine." And followed it with: "And I don't need a thing."

He pictured her on the couch as he'd left her the night before, her tablet and phone at hand as, propped up by pillows, she worked. She was the clinic's chief fundraiser and was setting up appointments with the boards of various corporations who supported The Parent Portal. She'd told him that the night before when, after dishes, he'd tried to hang around.

After her response, he'd been dismissed. Politely. Kindly. And he'd quickly said good-night, feeling as though he'd left a vital part of himself behind. His and Emily's baby could be in that house.

"Have you had lunch?"

"No, but I've got plenty of food here, Jamie. I

shopped before the procedure. I really am a big girl and perfectly capable of taking care of myself."

"I'm being a pain in the ass."

"No, you're a man who wants to be a part of his baby's life from day one. Assuming the implantation even took. I do understand. I just don't see any sense in us sitting around staring at each other."

"I was going to offer to bring you the best turkey wrap you've ever had. I can drop it and go," he offered, trying to sweeten the deal.

"The best turkey wrap I've ever had is at the country club," she said. "If you can beat that, you're on."

"How about if I tie it? That's where I am."

"I didn't picture you for a golfing guy."

"I'm not. Takes too long. I was here to play tennis, but my match got canceled." He had a life. A good, full one. Why it was suddenly important to him that she knew that, he wasn't sure. Didn't care to ponder the situation.

She'd already accepted implantation of his child. He didn't have to impress her.

"Oh."

"Tom Sanders, my father-in-law, and I play most Saturdays." He was suddenly moved to put his family—his baby's family, too—into the picture.

"Tom Sanders is your father-in-law? Judge Tom Sanders?"

"Yes." A heat wave of worry passed through him. As though he'd done something wrong. Talking to the woman carrying his child about his wife's father… "You know him?"

There was no reason for awkwardness. The child he'd had implanted in Christine was Emily's as much as it was his. He was in no way being unfaithful to his wife.

It wasn't wrong to like the woman who'd be bringing their child to life. To admire her.

What kind of fool would choose someone he didn't like, trust a woman he didn't admire, to keep his baby safe?

"I met him once," Christine was saying. "At a fundraiser, actually. A dinner put on by the Wentworth Corporation."

Lionel Wentworth, a local financier, was a friend and golfing buddy of Tom's. Jamie had seen him once or twice, in passing, at the club.

"You know the Wentworths?"

"Not really. I know Margot Simmons, an employee of theirs. She's in charge of their charitable donations. I sought her out several years ago, asking for a donation, and she's graciously included us on her recipient list every year since."

A thread tying them all together.

Relaxing back in the seat of his dark blue SUV, he watched a couple get out of their luxury sedan and head into the restaurant. He was no longer part of a couple. But he was going to need a car seat.

"I'm house hunting this afternoon, but I'd be

happy to drop a wrap off to you," he said. More eager than ever to see her. A decent guy felt gratitude toward those helping him.

"I'd eat it, if you did," she said.

Not quite a request—Christine was far too independent for that—but Jamie was already out of his vehicle, phone still to his ear, heading in to place their order. He'd eat his on the way—saved him from sitting alone in the restaurant, noticing all the couples enjoying their Saturday relaxation time together.

He wasn't ready for that yet.

He'd get there at some point… With another woman.

"You like pickles?"

"And onions and tomatoes."

As did he. Easy order.

"I'll be there shortly…"

He rang off, happier than he'd been in a long time. He was on his way to being a father.

Alive. With a future stretching before him.

He'd definitely made the right decision.

On Sunday Christine watched her phone. Carried it with her from room to room as she dusted the rooms she'd missed for two days. She took it easy. Did light dusting where necessary, using a wand instead of climbing up to get the scrolls at the top of the grandfather clock in the dining room.

When she found herself carrying her phone with

her to the bathroom, she had to acknowledge that she was waiting for Jamie to call. The wrap he'd dropped off the day before had been enough for two meals. She'd thoroughly enjoyed it. Took a moment to wonder what he might offer to bring over for dinner.

And realized that she was enjoying being spoiled a little bit.

Not good.

Yes, she had to give him access to the intimacies involved in her process of giving birth. Not physical intimacies, of course, but the information involving them. And physical access…

She could even enjoy the process, like she enjoyed her work in general. And certain aspects of it more.

But there had to be a balance. Clear boundaries.

Allowing him to tend to her some was fine. Looking forward to that attentiveness crossed boundaries.

Which was why, when he called a little after noon, and her lower belly jumped with approval just at the sight of his name on her screen, she accepted his offer to bring over a healthy portion of a mixed green salad with mangoes and grilled chicken, but didn't invite him in to eat with her.

And as soon as she'd finished her solitary meal, she got in her car and headed over to the women's center. It wasn't her night to be there, but she knew what to do when she started to struggle with anything. Go help someone.

That night she watched a couple of toddlers, sitting on the padded floor of the playroom and interacting with them, distracting them, while their bruised mother sat a couple of doors down. She was talking to the police and accepting arrangements for overnight housing for her and her children.

Christine was there until after ten and half fell in love. And when the embattled little family waited to hear where a room was available, she thought about offering to take them home with her.

She couldn't, of course. She wasn't licensed nor was her home equipped to serve as a safe house. But it felt good to care.

It always did.

On Monday, Christine was at her desk at six, getting her mind fully back into her life's focus. She might be pregnant, she might not be. Either way, her life would only be impacted short-term. She'd continue to take the uterine lining thickening hormone she'd been prescribed, and she'd abstain from wine and fried foods, but otherwise, she had to continue moving forward with her own life. Until her appointment a week from the upcoming Friday—two weeks after implantation—there was absolutely no further reason for her to have contact with Jamie Howe.

She told him so, as gently as she could, when he called.

"At this point, I'm supposed to resume normal activities." She gave him a pretty close rendition of the version she'd rehearsed in the shower that morning.

"I agree..."

"And I might not even have anything of yours living inside me," she interrupted, reminding them both.

"Exactly..."

"We might just be going through the process again next month." She cut in, again.

He could change his mind. Or she could. The contract gave them each that choice. She'd just be required to return the money already deposited in her account.

Which was why she wasn't starting on any major renovations until they heard a heartbeat: roughly six weeks from time of successful implantation.

"So... I'll see you at the doctor's office for the urine test?"

They'd already made the appointment. Together. Friday, by phone from the fertility specialist's office, before the procedure.

"Yes," she said, swallowing disappointment. Did he have to be that eager to have time apart from her?

Show that little interest in seeing her, even once?

Maybe getting to know her a little bit better? After all, she was hopefully going to be carrying his child.

He'd hung up before she could speak further. Or even come to her senses and choose to keep her mouth shut.

Leaving her unusually disgruntled, even a bit put out.

She was a person. With feelings. Not some… Some…

Shaking her head, Christine got up from her desk, heading out to see where she could be of service in the clinic for a few minutes before getting back to the fundraising correspondence. She had an inbox full of responding emails. Had functions to schedule.

Of course she was only a body to Jamie Howe. A machine. She'd known that going in.

It was the only reason she'd agreed to help him in the first place.

But after the weekend… His attention…

Most definitely, they needed the space between them.

Implantation, the beginning of any new project, tended to prompt emotions to run high. Add in the element of the intimacy involved with her part of the process, along with hormonal increases, and it was natural for her to feel a little different than normal.

To begin to accept a familiarity between her and the man whose child she intended to carry. It meant nothing more than that. Wasn't a permanent change in her life. She'd feel the same for Emily Howe, too, were she still alive.

Maybe more so. She could see herself becoming friends with the other woman, had circumstances been different.

And spent that next two weeks training her brain to immediately switch to thoughts of Emily—whose embryo was trying to take root inside of her—anytime she found herself thinking of Jamie. After about ten days of no contact, thoughts of Jamie translated to thoughts of Emily.

Problem solved.

Chapter Nine

Jamie looked at eight houses over the next ten days. He'd had twice that many people going through his home. Every day it became more of an issue to him that he wasn't finding anyplace that felt like home to him.

He had to have a place to go in the event that he got an offer. He was in the process of making a baby and had to have a home for it. His Realtor reminded him that he could take his house off the market and just stay there, but that wasn't an option he wanted to consider. He'd never liked the floor plan of the place. The vaulted ceilings with the upstairs looking down over the living area, made the place feel more like a party house than a home. The house was always too cold upstairs in the winter and too warm in the summer. And when he and Emily had had the backyard surveyed for the pool they'd planned to put in, they'd found that due to city sewer lines, they couldn't dig deeply enough in their backyard in the only area where a pool would have fit.

She'd loved the place. Thought, if nothing else, it would be a great investment. Turned out, it wasn't even that. Due to recent ground settling that had cracked the foundation of a home in the neighborhood, all of the homes in their community had lost value. There was no danger to anyone living in here, but there was the possibility that a homeowner would have the added expense of having to have the home raised and the foundation repaired.

He wasn't going to start a family and then, with single dad duties, also take on moving into a new home. A father provided a home for his children. Gave the child a room that he could grow up in, move away from, and then come back to.

Like Christine's. The place just made you want to walk in the door and stay. Every home he looked at in their exclusive small town failed the "Christine's home" test. It wasn't until his Realtor, after a third frustrating foray out to look at houses, asked him to be more specific in exactly what he wanted that he even realized he'd had a standard.

He was just getting off the phone with the man, finalizing a plan to see three more properties that afternoon, as he pulled into the parking lot of the office building across from the private offices of Christine's ob-gyn.

As though programmed, his gaze immediately searched for her car. Found it parked toward the back of the lot.

Leaving closer spots for those who needed them, he'd guess. He hadn't known the woman long, but could already list several facts that told him she put others' needs in front of her own. The clinic. Her volunteer work. Having his baby.

She wasn't a surrogate who'd put herself on a list. She was doing a favor for him and Emily. On his request.

In deference to the importance of the occasion, he'd put on blue pants with a white polo shirt, instead of jeans or shorts and was glad he'd done so when he caught his first glimpse of Christine. The long, colorful, flowing skirt she had on with a short-sleeved T-shirt would have made him feel underdressed. Every time he'd seen her, even in her home on Sunday, she'd been dressed as though on her way out to some kind of classy lunch with friends at an expensive restaurant.

The outpouring of warmth he felt toward her as he entered the building and saw her standing there by the elevator shook him a bit.

As did his sudden desire to have her standing

there because she'd been waiting for him. Not the elevator.

"You ready for this?" He purposely kept his greeting casual as he approached. She'd made it pretty clear she wanted nothing to do with him other than that which was dictated by their contract.

Since that was all that he wanted, too, all that he needed, all that he'd agreed to, he had no problem with adhering to her stipulations.

"Jamie, hi!" Her smile, when she saw him, wasn't at all casual. At least its effect on him wasn't.

But then, getting ready to find out whether or not he was a father in the making, had him a bit flummoxed.

That had to be all it was. He was about to find out if Emily's baby was on the way.

The elevator bell dinged, the doors opened and they got in together. Both reached for the third floor button at the same time, bumping hands. She dropped hers.

Rather quickly, it seemed to him.

"So…" He held his hands down, clasped in front of him, in the way men did when standing respectfully.

Her lips pressed together, she nodded.

He needed more than that. The contract gave him the right to know medical specifics. Not to know how she was holding up emotionally. Was she still sure she wanted to do this? Having regrets? Okay and ready to go?

Panicked?

"I haven't heard from you so I'm guessing there's been no news…"

Glancing toward the lights showing the movement past the third floor, she said, "I spotted a little bit yesterday."

His stomach dropped. Details were necessary. They'd been told about two kinds of bleeding. One that was common during implantation. The other, a regular monthly cycle, that likely meant no baby.

"I'm sorry. I should have called," she said, glancing at him as the elevator stopped at their floor. "But it wasn't enough to indicate anything, and I knew we were going to be here today…"

They stepped off the elevator, his heart beating a little harder than normal.

"It just felt…a little awkward, you know?" she continued. "Oh, hi, it's Christine Elliott. I just went to the bathroom and saw this… How've the past two weeks been for you?"

Her gaze was open, searching as she pulled him aside. "I've never talked to anyone about my monthly cycle, other than my doctor and the high school nurse when I started the first time. I'm not…"

"Shhh." He shook his head. Aware of far more than he could consciously understand. Aware of her. "It's okay. We're in the learning stages here." Standing against a hallway wall, with doors into office suites around them, he spoke as though there was a microphone nearby. Barely above a whisper. "So… it wasn't like normal monthly stuff?" he asked, as delicately as he could manage.

She shook her head.

"So, do you feel anything?"

"Of course not. It's way too early for that."

He knew. He'd read. Just…

He wasn't ready to go in. Wasn't ready to move past the point of getting started.

Wasn't ready to be disappointed.

"Do you think you might be?" he asked, when what he wanted to do was grill her on her normal monthly cycle. Was she ever late? If so, how often? Did she ever spot first? If so, how much and how often? What kind of chances were they looking at here? How did the data figure into percentages?

With a crook of her head and a small smile she turned toward the door closest to them. "Let's go find out, shall we?"

Jamie followed right behind her.

She'd opted for both urine and blood tests. The first to get an answer quickly, and the second because it was the contractually required confirmation method. Minutes after she'd done both, she sat with Jamie in Dr. Miller's office, waiting for the results.

Jamie was to be present for distribution of all medical information relating to the pregnancy.

He sat unmoving, his hands on his thighs, not even a hint of the finger twitch she'd noticed in her office more than seven weeks before. He hadn't looked at her, or spoken, since he'd entered the office.

She wanted to ask him how he was feeling.

He seemed so alone and someone needed to care.

And then she noticed the wedding band he still wore. And remembered that in his world she wasn't so much a someone as a some*thing*.

That in order to get this job done well, she had to rein in her usual nurturing instincts. She had to quit being motherly to have a baby. She was chuckling inwardly over the irony of that one when the door opened and Cheryl Miller, a woman who'd known her mother and had been the original and sole doctor at The Parent Portal when she'd first opened, walked in.

She knew the second she saw the smile on Cheryl's face what she was going to say and so was looking at Jamie when the doctor spoke.

"Congratulations, Dr. Howe, you're going to be a father!"

His mouth open, he looked immediately at Christine, met her gaze, and for one brief second she felt like the mother of his child. Felt as though they'd just been told they were going to have a baby.

She wanted to jump up. To hug him.

To kiss him long and hard.

Then his gaze dropped reverently to her belly.

And she came to her senses.

“We need to celebrate.” Jamie could hardly get a hold of his thoughts as he and Christine exited the doctor’s office together. They had a list of dates, future appointments. She had prescriptions that needed to be filled. The plethora of information they’d been given regarding what to expect, what to watch for, when it would be necessary to call the doctor’s office—all of it reverberated through his mind, needing to be put on a spreadsheet of some kind.

“No.” Christine smiled as she shook her head. “You need to celebrate. I imagine Tom Sanders will be thrilled with the news,” she added.

Tom! He hadn’t even thought about his father-in-law! Yes, Tom was going to be overjoyed at the prospect of being a grandfather. Even though he didn’t think Jamie had made the best decision for himself.

Why hadn’t he thought of Tom?

Or worse, why wasn’t he thinking of Emily? They’d just reached the culmination of their dreams.

Thanks to the woman walking beside him.

“The blood test results won’t be back for a few hours,” he told her as they exited the building. “And I’ve got some houses to look at. How about if we meet at your office right before four?”

Dr. Miller had said she'd call Christine with the results at four.

He was going to be a father.

A *father.* For real. Not just in plans.

She'd stopped just outside the door, standing in the shade of the large awning covering the entryway.

"That's the second time you've mentioned looking at houses."

A statement. Not a question. "I've got my place on the market."

Her frown was unexpected. "You're going through all of this to have the baby you and Emily created, but you're moving from the home you shared with her?"

"I wanted to move from that place when she was alive," he told her, too het up to pay much attention to her remark. "It never felt like a home. And it's dropping in value so isn't a good financial risk, either." He brushed off her questions, wanting first to solidify the location of their four o'clock appointment.

To take her out to a fancy dinner and celebrate their humongous accomplishment. And to make a nonalcoholic toast to the future.

They'd brought an embryo to life.

They were embarking on a partnership. There was so much to talk about. Visitation to discuss. He was to spend time with the baby while in utero so that it would know his voice when it was born, for one thing. Plans to make. Schedules to set.

And all that the doctor had just said about birthing choices. Natural. Epidurals. Assisted. Midwife. Classes.

He was familiar with most of the rhetoric in theory.

In practicality, he knew nothing.

Hadn't discussed any of it with Christine ahead of time, which seemed remiss of him.

"So, your office just before four?" he asked when his thoughts slowed enough to allow him coherent conversation.

She nodded.

"And then dinner?" He'd taken a step toward the parking lot. She was right beside him. "We can go out," he said, hearing the supersonic energy in his voice. Hoped he didn't sound as frenetic to her as it felt to him. "Nothing personal. Just business. We have so much to discuss…"

When he glanced at her, she was grinning. And nodding. "Fine. We can go out. But Jamie…"

"Yeah?"

"Call your father-in-law. You shouldn't be celebrating this alone."

He wasn't alone.

He was with her.

But she wasn't celebrating.

She was doing a job.

Chapter Ten

With hands that were shaking for no good reason, Christine pulled out her phone the second she was in her car, checking for pertinent emails or voice messages that might have come through during the time her phone had been on silent.

There'd been a few of both. Important, but not urgent.

And Olivia had texted. Her friend had been heading into court but wanted to know the results.

Positive, she typed back, and dropped her phone into the pocket on the side of her brightly colored bag.

This wasn't life-changing news for her, just life altering for a short period of time.

The baby wasn't even hers.

She started her car, pulled out into traffic, thought about the emails she'd briefly skimmed. The voice messages she'd sort of heard.

Wondered if Jamie had called Tom.

Hoped he had. Now Jamie was one who'd just had life-changing news. He'd been so happy he'd almost been irritatingly talkative.

Except that she'd found his uncharacteristic lack of focus endearing…

The man really wanted this baby.

Such a great thing.

Men wanted children. She saw it every day in her business. So why was she glomming on to the way his eyes had glistened in that first second after the announcement? On the almost uncontainable energy coursing through him so quickly he couldn't seem to rein himself in?

Why did it hurt so badly that a man was feeling that way about a baby *she* was carrying?

No. She wasn't going there.

This most definitely wasn't about her.

And that fact made it much more difficult to smile at the barrage of faces entering her office, sometimes in duplicate, on and off for the rest of that afternoon. Her full-time staff of seven, the doctors who worked for them, the technicians who were assigned by their employer labs to clinic, even the crew from the cleaning company, one by one, came in to either hear the test results, or to congratulate her because they had heard them.

She smiled. Thanked them all for their support. And reminded every single one of them that Jamie Howe was the one deserving of congratulations.

The baby was his. Not hers.

Still in his dress pants and polo shirt, Jamie appeared at her office door at five minutes before four. The way she reacted to the sight of that athletic body with that dark hair tipping his collar, and the hazel gaze meeting hers, you'd think the man meant something to her. Personally.

She almost walked from behind her desk to give him a hug.

It was just the emotion of the day, she knew that, mixed in with a bit of hormonal fluctuation. Now that she was pregnant, her body, and prenatal vitamins, would be naturally producing everything her uterus needed, so she was to stop the fertility medication. It wouldn't stop the roller coaster of emotions, though. She'd forgotten that from the past.

Jamie had barely said hello and mentioned that he might have found a house, when Cheryl rang in. Putting the phone on speaker, Christine and Jamie listened together as the doctor said that the blood test confirmed what they already knew.

And reminded them that their due date was March 14.

Cheryl congratulated Jamie again, reminded Christine to call her anytime before her next appointment if she had any issues and hung up, leaving them standing there on opposite sides of her desk, looking at each other.

So much was going on inside her, both physically and emotionally. She struggled for words. Knew she had to find them.

She was the professional. Jamie was paying for her services, yes, but he was, in essence, a client. One not associated with the clinic for legal purposes, but still a client.

It was up to her to take charge.

"What time did you want to meet for dinner?"

Not quite the business discussion she'd thought to have. But that's why they were having dinner. To discuss business.

"March 14 is good." Jamie dropped to the chair in front of her desk. "You won't be heavily pregnant during the heat of the summer."

She nodded. Had already figured that into the plan before she'd been impregnated. And said, "March 14 is a bit long to wait for dinner."

He grinned. "Dinner can be whenever you want. This might be way too soon, but I've been thinking all afternoon about what Dr. Miller said about the actual birth," he said then. "We'll need to schedule classes, depending on which way we go." He was like an eager student as he looked over at her. She could almost see his mind racing. There was nothing personal in the look. He was just all in with the news he'd received.

Her heart warmed as she sat, too. And while she didn't have long, with another appointment due in fifteen minutes, she figured it was better to have this part of the discussion in her office. With a desk between them. Not in some restaurant where the staff mistook them for a couple.

"Obviously you have all the say on this one," he was saying, sitting forward with knees spread and his elbows on the arms of his chair.

Forcing her gaze away from his face, his chest, she shook her head. Looked at a gestational calendar on her desk. She kept it on hand for discussions with clients, but had pulled it out that afternoon to remind herself, in a businesslike manner, what lay ahead for her now that she knew her body was going to produce a child.

"You have a say, too," she said. "Some things are slightly riskier than others. Like home birthing, which I'm going to say right now is not my preference, unless you and Emily had some reason for wanting it that way. I know that a lot of couples are doing the bathtub birthing process, with good results, but since I'm not going to be bonding with the baby..."

She wasn't thinking about her body naked. She was merely discussing a human function.

"Of course not," he said immediately, clasping his hands. "I'm seriously fine with whatever you think. I didn't realize, until Dr. Miller said so, that more women are actually choosing C-section births..."

"Again, I'd rather not," she said. "If it's necessary for my health or that of the baby then, of course, but if not..."

She'd rather not have to deal with the recovery time. Or carry a scar as a reminder for the rest of her life. Although, to be reminded of the gift she was giving someone else shouldn't be a bad thing. With Ryder she'd pushed him out and had been up and moving around within hours. Had been home the next day.

"So, I guess, if all goes normally, we've decided on natural childbirth," he said, cocking his head slightly as he looked over at her.

She was going to have his baby. And he'd be there. Witnessing one of the most intimate moments of her life. Coaching her through the process.

Something happened when her gaze met his. Something electric. Warm. Compelling.

And not at all appropriate.

Jamie didn't want to leave her office. Not even for the hour and a half before they met up again at a restaurant on Main Street.

They'd just embarked on a collaborative venture that was changing his whole world. They were creating life—him with his embryos and her with the capability of turning a microscopic piece of genetics into a human being. He couldn't quite wrap his mind around the news. He just knew that she was a major component of it.

And knew that she'd always be a significant part of his child's life. Whether she ever wanted contact or not. She was the birth mother.

The child wouldn't exist without her. That mattered.

He called his Realtor. Told him to put in a full price offer on the home he'd found. A two-story in a quiet, gated neighborhood with a big yard, it was across the street from the ocean. He didn't call Tom.

Not yet.

He went for a run, instead. To work off some of the excess energy coursing through him. Late afternoon in June wasn't the best time to be running on the beach. Dodging kids and buckets and half-buried plastic shovels made the activity a challenge. He welcomed every obstacle. Every child in his path. That father half lying in the sand, covered with the raspy granules, next to his toddler, building a mound, would be him in a couple of years. The one dodging waves with a grade-schooler—him, too. His feet plodded in the sand as sweat trickled down his bare back and into the waistband of the black swimsuit he'd put on.

For two years he'd been coasting. That stopped

that day. The next stage of his life was upon him. Opening a future filled with new activity. New adventures.

New challenges.

He was up for every one of them.

He ran hard. Farther than normal. Trying to decide which of the three bedrooms upstairs in the new house, in addition to the master, would be best for a nursery. The one closest to him made the most sense. But it was smaller and on the east side of the house, which meant sun every single day. A lot of the day. Might be too hot. The one at the opposite end of the hall had only one northern exposure window. But it was too far away. And purple. He'd have to paint, multiple times, before buying furniture.

The one in the middle had an odd alcove in it to make room for the shower in the hall bathroom. And the closet in there was miniscule. Wouldn't matter so much when his little one was a baby, but as it grew…

He picked up his pace, careful to keep enough distance between his feet spewing sand and beach patrons. Rooms, decorating weren't his specialties. They'd been Emily's. And critical to making a house into a home. *Otherwise you just had a building with stuff in it*, Emily used to say.

The building mattered, too, he'd tried to tell her. The house they'd bought had had her touches, but still hadn't felt like home.

But without her touches, would the new house feel like one?

They'd been so good together because, other than buying the house, they'd always found solutions that came from both of them. Their differences, their strengths, had complemented each other, and only together had they found the perfect whole.

He'd given in on the house, though they'd both eventually realized the mistake of his having done so. And Emily had loved the place. He wasn't sure he'd have moved her away from it.

One thing was for sure, he was glad they'd bought it. That she'd lived out her last years in a place she'd loved.

Slowing, he stepped hard in the sand for a few steps, his velocity trying to carry him as his legs were stopping.

What in the hell was he doing?

Breathing hard, he leaned over, his hands on his knees.

He and Emily had made embryos so that they could raise a child, have a family, together. Both of them—each contributing their differences, their strengths, to a happy, healthy result. Making up for each other's shortcomings. Having each other's backs.

He couldn't even figure out which room to put the crib in without her.

How had he possibly thought he could raise their child alone?

Sitting down, he faced the ocean, forearms resting on raised knees.

We're having a baby. He looked toward the setting sun.

And started to calm. Watching the horizon, its endlessness. Waves that continued to move. Day and night. Always. Without stopping. Ever.

Like the love he shared with Emily.

We're having a baby.

He wasn't doing it alone. He was doing it differently than he and Em had imagined, but she'd be there. In the genetics of the child they'd created together. A child that would bring parts of Emily into their new home. Perhaps making up for some of his failings.

And if not, they'd still be fine.

"We're having a baby," he said out loud, softly, just enough to hear his voice. To know it was real.

Maybe it was staring toward the sun that brought tears to his eyes. Maybe it was the acute loneliness and the love he still felt for his wife.

Maybe it was gratitude for what life was bringing to him.

All he knew for sure was that he had to cancel dinner.

And call Tom.

He and Emily were having a baby.

Chapter Eleven

Jamie called Christine every day, just checking in. The calls were short, never more than a minute, and just him asking her how she was feeling. He didn't ask anything about her personal life, and didn't offer anything from his. He never said why he'd canceled dinner that Friday and she didn't ask. Presumed he'd been with his father-in-law. And knew in her heart that that was how it should be.

She'd cried herself to sleep that night, though, her hand cradling her belly. Just an overload of various emotions that needed to be expended. And then she got on with the business of growing a healthy baby.

With Cheryl's permission she was back to playing racquetball—though being careful not to hit a ball so hard it came back and hit her in the stomach. Exercise within reason was not only healthy for the baby, but would help her have an easier delivery, too. She went to bed an hour earlier every night, and if she couldn't sleep, at least she was resting.

And she heard Gram's voice every time she put a bite in her mouth, reminding her that what she ate, her baby ate. Gram had been willing to let her keep Ryder. Had been willing to have a crying baby in the house, to release some of Christine's trust money to support it. Gramps had been on board as well. And for a few months there, the first few months, she'd actually allowed herself to believe that she could keep her baby. She'd fallen in love with her son.

And yet she'd done the absolute right thing in giving him up. She'd loved him too much to force him to grow up with less than what adult parents could give him. And she'd loved Gram and Gramps too much to cut short their last years of life. With both of them in failing health, the stress of having a baby in the house would have killed them.

The choice to make the adoption private, without contact, had been her father's. He'd thought it best that she rip off the bandage, as he'd put it. That she be forced to forget about Ryder as best she could and get on with her life. She'd "gotten on" to The Parent Portal, where there was always a choice for contact.

And Jamie was allowing her contact. She thought about Jamie a lot. Because it was his baby growing inside her. How could she not? He wasn't hers, just as the baby wasn't hers, but there was something very intimate about having his seed alive inside her.

His and Emily's.

She struggled to keep the other woman in the forefront of her mind. The baby was Emily's as much as it was Jamie's.

But she'd only met Emily once. Christine had some key memories, but could only play them so many times over and over without anything new to add.

She was ready for Jamie's call Monday morning—between seven and eight, as they'd been the previous two days—prepared to tell him that she'd slept well, and everything else was status quo. She figured, after a week or so, his calls would cut back to every other day. And then maybe every three or four. He didn't have to call at all. Or see her. The level of contact had been left up to him.

She'd gone into the process knowing that she could do it on her own. And be just fine. She'd have her monthly checkups, do what she was told, and grow his baby for him.

"I had an offer on my house over the weekend," he told her, instead of wishing her a good day and hanging up after her report. "Closing is set for a week after my new place closes, so everything's going to work out on that end."

In her office, she sat back in her chair, studying

the pattern of ridges on her black, short-sleeved shirt. And then how those ridges lined up with the blue, white, black and purple flowers on her cotton skirt. She didn't love the colors. But the skirt was soft. And she loved how it flowed around her when she walked.

Jamie's housing situation was none of her concern. None of her business. Her clothes were. Still, she had clients tell her things about their nonbaby personal lives now and then. She was being too rigid.

"Congratulations!" she said. "Everything in your life seems to be coming together, Jamie. I'm happy for you."

The words were 1,000 percent true. And felt good.

"I was just letting you know that I've taken care of my immediate responsibilities and would like to set up a visitation schedule."

Oh. Oh! No. Just *oh*. She calmed the jump of excitement in her stomach. "Okay. What did you have in mind?"

"How much can you stand having me around?"

She wasn't even going to let her mind contemplate the answer to that one. "Seriously," she said. "Do you have some ideas of what you're looking for?"

"If I had my way, we'd see each other every day," he told her. "But I also realize you have a life to live and I'm not a part of that. I know the sacrifice you're making for me. I just…forgive me, but you've got my whole future there and it's hard to not be present all the time."

Her heart melted. For him. For her. Because she didn't hate the idea of seeing him every day.

"We said in the contract that you could be," she told him. The man had just found out that a part of his wife lived on. This wasn't about her.

Why did she have to keep reminding herself of that?

Maybe because, in the moment, her whole life was being disrupted. So, yeah, she was allowed a bit of having it be about her.

"I generally work twelve-hour days during the week," she told him. "But I take breaks for some exercise and other things that come up. We could choose a time to meet a few times a week." He wanted every day. The fact that she wasn't opposed to that much contact with him told her that it probably wasn't a good idea.

"I was thinking something a little more flexible," he said. It sounded like he was moving around. She'd pictured him in his car. On his way to... Where?

"Where are you?"

"Walking on the beach. I just finished a run."

An immediate picture of his strong thighs, his tight and perfectly shaped backside, came to mind. She shouldn't have asked. Had had no valid reason to do so.

And had to figure out how she was going to make this work. Seeing him. And yet not seeing-seeing him.

"Okay, so more flexible. You want to just play it

by ear? Call when you have a minute and see if I'm free?" She wasn't going to be in about five minutes since she had an appointment.

Yes. Think about work, about others… That had always been her panacea.

"I'm fine with setting up dates. I'd just like to vary the times of day, and the days of the week if we could. You know, so the baby hears my voice throughout the day, or, at least, hears it at night sometimes, in the morning sometimes…"

It made perfect sense. This baby wasn't going to have a mother. It most definitely deserved all the help she could give it bonding with its father.

When she realized she was cradling her flat stomach again with her free hand, feeling the same kind of ownership she'd felt with Ryder, she sat up to her desk.

Concentrated on the issue at hand. Being more flexible fit her better. She lived a fluid life. Told Jamie so. And offered to be free that evening to further discuss.

Somehow, in the hours in between, she was going to have to figure out a way not to like him and his baby quite so much. How to care for the baby without caring—caring for it.

The situation was understandably emotional. But those emotions were situation based, not lifelong commitments.

She was the professional here. The one doing a

job. So it was up to her to keep the situation from spiraling out of control. To remember that he'd hired her body.

Not her heart.

Christine called just before five to say that she'd have an hour in between work and an evening commitment and he was welcome to drop by her place for their chat.

"I'm actually at the college of art here in town, in the middle of hanging art on the walls of the classroom. Can you meet me here?" he asked. And then added, "I thought maybe it would be good if you could visit me in my world, maybe once a week at least, if that works for you, so that the baby becomes familiar with the surroundings." It all sounded slightly hooey to him, but he'd read a lot about the importance of environment during pregnancy. Professionals in the field seemed to pretty much agree that babies were affected, at least somewhat, by things that went on outside the womb during their gestation.

Even if it didn't help, it couldn't hurt.

Christine had agreed immediately, and he was outside in the parking lot, waiting to lead her into the building that housed his classroom and small office. While classes hadn't yet started, first year students were moving into dorms, preparing for orientation, so the campus had a sense of life about it. His building was completely empty, though, and he let them in with his security card.

He'd seen her just three days before, and yet it was all brand-new again, the sense of life picking up when she was around.

Because she was carrying his child. He knew that his attraction to her was because she was pregnant with his baby. Just like he'd have felt a new and energized attraction for Emily had she lived and was the one bringing their family to life. It was natural.

But that skirt she was wearing—purple, black and blue little flowers on a white background—the way those flowers molded her, flowed around her calves with every step she took…

He pulled at the hem of the T-shirt covering the blue shorts he'd put on, making sure that it covered any evidence of how much he liked that skirt. And the ribbed top… It was sinful, really, the way the fabric outlined those breasts so perfectly. Hugged them so softly.

The way he was reacting to her was sinful. One thought of the child who would be setting up his classroom with him the following year—probably in a swaddle attached to his body—and he had himself under control.

"So what are we doing here?"

With a shard of guilt spearing through him, he turned to look at Christine. Oh God, if she'd seen, or sensed… He wasn't a creepy guy. Didn't ever get all het up over the mere sight of a woman. Not even Emily. He saw younger women, with great bodies and far fewer clothes, pretty much every day during his run on the beach. Found them attractive, of course. He was human. But he didn't struggle to keep his reaction to them under control.

Generally, his body just minded its manners on its own.

Christine wasn't looking at him at all. She'd picked up one of the several pieces of art lying along a bookshelf that lined one whole wall of the classroom.

"I teach math to art students," he told her. "Right brain, left brain. Opposite ends of the spectrum, to some. But in reality, art and math are encompassing visual depictions of the universe around us..."

He stopped. Emily used to glaze over when he got his Math on. As did a lot of people. "Sorry," he said. "I forget sometimes that numbers, measurements, spatial science and the way they all depict the world isn't all that exciting to the general population."

She'd moved to a canvas with geometrical shapes. On the surface that's what it was. If you stepped back and looked at the colors, you'd see a face there. And a single tear. "I'm intrigued."

"I use art to teach mathematical concepts," he said. "Or rather, I challenge my students to use their art to show me the concepts I'm teaching them. I'm not an artist. At all. These were all final exams."

"So, your students did these?"

She'd stopped at a three-dimensional, digitally printed plastic dollhouse.

"Last semester. The top grades from all of my classes. I display them for the following semester, use them actually, as teaching tools when I'm introducing concepts, and then the students get them back."

She'd stopped at the poster-board-sized colored pencil drawing showing exponential math through pictures. A big bear with three little bears to show the concept of something cubed. There were thirty drawings in all. The bottom one showed an entire equation complete with solution through children's pictures.

"This was a math education class, geared for art students who want to teach middle schoolers," he said. He was standing close to point out a couple of the students' impressive highlights and caught a sniff of… Something flowery. Deliciously so. And stepped back. Quickly. The arm that he'd had outstretched to point to a part of the drawing brushed against her breast in his haste.

His brain froze. Did he apologize? Draw attention to the flame she seemed to ignite within him? Or pretend it hadn't happened, that it was no big deal?

"What's this one?" She'd moved on to an abstract piece and he had to struggle to come up with the mathematical concept found within it. Throughout it.

His blunder was no big deal. He had to see that his reaction to her stayed that way.

No big deal.

Chapter Twelve

She had herself in check. Had almost forgotten her core purpose when she'd leaned in a little too close to Jamie as he was showing her math in abstract art and he'd brushed against her, but she'd moved away. Moved on. Kept her mind on the job at hand.

Giving Jamie and his unborn child exposure to each other, helping them build the bond that would last them a lifetime and beyond.

It didn't take a lot of effort. No heavy conversation or soul-searching required. Just being physically present with her belly in his space. She helped him hang and display all of the artwork on his shelf in less than half an hour.

"Wow, thanks," he said, standing back with her to

view the results. "Seriously, this would have taken me a couple of hours or more, and the results would not have been so aesthetically pleasing," he said.

She chuckled at his self-deprecatory tone. "Aesthetically pleasing?" she asked. "Doesn't sound like a Dr. Howe comment."

He'd been grinning, too, but his expression sobered at her words. "Emily said it a lot," he said, his mood noticeably changed. Subtly. But still noticeable. It was like a fan had been turned off. Leaving the air in the room stale.

Going to the desk at the front of the room, he gathered tape and nails, a hammer and some tacks together and locked them in a file cabinet in the corner.

"It's okay to talk about her, you know. In fact, I think it's best if you do." It's what she would tell any couple in her office, facing their situation. Along with telling him to seek counseling, except that she knew he'd already done so.

As had she. Before she'd signed on to be his surrogate. And she'd go back if she ever came up against a struggle she couldn't handle.

Half sitting on the corner of one of the student desks in the front row, Christine folded her arms and let him see the compassion she felt for him. As she did with most of her clients. Her compassion was what she had to give.

He faced her, his bottom half mostly hidden behind his desk. The light seemed to have dimmed in his expression and she wished life had been kinder to him.

Reminded herself that it was about to get much better, but harder, too, as he faced the challenges involved in raising a child alone.

He straightened. Nodded. Put his hands on his desk in front of him. Like he was ready to make a point.

"I'm struggling a bit here, unexpectedly," he said, looking her right in the eye. As though trying to impart a particular message. "I think it's only fair, given the unusual circumstances between us, that you know."

She nodded, too. "Yes. That's good. Talk it out. We knew this wasn't going to be easy. Only that for you it would be worth it." A thought occurred to her, along with a stab of horror that left as quickly as it came. Still… "You do still feel that way, don't you? That it's worth it? You want this baby, right?"

If not, there'd be a family that did, she reminded herself. Lists of couples with loving homes, waiting to fill them with children, were miles long.

The instant sense of protectiveness that had come over her regarding the baby inside her was not altogether new. But it was a not quite welcome regurgitation of days long past. If he didn't want the baby, could she think about keeping it?

Could she make herself give up a second child to strangers?

"Of course I want my baby!" Jamie's stern, wide-eyed expression, his commanding tone left her in no doubt as to the truth of his words. "I admit to experiencing some unexpected emotional ups and downs here, but none of them, not a single one, have anything to do with wanting that baby. I did. I do. I always will."

Good. She nodded. Okay then, they were fine.

"The struggle I was referring to has to do with you."

Not fine? They weren't done here. "Me? Am I doing something that displeases you? If so, you definitely need to speak up. That's why we have the contract, to protect both sides. If you have a problem…"

His head shake stopped her words.

"You aren't going to get something like this to fit neatly into a contract," he told her. "I'm just…you're carrying my child…you went from a virtual stranger to…the woman carrying my child. There are feelings involved with that…and…and… God, I feel like a first-class ass, and…"

She recognized guilt when she heard it. Her heart softened. Opened a bit more.

"Jamie. It's fine," she told him, wanting to help him feel better. "I promise you it's perfectly natural that you'd feel some resentment toward me. Emily, your wife, the woman you've loved since you were eight, should be carrying this child. Not me. You can't help but have a part of you resent that…"

There were some things you just couldn't fix. But you could make them more bearable by sitting with those who were suffering. Offering comfort.

"It's not resentment I'm feeling." He was still standing straight. The intensity of his gaze hadn't lessened in the least.

"It's not?"

"No."

Her mouth was dry. She no longer wanted to continue the conversation.

"I'm finding myself attracted to you," he said. "We hardly know each other. But...you're carrying my child. The most important part of me is inside you, dependent upon you, and...like I said, I'm a first-class ass."

She shook her head again, tried to shore up the walls around her feelings. "It's just a product of the situation," she told him. Knowing that, above all else, to keep things professional, ethical, safe, she could not allow her own feelings to come into the situation.

She'd be betraying his trust if she did so.

And if she acted unprofessionally, she could do damage to the clinic's reputation as well.

"A form of transference, and completely understandable," she said, with a little too much breathlessness for her liking, as the words came to her. "Certainly nothing to beat yourself up about," she added, finding strength from within to give them both a solid piece of advice.

"You're not an ass, Jamie. You're a decent man who's owned up to something that you could have just kept secret. Which makes this situation safer for both of us. What we're doing here is a beautiful thing, a miracle, really, but with every great thing there's a shadow side, too. By nature of all that's involved, pregnancy, even a planned and traditional one, generates a lot of varying emotion. Nothing's free. We'll get through this..."

The words were powerful. She felt them. Saw his face relax and allowed relief to flow through her as he grinned. Nodded.

"I'm sure you're right," he said as he turned off the office lights and locked the door behind him.

They walked silently, side by side, several inches between them, out to the parking lot.

He stopped by her car, and she turned to ask him when he wanted to meet again.

"I do see real truth in what you said," he told her, just inches away, his gaze locked with hers as though he had some otherworldly mesmerizing power. "But you are a beautiful woman, Christine. I'd notice you whether you were carrying my baby or not."

Notice her. Like he probably noticed most women of an appropriate age, as men did.

"Jamie..."

He held up a hand. "Don't worry, I'm not hitting on you. I'm just keeping it all out in the open, as you said."

He could have been hitting on her. They were alone in a deserted parking lot with the sun setting romantically behind them.

But he wasn't. She believed him. One hundred percent.

And that didn't stop her body from wishing that he had been.

That he could be.

That she could lean in and touch her lips to his.

But of course, she didn't say so.

She wasn't going to get weak and blow this.

Too much was at stake.

The next several days settled into a routine of sorts. Jamie ran every morning. Worked with his tennis team most afternoons during the week. Started two of his online classes. Drove up to the university in Mission Viejo to his campus office to attend meetings and prepare for classes there that were due to start after Labor Day. He had dinner with Tom a couple of times.

And had dinner with Axel and his mother, Sandra, once, too. She'd made steak tartare. Was a great cook. A good mother. And an immensely attractive woman who did absolutely nothing for him. He enjoyed the evening. Figured, when she said they'd do it again sometime, that he'd accept that invitation.

He didn't tell them, or anyone in his life other than Tom, that he was going to be a father. Things were still so new. So private. He wanted to savor the news for himself, not answer questions about the somewhat unusual choice he'd made.

Which meant that, other than the brief time spent with Tom, the only time he could really be himself, live the life that was coursing through him, was during his visits with Christine. With his baby.

They had them regularly in various locations and during different times of day, and he got through everything else on his schedule just to get to those visits. Christine had been right. Bringing out his attraction to her, naming it for the transference it was, made things much easier between them. They'd been to the grocery store once, just chatting as they walked up and down the aisles together with their own baskets, each doing their own shopping. When they both reached for the same box of bran cereal, they might have touched hands, but he saved them from the collision just in time. He let her have the first box and took the second for himself.

A couple of days later they met at a bagel shop midmorning, for a quick snack. She liked her bagels plain with butter. He was a cream cheese guy all the way.

The Sunday after her visit to his classroom, they took a walk on the beach. He'd hesitated before suggesting that particular outing. The beach was a constant in his life, a part of every day, which meant that it would play an important role in his child's life as well and should be familiar.

It was also the place where he felt closest to Emily.

A place he reserved in his mind for just the two of them.

Needing Emily to be as much a part of their baby's life as possible was what eventually convinced him to suggest that Christine join him there. She was attending a fundraising cruise later that day, but had agreed to meet him just after sunrise. In his running shorts, T-shirt and tennis shoes, he waited for her at the parking lot to the Marie Cove resident public beach entrance.

And glanced away when his body immediately reacted to the feminine thighs shaped softly by the black capri yoga pants she had on. The colorful midlength sport top that outlined a stomach still completely firm and flat didn't help.

With a flip-flop in each hand, she walked up barefoot to tell him hello.

Maybe he should have run first, so he'd be smelly and not feeling at all sexy when she met his gaze and smiled.

An easy smile.

An understanding one?

As soon as they were on the sand, it seemed suddenly mandatory that he tell Christine that he sometimes talked to his deceased wife as he ran.

"Did she run with you?"

"No," he said as he noticed a series of little bird tracks left in the sand. Something he didn't generally see as he ran. "She was always a bike rider. When we were in high school, she'd ride her bike and I'd run alongside her."

"You didn't like riding?"

"I did. I still do. We used to take day, and half-day rides. I just prefer running for daily exercise."

"I hate exercising."

The news kind of pleased him. Seemed to put more of a separation between the two of them in real life, as if the only things they had in common were bran cereal and the baby she was carrying for him.

"Which is why I play racquetball."

That was in the tennis family. He left the comment alone in his mind.

"So tell me about her," she said next, seeming to understand that Emily was the reason he'd suggested the outing. Understanding him with him saying so very little.

Twenty minutes later, after having regaled her with various memories that had popped into his mind—their first dance at their wedding when she'd started to cry because she was so happy to finally be married to him; the time they'd sneaked out of town to go on a date without anyone knowing they were together, only to run into another judge who worked with her father; the entire Saturday they'd spent decorating Christmas cookies with his mother—he wasn't feeling any closer to Emily.

Christine was still there with him, though, his awareness of her a palpable thing.

"I looked you and Emily up in the high school yearbook," she said softly. "I don't remember either one of you from when I was in school, but it's clear she was pretty popular."

"Everyone loved her." And she'd chosen him. "But that's because she was so easy to like. Emily was just one of those people who was comfortable in her own skin and so made others so. She had a way of taking things in stride, seeing the best in people."

He was making her sound like a saint. In her own way, she had been. He'd loved her deeply. And maybe he'd wished that she'd been a little less easygoing when it came to her time. To always being ready to help out, leaving them so little time alone together. Or so it had seemed to him.

"So why did you need to sneak out of town to go on a date?"

He shrugged. Kicked up some sand with his tennis shoe. Noticed Christine's bare toes. He couldn't picture Emily's. Wasn't sure he'd ever noticed them. Knew for certain he'd never found them the least bit sexy.

What was sexy about toes?

Maybe it was the red polish.

A date. She'd asked about why he and Emily

had kept their relationship a secret. Seemed so long ago—a completely different world. When in reality, the two of them had shared their first kiss right on that same beach.

"There were people who thought that I wasn't good enough for Emily. This town…with all its Beverly Hills types…her father being a judge…the country club…she was raised in that world, vacationed with those families, spent weekends on yachts. Had a full ride to college before she was born. I lived in a two-bedroom house across town from the beach, would only get to college on student loans, if then, and the only vacations we took were when we went camping." He told it like it was.

"And somehow you say that without sounding like a victim. Or sorry for yourself."

"Because I don't." The response was immediate. "I might not have grown up with monetary riches, but I never doubted that my life was filled with wealth."

"Even though your dad was sick?" she asked.

For a second there he'd forgotten that he'd told her about the emergency room visit when he was eight. The day he'd met Emily.

"He was my dad. We played sports together. He taught me how to catch fish. Did everything other families around us did. His kidney problem was just something that he dealt with. It wasn't like it defined him or our family. He wouldn't let it slow him down—other than the times he was in renal failure, and even then, he was always certain he'd be fine and wanted to know everything that was going on with me. Keeping track of things. Holding me accountable. Encouraging me. I never felt like he wasn't there for me. He lived his life, rather than making a life out of being sick. He did what he wanted to do, almost until the day he died."

"He sounds like a great guy." The words could have been placating. Polite. Instead, they sounded wistful, like she was sorry she hadn't gotten to know him.

"Emily was kind of uncomfortable around him." He was surprised to hear the words come out of his mouth. Hadn't even been aware of thinking them.

"Why?" Christine didn't look over at him. Or sound judgmental. She'd been watching the sand pretty much since they'd stepped out on it.

Looking for treasure? Or for hidden pitfalls to avoid with bare skin?

He didn't have an answer. Wasn't even sure why he'd made the statement. "I think she just felt so sorry for him. Her dad was so larger than life and mine…spent months at a time getting healthy enough to just go camping again."

"I think that makes him larger than life," Christine said softly. "He certainly lived larger than most would have with his life."

She hadn't stepped any nearer to him. He hadn't moved over, either.

And yet Jamie felt closer to her than ever before.

Chapter Thirteen

She'd wanted to kiss him. They'd been standing there on the beach and she'd almost leaned in… knowing that, Christine should not have taken pity on Jamie, with all the packing he had to do. He was a big boy. Could tape and load boxes. There'd been no reason for her offer to help him. Christine knew, as soon as she'd heard herself make the offer as they left each other at their vehicles on Sunday, that she'd been out of line. Which was why she cringed when she saw Olivia's name come up on her caller ID the following Tuesday just as she was walking in the door from work. She had ten minutes to change into shorts and a T-shirt and get back out the door. Jamie was bringing enchiladas home for them to share before they got busy.

And Olivia would be calling to ask Christine to stand in for her that night at the center.

Olivia knew she could count on Christine as backup. And vice versa. More often the former, since Christine's job didn't often involve life and death emergencies.

"Hey there!" she answered with forced cheer. "What's up?"

"What's wrong?"

"Nothing. Just in a hurry to get changed." She didn't have to say why. She was busy. Olivia was busy. They didn't report in to each other with every move they made. Which was partially why they worked so well as friends.

"I'm rushing, too. I'm standing in for Mary in the kitchen before card class, but I just wanted to tell you, I saw Judge Sanders when I was at the country club for lunch today. Someone said the hottie he was with was his son-in-law."

"You saw Jamie?" Dr. Howe, dammit. Whatever she called him in private, to everyone else she knew him as Dr. Howe.

"Jamie?" Olivia said the word slowly. "You're calling a business associate, Dr. Jamison Howe, Jamie? Christine, what are you doing?"

"He's going to be in my hip pocket for the next

eight months," she reminded. "Coming to my doctor's appointments. He asked me to call him Jamie."

The pause made her uncomfortable. "You're sure this is a good idea? Spending so much time with the guy."

They'd already been through that particular discussion to the satisfaction of both of them, she'd thought. Which had helped her calm down over her growing feelings for Jamie.

"You were the one who confirmed that studies showed that babies could hear in utero. And that bonding with the father was particularly beneficial in this case."

"I know. And as a doctor, I do believe it's important. As your friend...hearing the way you just said his name... I just don't want you to get hurt."

She didn't want to get hurt, either. "My walls are up and fortified," she assured her friend. "Besides, you know me. I'm not looking for a relationship. Don't even want one. And guys like Jamie...they're made for them. I need my independence. My freedom to work twelve-hour days and spend time at the center and have drinks with you..."

No need to discuss the fact that she had the hots for her client/employer. Or that he'd told her he was attracted to her. She'd had hormone shots before she'd conceived. And now that she was pregnant, her body was producing more of them. That explained her increased libido. Just like the transference that he was suffering from.

None of it was real.

They just had to keep their eyes on the bigger picture.

"Welcome to the mess," Jamie greeted her, holding what looked like a piece of framed wall art, as he pulled open the front door at the address he'd given her. "Dinner's on warm in the oven, so we can eat first and then pack, or do some packing first."

In navy running shorts and a T-shirt, framed by cathedral ceilings and an expensive-looking light brown leather couch and love seat behind him, the man looked…melt her insides gorgeous.

"Let's do some packing first," she said in spite of the fact that she was kind of hungry. It was best to stay busy during the time she brought his baby visiting. And most important that she be occupied at that moment. Stepping into his home, even with things out of place and boxes lining one wall, gave her a much more personal sense of him.

She was already carrying his baby. She didn't need to get any more personal. "You said you were most intimidated by the china and glassware, so why don't I start in the kitchen?"

He'd mentioned his packing woes as they'd parted ways at their cars at the beach on Sunday. "Actually,

I was hoping you'd help me out in the bedroom," he said.

Her gaze flew toward his, eyes open wide, heart pounding. He'd already turned away, was settling the frame in his hand, backside out, against a wall. "The closet and drawers are filled with Emily's things," he said. "I had no idea what to do with them and it was just easier to leave them where they were, but you've mentioned this women's center you volunteer at. I like that the people in need earn spending dollars by taking classes to better themselves, and then spend them in the center's shop for things they need. I'd like you to take a look at Emily's things and see if you think women at the center can use them."

How a heart could change gears so quickly, she didn't know, but Christine was no longer suffering from inappropriate sexual needs. Instead, she'd just grown a little fonder of the man inside that incredible body as she followed him up the open staircase.

"You sure you want me in here, doing this?" Christine stood in Emily's walk-in closet, directly across the little hallway from the closed door of his identical in design clothes storage room. His was a bit less packed. The hallway, of sorts, was a small walkway of tile between the master bedroom and the attached huge room that had two full vanities with sinks and mirrors on opposite sides, with a garden tub and separate double shower. Another door led off to a small room that set the toilet off from the rest of the suite.

It had all been a bit much for him when they moved in. Who needed so much wasted floor space in the middle of a bathroom? It did nothing but hold a rug and collect hair. It wasn't like you were ever going to plop down there and play a game or watch TV.

But you could dance there with your wife… The memory came and he let it wash over him. The day he and Emily had first looked at the house, he'd told her straight out he didn't like it, had complained about the waste of square footage in the master bath. She'd pulled him against her right there in the middle of the room, pressing her hips against his and starting to sway. Humming the song they'd danced their first dance to the night of their wedding.

He hadn't been all that fond of the song, either. But she'd loved it.

And he'd loved her…

"Hey, do you want…" Christine's voice was muffled and then not as she came out of the closet. "What's wrong?"

He shook his head. Glanced at her and felt the melancholy fade. "Nothing. Just thinking about how much there is to do…"

"If you aren't ready to get rid of her things, just say so, Jamie. We can pack them up and you can store them…"

Because to hang them in the new house would just be weird.

Thing was, he didn't even want to.

He was ready to get rid of them.

And felt like crap for feeling that way.

Moving on from grief was not for lightweights.

"I'm ready," he told her. And added, "I wasn't, but I am now."

Standing in the doorway of the closet, he watched as Christine moved hangers along one wall of clothes. "These are some really nice things," she said. "You sure there's no one you know who wants them?"

He shook his head. "Emily and I…kind of lost touch with our friends after the accident. People cared, they stopped by, but it wasn't like we could do much. And after she died…a couple of her closest friends offered to help me clear out her stuff, but… I didn't want them around. I know that sounds awful, but their pity…and their grief… I didn't want the first and didn't know how to handle the second."

It seemed so long ago now. A different lifetime.

"Is there anything here that you want to keep? Anything that means something special to you?"

It all meant something special. Even the shirts he couldn't really even remember her wearing. He'd saved a few items, all of the good jewelry, her wedding dress, in case he had a girl who would want it. Or a son whose wife might. Maybe even a granddaughter someday…

"Please, take it all. It would make me feel good to know that other women are taking pleasure from it," he told her. "I know it would make Emily happy. The shoes, belts, costume jewelry, anything you think they'd appreciate and use." He grabbed a box. Started taping one end.

He wanted it gone.

He had their baby on the way. Would always love and honor her as the mother in their little family. And as his best friend and soul mate.

But the daily living, with Emily first in his thoughts—that was done.

He was letting go.

On Friday of that week, four weeks after implantation, Christine had another appointment with the fertility specialist. She'd be followed by both Dr. Adams and her ob-gyn until twelve weeks or so, when the former passed off all care to the latter. Until then, the two were consulting with each other.

Christine liked Dr. Adams quite well. She just wasn't as familiar with her and wasn't quite as relaxed as she'd liked to have been when her name was called. Jamie was going to get his first glimpse of his baby with an early ultrasound—something Dr. Adams always did at four weeks after implantation—and Christine had purposely chosen the primary colored flowered skirt and short-sleeved yellow cotton top on purpose because of the elastic waistband and ease of raising the shirt. And maybe, just maybe she'd chosen the outfit because Jamie was going to be there and she felt like she looked good in it. She hoped not, but couldn't deny that she'd wanted to feel good about herself.

And he'd be the most likely reason. The ultrasound technician sure wasn't going to care.

Jamie, who looked too—everything—in his tan pants and black short-sleeved shirt, stood as soon as she did.

He walked just behind her as she followed the technician down the hall and into a fairly large shadowed room. This was it.

Visual proof that there was actually a little body forming inside her. Hopefully confirmation that, so far at least, it was growing as expected. Was healthy.

And then came that moment when she had to get up on a table and have her belly bared down to her pubic hair while Jamie was watching.

Not the way she'd like to be getting partially naked with the man. Or have him see her naked.

But the only way that it was ever going to happen.

She wanted to be relieved about that.

Jamie's first glance of Christine's belly exposed on the examining table might have been a bit of a struggle for him to get through, except that he couldn't really see her. Not her belly. If he leaned slightly, he could see her face. The technician, Danielle she'd said her name was, had positioned him in the best place to see the monitor, and it happened to be right behind her, the technician, who mostly blocked his view of Christine.

She talked to them about the coolness of the gel, about the process, and then said, "Let's see what we've got," in an almost singsong voice.

Heart pounding, he stared at the screen. Hard. Saw shadows, some much lighter than others. He'd seen sonograms on television, had seen one that friends of his and Emily's had shown around a few years before when they'd been expecting their first child.

He'd looked at some pictures during his reading over the past few months.

But this wasn't like any of that. The screen in front of him—that wasn't just a picture. It was his life. More valuable than his life, though.

"Here we are," Danielle said, seeming to direct her words over her shoulder to Jamie, not to Christine who, other than saying she was fine, hadn't spoken a word. He glanced at her face. She was lying there with her eyes closed.

Not looking at the screen.

Not sharing the moment.

"This is your baby," Danielle said, pointing to the screen. He could barely make out the form that outlined the baby, but he got there. Stared. Could hardly believe it.

When he looked closely, he could actually make out a head. A torso. The beginnings of a human being. And it hit him so hard he lost the air from his lungs.

He was going to be a father.

A real, flesh and blood father.

He glanced from the screen to Christine, needing her to know how much her gift meant to him. He'd never be able to thank her enough. To repay her.

Her eyes were still closed, but he thought he saw a tear slide down the side of her cheek. He could have been wrong. The room was illuminated only by under cabinet lighting above the counter along one wall. He hoped he was wrong.

The last thing he wanted was for his future joy to be causing her pain.

Clearly Danielle had been told that the baby wasn't Christine's. That she was only the surrogate. The woman had been completely respectful and attentive to Christine's physical comfort, but she'd placed the monitor so that Jamie could see it clearly. Christine would have had to turn her head over and up to see.

She discreetly thanked the technician as they left the room less than ten minutes from the time they'd entered. Jamie already had a strip of printed photos in hand. She could see them if she looked.

She didn't.

She'd prepared herself to feel the baby kick inside her. To care about it and then, as soon as it left her body, to move on down the road.

For some ungodly reason, she'd failed to think about how watching the miracle of its growth would affect her. She'd only had one ultrasound with Ryder.

She'd stared at that photo for hours, slept with it under her pillow, carried it in her purse, all those weeks she'd thought she would be keeping her baby.

And when she'd made the difficult decision to give him up, she'd put the photo away, upstairs in a trunk in the attic, and had never looked at it again.

"Right in here," Danielle said, leading them to an opened door leading into an office with a big messy desk and two chairs directly in front of it, telling them to have a seat.

She didn't want to have a seat. Not in the enclosed space, alone with Jamie. She just needed a minute or two by herself. To breathe and distract her mind from things she couldn't change and guide it to that which made her happy. Her work. The clients at The Parent Portal. The lives of the healthy children she'd helped others bring into the world. The families her work helped create. Picturing the bulletin board filled with their pictures on a sidewall in her home office, she took the seat closest to the door.

And talked about the fact that it looked like it was going to rain. There was a window in the room. She focused on the sky and tree limbs she could see beyond it.

Dr. Adams didn't keep them long. She didn't have a lot to say, other than that everything looked pretty good. She was a little concerned about the lining of Christine's uterus, wasn't sure it was thickening as much as she'd like. Said she wanted them back for another ultrasound in a month and said that while there was absolutely no worry, she might put Christine on progesterone shots as the pregnancy progressed.

"I don't understand," Christine said, sitting up straight. "I had no problems whatsoever when I carried my son. I'm older now, but still well within healthy childbearing years..."

She was making too much of a small thing. She knew it even as she said the words. This whole thing was hard enough, though, without finding out that there was something lacking in her.

Dr. Adams smiled, shaking her head. "If you'd conceived naturally I suspect there'd be no issue," she said. "And there might not be one at all. If this were a natural conception, I wouldn't even be concerned. But we see this sometimes when we're dealing with implantation. The surrogate's body doesn't produce the hormone quite as profusely as it might normally do. It's just something we watch."

She nodded. Feeling like she was going to cry anyway. She'd never even considered the fact that she might not be good enough to get this job done. This was what she had to give. She'd damn well get it right.

"The progesterone has no negative effect on the fetus," Dr. Adams explained, "although in rare cases, if the baby's a boy, he could have one of the most common birth defects we see. It has to do with his urethra placement, but even if that were to happen, it's generally easily treated with no adverse effects."

"And the side effects for Christine?"

"The injections themselves can be painful. There might be discomfort at the site. But otherwise there are no negative effects."

"And if she needed the injections and didn't have them?" Jamie asked.

Christine felt his glance on her, but couldn't look at him. She really just wanted to get out of there. Get herself together. Hit some balls against the wall until she was her normal self.

"Then you risk her losing the baby."

"Well, that's not going to happen," she said. "Not if I can help it."

She nodded. She'd already been given progesterone before the implantation. "So, are we done here?" she asked, looking from the doctor to Jamie. "Or, at least, done with me?"

The doctor nodded. Jamie stood.

And Christine got the hell out of there.

Chapter Fourteen

Jamie wasn't all that surprised when he walked out into an empty waiting room. Christine wasn't in the parking lot, either. Nor was her car.

Disappointment settled around his edges at a time when he should be flying to the moon. Or, at least, be fully focused on the family he was making. Feeling a bit bittersweet was understandable, probably even healthy, considering that his wife wasn't there physically to share the experience with him.

Feeling let down because his surrogate wasn't sharing the moment could not be healthy. He needed her to have her own life. Because he expected her to deliver the baby and hand it to him.

She'd been right to leave.

The reminder of who and what they were to one another had been a kindness.

He went to Mission Viejo, sat in his office on campus and met with a few students, individually, who were in town prior to classes starting and needed to discuss their academic futures with him. Thought about calling his mother and letting her know she was going to be a grandma, but wanted to wait until they'd surpassed the three-month mark. Between one in four and one in ten natural pregnancies, or 10 to 25 percent, resulted in miscarriage. And more than 80 percent of the lost pregnancies occurred within the first twelve weeks. Some authorities said those risks increased with implantation.

He'd done his reading.

And needed the stats to back up the material. He made sense of his world through numbers.

And, perhaps, numbers failed to consider key factors that could leave him with less than expected.

The thought shot through him as he was on the freeway home to Marie Cove. Emily had often teased him, laughed with him, about the spaces she filled up for him. Like their first dance at their wedding. He hadn't given a single thought to a song he'd like for that dance. It just hadn't factored in to his thoughts concerning that day.

He'd wanted to be married and be done.

He had wanted to celebrate. The wedding just hadn't seemed like some humongous, life-changing moment to him but rather a continuation of a life that they'd already been living, another milestone on the road they'd been traveling since they were kids.

And then there was the time he'd been in a car accident and hadn't called her right away. His vehicle was totaled, but he and everyone else involved, including the young kid at fault, were fine. She hadn't laughed about that one. She'd been truly upset with him, telling him his calm was a wonderful asset most times, but there were moments that required more. She hadn't been able to fill the gap in his emotional maturity for him that time. She'd fallen into it.

So was Christine Elliott doing the same? Had he pushed this whole baby thing, certain of his "life" calculations, without considering key factors? The things you couldn't measure?

Like love? Sacrifice? Pain?

He'd asked a woman who spent her life caring for others and helping them have the families they wanted, to grow and protect his child, without considering the emotional ramifications to her. Not that she couldn't take care of herself, but he should have taken Christine's well-being into account…

And he hadn't given nearly enough weight to the physical impact it would have on her. The energy it would take to carry around all the extra weight every second of every day. Weekly injections that would not only be uncomfortable to receive, but left discomfort in their trails. The birth.

Why those possible shots brought it all home to him, he didn't know. Maybe it was the reality of having seen the baby inside of her. The concrete proof that there was more than just a flat stomach going on in Christine's midsection.

The almost panicked way she'd left the doctor's office…

As soon as he was back in town, he went straight to her office. Told she was at the racquetball court, he drove there.

He texted her. Let her know he was outside. Would have left immediately if she'd asked him to do so. When she sent back You up for a game instead, he quickly grabbed his bag out of the back of his vehicle and headed inside to the locker room.

The silver shorts and black T-shirt were clean. He changed out the contents of the bag every night—part of his bedtime ritual. He was at the door to her court in five. Planning to go easy on her—and his baby—he hoped to find a way to apologize for his lack of more thorough emotional forethought where their situation was concerned. And to talk to her about the injections.

Just because he took things calmly didn't mean others were capable of the same. It had taken Emily a long time to help him see that one can't choose which emotions to feel.

How one deals with those emotions is their choice.

The first sight of Christine in black spandex shorts

and a purple, close-fitting T-shirt sent a slew of feelings raging right down to his crotch.

He knew what to do with them. Wasn't sure telling them to be gone was enough. Ignoring them helped. Nothing really worked.

He still wanted her.

"You serve," she said, tossing him the little rubber ball and grabbing an extra paddle out of a bright yellow duffel bag in the back corner.

He did. Lightly. Barely giving effort to his movement.

And was promptly scored upon.

So noted. He'd give his attempt a bit more oomph. Racquetball required finesse. And physical effort. But not the strength he used to serve an ace out on the tennis court.

By the fourth serve, he was using every bit of strength he used when he was playing to win on the tennis court. Neither of them had said a word, other than to announce score. Christine didn't run all over the room. For the most part, she hardly moved, other than with her upper body. She just commanded the room from where she stood. Knew exactly how and where to place the ball, with how much punch, in order to make it hardest for him to return.

She didn't move, but she had him running all over.

By the second game, he'd caught on. Paid attention to strategy. Power. Placement. He still lost, but this game was a lot closer.

And then, when he was gearing up for the best three out of five, she stopped. "That's it for me," she said. "I'm giving myself an easy hour or a hard half hour," she said. "I'm not going to overdo it." Hardly sweating, she approached him, took his racquet and grinned at him. "I'm pregnant, you know."

His penis hardened at the sight of that grin. Thank God for loose T-shirts. And the support of boxer briefs.

As her gaze met his, he grew serious. "I wanted to see you, to let you know, seriously, that I don't just expect you to do the injections as a precaution. Obviously, if the baby's life is seriously at risk, I'll ask for them, but your comfort, both emotionally and physically, are equally important, Christine. You're a person, not a machine. You matter, and your well-being counts as much as anyone's."

He'd repeated the words in his brain all the way home from the university. By the time he'd given them voice, they sounded rehearsed. Not sincere.

The whole point in seeing her, rather than calling, was so that she could see how much he meant what he said.

"It's all in the contract, Jamie," she told him, sandwiching his racquet together with hers and putting them, and the ball, in her bag—her backside in full view as she bent over.

Wrong of him to notice. He cleared his throat. Turned a bit. "I'm not talking about the contract," he said. "I'm talking about two people, you and me. And I'm telling you, I'm not going to hold you to sentences in a contract that give me the right to decide matters like these—choices that don't affect your health, but could affect the baby's. The injections won't affect your health, according to Dr. Adams, but they'll affect your physical comfort. I'm telling you that we will consider together whether or not you do them."

Turning, her bag strap on her shoulder, with one foot propped up behind her, she leaned against the wall. Her short dark hair was mussed, looked windblown and far too sexy.

It also made him want to wrap his arms around her and protect her from anything in the world that might cause her pain.

Like what—he was some he-man of old and she was a damsel in distress? The idea almost made him laugh inside. He'd never been one of those guys that had to prove their masculinity by thinking there were others who were weaker than him. And Christine would never resemble a damsel in distress. Or any other kind of person who couldn't take care of herself just fine.

"I appreciate your consideration," she said, after watching him for a moment. "It's nice," she said. "Really nice. And noted."

He heard a "but" coming and waited for it.

"If something comes up that becomes an issue,

then I hope you'll still feel the same," she said. "But the injections won't be an issue, either way," she told him, her expression easy. Calm. "If I need them, I'll do them. It's not a big deal."

Painful injections on, at minimum, a weekly basis? Okay, so it wasn't peeling off skin or anything, but…

"They won't be nearly as painful as giving birth," she told him, with a cock of her head. Reminding him that she knew what she was talking about.

He'd never witnessed a birth live. She'd done more than that.

"It'll be an extra minute out of my day once a week," she said.

She'd been so upset in Dr. Adams's office that morning. But it apparently hadn't been about the injections. Maybe he'd known that from the beginning. Maybe he just wasn't sure how to talk about the emotional pain being pregnant seemed to have been causing her that morning.

Maybe he'd been wrong about that tear he'd seen.

And her abrupt departure from their appointment?

"More than a minute. You'll need to make weekly trips to the doctor's office and…"

She was shaking her head.

"Progesterone shots can be given in the thigh. I can do that myself."

He shook his head. Sure, some diabetics and others learned how to give themselves injections, but it took time. He'd watched his father's struggle when he'd had to do at-home injections. He knew this one. "You'd have to learn how to..."

Her headshake back interrupted him. "Enough already, Jamie. I knew what I was doing when I signed the contract and I'm fine. I'm a pro at giving injections," she said. "I've been doing them since I was in junior high. My grandmother was diabetic," she said. "I spent all of my junior high and high school years coming home for lunch to give her her shots. She said Gramps hurt too much when he gave them and she had a needle paranoia and couldn't give them to herself. Her hands weren't really steady enough, either."

"You left school every day?" He stood there, wanting to stay and chat for as long as she'd allow it. "You never had lunch with your friends?"

Shrugging, she said, "I had great lunches. Gram was a phenomenal cook, and she always had something good waiting for me."

He wanted to say more about how she'd missed out on some of the most important teenage socialization time, but knew that no good would come from pointing that out. Realized, too, that she'd know more than he what she'd sacrificed. "Maybe that's why I don't remember you from high school," he said. "Emily and I looked you up in our junior and senior yearbooks, and neither of us recognized you."

"I was two years younger, not in any of your classes."

"And never in the cafeteria," he said, beginning to understand a bit more who Christine Elliott really was. A woman who'd been sacrificing herself seemingly most of her life, to tend to others.

He didn't like being one of those using her to find his own happiness.

Who tended to her beside Christine herself?

Who sacrificed for *her*?

Jamie didn't like questions without answers.

Problems without solutions.

But he sure as hell liked her.

Too much.

Chapter Fifteen

The next seven weeks settled into a routine that transitioned to a sense of normality. Christine lived her life as she had before impregnation: working, volunteering, spending a couple of evenings a week at the center, having dinner out with friends. Racquetball changed from focusing on rigor to precision. And her diet changed a bit, with the addition of vitamins and the omission of foods she used to like but suddenly had no taste for, plus those she could no longer eat. Tuna was first on her list of foods no longer welcome anywhere near her. The smell made her nauseous, exactly as it had the first time she'd had a baby—and that was the extent of any signs of morning sickness. Just like back then.

So many similarities. Right down to giving up the child at the end of the pregnancy. She'd done it before. She could do it again. And it should hurt less this time. The baby wasn't biologically hers; she knew it was going to a loving home. And she had the chance to see it if she wanted to.

Her clothes were getting a little tighter, and her stomach developing a paunch so slight most wouldn't even notice.

Olivia continued to be her dear heart. It was like the pregnancy was drawing them closer. The pediatrician was in clear support of her "project" but was focused on Christine's emotional well-being more than anything.

The biggest change in her life, though, was the few times a week she met up with Jamie Howe. They'd have a bagel downtown, meet up at a big box store if they both had shopping to do. A couple of times he filled her car at a gas station, saying that this was part of her living expenses. She'd argued, telling him that she was receiving a monthly stipend that covered those, but gave in when he agreed to only catch a few of the tanks full along the way, because of the extra driving she was doing to meet him.

He'd been to her house once, to interview a plumber with her because it was someone she didn't know, but whose bid had been the most economical, and with her pregnant he hadn't wanted her alone in the house with a stranger, but he'd left almost as soon as the plumber had. They'd agreed with a look and a mutual shake of the head that she wasn't going to hire the guy. Sometimes the lowest bid wouldn't be the cheapest way to get the job done in the long run.

The sale on his house had closed, but a week before he was to give up vacancy, thirty days after closing, the inspection on the home he was purchasing came back with possible foundation problems. His old home's new owners had made a deal to allow him to stay put, renting the house for two months, while possible repairs were completed. She'd been with him to meet the inspector at the new house only because they'd gone three days without seeing each other and that was the only time they both had free.

She'd taken the baby to see his or her new home. To hear Daddy's voice. Jamie didn't have to be speaking with her to make that happen. She only needed to be near.

Their arrangement could be considered a bit overkill. She got that. And yet, with current studies showing how much a baby could be affected by environment in utero, she wanted to give Jamie every chance to bond with his child.

They tended to do things where there was no chance for a lot of personal conversation, and instead they ended up discussing how their days had gone, how his math as a way of art design classes had overfilled and he'd agreed to open one more to take up the slack. They kept a professional boundary between them, separating them at all times.

And that was good.

When Jamie called the Sunday morning before their twelve-week ultrasound appointment the upcoming Friday, inviting her to lunch at the country club, Christine balked for the first time.

"You really think that's a good idea?" she asked him. "I mean, downtown, anywhere we're out and about, we're going to be seen together, but at the country club...that's your tribe. You'll know pretty much everyone and..."

It just seemed awkward to her.

"I spend a lot of time there, and we've never been. The baby's going to be growing up there. And...they have a phenomenal Sunday brunch. We used to go every week. It was like a thing. You'd see a lot of the same people. I've been avoiding it since Emily died and figured that now would be a good time to get back out there. In another week, I'm going to start telling people that I'm going to be a father," he said. "My employers. My associates. Friends. My mother and stepdad. It's not like I'm just going to start showing up in everyone's lives with a baby in tow, like it appeared in the night by immaculate conception."

She'd wondered how he was going to handle that. But...

"A lot of these people are going to hear through the grapevine, Christine. I'd like them to see that

I'm out, I'm fine. To have a heads-up, sort of, before they hear the news."

"I just…don't want people to think that you and I…that we…"

The thought of people seeing them together and thinking they were a couple… Assuming they were…

She and Jamie had been out and about for weeks. She'd never worried about what people thought. Those who knew her knew what she was doing.

So why did she suddenly think it mattered what people thought?

She didn't know what she was thinking. Just…the country club…the sense that everyone knew everyone…the gossip of powerful people…

The idea that what they'd think wasn't true and that she didn't want them to know it wasn't…

Because she *wanted* it to be true?

She gave her head a vigorous shake.

"How about if I introduce you as a business associate?" he asked. "Then people won't try to make us out to be more than we are."

Maybe. It could work.

But the country club…

She'd been there for business purposes before. In a group, not one-on-one. Those tables for two—they'd always seemed so romantic to her. People living a life she'd never have—not because of the cost, but because she wasn't going to be part of a couple.

It was a life she didn't want.

Those couples at those tables, they'd seemed so intimate. Letting themselves be seen out together in a room filled with their peers. Not just with patrons, but with people who knew them. Like they were making some kind of announcement.

She had no real reason to object. But felt pressure closing in on her. Because when she pictured herself with Jamie at the country club, she'd suddenly wanted to be there as herself.

Not as the body carrying his child.

And that was all wrong.

As it turned out, it wasn't just her and Jamie out for lunch, and they weren't at a table for two. Christine chided herself as she sat down at a table for five and was introduced to Tom, Judge Tom Sanders; his lawyer and close friend, Michael Waterson; and Jamie's lawyer, Tanya Brennan. In her brightly colored floral sundress and red sandals, she felt a bit foolish for the extra attention she'd given to makeup and matching jewelry, thinking that she was going to be on display at a table for two.

"I hope you don't mind joining the others," Jamie had said quietly to her as he'd walked her toward them from the parking lot where he'd been waiting for her. It wasn't like she was a member of the club and could walk right in like the rest of them. She could be if she wanted to be. She could use her mother's inheritance for her own aggrandizement. She just didn't want to. "Tanya and Michael work in the same firm and were having lunch with Tom. When he saw me in the parking lot, he was delighted I'd rejoined Sunday brunch and invited us to join them."

"It's fine," she said, had to say, really. Reminding herself that these get-togethers with Jamie were at his pleasure, part of the contract, allowing his baby to become familiar with sounds from the life he or she would be living. Part of why he was paying her such a hefty sum.

Yes, she had a say in the when and where. She didn't just have to show up wherever or whenever he told her to. But, she did have to agree to show up on a regular basis. His money guaranteed her cooperation.

She'd kind of lost sight of the funds along the way. Because, other than living expenses, she wasn't spending any of it until she'd passed the first trimester. She wasn't just being a good Samaritan, helping him out. She'd been hired to do a job.

And that job didn't entail noticing how delicious he looked in long, very nicely fitting tan pants and a brown polo shirt that hugged his biceps. Nor did it entail the peek at his butt when he moved in front of her to greet the people at the table. She hadn't meant to do that. He'd just leaned right when she'd been assessing seating arrangements and there he'd been. In her line of vision.

It didn't take her long to figure out that Judge Sanders's personal lawyer, Michael, and he had lunch often. While it wasn't clear to Christine why Tanya, Jamie's surrogacy attorney, was having lunch with the judge and Michael, she figured it wasn't her business.

Until, five minutes after they'd all made polite introductions and ordered beverages to accompany the three-room, sumptuous brunch buffet, Judge Sanders, instead of heading toward the food as their waitress had suggested, looked across at Jamie and Christine, who were sitting side by side—with Michael next to Jamie and Tanya next to Christine.

"I asked Michael to do some research for me, and he sought Tanya's expertise as well," he said, somehow looking as powerful as if he'd been in a robe and up on his bench, even in a light green polo shirt and white pants. "They're about to tell me what they found out, and I figured, since you two are here, you might as well hear it as well." He glanced from her to Jamie. "That way if we have any action to take, we can be in agreement on what it should be."

She didn't want lunch. Or the juice she'd just ordered. "Do I need my lawyer here?" she asked, glancing at Tanya and Michael, too.

"Not at this point," Tanya said. "May I?" She looked to Michael, who nodded and then at the judge, who also gave his okay with a lift of his hand.

"The judge was concerned about his rights to the

baby, in the event that something ever happens to Dr. Howe," she said, smiling toward Jamie.

He smiled back. Not a sexy smile. A polite one. And she was reminded that they knew each other. That they'd worked together on the contract that bound him to Christine. Them against her, if there was ever a legal battle between them. A need to enforce the contract.

Shards of jealousy shot through her, shocking her. Christine didn't *get* jealous. Found the emotion a complete waste of time. Counterproductive to... productivity.

"Isn't it a conflict of interest for you to be advising the judge and Dr. Howe at the same time?" she asked. Because she was feeling stupidly defensive.

Stupidly wanting to put some kind of distance between Jamie and this...this...perfect woman. His professional equal. Which could matter a lot to him, being a college professor and holding a doctorate like he did. Her little master's degree in health management suddenly seemed less significant.

Which was ludicrous. She knew it even as she acknowledged the strong and completely unfamiliar negative emotions passing through her.

What in the hell was wrong with her?

The only answer that made any sense was hormones.

The seconds it took her to come up with an explanation she could live with had her missing the first bit of Tanya's reply.

She checked back in at, "Since I'm not in any way representing the judge, just reporting what I know about this particular area of the law, and because Dr. Howe knew when he sought out our firm that we represent Judge Sanders, it's within my legal jurisdiction to have the conversation. I'm not in any way reporting any parts of Dr. Howe's agreements, contracts, or dealings with our firm to the judge. Only giving general information regarding the law."

Wow. The woman had that down. Christine nodded, feeling stupid for having asked the question. After all, they were sitting with a superior court judge. But as the surrogate, she knew she was within her rights to question legalities.

"The bottom line is that California law states that grandparents have the rights to visitation of their grandchildren if certain requirements have been met. One is that the grandparent would need to show that there is an existing bond between the child and the grandparent. It would be up to you, Dr. Howe, to provide Judge Sanders with that opportunity..."

"I included Tom in this process before I'd even consulted Christine," Jamie said, looking to Tom and between the lawyers. "Of course he's going to have a bond with my child."

Tanya nodded. "Again, I'm not here to advise on particular circumstances, just to give you generalities in terms of the law, and I'm trying to lay them out in as clear a way as possible so that there are no surprises."

She was covering her own backside, Christine thought. And was ashamed of herself. The other woman was doing her job. Well.

And with compassion.

Feeling surreal, sitting there in that situation without forewarning, Christine tried to rein in emotions gone haywire. To find her zen.

"Excuse me," the judge spoke up, glancing at Christine. "Please understand, I didn't foresee this meeting happening with you sitting here, though I'm glad that you are here so we can all be on the same page. I want you to know that I am immensely grateful to you for giving of yourself so unselfishly and making it possible for our family to grow." It was the first time he'd looked in her direction since he'd said a quick hello and briefly shaken her hand during introductions. "I'm also a lawyer, and a judge who's seen all kinds of things in my courtrooms over the years. But never surrogacy. I can read the law. I wanted to know current surrogacy case law…"

"You're fine," Christine said. "I'm just having lunch per my surrogacy contract." She could feel Jamie's eyes on her. Found a professional smile and pasted it on.

"Surely you don't think I'd ever deny you rights to

your grandchild," Jamie stated, his gaze compassionate, not angry, as it moved to his former father-in-law.

"Of course I don't," the judge said, patting Jamie's hand where it lay on the table. "You're as much a son to me as Emily was a daughter—you know that."

Already feeling like an interloper, Christine hadn't thought it could get any worse. But there it was, taking everything she had to stay seated at the table.

Even while knowing that no one had said anything designed to make her feel unwanted. Anything that should even have had that effect on her.

She'd thought she was coming out for lunch with Jamie. Just the two of them. Being the nebulous "them" they'd somehow become.

"The judge's concern had more to do with if something happens to Jamie," Michael said, repeating a key point from the beginning of the conversation. "Before the baby's born. Or afterward."

"Before it's born… I didn't even think of that," Jamie said, frowning as he glanced around the table. "I should have thought of that."

"You're talking about estate planning," Christine said, jumping into the conversation at the sound of his consternation. "A lot of people don't think about it until after they've had children. And even then, it's not the first thing they run out and do."

While, after research, she'd made the decision not to include estate planning counseling as part of

The Parent Portal, she had added the requirement of legal documents regarding embryo ownership in the event that a spouse died. That was why Jamie had been able to use Emily's embryos in the first place.

"I was planning to talk to you about it as soon as I gathered the necessary information," Judge Sanders said. "That's what this meeting is about. Finding out what we need to do to protect ourselves." He glanced at Christine again, assessed her, and with a frown, moved his glance toward Jamie. "I need to be certain that we're protected in case something happens to you before the baby's born. We need to know that in the event that that happens, the child stays in our family. With me. With your mother..."

She wasn't a lawyer. Or a doctor of any kind. But she got where this was going.

"You're afraid I'll try to keep it."

"There have been cases where the surrogate tries to keep the baby, yes," he said. "But with legal contracts in place beforehand, the baby will be protected from being a ward of the state while any lawsuits or custody battles are fought."

Thoughts flew through Christine's mind as the conversation continued around her. She had to take a step back. She was the professional here, not a member of the family. Not anyone personally involved.

She wasn't going to try to keep anyone's baby. She was the one who'd already given one away. They had no idea who they were dealing with.

And…if something happened to Jamie…their agreement that she got to have contact with the baby this time…would that change?

Jamie had asked Tanya if they needed a separate contract to determine estate matters in the event of his death. Michael was talking about a case he'd read about, something recently on the books having to do with an adopted child…

Not a surrogacy case. Not her concern.

How in the hell had she thought she could do this?

And why was she struggling so hard to do it? It wasn't like she'd considered, even for a second, that the baby inside her was hers. Or that she'd have any connection to it once she birthed it.

But she cared about it. Deeply. As would a nurse in a NICU, taking care of a patient. She'd remember this child for the rest of her life, think of it now and then, pray that it was doing well…

"So I can handle this through an estate attorney?" Jamie was asking. "I just need to name a guardian for the child in my will. And that will cover us in the event something happened to me before the baby's born and afterward as well."

"In conjunction with the surrogacy contract, that's correct." Michael answered that time as well.

Christine didn't know if she liked him or not. Mostly she just wanted to be done with the brunch obligation and on with her day.

If she didn't step foot in the country club again anytime soon, that would be fine, too.

No one seemed to be giving them curious glances, as she'd imagined they might, but she figured those who were curious would find other ways of sneaking peeks without being overt about it. They'd be sure to wonder why the judge and his former son-in-law were meeting with attorneys. And maybe wonder who Christine was.

She'd been leaning away from Jamie—not wanting them to think she was there specifically with him. It helped that he hadn't looked at her since the judge had spoken to her.

"Okay, good, let's go get some lunch," Judge Sanders said, standing while the others followed suit. Jamie turned to her; she saw him do it from the other side of the table. She'd scooted ahead of Tanya, to put herself between the two lawyers. She'd need to sit next to Jamie, to give the baby as much chance as possible to hear his voice. Maybe she should sit between the two men, so the baby could get familiar with both voices…

"Ms. Elliott?" Judge Sanders's booming voice called her to attention just as she was reaching for a plate—and noticed that the others had all moved on, taking plates from the identical stack of them across the room.

"Yes, sir?"

"I just… I'm sorry."

She smiled, just wanting to get away. "You have nothing to be sorry for," she said, picturing herself behind her desk, speaking with a client.

Any client but Jamie.

"I was harsh," he said, and the catch in his voice drew her attention. She glanced into his green eyes and saw pain there. "Harsher than I generally am. You're unselfishly giving us a great gift, and yet… I look at you and I feel resentment…"

His voice broke. And she understood. Hearing a replay of a conversation she'd had with Jamie many weeks before.

Nodding her head, she started to speak, but he said, "It's so hard…my Emily should be…" His voice broke and his eyes moistened.

"It's okay, Judge," she said, reaching out to touch his hand without questioning herself. "I truly do understand. This isn't an easy situation. It's going to have hard parts for all of us. I just hope that, in the end, it brings you and Jamie, and the little one, more joy than any of you could imagine."

Because that's what families did.

She knew. She'd had one once. With her mom and dad. And then again with her grandparents.

And had almost had another—before she'd given him up to a family that had a much better chance at bringing him more joy than struggle.

She just had to keep her mind on the prize—giving two very nice men a new family member. And in so doing, giving them a piece of their family back.

Chapter Sixteen

The twelve-week ultrasound went about the same as the first. Jamie couldn't see much but the screen and Christine's face. The technician had spoken mainly to him again. As far as he'd seen, Christine had kept her eyes closed. She'd left as soon as they met with Dr. Adams, though he'd known this time that she'd scheduled the appointment in between meetings at The Parent Portal.

Good news was that the fertility specialist was pleased with her uterine lining and Christine shouldn't need injections. Dr. Adams had turned over the remainder of the prenatal care to Dr. Miller, Christine's regular ob-gyn. The sonogram had been inconclusive regarding the sex of the child.

He hated that Christine hadn't been there to hear the report with him. It hadn't seemed right, her having left before he'd heard the results.

He suspected she'd done so on purpose.

And didn't blame her.

He hadn't been able to stop grinning, looking at the film of his little one's movement, and when the sound of the baby's heartbeat echoed through the room, he'd teared up as chills shot through him. How did you know that life was growing inside you and also be okay with having no claim to it?

No right to it?

He wished he'd been more aware of what he'd been asking when he'd come up with the surrogacy idea. It could be that he'd have asked anyway, but at least he could have been more sensitive.

Exactly what he'd do differently, he didn't know, but, seeing how loving Christine was, how nurturing, he knew he'd have tried to do something.

They continued their thrice-weekly meetings without change on into September. As busy as he was with the additional class, along with tennis practices and driving into the university in Mission Viejo a couple of times a week, those hours with Christine were the highlight of his life. Partially because she was carrying his baby.

And partially because… He hoped to God he was suffering from transference. But as time went on, he didn't think so. She drew him like a magnet, and he knew all about the molecular structure that defined many magnetic properties. Physics made more sense to him than emotional transference. And still didn't explain why this one woman called out to him.

So he let it go as best he could. Lived his life one day at a time. Enjoying the days with Christine in them more than the ones from which she was absent.

He'd passed on the house he'd wanted to buy, having seen that the structural damage was just too great to be a good investment. He had had to put most of his things in storage and move in to a little rental property while he looked for something else.

Other than the fact that he was aware he needed a place to put the nursery furniture he'd ordered, as well as the various other baby items he'd been buying—a stroller, a year's worth of disposable diapers, lotions and towels with hoods, car seat and… The list went on and on—he wasn't hating the rental. He'd found a little cottage right on a stretch of the private beach that made Marie Cove so desirable to many of Los Angeles' elite. It was only a mile from Christine's house, and he liked the vicinity.

Liked that she was close.

He'd have to get a bigger place eventually, but until the baby was two or three, they'd be okay there.

He'd spent Labor Day with Tom, and video chatted with his mom, who'd wanted him to fly up to Oregon. She'd been calling him at least twice a week, and texting almost daily since finding out he was going to be a father. That she was finally going to be a grandmother, and was already making plans to fly down and stay with him after the baby was born.

He was grateful for the love. And for the help.

He just needed space left in his life for…

Christine.

She and her friend Olivia had spent the holiday at the women's center. He didn't actually speak to her, but when he'd texted to wish her a happy Labor Day, she'd sent a picture of her and the pediatrician standing behind three grills filled with burgers and more coleslaw than he'd ever seen in one place. They'd both been wearing aprons, and the huge grins on their faces had brought a smile to his. He'd saved the photo in his gallery.

His first photo of her.

On the Friday after Labor Day he invited her to his little cottage. He wanted to talk to her privately. And not in a business setting. He told her so right up front, giving her the chance to refuse, and then had difficulty maintaining his calm when she didn't.

He'd never had trouble remaining calm. Not until Christine had come along.

Until the baby had.

He'd like to believe that his emotional upheaval was more in line with sympathy pregnancy than anything else. That he was on the normal, preparental roller coaster.

And there was some of that, to be sure. The highs

and excitement, mixed with worries and insecurities about being a parent. A single, male parent.

None of it made him jittery. Anxious. Or manically active.

Only thoughts of Christine did that. He'd never been jittery with Emily.

He didn't get it. He'd never so much as held Christine's hand.

And yet the second he opened his door to her that next afternoon, he reached for her hand, guiding her inside like she couldn't find the way herself. All two steps of it.

Realizing what he'd done, he pulled back almost immediately, but his hand knew the soft touch of her skin. And his mind was holding on. It wasn't going to let him forget.

"Wow," he said then, standing back to stare at her. "You look...great!" She wore capri pants with a tight, long, colorfully striped top and wedge shoes.

It was the first time he'd seen the shape of her stomach so clearly. "You're...showing..."

He stared. Knew he was staring. Couldn't stop.

Her chuckle only served to make the moment more potent. "You've seen the sonogram, Dad," she said.

Silence fell and as his gaze rose to hers, she instantly sobered, her deep brown eyes locking him to her.

He was the host, but she recovered first. "So, what

did you want to talk to me about?" she asked, looking beyond him to the L-shaped great room that encompassed living, kitchen and dining areas. A small hall led to two bedrooms with a rather large bathroom in between. A side door off the kitchen led to a two-and-a-half-car garage—which was one of the reasons he'd landed on the place. It had lots of space to store the boxes he'd wanted closer than his rented storage facility.

He wanted to show her the spare bedroom, currently consumed by his baby purchases. Wanted her to ooh and ahh over them. To want to see every single purchase. To touch and feel. To voice her opinions and suggestions.

He wanted to hear them.

And to get all gooey at the sight of the tiny little onesies he'd picked up in the university bookstore.

"Right," he said instead, moving toward the couch and love seat that was fine for his home, but consumed the cabin's much smaller space. "Have a seat."

He offered her something to drink, but she lifted the aluminum water bottle she'd brought in with her and politely declined. Settled onto the edge of a cushion at one end of the couch.

Not planning to stay long.

Getting back to business.

A place he didn't want her to go.

"I wanted to talk to you about the future," he

started, settling with some difficulty onto the love seat cushion closest to her. He needed to walk. To move.

A reaction only she seemed to instill in him.

"What about the future?" Her frown was softened by the smile he'd grown to dislike: the one with professional stiffness about it. Not something he'd noticed when he'd first been a client in her office, but one that he'd learned well in the months they'd been together.

Learned well and started to dislike it being directed at him. Vehemently.

"I'd like you to play a part in the baby's life." When he put it starkly like that, all alone out in the world, he stiffened inside. "It's kind of a reverse surrogate wanting to keep the baby thing." He tried to lighten the moment and heard the miserable fail.

She hadn't moved. Just watched him, that horrible smile on her face.

"It sounds bad," he said. "You're already sacrificing so much, putting parts of your life on hold, to give me my chance at a family, and here I am asking for more. I just…now that we're in this situation… I'm seeing what I was really asking of you…"

Yes, but that wasn't what this was about, either.

"…So much more than to hire your body for nine months.

"You deserve to get to know the child you're carrying. What I'm trying to do is establish your relationship with the baby, if you want one. One of your choosing."

She still said nothing. Just sat there. Smiling at him. He saw no tremble in her lips to indicate she cared, no change of expression that let him know she'd even heard.

"I'm not asking you to give any more of yourself," he said. "I'm not asking you to do anything for the child, to sacrifice any more. I know our contract states that you can request the chance to see the child at some point, if the need arises. But I'm saying, the door's open for you to have the child in your life on a regular basis, from birth. Not as the mother, necessarily. Not with legal custody rights. But…there."

There. He'd finally gotten it right.

Partially.

Her smile had faded.

"I've… I like you, Christine. I like having you in my life. I'd like to think we've become friends. And that we can remain friends…"

And that was the other part. He didn't want the birth of his child to mean that he'd lose her.

She was blinking regularly. Breathing.

"Say something…"

Pursing her lips, she rocked a little bit, forward and back, the movement almost imperceptible. But there. Was she nodding? Comforting herself?

"I…uh…" She cocked her head, smiled at him

again. Mostly professionally, accompanied by a more personal glint in her eyes.

"Ever since that brunch with Tom at the country club..." He'd apologized profusely after that god-awful hour. She'd brushed him off as though the meeting had been of no personal concern. Had said she understood where Tom was coming from and was fine.

He'd had no choice but to let it go. To try to believe her. But...

"Before that even... I've begun to realize how selfish I've been and... The Parent Portal is all about the human element in fertility choices. It's what sets your clinic apart. You've given your whole life to the cause, and I've managed to put you in a situation that takes your own humanity out of it..."

"It's okay, Jamie."

No it wasn't. "Please, Christine, don't go all Ms. Elliott on me. I'm not a client here."

"Technically, I'm your employee."

He shook his head. "You've become a friend. One that means more to me than I can even understand..."

"Don't." Shaking her head, she held up a hand. It was trembling. "This...this is what's not okay," she said. "This is what's hard. I have a role to fill, Jamie. A job to do. And a reputation to uphold. Not just for me, but for The Parent Portal. My employees. Our clients. And future clients. The future families we can help bring to life..."

"I know."

"What you're saying here...it's like tempting a dog with a pork chop bone when, after he takes it and enjoys the moment, it's going to splinter inside him and could kill him."

His offer was like a bone to a dog. That's what he heard. She coveted what he wanted to give her. Was licking her chops and...

"I'm being selfish again." His brain finally got to the point she'd been making. His offer only made things harder on her. Not easier. While attempting to be kind, he'd ended up being kind of cruel.

"You're being human, and very sweet." The way she smiled at him, her trembling lips only slightly tilted, changed his world. "And if we weren't under legal contract, if we weren't dealing with a situation that was conceived at The Parent Portal..."

The conversation seemed to have ended as she trailed off, and the room seemed to darken. To lose air. Jamie glanced out toward the ocean. Wondering how to extricate them both from the very awkward situation he'd created. How to hide his already-exposed vulnerability once again.

"If...after the baby is born...you still want to make your offer, offers—friendship and a relationship with the baby—I will at least be open to having the conversation." She stopped. Just kept watching him.

Thinking? Assessing? He withstood the scrutiny. Waited for what she'd bring next.

"It actually does help, knowing that the birth might not be the end. Knowing that there's possibility." Her hand cradled the slight bump in her belly.

And the lights came back on.

Chapter Seventeen

During their sixteen-week visit Cheryl offered Jamie the opportunity for another ultrasound, to determine the sex of the baby, but he declined after looking at Christine.

"I don't mind," she'd told him, while they were still sitting in the doctor's office. "Truly, it's not a big deal." Not physically. And the rest… She was a pro. If there was any momentary residual emotional discomfort, she'd quickly get over it.

Besides, he'd offered her the chance to actually know the baby she was creating. He might change his mind. She wasn't the mother and had no legal rights. But the idea dangling out there made the pregnancy easier.

Not for any logical reason. It wasn't like she'd be a mother this time around. The child wouldn't know her as such. That would be too confusing. And unfair to all of them. But to actually be able to see the child, to see for herself that it was well, happy, thriving…

She brought up the ultrasound possibility again a couple of days after their Wednesday doctor visit, five days after he'd made his sweet offer in his cottage. They'd been for a walk on the private stretch of beach attached to his cottage—and several others along the way—and were sitting, in jeans and long-sleeved shirts, in the sand, about halfway between the ocean and the cottage. The Friday late afternoon air held a chill that was more invigorating than cold.

She was meeting Olivia for dinner at seven. Had to get home and change, but had been struggling to find a way to talk to him about things she really wanted to discuss, without compromising that professional glass wall standing between them.

Having asked if they could sit a moment, she suddenly felt like she'd created a hot seat for herself.

The ocean was rough, roaring into the beach in waves strong enough to knock over sandcastles and sweep them away. She and her father had made an entire colony out of sand once—huts and a store and a school with little twig benches…

"I want to order the ultrasound," she told Jamie. "I won't do it without your say-so, as you have to foot the bill since it's not required prenatal care at this point, but you wanted to know the sex of the baby the last time, and now they can tell."

He was shaking his head before she'd even finished. "I can wait."

"Jamie..." She turned her head, waited for him to look at her. Hadn't realized how close they were. Their shoulders weren't even touching, but his face was so close. A lean and a scoot and her lips could touch his. Could talk in a whole new way.

"You think I don't know it's hard on you to lie there and hear that heartbeat and divorce yourself from what's going on inside you?" he asked. "I've done more reading...the hormones that protect the baby affect you, too. There's natural bonding going on between you and the baby... I'm not going to put you through any more than absolutely necessary."

"You need to quit thinking about me, and let yourself get everything you can out of this," she said, a passion in her tone that surprised her. And seemed to knock him a bit off course as well. Wide-eyed, he glanced at her and kept looking.

"I signed on for this," she told him. "I've been pregnant before. I knew what I was letting myself in for. The nine months will be over and I'll go on with my life. But you...you're missing out, Jamie, by not letting yourself revel in it. Or celebrate it."

"How do you know I don't? You're only with me for short periods at a time a few times a week. That leaves a lot of celebration time."

He was right. She didn't know. The idea didn't sit well. Had she been so certain she really knew him? That she knew what he did with the majority of his life?

Confused, she forced her mind back on track.

"You're dying to know if you're having a boy or girl." She couldn't be wrong about that. She'd listened to the things he didn't say.

And the little things he had, like the time he'd mentioned a future with dance classes or fishing poles… It wasn't like he'd had a preference for one or the other, or even a need to have fishing poles if it was a boy; he'd just seemed to need to know. Because he was a guy whose numbers had to be concrete. Had to fit neatly within their formulas.

He was taking on solo a job for two. Not just a job. A lifetime commitment. With no professional boundaries.

He hadn't denied her statement.

"I'm scheduling the ultrasound," she said, standing.

He stood, too, and their hands brushed. Just briefly, they both froze. Looked into each other's eyes.

And she was glad she was pregnant with his child.

Jamie wasn't a reveler. His celebrations tended to be of the quieter kind. A sense of rightness inside him. Well-being.

But that next Friday, when he stood just behind a new technician, Molly, in a different ultrasound room located within Cheryl Miller's private practice clinic, and heard the words, "It's a boy!" he whooped right out loud.

He'd kind of been hoping for a girl who'd take after Emily. But there wasn't even a hint of disappointment in him as Molly pointed out the evidence.

"I'm going to have a son!" He couldn't believe the near squeal came from him, and instinctively, his gaze went to Christine. To share the miracle with her.

Her eyes were closed. There was no mistaking the couple of tear drops coming from their corners.

But she was smiling.

Christine had said he needed to celebrate, and he wanted to. But only with her.

The fact brought him up short as he drove away from the clinic that morning and headed straight to the public beach he'd shared with Emily all those years. To commune with his wife and sit with their baby news with her in the only way left to him.

Walking down as close to the shore as he could get without waves washing up on him, he plopped down in the dark brown dress pants and beige sweater he'd worn to class, and looked out to sea. To Emily.

The horizon met him with a blank stare. He looked for her face and saw Christine, eyes closed, with tears and a smile. Saw her on the private beach outside his cottage, looking at him like she needed to kiss him as badly as he needed to kiss her. And in her office the day he'd first made his request of her to carry his baby. Remembered her telling him that she was certain his request would be on her mind for years to come.

"We're having a son, Em!" He said the words aloud, releasing emotion that had been clamoring inside him.

He listened for Emily's response in his head, her excitement, and instead heard Christine's voice thick with emotion as she told him that he was offering pork to a dog.

What kind of an ass was he that a woman he'd only known for months was able to drown out the memory of the wife, the woman, the girl he'd loved for more than half his life?

What kind of a fool?

As the baby grew inside her, Christine worked longer hours at The Parent Portal and volunteered more. She was doing the healthy thing—keeping herself occupied with pursuits that brought value to her life. She took care of herself. Rested on the couch in her office at least a few minutes every morning and afternoon. Was eating like a health nut, down to measuring and weighing when she was at home to ensure that she got recommended amounts of all the nutrients that would help the baby boy to grow, and none that could hinder his growth.

Her body was his temple for the next few months, and when he returned it to her, he'd be leaving it in better condition, healthwise, than he'd found it. She'd have a few pounds to lose, some baby fat, but her cholesterol levels would be stellar.

At four and a half months pregnant, she'd gained seven pounds. Was aiming for a pound a week for the rest of the pregnancy. The last ultrasound hadn't been necessary but she'd been glad to have the confirmation that all was well. The baby's growth was right in the middle of the normal chart. Her uterine lining was nice and thick and protecting him. Her blood pressure was great, his heartbeat strong and steady.

She was having another boy. Very similar to something she'd already been through. Jamie's baby should have been the only thing different in her life. Her only focus. But how did you control your subconscious? She was waking up nights with Jamie Howe on her mind, as though he was in her bed with her, but when she opened her eyes, she lay there alone. Sometimes she remembered dreams. Sometimes she didn't.

It was all very confusing.

As was sitting in the most luxurious SUV she'd ever been in. But that Wednesday evening, he'd invited her to a musical being put on at the university in Mission Viejo. A couple of his students were working sound, another was a dancer, and Jamie was friends with the choral director—a man almost as old as Tom Sanders.

They'd eaten in the car on the way in—the dinner she'd packed was all healthy finger foods—because she'd had a late-afternoon appointment already scheduled.

Jamie didn't say a lot about the cucumber sandwiches and avocado deviled eggs, but he ate them until they were gone so she took that as a win. He talked almost the whole way—filling her in a little bit on each of his students who were involved because she might meet them. And talking about Daniel, the choral director's, operatic singing career. As they were parking, he let her know that Daniel knew about the baby, as did the college president who employed him.

He'd failed to tell his students, apparently, or hadn't found doing so appropriate, and she'd felt their eyes boring into her belly as they'd come in a group of three to say hi to Jamie in the vestibule after the show.

She'd just been getting used to the idea of accepting that strangers would naturally assume they were a couple and that the baby she was carrying belonged to both of them, not minding that they thought that, when he'd introduced her as his surrogate, and explained that she was carrying his and Emily's baby.

Apparently they'd been in his life long enough

to know about his deceased wife. As they were all three seniors, it made sense.

And after the play, her good mood slowly dissipated. For a bit there, she'd forgotten that she was only at the university so that the baby inside her could be exposed to the sounds. She'd forgotten she was working. She'd simply enjoyed the show, being with Jamie, hearing him laugh out loud.

She'd been in Mission Viejo so his baby could hear him laugh out loud.

Jamie kept up a string of conversation all the way home, too. Mostly about the play—an original, non-holiday tale about scientists and animals that was the culmination of a semester's work. He'd told her about sound levels and how his students used mathematical skills in their artistic creations in Mission Viejo as well. And how the dancer, who had sprained an ankle a month before, had been afraid she wouldn't be able to perform. There'd been more. She let it roll over her, hoping the baby inside her was paying attention to his voice.

And then she was waking up in her driveway, feeling as comfortable as if she'd been in her own bed.

"I'm so sorry! I didn't mean to drop off on you," she said. "I've been doing that lately...falling asleep anytime I'm sitting doing nothing."

"So, what, it's happened once?" he teased her.

His smile was illuminated by the streetlight in front of her house. She was as focused on the warmth those lips sent through her as she was on the fact that he'd turned off his SUV.

"I have something to talk to you about," he said, staying on his side of the vehicle, looking straight ahead, though the way he said the words sounded really personal.

Her heart started to pound as anticipation thrummed through her. Inappropriate anticipation.

"If this is more about the future… I meant what I said, Jamie. We can't…"

He was shaking his head.

"It's about now," he said. "I'd like permission to touch your stomach," he told her. "I was reading about the fact that mothers can feel their babies from the outside as well as inside, and that babies sometimes move to the touch."

She should have offered. She knew this stuff.

"Of course you can feel it, Jamie!" Loosening her seat belt, she let it slide back into its holster. "I'm sorry I made you ask." Pushing up the console between them, she moved over slightly and offered him access to her protruding belly, covered by the dress yoga pants and black, red, yellow, blue and white floral, formfitting tunic she'd put on because she'd thought they were festive.

Offering a new daddy the chance to bond with his baby.

She was not—absolutely not—wanting the feel of

Jamie's warm hand spread across her stomach. And if she was, then she would make the wanting stop.

She had to make it stop.

Because when those fingers lightly brushed against her top and then settled with confidence on top of her belly, her entire lower body melted.

Chapter Eighteen

She wasn't huge yet, but he'd been able to reach her baby bump easily.

From there, Jamie just froze. He'd read that if he moved his fingers, applied a very slight pressure, he might be able to distinguish parts of the baby. And might also be able to convince him to move. Chances of that were better as the pregnancy progressed.

He was struggling to separate Christine's stomach from the baby inside her. He'd feared his reaction from the moment he'd known he needed to bond with his son in this way. He trusted his ability to be a great father.

What he didn't trust was his libido. Not where this woman was concerned.

How did a guy feel his baby in a woman's stomach and want to have sex?

How could he feel his baby in a woman's stomach and not want to have sex?

As his body reacted to the feel of her beneath his palm in the quiet darkness of his car, he slowed his mind. Closed his eyes.

And knew that he'd never separate Christine from his son. She was helping to create him.

In the darkness behind his lids he couldn't hide from another truth. He was falling in love with the woman. Had already fallen in love with her.

It wasn't transference. It wasn't gratitude.

It was her.

Igniting things in him he'd never felt before. Not ever.

Not even with Emily.

What he did with any of it, other than calculate and catalog, he had no idea.

Moving his hand slightly to the left, he tried to make out a shape and… He jumped, pulling his hand off of Christine and then immediately putting it back down.

"What was that?"

"He just moved…" Her words ended on a lilt—a sound from her that was unfamiliar to him. "How cliché is that?" He heard clearly forced levity in her tone, and then, "It's like he knows you, Jamie. I've felt bubbles over the past week or two, but this is the first time I could really feel him move. And he did it for you…"

Her face was turned to his in the streetlight, her eyes glistening.

"He did it for both of us." The words slipped out in a reverent moment.

"No." Her tone had changed. Hardened, but not in a mean way. Just firm. She placed her hand over his, holding his hand in place when he might have lifted it. "He's doing this for you, Jamie."

She couldn't possibly know that. And most likely wasn't right, considering that the baby had no idea that the woman carrying him, protecting and caring for him, hadn't contributed an egg. Maybe the warmth of his bigger hand was a contributing factor, but…

He felt the tear drop on the side of his hand, a bare portion not covered by her smaller hand. She didn't pull away, or push him away, just sat there silently.

"We're human beings," he said softly, the words pouring up from a new source within him. "I can't possibly sit here and experience the first touch of my baby all alone. You're a part of it. Just as you can't sit there and endure whatever it is that hurts you and have me unaware."

Her hand slid off from his.

He continued to cradle her stomach.

"Let me share it with you, Chris."

"Only my mom and dad and Gram and Gramps call me that."

The news wasn't surprising. Only family was allowed to occupy the inner circle of her heart. Using her full name was a shield by which she kept the world from getting too close.

He'd grown to know her over the past months, in all of their innocuous conversation.

Their refusal to allow anything physical between them had left open another avenue of intimacy.

An emotional, mental recognition that he couldn't prevent.

"Let me share it with you, Chris," he repeated, not able to allow himself to be deflected from that goal. If she told him to go, he would do so. But if she let him stay, he was doing so as a friend. A man who cared about her.

Not as the father of the child she was carrying.

"I wanted to keep my first son."

What in the hell was she doing?

Reaching for the door handle, Christine held on to it. Ready to get out. The hand on her stomach compelled her to stay.

She was there to help Jamie bond with his baby, and he was doing so in the most incredible way. There was no mistake that the fetus had chosen right then to kick for the first time. To reach up from the womb that was giving it sustenance for the moment to the hand that would feed it for a lifetime.

She would not make the moment about her. Had to focus on him. On the goal at hand…

"Did you tell anyone?" His voice, soft in the darkness, oozed over her like warm chocolate. Soothing. Sweet. A reminder of happier times.

Of childhood.

She'd been such a happy kid.

Which made the sadness that had followed seem so much more acute.

"Yeah," she said. "My dad and his wife knew. I had my grandparents to consider, though. By my senior year they were both failing. If I wasn't there, helping them, they'd have had to sell the family home and move into assisted living. I couldn't do that to them. Not because I'd made a mistake. I couldn't abandon them, or force them to live out the end of their lives in what would have been, to them, a prison, not after they'd spent their lives taking care of all of us. Taking care of me. They were both mentally sharp. I went to my dad for help, trying to figure out a way to make it all work."

She'd already told him and Emily a bit about Ryder. Telling him a few more details didn't need to change anything in their relationship.

Except it did. She was letting him see her, the person. The woman who grieved, every single day, for the child she'd birthed and given up. And in his seeing, she had to see, too. Had to see how devastating it had been for her to let them take Ryder. And how incredibly painful she was finding the idea of knowing that when she gave birth to Jamie's child, she'd be losing that baby, too. Even as she justified herself, she rejected the justification. Knew she needed to just shut up.

The baby moved again. Not as energetically, but still completely decipherable, sending muscle memory waves through her entire body.

Resurrecting a memory so vivid it took her breath. And all of her focus. She was there again, lying in her bed, curled in a fetal position, cradling her belly with her hands, promising herself that she wouldn't give up her baby. Her father was taking her the next day to sign the adoption papers, and even while she sobbed and told herself she wouldn't do it, she knew she had to.

Because she loved her baby, and her grandparents, that much.

"Just because a person is old doesn't mean their life is less valuable," she said aloud. "I was in a position to tend to my grandparents. If they were in a home, I'd have no home. No way to provide for a baby. At least not in a way that would give him a happy, secure life. I was seventeen. And while I had a trust fund, I had no access to it until I was twenty-three."

"And your grandparents wouldn't let you use it? Not even to support your child?"

The judgment in his tone was probably unintended, but she heard it. And was oddly comforted. "Gram was willing to give up the part of it they received for my care. She thought she could talk my dad into giving me more. But it wasn't up to them. My father had full custody of me after my mom died. He set up the trust, with court approval, and he was the executor of it. My grandparents got a monthly stipend for my care, but that came from my father, not from the trust. He also helped pay for any house repairs or other unexpected expenses that came up for them."

Dad was a decent guy. He'd just eventually made a different life for himself. One that hadn't fit her. And he'd been kind enough to facilitate her need to stay in Marie Cove.

Life wasn't always neatly tied up in a pretty bow.

With his hand on her stomach, the telling seemed almost natural. Two boy babies. One in the now. One in the past.

But connected within her.

"So you went to your father for guidance, and he basically forced you to give up the baby."

She'd been an unwed teenage mother. The situation had been of her own making. The consequences of a completely thoughtless and selfish choice. His defense of her...

She had no idea what to do with it.

Gram and Gramps hadn't blamed her. They'd told

her over and over that she needn't feel shame. That her heart was good and pure. She'd loved Nathan with all her heart, and that wasn't a bad thing. They'd all loved him.

"Tammy, my stepmother, offered to keep him, to raise him," she said, hearing her voice as though it belonged to someone else in the darkened vehicle. "She cried with me…"

Her throat tightened and tears sprang behind her lids. She pushed against them. Waited until she'd won the once-familiar battle.

"My dad said no. He felt that it would hold me back. That I'd never have closure. He also didn't think it would be fair to Ryder, being raised by his grandparents with his mother in and out of his life. Or, an alternative, to lie to him about his parentage. He said that it would be kinder to give the baby a family that was ready to love and raise him. And kinder to me to put the pregnancy behind me and move forward with my life. To give me a fresh start. To that end, he purposely arranged a private adoption so that I'd have no chance of contact, forcing me to let go."

She'd been forced to move on. And was only these last months realizing that a mother never let go. Or, at least, she hadn't.

And couldn't. Not completely. She'd always love the baby she'd never known. Always wonder if he was okay…happy…loved. If he knew he was adopted…

"And you started a business whose emphasis is on open fertility donations, focusing not only on the parents' rights, but on the rights of those who contribute," Jamie said.

She shrugged. Life taught you lessons and if you wanted to be happy, you used them for good.

"But you know his name. Ryder."

Shaking her head, she stopped when the movement affected Jamie's hand on his baby. "That's just what I called him. To myself." She didn't like how pathetic that made her sound. She wasn't pathetic at all. She was a strong woman with a great life that she loved.

"So…" He moved his hand and she stiffened, expecting him to take away his warmth, and relaxed when he settled his palm on the left side of her stomach. Then his fingers moved slightly, adding a little pressure, as though playing with his son, and a fissure passed through her. Lighting up her body. "What happened to the father?"

She should have expected the question. Hadn't. Nathan wasn't part of a baby discussion. Wasn't a detail she'd ever have shared with clients in her office.

Weighing the advisability of staying in the SUV with Jamie or going in the house, she searched for words.

"Chris?"

She turned automatically to look at him. Then realized maybe she shouldn't have done so.

"You're sacrificing so much for me, changing my entire world. Please let me give back."

Sirens went off inside her. They didn't come with particular words. Just clear warning. "You're giving me far more than most surrogates get," she said. This was a business deal.

She'd lost sight of the goal. That wasn't good. No way that was good.

"I think you know I'm not talking about money. But what do I get to give for the maternal gift you're bestowing upon my baby?"

She didn't love his baby.

He hadn't said *love*.

"I care about you, Chris. It's ridiculous for us to keep pretending that's not the case. I get that there are boundaries we can't cross, but let me at least be your friend. Accept my gift of caring as I'm accepting yours."

She had friends. A lot of them.

None that had ever called her *Chris*. Not more than once. She always corrected them. Always. She was Christine. All grown-up.

A grown-up could tell a little story from the past.

"His name was Nathan. I met him my senior year. He was a foster kid, also a senior, but new to Marie Cove and the high school so you wouldn't have known him."

Jamie and Emily had gone to USC and hadn't even been in Marie Cove during the year and a half she'd known Nathan and then spent birthing Ryder.

"Nathan was responsible, grounded. More like me than any of the other kids. He knew life's realities and thought of others. Life wasn't just all about him. He wanted to join the military and loved talking to Gramps about Gramps's time in the service. He wanted to spend time with me here, at the house, with my grandparents, and jumped right in and did things for them when he saw a need." Had she reinvented the guy over the years? Romanticized him?

She'd certainly replayed those months over and over and over again. Far too many times.

"He told me repeatedly that it was so great to be part of a real family. When I got pregnant a few months before graduation, I was scared, of course, upset with us for not being more careful, but I was also kind of excited. I figured life was going to be different than I'd thought, but still be great for all of us. Until he balked. He didn't want a baby. Didn't want me to have it. Didn't want to have anything to do with it. He'd been planning to see the world. Was just biding his time until he turned eighteen and could get out of Marie Cove and start living. His whole plan to join the military was so that he could travel to faraway places. He turned eighteen a couple of weeks before the end of the school year and left town the day after graduation without even saying goodbye."

There. She'd given Jamie what he wanted.

His hand moved. Or the baby did. And the next thing she knew, she was sobbing. Big, gross, childish sobs all over the man who'd somehow found a way past the thirteen years' worth of thickening walls protecting her heart.

Chapter Nineteen

Sliding his hand from Chris's belly to her back happened naturally. Jamie didn't consider options or consequences. The second she broke, he had her, pulling her to him, cradling her head against his shoulder. He was no psychiatrist or trained counselor, but he'd seen this one coming.

There was nothing to say, no words that were going to help. He could only sit with her. Share her pain as best he could.

He'd known his own kind of grief. Sometimes being with another while the onslaught raged was just better than being alone.

Time passed; he wasn't counting it.

The neighborhood around them was quiet, unaware of the storm inside their cocoon of darkness. At one point as she sniffled, he leaned over enough to grab some napkins out of the glove box, handed them to her and then wrapped his arm right back around her. Shielding her from the outside world just long enough for her to purge some of the pain trapped inside her.

And feeling some of that pain. At first, when his throat tightened, he didn't get what was happening. But as his gaze on the street outside started to glisten, he recognized the sorrow gathering up inside him. Not for him. Not for Emily or their losses. But for Chris.

All for her.

"I'm so sorry." She didn't pull away as her sobs eased. Just lay against him for the moment. He wanted to be her support for as long as she needed him.

"Don't be. Please, don't ever look back on this moment with remorse," he told her softly.

She turned her head to look up at him, her eyes raised in question, and he lifted his thumb to the tears on her cheeks, wiping them away as though he could somehow take away the pain that had caused them.

He couldn't return her to thirteen years in the past. Couldn't reverse choices or return her son to her.

She continued to hold his gaze, letting him see the woman behind the mask, while he gently brushed her skin. She was so ungodly beautiful he ached with it.

Drawing his thumb down the trail of her tears, he ended up at the corner of her mouth. Gently moving from her mouth, over an inch and down, to return and repeat the gesture.

There was no motive anymore. No forethought. Just a need to be there, connected to her. Her lips opened when he brought his thumb back to them, only inches away from his own, and he lowered his head.

The kiss was instinctive. A way to bring them closer still, to join their pain, their lives. He didn't ask what he was doing, he just did it. And when her lips opened farther, moving against his, he deepened the touch, opening his mouth fully, finding her tongue with his, melding them. He wasn't going anywhere with any of it. Just living in the moment that was there.

Doing what felt natural. Right.

His arms pulled her closer, cradled her neck, as he broke contact only to deepen it more, to kiss her in a way he didn't know, didn't recognize. Fire burned through him, need so hot it erupted, obliterating any thought he might have had. He had to take them further, go with her into an unknown. His erection straining against his pants, he moved, straining toward her pelvis, her hip. He didn't know until she pressed forward, joining their intimate parts through their clothes, how badly he'd needed his penis to find welcome against her.

"No!" With an emotion-filled cry, she pulled away from him. Her eyes glinted with tears in the streetlight as she wiped her mouth. "No," she said, more calmly.

Christine had just entered the vehicle. He didn't have to ask or wonder—he knew.

And instantly respected her right to be there.

Feeling blindsided, like a deer in headlights, he tried to make sense of what had just happened. When what he'd just been denied had him in such a stronghold he could barely form coherent thought.

"This is wrong."

He didn't deny the point. Couldn't. He had no frame of reference for what he'd just experienced. It didn't feel wrong. But it made no sense, and in his world if it didn't make sense, there was something wrong.

But…

"Caring about someone isn't wrong," he said. "Chris" almost slipped out of his mouth. He refused "Christine." "Being present when someone is hurting is one of the purest forms of expressing humanity."

Where in hell were the words coming from? Certainly no math equation.

Her nod was the first thing that had made any sense to him since he'd been brushing a tear off a cheek.

"The kiss," she said. "It's wrong and it can't happen again. If you even try, I'll have to enforce the clause in our contract that states that I can, with cause, refuse to see you, which would deny you access to your son until his birth."

He heard the words, saw her hand reach for the door.

"It won't happen again." He wasn't going to lose her. Or these months with his son.

She nodded. Pulled up on the door handle.

"But, just for the record, it wasn't all me."

His parting shot was cheap.

But it was also the truth.

The consequences of sexual passion had almost ruined her life once. Almost killed her, if she were honest and considered the darkest hours just after she'd given birth to Ryder. They'd given her something to help her sleep and for a moment there, as she'd been drifting off, she hadn't wanted to wake up.

Falling for the notion that she had a good partner who would hold her when she had a weak moment had been the catalyst that led her to having sex with Nathan. They'd only done it once. It hadn't been planned. She'd been crying because her grandfather had had a dizzy spell and had fallen that day. She'd seen it happen, been unable to help him.

The doctor had said he'd be fine. They'd only kept him in the hospital overnight as a precaution. Gram, of course, had insisted on staying with him. As was right.

And Christine had been home alone, reliving the moment. Coming face-to-face with the proof that the source of her strength was getting weaker.

That Gramps wouldn't be around forever.

When Nathan called and she told him what happened, he'd come right over. Had held her as she'd cried…

She'd thought he was the real thing. Her soul mate. The man she'd been meant to find. The "Gramps" to her "Gram."

Then she'd grown up.

That first night after Jamie had kissed her, she'd taken a hot bath and had gone to bed. Determined to be kind to herself, and others. To get up in the morning and go to work. To help others have children to feed.

She didn't sleep all that well.

By noon the next day, she couldn't sit still and pushed Jamie's speed dial on her cell phone. If work, helping others, wasn't sufficient, she'd done something wrong.

She knew she had.

"I'm so glad you called," he said, picking up on the first ring. She'd waited until his lunch break from class. It would have been wrong to do otherwise. She knew his schedule. "I apologize profusely, Christine. I can guarantee you it won't happen again."

It sounded as though he'd rehearsed the words.

Or listened to them repeating in his brain too many times for too many hours.

"Christine." Thank God he'd reverted.

And to the sadness within her at the loss of his "Chris," she told herself to grow a pair.

"I'm calling to apologize for my overreaction last night," she said, hearing the stiffness in her voice and finding that a good thing. "I realize I am as much or more to blame as you were and that it was wrong and weak of me to threaten you with the 'cause' clause."

Silence hung on the line and she took advantage of it. "That said, there cannot be a repeat of last night. Not any of it. We have an emotional project going on here. It was bound to bring forth intense feelings in both of us. But we're aware now. We're adults. And I have complete faith that we can both handle this."

He answered immediately. "I agree. I'm embarrassed, ashamed, and I do apologize. You were having a low moment and I pushed my way in to a space in which I didn't belong. It won't happen again."

His tone, the distance and sincerity, spoke volumes. Grateful that the call had gone better than she'd imagined it could, she hung up.

And started to cry.

"I wanted to have sex with him." The words flew out of Christine's mouth the second Olivia slid into the booth that night at a pub they often frequented. Christine had been facilitating a women's health class early that evening, with the volunteered help from Cheryl Miller, but had called Olivia to ask if her friend could do a late dinner.

"Did you?" Olivia hadn't even put her purse on the seat beside her. It hung suspended in air, as her friend looked over at her.

"Want to? Yes."

"No, did you do it?"

Would Olivia be disappointed in her if she had?

"Of course not."

"But you wanted to." Purse on the seat beside her, Olivia leaned forward, her hands folded on the table.

She'd just said she had. What more did the woman want?

Orange and black garlands hung between their booth and the ones behind them on each side. Streamed mellow pop music played softly in the background, and the staff was all wearing spider antler headbands. Christine had helped the staff decorate the clinic for Halloween, but she hadn't even so much as put up a Christmas tree at home since Gram had died.

"So, why didn't you?"

"You know why! It would have been completely unethical! Unprofessional!"

When Olivia nodded, she calmed. And added, "And because I'm not going to make the mistake of letting a man comfort me into sex twice."

She knew, when she said the words, what she was

doing. Opening the door to the question she'd known Olivia would ask…

"There was a first time?"

And it all came out. The waiter came to take their order. Olivia asked for more time without interruption. Christine was aware, but didn't get involved. And as soon as the young man was out of earshot, continued with her story. All of it. Every single detail she could remember.

At some point Olivia ordered club sandwiches for both of them. Christine ate every bite. She had a baby to feed.

And when she was done with her story, she felt physically full, and otherwise, no better. If anything, she felt worse. Weak. Like a victim instead of the survivor she was.

She pulled out her wallet to pay and get the hell out of there. She needed rest.

Olivia's hand covered hers on the little tray holding their bill. "Whoa, wait, what are you doing?"

"I'm paying," she said firmly. "I asked for this dinner. I spent the whole time whining. I'm paying."

"We aren't done yet."

Christine frowned. Looked across at her friend. "We can be done."

Shaking her head, Olivia asked, "Why did you tell me all of this?"

Yeah, it had been a mistake. They'd been friends for years and didn't spill beans that had long since been consumed. "I'm sorry. I know it's not like me. All I can do is play the hormone card and get this baby birthed." She still had a little over four months to go. Tried to chuckle.

An image of Jamie, his face so close it seemed like she could read words in his eyes, sprang to mind.

And she longed for him. Right then. Right there. Longed to be near him. To hear his voice. To kiss him again and not stop.

She was birthing the baby he'd created with another woman. A baby they had created out of deep and abiding love for each other.

What in the hell was the matter with her?

"No, seriously." Olivia's tone was soft, soothing. "Why did you tell me this?"

She didn't know. Wished she hadn't. She shook her head. Wanted to go. And to stay.

"It wasn't right, sweetie, what they did to you back then. A teenager, being left to care for aging grandparents. Not only taking on the day-to-day responsibility, but bearing the weight of it in the bigger picture. It might have been what you thought you wanted, but they were adults—they should have known better..."

"It was my home. Is still my home. I love it there." And truly couldn't imagine wanting to live anywhere else.

"So maybe someone else should have borne the

responsibility of their health so that you could live there and still be a kid."

Maybe. But like she'd told Jamie, life wasn't always neat and perfect.

"Taking care of them… I love that about me. I don't resent one single second of it."

"You don't regret not getting to sit in the lunchroom with friends and be privy to the gossip? Or to try out for cheerleading or band? You must have been lonely. Didn't you ever wish it could have happened differently?"

Of course she had. The loneliness had been acute. Which was why she'd been so ripe for Nathan's support and companionship. "They couldn't help getting sick," she said. "Just like Mom couldn't help dying in childbirth, trying to give me the sibling I wanted. Or like any of your patients can't help getting diseases that end up requiring great sacrifice of, and pain to, their parents."

"So if you weren't looking for a clearer understanding of the past, why did you bring it all up now?" Olivia's glance was serious. Firm.

"Because you and I are the same," she said. "Because you get that a woman can choose to give her life to a career and others, and have that life be as valuable, as happy, as one who chooses not to live alone."

Olivia's gaze darkened. "Oh, sweetie," she said.

Appeared to have some difficulty swallowing. "We aren't alike at all in one very important way..."

Their waiter came close, looking at them, and turned away.

"Yes, I believe a woman dedicating herself to her career can be vital, but that's very different from choosing to be alone. You can be all those things you described and still share your life."

Christine opened her mouth to argue. Figured she'd said enough. Until you'd lived without any freedom because you were tied to loved ones, because you were all they had, because they meant so much to you, you probably wouldn't understand.

"Nine years ago, when I was still in med school, I was married." Olivia's words shocked her. Olivia had been *married*? "My husband was ten years older than me, and wanted to have children right away. He was also quite wealthy and thought it made more sense for us to start our family, and *then* for me to go to med school. It was our only real issue—my dedication to a career—and I adored him. We compromised—we'd start our family, but I was also going to stay in school. Our baby was born with severe birth defects. She lived almost four months, but then we lost her." Olivia's tone didn't change. She was speaking facts, not feeling the emotions they created. Christine knew because she recognized herself in her friend.

"Don't tell me the jerk blamed you…because you were in school or something…"

"No." Olivia's smile was tinged with sadness. "And he wasn't a jerk. But Lily's death was hard on our marriage. I ended up specializing in pediatrics and buried myself in saving other people's children. The last straw for us was when we found out I couldn't have any more babies." Olivia explained that the problem was not with her eggs, but in her body's inability to successfully nourish a fetus.

"I admire the hell out of what you're doing here," she said, leaning in with arms crossed on the table in front of her as she spoke to Christine. There were other people around, parties coming and going, but Christine had hardly been aware of anyone. "Giving a man a chance to have his child…it's incredible. Being able to have a child at all is an incredible thing to me…"

So they weren't alike. Something awakened in Christine. She couldn't define it. Didn't recognize it. But felt enlightened just the same.

"But I'm telling you this because I'm not alone by choice, Christine. I adored my husband when I married him. And I adore him still. He's a good man. A great man. We just weren't good together after Lily died. We handled it differently. I needed to work. To bury myself alive or die of grief. He needed more of me. More from me. You know the statistics…how many marriages fail when a couple loses a child. It doesn't kill the love, though. And I haven't met a man who even comes close to instilling that kind of love or passion in me."

"Do you ever see him?"

"Sometimes. Not often. It's too hard." She waved her hand and then leaned in again. "When I asked you why you didn't sleep with Jamie, you immediately spouted off about professional ethics," she said. "But those are only going to be an issue until after the baby's born."

Tension passed through her system. Grabbing hold.

"I'm thinking there might be more to it than that. You didn't need to speak to me, someone who you thought was like you, if your only concern was professionalism," Olivia continued, and Christine felt like a woman tied to a train track with an engine veering down on her.

She needed to stop her friend before she said anything else. And needed to hear what was being said, too. Olivia was right. She'd told her about her past for a reason.

Because it seemed to be looming in her present, and she couldn't put it to rest. From the time she'd graduated from college and opened the clinic, she'd never looked back. Never had a problem leaving the past behind. She'd been happy.

Content. At peace.

"Is it possible that you've been hiding behind professionalism all these years, finding enough satisfaction in The Parent Portal and the family you've built there to keep from being hurt again?"

"Of course not." She was a woman with her eyes wide-open. Had been since the moment she'd given birth and allowed the nurse to take her child away and never bring him back.

Sitting back, Olivia reached for her purse. "Okay," she said. "It was just a thought. So, if your only problem is the professional relationship between you and Jamie, the solution is simple. Wait it out until you recover from having the baby and then sleep with him."

No. She frowned, putting her credit card on the tray with the bill. No, she was not going to sleep with Jamison Howe.

"I'm having his wife's baby. She's the one he loves. I'm just a stand-in."

"Maybe." She seemed to be waiting for more.

"The last time I felt this way, my heart broke."

Olivia just nodded with her whole upper body, back and forth.

And the peace in Christine's heart shattered, engulfing her with fear.

She'd believed in happily-ever-after once. Had given her whole heart to her mom and dad, her grandparents, Nathan. Ryder. And had it shattered. Again. And again. And again. And once more after that.

She'd survived. And other than her mother's death, she'd handled it all alone.

She couldn't do it again. Couldn't open herself up to another possible loss.

She just couldn't.

Chapter Twenty

Jamie went running first thing Saturday morning. In athletic shorts and a long-sleeved T-shirt, he put on his newest tennis shoes and took off down the beach from his little cottage. He'd spoken to Christine twice since their Wednesday night skitter off course. Normally he'd have requested to visit with her.

He didn't.

He missed his baby like crazy.

Missed Christine almost as badly.

Felt like he'd been unfaithful to his wife. To her memory. Kissing the woman who was carrying Emily's child.

Even wanting to kiss her.

Wanting to make love to her with a fire that burned hotter than anything he'd ever felt before. The truth poured through him as he ran, consuming him with shame.

He couldn't hide from what had happened. Or how he'd felt.

Didn't even attempt to try.

He just didn't know how he could come to terms with either Christine or his son, feeling as he did.

Half an hour into the run he came face-to-face with waves slapping up against a cliffside at the beach's end. He could turn around. Head back. Or go up and over, with the hope that he'd be able to reach sand on the other side. The shoreline had more beach. For more than a hundred miles. He just had no idea what cliffs came in between sandy stretches.

Feeling as though his whole life was suddenly filled with unknowns, unable to tolerate not knowing what lay ahead, he started to climb. Slid a couple of times, scraping his arm pretty badly, bruising a knee, but he kept going, and twenty minutes in, saw a way that would have been quicker. And saw beach, too. As soon as his shoes hit sand, he started running again. Only briefly availing himself of the waterspout attached to the pack on his back.

Em?

Where was she?

Where was *he*?

Why didn't he feel even the slightest bit of resentment that Christine was carrying the child Emily had been meant to carry? She'd assumed, near the beginning of the pregnancy, that he would resent her.

And the house… He couldn't wait to get out of the house he and Emily had bought together. The home she'd loved. Yet, here he was, still just looking at homes like he had all the time in the world, feeling no rush to find a new one, happy in his little cottage.

He'd been told the owners were willing to sell, and he'd actually been thinking about buying it. It would be great for a weekend at the beach. For his and Tom's visitors. Or for his mother to stay in when she visited.

But if he wasn't in a hurry to get into the new house, why rush out of the old? He'd told Christine that it hadn't ever felt like a home to him. And felt badly afterward.

But the words were true.

He wanted their child, but not the home Emily had created for it?

Sand flew behind him as he ran on mostly deserted land. If he got to a public beach, there'd be a few people milling about. There always were, no matter what time of year.

Emily had loved the beach best in nonsummer times. She'd liked the brisk air. The fact that people weren't there to worship the sun, but the water.

The house—there'd been no passion there. He'd always thought, once he and Emily finally bought their "forever" home, it would automatically warm with their love in every room.

He'd wanted the type of intensity he'd witnessed between his parents anytime they'd been in the same room in their home.

Because at home they could let down all barriers and just be completely themselves.

The apartments he'd shared with Emily had all been owned by others, and they could hear others through the walls. But their own home…

He ran as though angry with the sand. Barely aware of the water off to the left. Or the slight cliff leading to grass and hopes to his right.

Em?

The intensity between his parents…

It reminded him of the other night in the car with Christine…

He stopped. Bent over, his hands on his knees, gasping for air.

Shook himself off. Tried to start running again. And fell to his butt in the sand, knees raised, facing the ocean.

He'd loved Emily with all his heart. First as a friend. A best friend. And then forever.

And Christine…

She had brought passion to his life.

She was carrying the baby he'd created with his wife, and he'd fallen in love for the first time in his life.

What in the hell was he going to do with that?

* * *

When Jamie didn't suggest an outing by Sunday afternoon, Christine called him. She'd been completely out of line threatening to enforce her right to not see him for the remainder of the pregnancy.

He must be treading carefully, afraid he'd do something to set her off, and she couldn't have that.

"I have to decide by tomorrow what finish I want on the floors, either just a clear gloss, or tinted coating, and I could sure use some help," she told him about her renovations, including the fact that she was being mindful of chemicals that could affect the baby, keeping things just as they'd been before the night of the show. They'd meet up in the midst of normal life, and then go on with their separate lives.

When he didn't immediately respond in the affirmative, she added, "He's been kicking up a storm all weekend. He needs to hear your voice."

The baby was his. She couldn't fall in love with it. Which meant that he had to cover that part.

So, they'd kissed.

And she'd cried. She was pregnant. She was allowed to be out of her head a bit. Once the baby was born, her hormones leveled out, she'd be happy with her life again.

And even if Olivia *was* somewhat right about some things, Christine had already made her choices. Luckily she'd had warning to guard herself against

Jamie before she'd done something really stupid like fall in love with him.

That's all the kiss had been. A warning to herself.

She'd dressed in a baggy denim dress with colorful flowered lace trim, and as soon as he stood, in jeans and a short-sleeved polo shirt in her living room, his hazel eyes assessing her in a way that felt far too personal, like he knew her too well, she started to panic. And quickly calmed herself with the knowledge that fear was a warning and she was taking heed.

"It's good to see you," she said, to put him at ease. To let him know that nothing had changed between them.

He smiled. "It's good to see you, too." His words were warm. And that gaze… It was like he was leaning in to kiss her without moving. So she turned away.

Cut off anything that might be misconstrued or cause trouble.

She walked through the downstairs, which was all hardwood. Showed him sample colors. Didn't give an opinion. And he chose the clear gloss—her own first pick.

Then it was time for him to go. Except that he asked what she was doing with the upstairs.

"Nothing. It's all carpet and I don't know if I'll have enough to do the whole place this year." Which wasn't really the case. With what he was paying her, she'd have plenty to do both. But she'd been thinking about new tubs and showers. And she wanted to put some of the money away. Maybe invest it.

A girl could never be too sure of her future.

When he asked to take a look, she took him upstairs. Waited in the hall at each door as he peeked inside.

"This place is a castle," he said, as he glanced into the master suite she'd moved into after opening The Parent Portal. Her grandparents had moved back into it after her father moved out. And they'd been gone, within months of each other, since her sophomore year of college.

There were five bedrooms in all. "You can just hear all the kids making noise up here," he said.

And she started downstairs. "There's never been more than just one," she told him, shutting down the picture he'd painted before it could take on color. "My grands bought it from a couple who'd been in the movie business in LA and had it built to have a place to entertain quietly, outside the city." She turned around and grinned at him, holding on to the handrail as she traversed the steps with her bigger belly. "In other words, so they could entertain without everyone who was someone knowing who they were with." They'd reached the first floor and she moved toward the front door. "And then Gram and Gramps only had Mom, and she only had me," she finished, efficiently obliterating any idea of those upstairs rooms filled with noisy kids.

"Don't you get lonely here all alone?"

"Nope." It was home. Filled with all the love she'd ever known.

The baby moved as she reached for the door handle, and pulling back, she said, "He's kicking," and turned her stomach toward him. The baby was his purpose for being there.

Jamie's hand connected with her stomach immediately, no hesitation, and while she braced herself to remain immune, to take herself out of the picture, she also relaxed into his touch. This was them.

She was good.

"I've decided on a name for him," he said.

She nodded. None of her business.

"I figure, if he can hear us talking, he might as well start learning it."

Made sense. Good sense. She looked up at him.

"I'm going to call him Will, after my father." She smiled. "And Ryder, after your son. To honor what you're doing for us."

William Ryder Howe.

Her smile faltered. She teared up. Put some kind of "you don't have to" sentence together. Suggested naming the baby for Emily's father, or to at least think about it.

And when he hugged her goodbye, holding his

baby close to his stomach through her skin, she hugged him back.

Then made herself let go.

Jamie couldn't push her to admit it—if he did, he'd push her away. But after that Sunday visit, the couple that followed that week, a quick stop in her office and a toned-down game of racquetball, he was fairly certain that Christine had feelings for him.

The truth came not so much in the things she said, but in the sometimes stilted, almost rehearsed, way she said them. The careful way she guided their times together—not at all the naturally compassionate professional he'd once known. In the memory of the hunger in her kiss. New to passion as he was, there was no doubting that she'd been as hot for him as he'd been for her. The truth came to him through her eyes when she'd meet his gaze and say nothing at all.

The truth was more than just an awareness of her attraction to him. Her caring about him. Unless something changed for her, she wasn't going to be able to open her heart enough to love anyone intimately. She'd given all she had.

Unless he found a way to show her that she didn't have to go through life, or bear life's challenges, alone.

And the only way he could figure out to show her that, to prove it to her, because telling certainly wasn't going to do it, was to do for her the one thing that mattered most. And that she deemed impossible.

He had to find her son, Ryder. Or at least do all he could to try. To see if there was any way he could at least give her some peace of mind about the child's welfare.

It was a tall order for anyone, let alone a guy who had no rights in her private life at all.

Over the next couple of weeks, he alternated between searching keywords on the internet and telling himself to stop being a fool and get on with his life.

He called a couple of old friends from high school who'd been younger than him, ones he hadn't spoken to in years, shared the news of his impending fatherhood, and, when congratulations were done, he'd caught up on their lives and then awkward silences had fallen on the line when he'd asked about a girl who'd gone to high school with them. Nobody remembered Christine.

He saw her three times a week, both of those weeks, including a routine doctor's visit, and all six times, he came home more determined that he had to find her son. For every pound she gained she grew more vulnerable. More fragile. And more determined than ever that when the baby was born, their lives would return to normal.

And while his would be a brand-new normal, hers would be the normal she knew.

He could touch her stomach. He could even hug

her goodbye fairly regularly. But he absolutely could not talk about any kind of future that included her postbirth. There were times when he caught her looking wistfully at her own stomach. When she asked about his house search and worried that he wouldn't get in in time for the baby to have a nursery. Times when he knew she was hurting. But she played her part without fail.

She'd let him in once. It was clear she wouldn't do so again.

Christine Elliott was a strong woman. She knew what she knew. Believed what life had taught her. And was true to herself.

He'd never met anyone who really believed, to their core, that they could, and should, go it alone. Nor one who would be so incredibly great at more. So ultimately happy.

How he knew that, he didn't question.

He just knew that Ryder was the key to helping her find the happiness she deserved. The key to unlocking her heart so that she could let herself be loved. By him or not. At that point, it didn't even matter who she loved, only that she knew she could. She'd never believe she wasn't alone when alone was all she knew. All she felt.

He had to find her son.

Desperation had a way of pushing a guy forward even when the order was too tall, it seemed. That was the only reason he could give himself for the fact that three and a half weeks after he'd felt bone-deep burning passion for the first time in his life, Jamie was in Los Angeles, waiting to be shown into the office of a man he'd never met.

Playing scenarios through his mind. Did he introduce himself as the father of the baby his daughter was carrying?

In some scenarios that seemed the most powerful way to go. And in others, it was far too messy. For all he knew her father wasn't happy about her choice, would resent Jamie, which would make the trip another lost cause.

A hugely disappointing one. He was out of ideas.

"Dr. Howe? Mr. Elliott will see you now."

The financial manager, dressed impeccably in a gray suit with white shirt and sedate silk tie, stood from behind his desk as Jamie, feeling decidedly underdressed in the brown pants, beige short-sleeved shirt and tie he'd worn to class in Mission Viejo that day, entered the room with a confidence that wilted with every step.

He didn't let it show, though. He'd learned from the best over the past few months how to be who you had to be, regardless of the personal toll.

"I understand you insisted on speaking with me personally," Dennis Elliott said. He had graying short hair, but his dark eyes were exactly like his daughter's. He didn't hold out a hand. Jamie didn't offer one. Nor did he sit down. And Jamie followed suit.

"Yes, sir. I..."

"I think I can save us both some time here. While the firm is always happy to take on new clients, my book is completely full. I can, however, give you a personal reference to the broker who's been with me the longest. I'm happy to show you his portfolio, that which isn't confidential, to give you an idea of his accomplishments and capabilities."

Jamie wasn't the least bit deterred. If anything he'd gained strength with every word the man said. How dare he leave his little girl's heart to just suffocate and die?

The anger that assailed him came as much of a surprise as had the passion in his SUV weeks ago. And the jitters that had assailed him at his first meeting with Christine more than five months before. Maybe he'd always been a calm man because he'd never loved as fiercely as Christine had loved others all of her life.

"I'm not here to make either of us money," he said. Dennis Elliott could very well be a wonderful husband and father, a great man, but, standing there, Jamie resented the hell out of the man who'd chosen making money over being there for his daughter. Who'd assuaged his own grief rather than helping his daughter pick up the pieces of her shattered life.

Again and again.

"I'm a...friend...of your daughter's." Not rehearsed rhetoric. He had no idea if Elliott would pick up his phone the second Jamie left the room and get his daughter on the phone. If he was, in essence, putting the nails on his own coffin.

He only knew that, even if he was, he had to do it. He had to show Christine that someone would move mountains to try and be there for her.

And with that thought, the way became completely, calmly, clear to him. "In fact, sir, I am in love with her. Completely."

The man sat. "Christine's in love?"

Was there relief mixed in with the incredulity in the man's tone? Jamie couldn't take the time to find out. Or allow the distraction.

"I want to marry her," he said, as though the idea had been consciously in his mind when he'd walked in that door.

He hadn't even thought about marriage. Maybe he should have. Emily would be shaking her head with that grin of hers and teasing him about his emotional denseness.

The thought of his wife didn't bring shame. Strangely, the memory of that grin comforted him.

"I don't know a thing about you, but if you managed to get past Christine's independence, then you have my full support," Dennis said. "I can't tell you how…"

"Sir, if I may…" Jamie interrupted, his tone filled with the confidence of the man in charge of a class filled with exceptionally smart people. "I've come seeking your help. You mention Christine's independence, but it's more than that. Her independence masks pain that was too much for her to bear. I think it stems from losing her mother and son."

He sounded like some kind of therapist. Funny, how smart love made you when you cared enough to see.

"But…she hasn't mentioned me to you at all, I take it?" Dennis asked.

"No, she has not."

Had she mentioned the pregnancy? Surely her father knew…

"When was the last time you saw her?"

"Several months ago. Christine's like that. We'd love to see her more, but we generally have to settle for once or twice a year."

Good to know. He was betting the man didn't even know his daughter was pregnant again. Which made him all that much more determined to be successful in his quest. At whatever cost to Dennis Elliott. Or himself, for that matter.

"I believe Christine loves me, but she won't listen to her heart," Jamie said. "All that's ever done has brought her pain. Hurt her. And she won't let herself need anyone. Or believe that anyone can be there for her."

When the man nodded, eyeing him with fingers steepled at his lips, Jamie continued.

"I need to find her son, sir." Jamie held up a hand

when the man opened his mouth. "I understand that the adoption was closed. I also understand you handled all of the details. I'm not asking for the impossible here." Okay, maybe he was. So be it. "I understand that you might not know who the parents are, and even if you do, you have no way of forcing whoever adopted her son to allow her to see him. I'm just asking you for any information you can give me, the name of the agency through which we could request someone contact the parents. We don't need a picture. Or to know where he is. We don't even need a name. If I could just let her know that he's okay. That he's loved and happy…"

He was a man in love. Fighting for the woman he loved. Not for himself. But for her.

Even if she hated him for doing what he was doing, if he could give her back even a hope of opening her life to love again—any kind of love. Partner. Parent…

"Her whole life, her family, is that clinic—where she makes sure, every day, that no biological parent, or child, under her jurisdiction, and in conjunction with the law, is ever prevented from knowing of one another. Her whole life, sir. She gets up every day to make sure that in her little part of the world, no one suffers as she does. Every day."

Dennis Elliott stood. Sat on the corner of his desk.

"What do you do?" he asked, studying Jamie. "For a living?"

Jamie might have been more put off by the question, in response to his plea, if he hadn't spent the past several months with Christine. In at least one way she appeared to have learned from her father to avoid internal emotional warfare by changing the subject to something innocuous. He knew the drill.

"I'm a college professor. Mathematics." Sweating, Jamie was inordinately thankful he'd opted not to mention that he was also the father of Christine's surrogate child. Or even that she was carrying a child.

"Where do you teach?" Jamie named the university branch in Mission Viejo and the college in Marie Cove.

Dennis nodded. "You're local a lot of the time, then."

"I am."

"You own a home?"

"I did. I sold it." And then he added, "I'm making an offer on the little cottage on the beach I'm renting until I find something. It'll be nice to have for romantic weekends, or summer days at the beach. And for out-of-town guests."

He hadn't even told Christine his plan, and he was telling her father?

"She'd love that. But, you know, she'll never leave that house she's in."

He nodded. "I think part of my problem finding a house is that none of them measure up to that one.

I've never been in a building that feels so much like home."

"So she hasn't asked you to live with her?"

He didn't answer. But his gaze didn't back down at all.

"She doesn't know I'm here, sir, and might never speak to me again when she finds out." A bit of an exaggeration. He hoped. Though, technically, she didn't need to say anything to him during doctor's appointments and the birth.

Dennis wiped a hand slowly down his face. Glanced at a picture on his desk. Jamie could only see an angled back of the frame. Wondered if Christine was in it. Or if it was just his current wife and son.

"I can't promise anything. I'll have to make a call. But I know who adopted Chris's baby."

Chapter Twenty-One

Chris wasn't all that happy about going with Jamie to Anaheim, over an hour's drive from Marie Cove, one Saturday in her sixth month of pregnancy. She'd put him off the first time he'd asked her to accompany him to see the same group of students who'd performed in Mission Viejo be guest artists on the main stage at Disneyland. But when he'd asked a second time, saying he wanted to support his students, but really didn't want to show up to the busy park alone and then added that it would be good for the baby to hear his voice in a crowd of voices, she reluctantly gave in.

She wore yoga pants, a long, colorful, tight-fitting tunic top and tennis shoes without socks and was kind of looking forward to the day as she climbed into Jamie's SUV and strapped herself into that so comfortable seat.

But she dialed her enthusiasm down the second he smiled at her. In jeans and a T-shirt, with his dark hair curling at the collar, he definitely needed to be some woman's husband. Her stomach warmed, her heart pounded harder and she knew the fear was her mind's way of telling her to be careful. To guard herself. It wasn't like she'd be getting much out of the theme park anyway. They weren't staying long and she couldn't do many of the attractions due to her condition.

And the last time she and Jamie had taken a trip out of Marie Cove—the only other time they'd been in a vehicle together—had nearly ended their relationship.

It had thrown her life in a quandary that she didn't care to repeat.

"I talked to my mom today," Jamie said as he set the cruise control for highway driving. "She's planning to stay a month after Will's born."

"That gives you three months to find a house or you'll be sleeping on a very big couch in a very little room." His little rental had two bedrooms, but from what he'd said, one was nearly full with baby stuff already.

Not her business.

"I bought the cottage."

Turning to look at him, determining that he wasn't kidding, she didn't try to hide her shock. "Why? That place isn't big enough to raise a child. Besides, it's too close to the water. A toddler learns how to open doors anywhere from eighteen months to two years, depending on his height and it only takes a second with your head turned..."

When she heard the vehemence in a statement she had no business making, she cut herself off. Stared straight ahead.

And realized her hand was cradling her baby bump. She snatched it away. But it was *her* stomach and where else was she going to put her hand? She tried the door handle. Around her belly to her thigh. The edge of the seat beside her thigh. And back to her belly.

Then, at Jamie's silence, turned to see him alternately watching her and the road. Back and forth.

She wasn't saying another word.

"I'm hoping to be in a new house by the time Mom comes," he said. "And she can use the cottage. It can be a weekend fun spot, you know, for days at the beach. And a place for Mom to stay. My house won't ever be big enough for me to have her watching over my shoulder like she's done ever since my father died."

"I'm sure it's just because she loves you and knows the pain of loss..."

He glanced at her again, and she swore she

wouldn't take her gaze off the road in front of them for the rest of the day. "I'm sure you're right," was all he said.

His mother had lost her husband. Her father had lost his wife. Each parent had a child, about the same age, at home.

She hadn't ever put the facts together quite like that. Realizing that she and Jamie had something kind of deep in common. He'd had Emily's parents watching out for him. She'd had Gram and Gramps. Both of their single parents had remarried, but there'd been one major difference. Jamie's mother had kept him with them.

Thinking of which brought back to mind her father's odd phone call a few days before. Him calling every month or so to check in, if she hadn't called him or Tammy, was normal enough. But before he'd hung up, he'd told her he loved her. Out of the blue, just said the words.

She hadn't known what to do with them. Had pretended she hadn't heard. She couldn't remember the last time he'd expressed any deep emotion around her, and he chose then, when she was hormonal and not herself?

Not that he'd know that. She'd purposely chosen not to tell him about her surrogacy. Just hadn't wanted to go there. It meant she was going to have to make up some kind of excuse to miss Christmas dinner, but she could always say she was volunteering over the holiday. He'd believe that.

Jamie streamed music most of the way, mellow country mostly, and she put her seat back and napped a little bit. She didn't remember being as tired when she'd been pregnant before, but it wasn't like she'd spent a lot of time hanging on to, or cataloging those memories.

They got stuck in some traffic heading off the freeway and into Anaheim. He kept watching the clock to the point that she said, "We're going to be fine, Jamie. It's still an hour before they're due to go on. We've already got our tickets so we'll be able to go right in…"

"It's like getting on a plane now," he said, more tense then she'd ever seen him. "You have to go through security and have bags checked."

"We've still got plenty of time. Even if we have to park far out in the lot, they have shuttles still, I'm sure… And even if we're a minute or two late, it's not like they're going to know. I'm sure that it will mean the world to them just to see you there afterward…"

His impatience was almost comical—except that it wasn't kind to take pleasure in another's discomfort. He didn't swear, or suddenly start to drive erratically, but he definitely wasn't her Jamie.

No.

Not *her* Jamie. Just the Jamie she was usually with. And really, what did she know? They saw each other a few minutes or a little more, a few times a week. And at the doctor's office, where she was merely a conduit, and he and the doctor were the people with roles to play.

As she'd known would be the case, they were inside the park, heading from the locker area up front, past the first couple of stores—or that last chance to buy souvenirs if you were on your way out—toward Main Street, with almost half an hour to spare.

Excitement lit inside her, on a small scale, as she looked around at the fantasy town where everything was colorful and beautiful and perfect looking. "It looks pretty much like I remember it," she said, smiling at Jamie, who was keeping close beside her. "How can that be?"

The place was crowded, of course, and he seemed more intent on watching out for her than giving any hint of enjoying his surroundings.

Like, at any moment, someone might bump into her stomach and hurt her.

Or the baby. It was about him, not her, she reminded herself.

He knew right where the main stage was and didn't let her veer off course even long enough to take a peek at a couple of Disney characters dressed up for photo ops.

"I have a picture someplace of me and Mom and Dad here," she told him. She'd forgotten that she had it. Figured it was probably in the photo trunk in the attic. She was going to look when she got home. Get it out.

Those were the types of photos that she should frame and put on the hallway walls upstairs—after she got them repainted.

She figured they'd find a seat in the back of the arena, leaving lower seats for guests there to see the whole show, but Jamie led them straight to the front row.

"We're going to block the view of those kids." She leaned over to whisper, getting a whiff of his musky cologne in the process. The scent that seduced her that night in his SUV. She pointed to the bleacher two up behind them.

With a nod, he scooted a couple of feet. But stayed right there in front. Like he thought his students would be looking for him and he wanted to make certain they saw him easily. She hadn't realized how close he was with them. They'd really seemed kind of formal with him when they'd been to their last show.

An emcee came out. Asked the crowd if they'd enjoyed the break. Said he hoped they'd had enough time to get refreshments from the carts she and Jamie had passed on the way in. Jamie scooted closer to her. Put an arm behind her, touching her back, but resting on the metal bench on the far side of her.

No one was going to bump her from behind. And she had support for a back that was starting to ache now and then. So thoughtful.

"Up next in our competition is a thirteen-year-old from Santa Barbara," the emcee said. "Shawn Bretton."

"Competition?" she asked Jamie, looking at her watch, as the audience clapped. "I thought there was a show due to start. Your kids are up in ten minutes."

"This is the show they're in," he said, staring at the stage, his voice a little short. "It's a music competition put on in conjunction with schools and talent agencies."

A young man had walked out onstage dressed in black pants and a white button-down shirt with the sleeve cuffs rolled halfway up his arms. He walked with confidence and stood a bit awkwardly. A combination of adult and kid.

"Tell us a little about yourself, Shawn."

"I'm a student at Shelby Junior High, in the eighth grade. I play baseball, and I hope to study law."

"And what are you going to sing for us today?"

"A song my dad wrote when I was little..."

"Your dad. He's a songwriter?"

"Yeah, but he told me not to say any more about that. I'm me, not him. But can I say one thing?"

"Of course."

"My dad, he's like this man that..." The boy stopped. Pulled the mic he'd walked out with away from his mouth. Looked off in the distance, and then pulled the mic back. "He used to sing. Until the car accident that killed my sister and hurt my dad so he couldn't sing anymore. My mom was hurt, too, and couldn't have any more kids. My dad wrote this song about how life is hard, and it's beautiful, too. It's kind of about our family..."

The kid was so...real. So... She didn't know what. He was cute as could be with dark hair and eyes. She was close enough she could see the expression in those eyes as he glanced down at the first row just before he started to sing.

And the words—about the joy a little boy brings to a family. From his first grin, his first tooth, his first step. How all the firsts teach his parents that everything will be okay as long as they don't let death win. No matter what the future holds, there will always be a first grin, a first tooth, a first step that will bring joy. Because while death was a part of living, so was birth. New life. First grins, first teeth, first steps.

As the boy's perfect high pitch, not yet deepened with puberty, drew to its final close, Christine became aware of herself sitting there. Mesmerized.

And sobbing. With Jamie's arm wrapped tightly around her.

The crowd gave the boy a full second of reverent silence and then exploded into applause around them. Christine sat there, unable to do anything but feel.

How could a child bring such truth to her world? And slap her at the same time?

She'd lost so much. But not a child to death. Her

child lived somewhere. And she hadn't lost her ability to carry a child, as Olivia had.

But had she, in her pain, robbed herself of first grins? First teeth? First steps? Had she robbed herself of the joy of new life because of her loss? Was she letting death win?

"I have to tell you something. Right now," Jamie said, suddenly, looking from his phone, which had signaled a text, to somewhere off to the side of them, and back to her. "And I think you're going to want to hold yourself together."

Of course. That she could do. With a sniffle and a deep breath, she sat up straighter. She was there for him. For his students. He must have seen them off to the side of them. Ready to go on.

Jamie's hand squeezed her shoulder, pulling her so tightly against him she could feel his heart beating. "Shawn Bretton is your son, Chris. And I was under the impression that while you could watch him, you weren't going to get to meet him. His parents offered him the opportunity to meet his birth mother and he chose not to do so. But his parents told me he'd be here today and invited you to come watch him, just not meet him. But I just had a text that his parents saw you sitting here and they're willing to introduce you to him. He just can't know who you are. Anywhere else it would be hard to explain, but here, you could just be a fan of his song."

She heard the words. Listened hard inside her

brain and heard them again. Still reeling from the music, she started to shake. Looked off to the side where Jamie had looked, saw a couple standing there, looking toward her and toward the back of the stage as well.

The boy on the stage. The love. The voice. He played baseball.

And… He was *hers*?

Not hers, but he was who Ryder had become?

She stared into Jamie's eyes. "You found my son?" The words stuck in her throat. Came out in mostly a whisper that he probably couldn't even hear over the crowd talking around them as they awaited judges' scoring and the next act.

Jamie nodded, but the tears in his eyes were her real answer. "Because you don't have to do it alone, Chris…"

Leaning in, she planted her lips on his. It didn't matter that they were on the front bleacher with a crowd behind them. That her son's parents were watching. That she was in his employ, pregnant with a child he'd created with another woman.

She just didn't have any words to thank him.

Jamie fell in love all over again as he stood with his arm around Chris and watched her smile from ear to ear, as she was introduced to the young man she'd birthed. There was no hint of the emotion that had to be roiling inside her, just a self-conscious wipe of her eyes as she told him what a great job he'd done. And thanked him, too.

"I…lost a baby once," she said. "And until today, when I heard you sing… I've been letting my sadness win…so, thank you." The words explained the sign of tears on her face without, in any way, giving a hint that it had to be taking everything she had not to grab the boy in her arms and not let go.

His parents stood on either side of him. But both of them met her gaze as they thanked her profusely for sharing her story with them.

They were thanking her for a lot more than that.

Jamie knew. And in the car, on the way home, Chris said, "How can I mourn a past that not only gave him a much better life than I could have back then, but gave them back their lives, too?" Her head lying back on the rest, she had a small smile on her face as she turned and looked at him. "I won't ever be able to thank you, Jamie. Not ever."

He didn't say a word, just sped as fast as he could to an exit he knew that took him to a road that led straight to the beach.

"Why are we getting off?" she asked, as he exited the freeway. "Do we need gas?"

He nodded. Shook his head. And drove.

She didn't say a word as he pulled into the partially full parking lot and stopped the SUV. A group of teenagers was unloading a cooler out of a van, heading toward the beach just yards away. The ocean roared to shore and receded in the distance.

Unfastening his seat belt, he reached over to unbuckle hers, and then, leaving the console down between them, said, "You're giving life to my son. So I found yours. You owe me nothing..."

He didn't want her gratitude.

Her lips trembled as she teared up, and he noticed her hand cradle her belly. His son. Who she was caring for so carefully. Because that's what she did. Never asking for any emotional sustenance for herself. Or expecting any.

"I love you, Chris. With every fiber of my soul. That's why I found your son. Not for anything for me, but because it's what I know you needed. That's what love is. And I might not live through the night, or I could live to be a hundred, but I will always be loving you and doing everything in my power, wherever I am, to give you moments of joy. It would mean everything to me if you'd share my life with me, raise my son with me, but if not, I'll still be loving you."

She shook her head, and he closed his eyes as his heart sank. And yet, it didn't sink far. Because he'd done it. He'd given her what she'd needed most. And if that meant she went on and opened her heart to someone else somewhere down the road, then that would be enough.

It would really be enough.

Just like an enduring love minus jitters and emotional intensity had been enough of him for Emily?

When her finger brushed against his mouth, and then up to the corner of his eye, he opened them to see her gazing at him, the look in those brown eyes so filled with emotion they glistened, but not with tears.

"I'm not good at this, Jamie. I want to spend a life with you, to raise this baby with you. I don't even know how to start. All I know is being alone."

With one hand he had the console up and was already reaching for her. "I can be patient," he said, moving over as he pulled her to him, until they were away from the steering wheel and her pregnant self was on his lap. "And I have it on good authority that I'm an excellent teacher," he said, knowing when to give her what she needed. In that moment, she was her father's daughter. Needing a minute of distraction from an intensity she'd forgotten how to trust. To embrace.

"I love you, Jamie Howe."

Her words dropped softly into the vehicle, wrapping around him. Words he hadn't been sure he'd hear. Words he hadn't been sure she'd ever be able to say.

"I love you, too." He didn't bother to try to hide the tremor in his voice. Or the arms that held her.

She nodded. Settled more firmly against him and said, "I want to wait to have sex with you until I'm just me again. I need to know you see me as me, not as his incubator..."

"I've never seen you that way," he interrupted. He'd done his own reading. About transference, too. But he also understood.

Chris was Christine. She needed that part of herself. And more, the world needed her. She had a purpose that served far more than just him.

"I was going to say that as long as you agree that there will be no sex until I've recovered from the birth, then it would probably make sense for you to move out of the cottage and storage and into the home that it looks like we'll be sharing for the rest of our lives...my house."

He chuckled. He couldn't help it. And then laughed out loud. Chris might be coming back to life, but Christine was right there with them. Just getting right down to the practical.

"What?" she asked, pulling back.

"You," he told her, kissing her. Long and deep. Without any humor at all. And yet, he was pulsing with a euphoria all new to him. "If you're okay with it, I'll start moving in tomorrow. And I hope you have a room in mind for William Ryder's nursery because I have a load of boxes to open and furniture to start putting together. Our son's going to be here before we know it." He placed his hand on her belly, and while she placed hers on top of it, she shook her head.

"The next one will be ours, Jamie," she said.

"I will love William Ryder as much, I will mother him with all of my being, but he belongs to you and Emily. When he's old enough to understand, he has to be told. And to honor her."

"I see it a different way," he told her, tracing her lips with his finger. "I see us all back in high school. Emily is my best friend. And you're my girlfriend. And the two of you meet through me, and form your own sisterly closeness. And together, the three of us, go out into the world and support each other throughout our lives, and love each other's children."

"She'll always be a part of us."

"Yes, and you'll always be a part of us, too," he said, not sure how that worked in the real world, but knowing that it all added up to him.

And that his total was right.

"Together. Forever. As a family." Christine's tone was firm.

"Forever." He knew the promise he was making.

And that was real life—and it didn't get better than that.

* * * * *

MILLS & BOON

Coming next month

A YEAR WITH THE MILLIONAIRE NEXT DOOR
Barbara Wallace

"Stella…" He breathed her name into her mouth like it was a prayer. She felt his fingers sliding along her cheeks until they cradled her face. He combed back her hair and pulled away.

"Stella," he repeated.

He was rejecting her.

"Well, isn't this humiliating," she said, backing away. "I…"

Linus backed away, too. The tenderness she imagined in his gaze had morphed into embarrassment. "I should go," he said.

"Yeah, I think that's a good idea."

She kept her attention glued to the coffee table while Linus got up and limped toward the front door. "I'm sorry," he said when he reached the landing. "But I don't think either of us wants to do something we'll regret."

Not trusting herself to speak, Stella only thanked God for that. She'd rambled on about her failings and made a fool out of herself, but at least she hadn't done something she'd regret.

*

Linus closed his front door and collapsed against it. That might have been one of most difficult things he had ever done. *Give yourself a pat on the back, old boy. You behaved like a gentleman.* Eighteen months ago, if a beautiful woman threw herself in his arms, he would have kissed the daylights out of her. Lips that soft and delicious? How could he resist?

But he did resist. Had to. It was clear his neighbor needed a friend far more than she needed sex.

I need to prove I'm not a disappointment.

How could the woman with whom he'd spent the evening disappoint anyone? It was inconceivable. She was funny. Beautiful. Smart.

His rejection probably hadn't helped her self-esteem issues. Still, he'd done the right thing. Maybe that meant he was evolving into a better person. Because for once he cared more about helping a woman than seducing her.

Now if he could only stop thinking about how amazing Stella's lips tasted, he'd be fine.

JOIN US ON SOCIAL MEDIA!

Stay up to date with our latest releases, author news and gossip, special offers and discounts, and all the behind-the-scenes action from Mills & Boon...

millsandboon

millsandboonuk

millsandboon

It might just be true love...

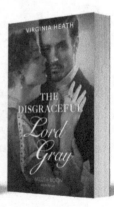